Jass

ALSO BY DAVID FULMER

Chasing the Devil's Tail

Jass

DAVID FULMER

HARCOURT, INC.

ORLANDO   AUSTIN   NEW YORK   SAN DIEGO   TORONTO   LONDON

www.HarcourtBooks.com

Map of Uptown New Orleans and Storyville
reprinted by permission of Poisoned Pen Press.

Library of Congress Cataloging-in-Publication Data
Fulmer, David.
Jass/David Fulmer.—1st ed.
p.   cm.
ISBN 0-15-101025-0
1. Police—Louisiana—New Orleans—Fiction.   2. Jazz musicians—Crimes
against—Fiction.   3. New Orleans (La.)—Fiction.   4. Creoles—Fiction.   I. Title.
PS3606.U56J37 2005
813'.6—dc22   2004011620

Text set in Sabon
Designed by Cathy Riggs

Printed in the United States of America

First edition
A C E G I K J H F D B

As always, to my family,
near and far, before and after me.

"I don't know where it come from. And I can't say what it was, 'cause it was one of them things you know without sayin'. I sure knew it when I heard it, though. I sure did. Back then it was called jass. Later on they called it jazz, but it wa'nt the same no mo'. It was somethin' else. Ain't but a few that 'members the way it was befo'. Pretty soon there won't be no one at all. Not a one."

—D. O. DELAREAUX
New Orleans musician, shortly before his death in 1950

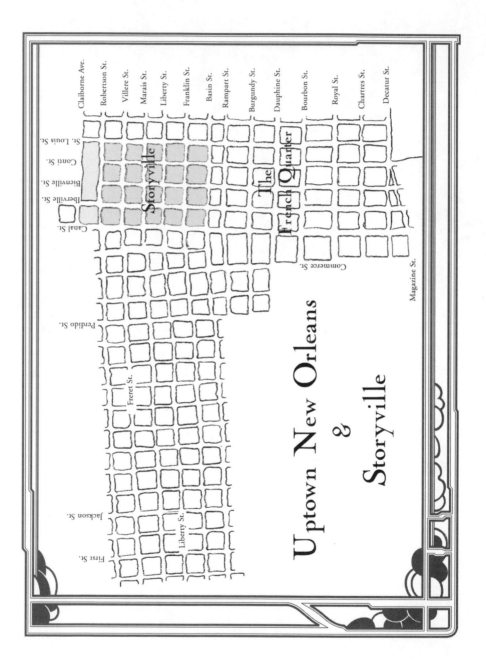

Uptown New Orleans
&
Storyville

Jass

ONE

Antoine Noiret came awake with a start, as if he'd been jerked out of sleep by a rough hand.

He groaned, dead tired. The crazy bitch had kept him up for two hours after they had stumbled home from the saloon, and that was after playing for six with nary a break. He thought she was going to let him pound her hips for his trouble, but all she wanted to do was rail at him, and once she got going, she screeched like she was mounted on his yancy and thrashing for all she was worth. He didn't quite understand what all her fussing was about. At one point, she pulled open her shirtwaist and hiked up her petticoats, demanding to know if that was what he wanted.

Indeed it was; otherwise, what was she doing in his room at that hour? She was the one who had come sniffing around him, after all, first watching from the back of the hall, then coming around to whisper in his ear as she made promises with her eyes. He had hoped to finish out his grueling night with a good fuck and then sleep like a dead man through the dawn and well into the day.

She had other ideas, and when he reached for her, she dropped her skirts and went to stalking about the room, a sweaty, half-dressed mess, her rouge and mascara running in clownish streaks, calling curses down on his worthless self. After a few minutes of this abuse, she wound down and lurched into the hall, slamming the door so hard it shook the walls. Antoine was baffled.

It didn't matter. He grunted with relief, glad to be rid of her and her noisy, filthy mouth. It was just as well; he had no business bringing her there in the first place. Not after what had happened before.

Her steps had barely faded off in the hallway when he dropped into an exhausted slumber, like he had fallen into black water. Time passed until he came half awake to someone moving about in the darkness. He let out a silent groan, praying that she would just go away again and leave him alone. He was done for the night.

He pulled the damp, dingy pillow over his head, hoping she'd get the idea. The air stirred as footsteps padded up to the bed. Then he heard a dark cough and felt something push into the pillow, a finger perhaps, poking for attention, and it began to dawn on him that there was something wrong about it.

Because it wasn't a finger at all—it was the tip of the blade of a ten-inch hunting knife. With a certain and sudden precision, the blade plummeted through the pillow and tore into Antoine's neck, just behind the jaw and below his ear. He felt a raw shock of pain and tried to bolt up off the mattress. Though he was a big man, a bigger weight held him down as the knife pinned him like some insect. He thrashed about, his thick arms going weaker and weaker as blood soaked the sheets.

In less than twenty seconds, he had gurgled a last breath and his hands flapped a final time before dropping over the side of the mattress.

The knife slid back through the pillow that had muffled his dying grunts. A moment later the door opened and closed like a quiet breath and the footsteps pattered away.

TWO

Valentin St. Cyr spent the week working the big room at Anderson's Café, keeping an eye and putting the occasional rough arm on a selection of the card cheats, pickpockets, drunkards, hopheads, and other stray scofflaws who swarmed along Basin Street every night when the sun went down.

Come Thursday, they were serving drinks as usual and the usual crowd was there. Louis the Lifter and his partner Charlie Bow-wow huddled by the door, taking the measure of the proper gentlemen, young sports, and nervous out-of-towners who were passing inside. Coke-Eye Johnny, once known to the whores as the handsomest man in Storyville, shuffled up and down the bar, all drawn and ragged, seeking another victim upon whom to foist his woeful tale of slavery to the white powder. In the back corner, Chez Boday, sporting a mouthful of gold teeth and a razor scar from ear to chin, was employing his famous dice to relieve a fat Dallas cotton broker of his last dollar.

Rich white men sat at the private tables drinking the good stuff. The high-rolling gamblers were at their cards, decked out in their finest, and with plenty cash in their pockets, while eager young would-be rounders worked the fringes of the room with a game or a woman and, as always, those few no-account, penny-ante hustlers, grubby sots, and dead-end dope fiends who had not yet caught St. Cyr's eye scurried in and out of the corners, as furtive as rodents.

Up on the stage, a five-piece band chugged merrily through a bubbling jass number, and the bartenders shouted back and forth over the happy noise. All around the room, gazes shifted when some well-heeled fellow strolled by with a comely octoroon on his arm.

At some point amidst the frivolity came a hard glance that was met with a sharp word, and, like a swirling eddy, a circle opened in the middle of the polished floor. Two rounders faced each other, one waving a straight razor, the other grasping a thin stiletto. Wicked steel gleamed under crystal chandeliers as the racket in the room dropped a startled notch or two, but it was all over before it began because Valentin stepped out of the crowd and, without a moment's pause, swung his whalebone sap one way and then the other, first catching the knife-toting rounder hard over the ear and then laying it flat against the forehead of the sport with the razor. They went down like two sacks of Louisiana rice and lay groaning on the marble tiles, blood seeping from their misbehaving skulls.

Valentin waved a hand and a roughneck dragged the miscreants through the crowd and out to the back alley, where they could come to and spend the rest of the night slicing each other like boudin, for all anyone cared. There was a rush of chatter and laughter over the added entertainment. They'd gotten their money's worth this night.

In his second-floor office, Tom Anderson, known far and wide as "the King of Storyville," heard the commotion from the room below dip like a passing train and straightened in his chair. Ten seconds went by, and the noise resumed at its previous volume. Whatever happened had been met and dispatched.

Anderson let out a short sigh of annoyance. Though it was exactly what St. Cyr was getting paid for, sometimes the man could be too damned efficient. It was a fine time for a distraction.

He used it anyway, interrupting the gabbling on the other end of the line with an excuse of pressing business. With a quick promise to deal with the problem forthwith, he laid the ornate wood and brass handpiece into its cradle. He massaged his earlobe absently for a few seconds, then pushed back from the desk and stood up.

Moving with the deliberate steps of a man who had passed fifty years and 250 pounds with power to spare, he made his way out the door, down the narrow stairwell, and along the back hall to the steamy kitchen, where a staff of eight Negro cooks and a French chef sweated over hot stoves. The waiters banged in and out, yelling for their orders. Anderson steered clear of their bustling way and stepped up to the swinging doors for a peek at the main floor of the Café.

It never failed to stir him. The room was huge, fifty feet wide and the length of half a city block. Along one wall was the bar topped with Italian marble and fitted with a rail of polished brass, and behind it was a mirror that ran its length and reflected a rolling landscape of liquor bottles, with kaleidoscopic swirls of motion and colored lights beyond. The floor was also marble and crisscrossed with paths of thick carpeting that was spared the indignity of tobacco stains by way of spittoons that had been planted every ten paces. It was a grand sight to be sure, and there was nothing quite like it anywhere on the American continent.

Anderson shifted his gaze. It was a good crowd, mostly heeled and well-dressed, and every time a bottle tipped, a card turned, or a tune played, he got a little richer.

He caught sight of St. Cyr in the far corner, scanning the room, as watchful as a hawk. Whatever the earlier nuisance, it had been swept out into the night.

So all was well. Anderson spent another few moments relishing all this grandeur. Then, with some reluctance, he started back upstairs to pour himself another small glass of brandy and ponder the problems that had been dropped in his ample lap earlier this night.

It was 3 A.M., the band had long since stopped, and Valentin was waiting for the last of the stragglers to leave when he saw the kid they called Beansoup come strolling in the door like he owned the place. He saw the Creole detective staring at him and raised a grimy hand in greeting. "I got a—"

"What are you doing out at this hour?" Valentin said.

"—message from Mr. Jelly Roll," Beansoup stuttered, flinching at the Creole's rough tone.

"I asked what you're doing out at this hour."

The kid sniffed and jerked a thumb. "I'm helpin' out over to Miss Burt's. She gimme a job."

Valentin eyed him up and down, taking in the moon face with the blond hint of a mustache, the pale hair oiled and plastered like wet straw, the body an assembly of angles that didn't seem to connect. With his cracked leather shoes, a suit coat and trousers that were already too small, and the dingy gray derby that perched high on his round head, he looked like nothing so much as the buffoon in a vaudeville routine.

Valentin put down an urge to snicker at the comical facade, keeping his face stern. He said, "What about Morton, now?"

"He told me to fetch you. He's asking could you come by on your way home."

"You wait for me," he said.

Beansoup gave a nod and a wink, once again all full of himself, put a foot up on the brass rail, and leaned his elbow on the bar like a regular rounder.

Miss Burt's mansion was only two doors down from the Café. Even at that hour, when almost everything else in Storyville was closing, electric lamps still blazed from the chandeliers in the front rooms, casting arrows of gay light through the tall windows and onto the banquette.

When Valentin stepped into the foyer with Beansoup at his heels, the two girls who were standing in the archway that led into the parlor turned around and began arranging their smiles. Then they saw who it was, and their thin smiles dissolved. The detective caught Beansoup giving the girls the eye, so he poked the kid's shoulder, pointed to the chair next to the wall mirror, and said, "Sit." Beansoup's face flushed and he huffed angrily. Then he saw the Creole's look and did as he was told.

"And take off your hat," Valentin said more gently.

He left Beansoup and went into the parlor. It was a big square room with a high ceiling that held a heavy chandelier of tinkling crystal. The floor was covered with thick Persian carpet, and curtains of heavy brocade hung by the windows. All the furniture was of French design, with rich upholstery in bloodred and gold. Lamps with tasseled shades cast a buttery glow along the walls.

In the opposite corner, three men in evening clothes sat in café chairs, watching the doves cavort before them, their cheeks flushed giddy pink, like they were schoolboys up to some mischief. The girls, all in their evening dresses, looked plenty tired. It was no wonder; in the course of this night, each of them would have serviced as many as a dozen customers. Still, they managed to put on bright faces and make their weary limbs flutter as they performed prancing little dance steps to the music from the piano.

Even angled into a corner, the instrument all but dominated the room: a beautiful concert grand, pearl white, custom-made to Miss Burt's exacting specifications and transported by train from New York City. Though every professor in New Orleans lusted to lay fingers on the perfect ivory keys, that privilege had for two years been accorded to Ferdinand LeMenthe, who went by the moniker Jelly Roll Morton.

As Valentin approached, Morton looked up from the key-board to treat his visitor to a toothy smile that glinted with gold. He winked and murmured, "'Nother minute, all right?"

Valentin leaned on the sound box to admire the effortless ballet of fingers on keys, thinking about what a complete sport Morton had become in the few years since he had first been hired to play in the parlor of a Basin Street mansion. He had been a gangly kid of sixteen then, a gawky sack of bones who just happened to have sure fingers and a decent voice. So there he was at that tender age, entertaining the sporting women in the finest bordellos in one of the world's most notorious red-light districts and their customers, too, including some very dangerous characters. He played with equal ease the popular tunes of the day, waltzes and ragtime numbers for dancing, the occasional gutbucket blues, and of course a selection of those late-at-night bawdy songs that sent the whores and their sports off shrieking with dirty laughter.

Young Ferdinand had started using the nickname "Jelly Roll" to hide his profession from his maman and because he thought it sounded just right. A common slang that gutbucket singers used for a certain part of the female anatomy, his moniker had been lifted from a professor he heard on a Mississippi riverboat. The fellow, a fine piano player but a falling-down drunkard who was regularly fished out of the muddy water after toppling over the rail, ended up in the bughouse from drinking too much hot whiskey. Ferdinand decided it would be a shame to let a moniker like that go to waste, and so the classically trained scion of a pious and upstanding Creole family became "Jelly Roll Morton," Storyville piano jockey.

He had played in all the high-dollar houses at one time or another, hiding his employment from his mother and grandmother. He didn't quite escape the maternal doting, though, because the madams tried to protect his tender eyes by setting dressing screens between him and the girls and their customers.

Ferdinand simply poked holes with his pocketknife and got an education that other young men could only dream about. Once he was eighteen, he was on his own and could drop the ruse. Now, at twenty-one, he was quite the Storyville veteran. He was, in fact, the best-known piano man in the District.

Best known though not best. That title went to Professor Tony Jackson. Whatever Morton played, Professor Jackson could render twice as clean and twice as fast. The professor was a regular marvel and everyone in the District knew it. Morton knew it, too, and it gave him no mean distress.

Leaning there and listening to the cascade of ragtime notes, Valentin recalled the story of a young Ferdinand swaggering up to the famously shy professor and offering to show how well he had mastered the older man's "Mississippi Crawl."

As the tale went, Morton sat down on the bench next to Jackson without being invited, then flexed his knuckles and went to it, his fingers fairly dancing over the keys in a slick, near-flawless rendition of the intricate composition. Jackson paid polite attention to the music as his bulbous eyes flicked, taking in Morton's lank frame, tawny skin, and green eyes.

Morton ended the tune with a magnificent crescendo and crossed his arms as if waiting for applause. The room stayed quiet.

"That's fine." The professor spoke softly, in a lisping whisper. "Though if you want to make it right smooth, you need to practice it double time." He proceeded to demonstrate. After twelve bars, Jelly Roll let out a cry, jumped up, and ran out the door.

He had learned his lessons in the years since. He could now double-time the "Mississippi Crawl," too, though he could never quite match the professor's fluid touch. So he contented himself with being the flashiest piano man on Basin Street, a sport and a rounder, as brash and boastful as Tony Jackson was modest and retiring. He was known to play the pimp, with sporting women at his beck and call. He could but snap his fingers and have a pill of hop or a card of cocaine delivered directly into his hand. He dressed in forty-dollar suits, tailored precisely by a Jew on Ursulines. Everyone in the District knew the name Jelly Roll Morton and he liked it that way.

He arrived at the song's final tinkling notes and glanced over his shoulder at one of the dancing girls, who swirled to the Victrola and began to crank the handle. The record disk went around and the ornate horn gurgled out a rendition of "You, Only You." Morton stood up, stretched, and tilted his head for Valentin to follow him. They went through a doorway and into the pantry that was under the back stairwell. The kitchen door stood open and they could see the Negro cook dozing in a straight-backed chair, her arms crossed beneath her heavy bosom, nodding her head up and down as if in silent agreement with whatever dream was swirling through her drowsy mind.

There was a bottle of sherry on the sideboard, and Morton poured a few inches each into two glasses and handed one of them to Valentin. They sipped the sweet wine and listened to the footsteps dragging up the staircase as one of the doves led a gentleman to her room. If the girl was still sharp, they would be hearing the same shoes descending in a matter of minutes. Unless, of course, the fellow had the cash and the vitality for a longer stay.

Though he had been at the piano since early evening, Morton still looked fresh, his light cotton suit a perfect fit, his tie knotted firmly at the neck, his face as bright as if he had just come from a decent nap. He was still a kid, of course, and could do that. On the other hand, Valentin, some thirteen years his senior, was ready to go home and end his day.

Morton eyed the detective. "'Preciate you stopping by."

Valentin said, "What's Beansoup doing hanging around here?"

"I don't know," Morton said. "Thinks he's a sport, I guess."

"He told me he has a job."

Morton chuckled softly. "He ain't got no *job*. He won't stay away, so Miss Burt lets him run errands." He smiled wryly. "He spends most of his time trying to sweet-talk the ladies."

"He said you wanted to see me."

Morton nodded slowly, his face falling into a worrisome mask. "You know Antoine Noiret?"

Valentin searched his memory and came up with a horn player, Negro or mulatto, a rough sort, with broad features and hard muscled like a gandy dancer.

"C.C. Ramblers?"

"That's right." Morton raised a cagey eyebrow. "Up until Tuesday night."

"What happened Tuesday night?"

The piano man dropped his voice dramatically. "He was murdered. In a boardinghouse over on Philip Street. He got stabbed in the throat while he was layin' in bed. I heard it was a hell of a mess."

Valentin nodded, though he didn't understand why Morton was sharing this information. For that he had to wait for the piano man to drink off his sherry, refill his glass, sit back, and settle a pointed gaze on him.

Valentin all but rolled his eyes to heaven. Now he understood. Lately, whenever some no-good Rampart Street jass player died or disappeared, Morton started muttering about someone hunting down and killing Negro musicians. The murder of this Noiret fellow would be yet another chapter in the grim tale.

While there was no doubt that members of that crowd dropped with an astonishing regularity, it was also true that a good share of them were nothing but low-down rounders who, when they weren't raising a hellacious ruckus in some saloon or dance hall, could be found drinking anything they could put down their throats, smoking hop or whiffing cocaine, throwing away their dirty silver at cards and dice, laying about with the cheapest whores, or engaging in drunken, often bloody brawls. They all packed a pistol or at least a straight razor. It was a wonder more of them didn't end up murdered in dreary rented rooms.

To Morton, it was sinister business. He had somehow gotten it into his head that these particular murders were attacks on those Negroes who had the gall to cross over Canal Street to play in bands, not with coloreds and Italians, but with white men. He saw the work of the Klan, the Regulators, or perhaps a single malcontent, depending on his mood. Valentin, on the other hand, was fairly certain that it was nothing more than band characters meeting cruel, though well-deserved fates.

They'd argued over it before and he really didn't want to do it again this night.

Morton did. "I tell you, there's something goin' on," he said, his whisper so cryptic that Valentin gave out a short laugh. Morton put on a pinched look of frustration and threw up his hands. "All right, forget about it, then," he sulked. "But you're gonna wish you listened to me. Something ain't right about it."

Valentin got to his feet, leaving his drink. "It's late," he said. "I'm going home. I'll take Beansoup with me." He walked out of the pantry.

They ambled south on Iberville Street in the dead of night. Beansoup yammered a blue streak for the first few blocks, then began to wind down as they made their way through the Quarter. By the time they turned the corner onto Magazine Street, his shoes were dragging.

When they got upstairs, he headed for the couch without being invited, and in the time it took Valentin to creep through the bedroom, pull an old blanket from the closet, and get back to the front room, he was fast asleep and snoring like a root hog.

Valentin went back into the bedroom. The rear window that looked out over the narrow alley was open, allowing a breeze to waft in. Justine had pulled the baire up, even though it was too late in the year for mosquitoes. He went to the bed and lifted the netting a few inches to gaze down at her sleeping face. He could just make out the outline of her scar, right above the temple at the hairline.

As he stood watching her, she gave a little start, her eyelids fluttered, and she let out an anxious sigh. Her arm extended a few inches and her palm came out, as if to ward off something that was assailing her. Then the hand drifted down and she was quiet again.

He put the baire back, went to the window. Nothing was moving. From up on Gravier Street, he heard a dray horse snort and the creaking wheels of a hack. As he leaned on the sill, he thought back over his evening, arriving at Morton and his crazy notion that someone was out killing jass players, complete with a hint that Valentin use his skills of detection to ferret out the guilty party. It opened a door to a roomful of thoughts and pictures that made his brain begin a busy circle, and he whispered a silent curse at the piano man for dredging it all up again. Tired as he was, he knew he wouldn't be able to sleep for a while.

He went into the front room, walked softly past the sofa where Beansoup sprawled and snored, and slipped out the door again, locking it behind him.

The fittings for the gaslights on Magazine Street had been removed, but the Public Works Department had yet to begin installing the electric lamps in their place. So there was only a half-moon, hanging low over the Gulf and casting swaths of pale silver amongst the long shadows, to illuminate his path.

He headed south and east along the narrow streets. He often walked the city in the dead of night when he had trouble sleeping, sometimes all the way to the Irish Channel or Esplanade and back. He had covered most of New Orleans one step at a time and could swear he knew every dark corner, every side street and alleyway by heart.

On other nights, like this one, he would travel only as far as the banks of the river, where he would stand watching the ships and barges ruttle past, one after another, carrying their heavy cargoes, with spectral lights and wet metallic groans and clanks, out onto the dark waters of the Gulf.

He climbed the long slope of the levee and looked over to the other side and the little constellation that was Algiers. As he stood there, the glittering pinpoints melted into the vision of a smoky saloon, a table scattered with dirty playing cards, and the body of a good-for-nothing rounder named Eddie McTier stretched out on the sawdust floor, blood bubbling from the angry hole in his chest, a hole that had been blown open by Valentin's own Iver Johnson revolver. That had been what, two years ago? And the picture was as clear in his mind as if it had happened yesterday.

His thoughts wandered from the dead gambler to a dead prostitute named Annie Robie, and from her to Buddy Bolden, the jass-playing madman. Valentin knew if he didn't stop right there, the whole sad tale would play out in his mind and he would once again end up judging himself guilty of something.

Just then he caught a wisp of motion and looked over his shoulder, but it was just another vagrant shadow. He sometimes imagined that one night he would turn around and see Buddy standing there, the silver cornet dangling loose from his hand, wearing the wide, white, wicked grin that announced he was ready to claim the city streets for his own. It had never happened, of course, and it never would.

Out on the river, a freighter blew one low, mournful note, an echo of Bolden's down-and-dirty jass, rising and then fading into the night.

———

By the time he started back, the first muted streaks of dawn were edging over the flat horizon. The earliest birds in this corner of New Orleans were beginning a new day, and here and there piles of rags, some of whom Valentin knew by name, stood up and walked. The air smelled of the rolling river and the closer and more pungent odor of gutters filled with animal and human sewage.

He opened and closed the door and crept into the bedroom. He could make out Justine's form through the thin silk netting. She was curled around her pillow as if it was keeping her afloat in a stormy sea. She didn't move or make a sound when he slipped in beside her. He let out a long, tired breath as he felt his bones sag into the mattress. It wasn't long before day. He could sleep now.

THREE

Valentin heard music from somewhere, a soft tune, sweetly sung, rising and falling like a bird trilling on a far-off branch. It was such a pleasant sound that the corners of his mouth bowed in a drowsy smile as he followed the tune, up and down and around the lilting path of its melody. Then it faded, as if the bird had flown off, and he tumbled back into sleep.

He came fully awake an hour later to the smells of coffee beans and chicory brewing. By the patterns the sunlight had cast on the wall, reaching almost to the wainscoting, it was after ten o'clock. He had slept five hours, maybe a little more. Not a bad night for him.

He pulled on the linen trousers that were draped over the bedside chair and sat there for a moment, looking at nothing. Then he got up and ambled out the front room to stand in the kitchen doorway, his feet bare, his thumbs hooked over his waistband, his undershirt hanging loose on his lank frame.

Justine was at the table with her head bent over one of the books he had bought for a penny at the street market. Aside from the scar at her temple, she appeared the same sporting girl he had first met two years ago. Her milk-coffee skin, long, textured hair, and small, tight body made her look younger than her twenty-four years, as pretty a dove as had ever graced Antonia

Gonzales's mansion, and Valentin knew that the madam had been sorry to see her go.

He had taken her out of the sporting house and brought her to his rooms on Magazine Street in the middle of the string of killings of prostitutes they called "the Black Rose murders." When that nightmare ended and the case had been laid to rest, she stayed on. It had been over a year and a half.

He went to the spindly old cast-iron stove to pour a cup of coffee out of the blue enameled pot warming there.

"What were you singing this morning?" he asked her.

She raised her head and gave him a puzzled look.

"I thought I heard you singing," he said. "Earlier, I mean. I was still asleep."

"Oh, that." She blushed and smiled slightly.

"What was it?"

"Just something I heard somewhere. I couldn't remember the words."

Her smile lingered for a moment, then dwindled by slow degrees into something wan and distant. She closed the book and asked him if he was hungry.

By the time he returned from the privy and had finished in the bathroom, she had fresh coffee brewing. He sat down and she put a plate in front of him, with a buttermilk biscuit split open and topped with two eggs, sunny-side up. She took the opposite chair and picked up some sewing.

He broke the first yolk, musing for a moment on how normal it would appear, the two of them sitting there, him quietly enjoying his breakfast while she mended socks like a dutiful wife. It had been like that for some months, and he had just begun to wonder how long it was going to go on when he noticed that there was something amiss with her.

At first it was nothing much: odd looks, curious slips of the tongue, sudden laughter over nothing. One day she would be the woman he knew: quiet, quick to smile, busy with her days, content with her life with him, always eager to frolic on the bed. The next day she would be acting like another person, all agitated about something that he couldn't see or name. She got impatient over small things, her dark eyes flashing annoyance. She had always been on the quiet side, but sometimes she would go for the better part of a day without saying more than a few words. He studied her more closely and saw tensions hiding beneath her placid facade. When he asked her if there was something wrong, she would first look startled, then frown absently, as if the question irritated her, and so he didn't ask anymore.

Valentin St. Cyr's successes as a detective had come less from his powers of deduction than from his ability to see behind masks and divine what drove people this way or that. It seemed he had a sixth sense that allowed him to untangle the sordid webs that miscreants wove. Such was the reputation he had built; though it was true that there hadn't been anything to test it in a good while.

Justine had him bewildered. Though she had long since recovered from her injuries, she still complained of headaches, a leftover effect from a blow to her head. Her doctor prescribed paregoric, and Valentin noticed that as the months passed, she was employing the medication more and more. That wasn't like her, either. She had never been one to drink too much whiskey or smoke hop, like so many of the sporting girls; and yet she seemed to have acquired a yen for her prescription and filled it religiously every Saturday on her way home from Mass.

He had paid a quiet visit to her doctor, the same young Creole who had treated her at the hospital. He described her symptoms and asked if there might be any lingering effects from her injury. The doctor had at first looked dubious, as if he thought Valentin was exaggerating, then listened with growing impatience to the description of her shifting moods and odd behaviors.

With a brusque shrug he said, "These matters of the mind are still a mystery. Most likely, it's something that will pass in time. Let's stay with the paregoric for her pain and we'll see how she progresses." Then he excused himself and hurried off.

Nothing had passed in time. She was still behaving in such strange—

"How were things at the Café?" she inquired, breaking into his thoughts. She was often eager for news from the circus that was Storyville.

"The usual," he said. "Couple fellows decided to have a knife fight right in the middle of the floor, but that was all."

She nodded toward the front room where Beansoup was sawing logs. "Where did you collect him?"

"He was hanging around Hilma Burt's."

She cocked a curious eyebrow. "What were you doing there?" She knew he never went into a sporting house unless he was on business.

"Morton wanted to see me about something."

"About what?"

He didn't really want to go into it, so he gave her a short version of the conversation. In the light of day, it sounded all the more foolish. "This Noiret character was a bad sort," he told her. "Someone was bound to stick him with a knife or shoot him dead sooner or later. And it happened way out on the other side of Canal Street." He shrugged. "There's nothing to it, no matter what Morton thinks."

Her blank look told him she wasn't listening anymore. He went back to his eggs. "How did you spend your evening?" he inquired presently.

Now her eyes cut at him before she spoke. "I stayed here," she said. "Did the wash and read some. Then I went to bed." There was no mistaking the edge in her voice. He was about to say something about it, but her face closed again as she peered myopically at a stitch.

"You aren't going to eat?" she said after a moment, her tone softening. He picked up his knife and cut into the biscuit.

When he finished his breakfast, he put his plate in the sink and carried his coffee cup to the bedroom to dress. Some minutes passed and he heard her singing again, the same song, a sweet melody without words.

When it was time for him to leave, he called to Justine. If she answered back, he didn't hear it.

Friday was payday. In addition to the regular salary he earned working five or six nights a week at the Café, Valentin received a stipend from three of the finer sporting houses on Basin Street, the mansions of Antonia Gonzales, Countess Willie Piazza, and Lulu White. He had become something of an unpaid security man at Hilma Burt's mansion as well, due to her liaison with Tom Anderson. With the King of Storyville's most recent amours, he wondered if he would be taking on duties at Josie Arlington's, too.

He had a ritual. After his bath and shave, he would put on a light cotton shirt and dark linen trousers, attach his suspenders, lace up his brown leather walking shoes, and head out the door. He was one of the few gentlemen of the day who went on the street without a hat.

Downstairs at Gaspare's Tobacco Store, he'd purchase a copy of the *Sun* and a cigarillo that had been imported from Cuba. If the weather was good, he would cross Canal Street and spend an hour smoking and reading in Jackson Square. If it was cold or raining, he'd take his paper four doors down to Bechamin's Café and grab a table there. Afterward, he would catch a Canal Belt car north to the District.

Justine stepped out onto the balcony in time to catch Valentin as he came out of Gaspare's and sauntered toward Common Street, his newspaper tucked under his arm. He didn't look back and so he didn't see her watching him. He always used to turn around and wave, leaving her with a small smile as he went off to begin his day. He hadn't done that in some time. She tried to recall when he had stopped.

As she stood there, with the stream of pedestrians, the bicycles, wagons, streetcars, and the occasional motorcar busying Magazine Street, thoughts that had been lurking in the corners of her mind stirred once again.

Another night had gone by, another day had begun, and she had missed it all. The world had turned in a cascade of color and sound while she stayed home, passing the hours with chores, a bath, and a book. She had taken a small dose of her medicine after the sun went down and it made her feel a little better.

She hadn't stirred when Valentin came to bed, and she woke up just after the first light of day with a small headache. She helped herself to the other half of her dose. The tincture, a red darker than blood, went swimming in the glass of water. She had hummed a song she had heard somewhere while she waited for it to take hold.

She had lost herself in a book until Valentin woke up. She served him his breakfast and they chatted like strangers. When he got up and left, she was visited by a familiar emptiness. Now the day stretched out before her. She had to concentrate to remember what she was supposed to do first.

Valentin found a quiet corner of the square, sat down, lit his cigarillo, and opened his copy of the *Sun*.

A presidential election was in the offing, and the paper suggested that Mr. William Jennings Bryan had such a clear lead over Mr. William Howard Taft that the result was a foregone conclusion.

He saw that two local stories that had been the source of much chatter had come to a close. Daniel Roche, the scion of a respectable Garden District family, had pleaded guilty to embezzling nearly thirty thousand dollars from his employer, blaming his erring on a cursed addiction to opium.

The other story was far more grim. The Lamana kidnapping had come to an end with the hanging of Antone Scalisi. The Sicilian, in a feud with the Lamana family, had kidnapped seven-year-old Carlo. The boy had died, though whether by accident or intention was never clearly established. It would have been cold comfort to Scalisi as he went to the gallows that it was the state and not the Lamana clan extracting justice.

Valentin knew that he could have settled the dispute before it wound to its tragic conclusion. But he hadn't even been asked; yet another indication of how far he had slipped, in what little account he was held these days. With that doleful thought, he folded the newspaper, stood up, walked out of the square and down Decatur Street to catch a Canal Line car heading north.

In another ten minutes, when the car came to a stop at Basin Street, he was greeted by a familiar—and now famous—tableau.

The *Sun* and the politicians called it "Storyville." To everyone else in the city, it was "the District." The former moniker was the namesake of Sidney Story, the alderman who wrote the ordinance that had created it. Though this particular garden of earthly delights had been in full bloom long before Alderman Story arrived upon the scene.

Since the battalion of prostitutes swarmed to New Orleans in the wake of Andrew Jackson's ragtag army of 1812, red lanterns had been hung in the windows of the shacks of wanton women as a sign of invitation to pleasures of the flesh. The harlots in the rough hovels and the bordellos that came later were consigned by righteous citizens to the dirt streets "back-of-town," which meant beyond the basin that had been dug over the decades by city dwellers claiming dirt upon which to more securely found their French Quarter homes.

Through the better part of the century, the neighborhood bordered by Basin Street was a stage upon which a tawdry carnival was staged. In grand mansions along the main thoroughfares, champagne brought fifty dollars a bottle and beautiful

octoroons entertained the sons of Crescent City high society and
the royalty of foreign lands; while just around the corner, along
the line of filthy Gallatin Street cribs they called "Smoky Row,"
drunken whores would lure hapless customers, spit tobacco
juice in their eyes, knock them cold with bats, and steal everything of value that they carried or wore, leaving them to crawl
away with their lives, if they were lucky.

Though it was a vicious, sinful, disease-plagued slough that
evolved beyond the basin, there were no efforts to stamp out the
scarlet trade. It was a gold mine, after all, pouring hundreds of
thousands of dollars into the pockets of some of the city's most
respectable coffers, including those of the churches that owned
certain parcels of real estate. It took almost ninety years to de-
vise Storyville, a twenty-block square attached like an after-
thought to "downtown" New Orleans, beginning at Basin Street
and running northeast between Canal and St. Louis streets to St.
Louis Cemetery No. 2.

This year, 1908, marked the eleventh anniversary of Storyville as the only red-light quarter ever legally chartered in the
United States, its forty-odd bordellos officially licensed as "Residences for Lewd and Abandoned Women." In fact, the District
was created by the kind of delicious dance at which politicians
were, then as now, so cunningly adept. According to the law
that Alderman Story authored, prostitution was declared illegal
everywhere but the streets of the District. So that by the turn of
the century, at least two thousand "soiled doves" were dropping
their bloomers and spreading their thighs in houses that were
confined by design to that single neighborhood.

Valentin crossed over to the corner of Iberville Street, stepped
under the colonnade of Anderson's Café and Annex, and rapped
a knuckle on one of the cut-glass diamonds that were set into
the polished wood. After a few seconds, the lock slid back with
a crack and a Negro holding a mop held the door open for him.

Tom Anderson was seated at his regular table at the far end of the bar. He liked to do business there, reserving his office upstairs for his more confidential and delicate matters. He had papers spread out before him, a gold fountain pen in his hand, and a fine china cup at his elbow. As usual, he wore a silk dress shirt from Mayerof's, the collar removed and top button undone at his fleshy neck. Suspenders hung down on either side of the chair. His round face was adorned by a well-maintained handlebar mustache that had, along with his eyebrows and oiled hair, turned a stately gray.

At Valentin's approach, he looked over the tops of the wire-framed glasses that perched on his thick and regal nose. "There's coffee," he said, gesturing with his pen.

The Creole detective helped himself from the copper urn that sat atop the marble bar. He brought his cup to the table and they got down to business, Anderson inquiring about any hints of trouble, any whispers going around the streets that might bear attention. Valentin knew that he employed a small army of spies to feed him information from the District's narrowest nooks and crannies. He himself had nothing to offer on this particular morning.

It didn't seem to surprise the King of Storyville, though it did seem to annoy him. He pursed his lips and his bushy eyebrows dipped. "So you haven't heard about this trouble on St. Louis Street?"

"What about St. Louis Street?"

"I got word that some coppers have been trying to get extra payments from houses up there."

"Who are they?"

Anderson gave him a hard glance. "Well, if I knew that, it would have been handled by now." He went poking through his papers and came up with a slip with some names and addresses scrawled on it and passed it across the table. "Those are the madams who complained. Pay them a visit."

Valentin glanced at the paper. The addresses were on the

fringe of the District, low-class houses that employed low-class women. Anderson read his thoughts, and said, "I know. But if we let them get away with this, they'll be knocking on Lulu White's door. Then we'll never hear the end of it."

They both paused to picture the scene, then shared a quiet laugh that faded soon enough.

"Very well," the King of Storyville said, and handed over the white envelope that had been resting near his elbow.

It contained Valentin's pay for the week in gold Liberty dollars, and the King of Storyville always passed it across the table when their business was finished. In the past, the pair might have sat at the table for an hour, drinking coffee and discussing the latest news and gossip from the District, chuckling about some recent drunken buffoonery, winking over a fine dove, muttering about a bad actor who needed a lesson in manners. Only when they were done would the King of Storyville offer the envelope, sighing with reluctance at having to return to more mundane business.

That was before. Things had changed and these days they were ill at ease with each other. Now, by unspoken agreement, the moment they finished with the matters of the day, Valentin was paid and sent on his way, to the relief of both men.

The detective made his exit now, leaving his half-empty cup on the bar. He could feel Anderson's gaze following him as he walked across the tiled and carpeted floor and out into the midday sun.

The King of Storyville spent a long minute staring fixedly at the empty chair. St. Cyr had been his man for almost eight years now, and though he made it his business to know everyone else's, after all that time the Creole detective's shifting and cryptic presence still vexed him.

He knew the basic facts, of course. The man's given name was not Valentin St. Cyr at all, but Valentino Saracena. He was thirty-four years old. His father, a Sicilian dockworker, had been murdered in the midst of the Italian troubles of the 1890s, and his Creole-of-color mother had disappeared not long afterward. Saracena had gone away for a long while, then returned to New Orleans, bearing the fairly common St. Cyr moniker as he covered his tracks and separated from his past. He had become a police officer, of all things, and first came to Tom Anderson's attention when he was assigned the Storyville beat. Anderson took a glance and then fixed an eye on the young patrolman, watching how he worked the District. It took a certain special touch; for there was no place like it on earth.

As it turned out, St. Cyr was a good copper. Too good to last, in fact, and when he left the force over some nasty business with a sergeant, Anderson stepped in to offer him a situation. It infuriated some in the commissioner's office, but he wanted the best man for the job and St. Cyr was it. He was hired to handle matters of security at the Café and around the District in general, and he earned more of his employer's confidence as time went by.

They had an unspoken agreement that he would pass as a Creole on the European side of the line, rather than a Creole of color, which he could truthfully claim on his mother's side. Even so, most citizens took him to be a white man. Those who knew the truth either didn't care or weren't about to challenge Anderson over having a person of color tending to his affairs. The King of Storyville trusted him; any discussion ended right there.

All had been well until the Black Rose murders of the spring of the previous year. It was after that terrible business ended that St. Cyr began to drift. For over a year now, he had been going about his duties mechanically, doing what was expected of him and little more, and more often than not it seemed his mind was elsewhere. Lately Anderson had been hearing whispers about his young lady, the café-au-lait dove named Justine, and he wondered how that might be complicating the detective's life.

Too bad, but business was business. The detective was not the asset he had once been. Still, it was with genuine regret that the King of Storyville found himself regularly mulling over who he might find to replace him.

The onset of the weekend always created a jittery buzz up and down Basin Street. Making his way along the banquette, Valentin had a sense of being on the floor of a busy market just before the rush of buying and selling began, or on a stage with the curtain about to rise on a grand, tawdry pageant.

He knocked on Hilma Burt's door and stepped into the same foyer that he had visited not ten hours earlier. The house was still, all the girls upstairs sleeping or just waking up. The Negro cleaning woman straightened when she saw him and nodded in the direction of the sitting room on the far side of the parlor. He exchanged a few words with Miss Burt, collected another envelope weighted with gold coins, signed a receipt in her little book, and went on his way. He was not invited to sit down and the madam kept a cool eye fixed on him the entire time. Valentin understood; with the trouble brewing between her and Tom Anderson, he was suspect. He made a hasty exit before the madam decided to start bracing him.

At Antonia Gonzales's one of the girls was waiting with the envelope and the receipt book. As he descended the steps from the gallery, it occurred to him that for the last few weeks the madam had not been around for his Friday morning visit. It was odd, since she had always been happy to greet him, chat for a minute, and personally hand over his pay. A touchy sort might think he was being avoided.

He got the same treatment next door at Countess Willie Piazza's, but he expected it there. The madam tended toward secrecy and intrigue, and liked to handle her transactions through underlings. It was just as well; he wanted to keep moving.

Which was why he made the house on the northwest corner of Bienville Street his last stop. He knew he wouldn't be getting out of there with a simple nod and a thank-you.

A maid ushered him inside and through a parlor known far and wide as the most extravagant in all of Storyville, with dark and heavy furniture imported from France, Persian carpets on the floors, thick curtains of the most luxurious brocade, and a massive crystal chandelier overhead. Polish wood glowed and glass sparkled. There was a mantelpiece adorned with ceramic figurines and two gold candleholders. A grand piano of brown walnut occupied one corner. The smells of fresh flowers from the French Market wafted sweetly over all of it.

The moldings and jambs were all of dark, heavy hardwood, and the house had been dubbed "Mahogany Hall" by its proprietor. The other houses in the District carried the madam's name: Hilma Burt's, Martha Clarke's, and so on. That wouldn't do for Miss Lulu. Her palace required an appellation.

On the far side of the room was an archway that led into a sitting room, and it was there that he found Lulu White waiting for him, posed like a queen on her favorite love seat, an opulent affair of tufted burgundy satin.

Miss Lulu was quite an odd bird, even for Storyville. Short and thick, with brown flesh and distinctly African features, she swore up and down that she was in fact white, donning wigs in various shades of red in hopes of bolstering her claim. She professed to be a native of Jamaica, the progeny of an English father and a Creole mother, even though it was common knowledge that she had been born and raised on an Alabama tenant farm. Though Valentin judged her to be at least half crazy, he also knew that she was a genius at turning a dime into a dollar and was easily the richest of the city's madams.

She greeted him with a smile that was genuinely fond and beckoned him to join her on the love seat. Once he was settled, she leaned back and went into the end table for his envelope and the receipt book. He signed the pad and pocketed the packet of coins.

"Very good," she said, as she put it away. "Can I offer you a cup of tea?" She reached for a little bell.

Though it was the last thing he wanted to do, Valentin accepted politely. He didn't like tea, and the madam's prying drove him mad, but unless she had something pressing, he was obligated to suffer through these sessions once a week. Of late, it was always the same routine: she would launch into her latest gripe about Anderson and Josie Arlington as a way to pry information out of him. He had nothing to offer and wouldn't share it if he did. It never seemed to occur to her that she was barking up the wrong tree. She had convinced herself that the Creole detective had Anderson's ear and was dutifully passing her pronouncements on. That Anderson was hearing her complaints and ignoring them was all the more proof that her suspicions were well-grounded. And so it went, round and round in her mad mind.

As soon as the maid appeared with the service on a tray, she asked how things were at the Café.

"Fine," Valentin told her, also as usual. "Very quiet."

Small as it was, she took the opening. "Well, that's a good thing, isn't it? Tom Anderson doesn't need any more trouble. He's a busy man these days. What with having to service Josie Arlington, Hilma Burt, and who knows who else. He's no young rooster. You'd think he'd know better. It's simply unfair..." And off she went, running down her list of grievances. It was an old song.

Valentin nodded mechanically, barely sipping his tea, his mind elsewhere. After about five minutes, she slowed the tempo of her rant, closing with a dramatic huff. Her face fell, and cracks of age came creeping out. Valentin felt a twinge of sympathy for her. Though she had sports to squire her about in exchange for money and gifts, her life had to be lonely. There were just too many younger, prettier girls about for any rounder to stay long. So a fellow would entertain her for a little while, take whatever he could grab, and move on.

She was no longer the free-spending grand dame when it came to fancy men, and her charity diminished with each new leech. A black-hearted swindler named George Killshaw had put an end to those days.

"Enough about all that." She cut into his thoughts as she finished her morning diatribe and turned down another path, treating him with a frank gaze. "How are things with you, Valentin?"

"Things are fine," he told her, wondering why she was suddenly so serious.

She was waiting for more. When he didn't speak up, she said, "And how is Justine?"

"She's doing well. She still gets her headaches."

"Yes, of course," Lulu White said, nodding with concern. She sipped her tea, then dipped her head cagily. "Now, what's this I hear about someone out after jass players?"

Valentin grimaced; so that was it. He should have known. Of all the madams, Miss Lulu had the sharpest ear for gossip.

"Morton's got this idea in his head, that's all," he said. "I didn't know he was spreading it all over town."

"Oh, he's not!" the madam said in an even more conspiratorial whisper. "He was by last night, this morning, actually, visiting one of my girls. We were talking and..." She smiled with childish pride that she was the one Morton had confided in. "So there's nothing to it?"

Valentin said, "He has a good imagination."

"I see." There was disappointment in her voice. "Well, then, it's business as usual, isn't it?" She put her teacup aside and, muttering about the demands of her busy day, got up to see him to the door. "Give Justine my regards," she said as she let him out.

———

He finished the rest of his errands and got back to Magazine Street in the middle of the afternoon. Justine had put out a cold plate of andouille, cheese, vegetables, and French bread. After he ate, he thanked her with a quiet courtesy that made her feel like a servant and went off to the bedroom. She heard the springs squeak, then silence.

She stepped into the kitchen, opened the cupboard, and found the packet of Straight Cuts that Valentin kept there. She carried one to the balcony, where the rough smell of the tobacco would dissipate. Snapping a lucifer on a brick, she leaned in the doorway to blow out a long spiral of smoke.

When she touched an absent finger to the scar along her hairline, she felt the slight depression where the flesh had never quite healed back. It was a souvenir. A sudden memory of the moment when she had received it brought a spike of fear that was followed by a flush of anger. The feeling seeped away, leaving her all bewildered, as if she had lost something. She watched the street, trying to make her thoughts wind their way back the way they had come. When she felt the ember of the cigarette burning close to her fingers, she gave up. She tossed the butt over the railing. It left a tail of tiny embers before it landed in the gutter.

She looked over at the Banks' Arcade, four stories, brown stoned, and stately. With its gardens and ornate fountain, its fine dining establishment and elegant suites upstairs where gentlemen entertained their paramours, it was a place reserved for the well-to-do French and Americans of New Orleans. As she watched, a woman stepped through the tall wrought-iron gate of the side garden and onto the banquette. Justine stared; there was something familiar about the woman—her face half veiled beneath a Floradora, her fine silk dress and brocade shawl, the way she held herself, her head high and shoulders squared. Justine knew that the woman, a pretty quadroon, had spent the night with a gentleman of means in one of the upper-floor suites and was waiting for the cabriolet that was now rounding the corner of Gravier Street to carry her away.

The carriage pulled up and the Negro driver bent down to offer her his hand. As she pulled herself up, she must have sensed Justine's stare, because she raised her head. Their eyes met over fifty feet of air. Then the quadroon woman smiled slightly and settled back into the fine red leather seat. The driver cracked his little whip and the carriage clattered off to turn the corner of Common Street.

Standing above the morning traffic, her hands resting on the wrought-iron railing, Justine slipped into a reverie. She saw herself in a dress with a bodice that showed off her narrow waist and the curve of her bust. Her hair was up and she had on just enough mascara to bring her slanted eyes out over au-lait cheekbones. She smiled at the reflection and the woman in the glass smiled back, as if she was—

She jumped a little, startled by a singsong call from down the street. The greengrocer's wagon was rolling around the corner, the wheels creaking and groaning under a full load of produce. She stood still for a long moment, letting go of her crazy thoughts, letting them swirl away like bits of colored paper caught in an updraft. Her mind cleared and she was back on Magazine Street on a Friday afternoon in September. She went to find her bucket and rope.

Friday nights were always busy at the Café and Valentin left just after dinner. Before he went out the door, he kissed her gently on the forehead. Then he escaped, leaving her to see her own way through the long evening.

The sun was going down. Terrence Lacombe sat on the gray greasy mattress in the room in the hotel on Peters Street, breaking down his clarinet. Pawning it meant he wouldn't be able to work if a job came along. It didn't matter; he was getting sick. Already he had chills and a feeling of something crawling on his skin, the cold burning itch that would soon be driving him half mad if he didn't do something about it. He wanted to chase the pictures that kept coming into his head, too: a big black man sprawled all bloody on the bed, a butchered carcass. Just the image brought another shudder. He snapped the case closed and stood up.

He was pulling on his overcoat when he heard footsteps out in the hallway. He froze, figuring it was the manager coming around for the week's rent, money he didn't have. He took a step toward the window, then remembered that the fire escape was fixed so it didn't reach the ground, forestalling exits just like the one he was considering.

The footsteps drew close, stopped for a breathless instant at his threshold, then turned and padded back down the hall. Terrence fidgeted, grinding his long, dirty nails into his palms. It didn't matter if it was a trick. He had to go through the door to get to the pawnshop to get the cash to get the remedy he needed this night. He pulled his coat tighter around his throat and made ready to bolt if he had to, past the clerk and down the stairs and out onto the street and away.

He opened the door a few inches, then a little wider. He stuck his head out to peer up and down the corridor. It was empty and early evening silent. He was just about to step out and make his escape when he noticed the paper sack at his feet. He took another sneaking glance along the hallway in both directions, then snapped it up, ducked back, and closed the door.

His thin fingers were beginning to tremble as he reached inside the sock and drew out a glassine envelope that held a good tablespoon of crystalline powder, off-white in color. Terrence stared at it in wonder. He couldn't imagine who would present such a lagniappe or why. Then he didn't care; another wave of nausea was rising in his gut.

In less than a minute, he had the powder cooking in his blackened tin and had pulled his belt off his waist and strapped it about his arm. He forced his hands to stop shaking and, with a practiced move that was almost graceful in its delicacy, used his brass-plated syringe to draw off the liquid. Eyeing a place he hadn't yet ravaged, he guided the needle into the vein. Then he slipped the plunger back, sucking blood. He waited a sweet, agonizing second, then pressed with his thumb.

It came on like a dizzying rush of warm air through his head and then through every cell in his body. The sick feeling was washed aside and he felt like he had settled into a steaming bath.

He heard the door hinges squeak. He was turning his head to see who it was when he felt a blow to his heart like someone had slammed him in the chest with a sledgehammer.

A second blow came, this one knocking him sideways off the bed. He did not feel his head collide with the bare floor, only that he was looking up now and that a face was looming over him, already turning black around the edges. The mouth moved, biting off words that were lost in the roar of blood in his ears. Another shuddering wave came over him, bursting from the middle of his chest to the tips of his fingers. The face disappeared into blackness and he was gone.

A moment passed and the door to the room creaked closed.

It was near 5 A.M. and Anderson's Café was quiet. The band had long since stopped and the bartenders had all gone home. Mr. Tom had slipped off for his rendezvous with a girl from Gypsy Shafer's.

Valentin said good night to the old Negro watchman, then walked outside to stand on the banquette. None of the streetcars were running yet. He had money in his pocket for a hack but decided to walk the ten blocks south. As he crossed Dauphine Street, he heard rubber tires swishing up from behind. A surrey rolled to a stop and Jelly Roll Morton looked down from the rear seat. "You want a ride?"

"What are you doing here?" Valentin said.

"On my way home. Come on, we'll carry you."

"I'd just as soon walk."

"All right, then." Morton stepped down onto the banquette. He was a sight, all done up in his finest, as crisp as if he had just dressed for a night out on the town. He told the driver to go on and wait for him at the corner of Magazine. The carriage clattered away. After they had walked a few paces along the banquette, the piano man glanced at Valentin and said, "Well?"

"Well, what?"

"What about Noiret?"

Valentin gave him an annoyed look. "Is that why you stopped? Because if it is, you need to call him back before he gets too far on." Morton opened his mouth to protest, but Valentin cut him off. "I saw Lulu White this morning." He came up with a severe look. "You need to stop spreading rumors."

"They ain't rumors," the piano player sniffed. He looked around, as if someone might be lurking nearby, then dropped his voice to a deep whisper and said, "Why Noiret? Why him?"

Valentin wanted to say because most likely he was a good-for-nothing son of a bitch. He didn't, though, and Morton went ahead and answered his own question. "Because he was working on the wrong side of Canal Street." He took another furtive look around. "You know how those people are," he said urgently. "They ain't gonna allow it."

Valentin shook his head in exasperation. He was not about to get into another argument over this crazy business. Morton didn't understand. It wasn't just that Antoine Noiret was nothing to him. Or that the murder was already three days old and had happened far back on Philip Street, along a row of dingy houses that were broken up into tiny rooms available to transients by the day or week and to cheap whores by the hour. Without even seeing the place, Valentin knew Noiret wasn't the first dead body that had been carted out the front door.

Morton had his own ideas, of course, and if there was no

stopping him once he got going, it didn't mean Valentin had to listen to it. "I don't want to talk about this anymore, Ferd," he said. He was one of the few people who was still allowed to use Morton's given name. "I just want to get home and go to sleep."

Morton looked like he was about to come snapping back with something. Then he thought better of it and put his hands behind his back as they walked on. "You ever think about Buddy?" he asked ruminatively as they crossed Camp Street.

Valentin said, "I do, yes."

"They'll not make another one like him," the piano man said with a little laugh.

Valentin never knew what to say when someone mentioned Bolden, so he kept quiet. They walked the last block in silence, each thinking his own thoughts.

They stopped on the corner where the hack was waiting. Morton reached for the brass bar, then stopped to look down Magazine Street in the direction of Valentin's rooms.

"How's Miss Justine?" he inquired.

"She's well. Why?"

"I'm just asking," Morton said, and smiled curiously. "Make sure you give her my regards."

He pulled himself up into the wide rear seat. The driver snapped the reins and the carriage rolled away.

FOUR

Justine opened her eyes and stared at the cracks in the plaster wall. The pillow was damp where her face had pressed into it and she pushed it away. There was sunlight through the window that opened out over the alley; it had to be late, after ten. She had missed early Mass again.

She felt Valentin's warm breath on her back and rolled on her side to look at him. She could not count the mornings when she had lain beside him in the bed, wishing they could hide there like sleepy children while the world went on without them. She knew it was silly, a schoolgirl's daydream, and of course she never mentioned it to him. She studied his profile, now unguarded in repose, his olive skin bloodless with sleep, wondering if she watched long enough, she'd be able to read something in his face. Then she thought about shaking him roughly awake to catch him unaware and ask him exactly what was on his mind.

There was a time when she didn't have to puzzle over it. He would tell her about his days and nights, about the part of his life that she didn't see. He described the cases he worked and she giggled over the gossip he brought home. He had even told her about his past, about the tragedies that had rained down on his world as a young boy.

There was more. He had listened to her stories, too, intrigued by her tales of the life she'd led before she landed in New Orleans. Unlike most rounders, who cared nothing for a girl other than to serve their basest needs, Valentin had shown true concern for her. He had taken her out of Miss Antonia's to protect her. He had stayed by her bedside while she recovered from her injuries. When it was all over, he didn't exactly invite her to stay, but he didn't put her out, either, and so there she remained.

She had a sudden memory of the moment she realized something had gone askew. He had come back from his last visit to the hospital in Jackson and there was a look on his face that she had never seen before. He wouldn't—or couldn't—tell her what was wrong. He just sat across the table from her and didn't say a thing. At one point he reached over and ran gentle fingers along her unhealed scar. His gray eyes were stricken, wounded, as if he was the one who had put it there. She never forgot that look, because it had lain so heavily on that moment.

She came to understand in the months since that he was carrying a terrible burden of guilt over what had happened to his friend Bolden—and to her. It started small, then grew to a presence between them, like a third person in their rooms, an intruder who wouldn't leave. Or so she imagined. She didn't even understand what went through her mind some days. Whatever it was, real or imagined, he had let it get the best of him.

As the time passed, they spoke less and of less important things. He didn't bring much of himself home anymore. They frolicked less often, and so she had to wonder frankly what she was doing there.

She thought of waking him up at that moment with a rough shake and asking him just that. Before she got foolish and actually did it, she slipped out of bed, maneuvering over him delicately until her feet touched the floor. She took the silk kimono that was draped at the end of the bed and pulled it on over her thin nightshirt. As she reached the door, she heard the springs squeak and looked back. He had turned on his stomach and sprawled his arms wide, as if reclaiming the bed for his own. She went into the bathroom to start the water in the iron tub, then went into the kitchen to put the coffee on.

The street was busy with hacks, motorcars, and the occasional streetcar milling up and down as the banquettes filled with pedestrians on Saturday morning errands. Bechamin's front door was standing open and from behind its counter the Frenchman waved a greeting as Justine walked by. She stole a glance across the street toward the Banks' Arcade, recalling the quadroon stepping into the fine carriage, and the way she'd held herself, all stately, a lady in charge of her affairs. Or at least as much as any woman in her world could be.

A breeze off the river greeted her as she crossed Canal Street. Slipping into the shadows of the Quarter was entering another world, quiet and still at this early hour. She walked more slowly now, meandering up one narrow street, turning a corner, and turning down another. It was pleasant there, shaded from the sun, and as she passed under the colonnades with their wrought-iron railings, she lost track of time.

Her thoughts again went wandering along with her, drifting away from the narrow streets of the Vieux Carré, out of the city of New Orleans, back along country roads, around the outskirts of little towns, and into the deep green shadows of the bayou. It was a familiar path. Sometimes the memories seeped in like slow water; other times, they jumped in with sudden and jarring focus. At regular intervals lately, she got an overpowering sense of something reaching out of that dark, lush tangle to clutch at her, all but making her heart stop. Then the feelings would pass and she would think she was just plain crazy.

It had not been so long ago that she was looking out the cracked window of the collapsing shack at the black water that crawled along beneath the ancient trees. No one who saw her parading through the city of New Orleans in her fine dress could guess how far she had traveled. She thought of her brothers and her sisters, wondering where they were now, and if they ever thought of her. It made her heart sink to realize that she might not ever see them again, not after what had happened that one awful August day.

The brakes of a steam engine shrieked and she all but jumped out of her skin. She looked around, blinking in the late morning sun. The bayou was gone. She was standing on the corner of Basin Street and Iberville, directly across from Anderson's Café. Behind her was Union Station, the trains chugging in from the south and chugging out to the north and west in a long half loop around the border of the District.

Somehow her absentminded wandering had brought her all the way through the Vieux Carré and to the main line of the red-light district. Basin Street was a noisy jumble of metal, the odd harsh music of the infant century. A hack went by, then a streetcar, the wires crackling overhead. She smelled ozone, burning coal, horse manure, the dirty smoke from the motorcars. Delivery boys hurried along the banquettes, sweating as they pulled wagons of goods for the sporting houses. It was the start of another busy Saturday in Storyville.

Justine peered up and down and across the street to see if anyone had noticed her. Then she realized that none of the people she knew would be out at that hour. Her eyes came to rest on the facade of Antonia Gonzales's mansion, across the street and a half block down. She knew it well. It had been her home for a year and she still thought of it fondly. She had been the fairest of the sporting girls there, and only gentlemen of class and sports who stayed flush won the pleasure of her company. Miss Antonia had been sorry to see her go.

She heard the faraway bells of St. Ignatius tolling three-quarters. She could make it to noon Mass on time if she hurried along Basin Street and then turned east on St. Ann. Once she stepped inside the chapel, the scent of the incense, the whispered prayers in sonorous Latin rising to the vaulted ceiling, and the pale tinted light through the stained glass windows would combine like a special potion to calm her mind. Her body would unwind, too, as the jumble of thoughts and images inside her head wound down, like a top at the end of its spin. It never failed; though just to make sure, she would stop at the apothecary on her way home and have her prescription filled.

Though she knew she need only put one foot ahead of the other and start walking, she didn't move. She kept gazing across at Miss Antonia's as she dropped her hand into her purse and brushed a finger over the three pale pink envelopes that were tucked away there. Inside each was a small card with *Miss Antonia Gonzales* printed on it in fancy script. In the space underneath the name, the madam had penned messages, each one polite, though insistent. *Please visit me at your convenience... Requesting a visit as soon as possible...Please contact me at your earliest convenience...*

It had started with a chance meeting at the French Market one afternoon a month or so before. Miss Antonia had greeted her kindly, warmly, more like a doting aunt than a former employer. They didn't speak of anything important, just an exchange of pleasantries. The madam must have sensed something, though, because a week later the first of the three messages arrived.

Justine had kept the notes for weeks now, so long that the first one was beginning to fray at the edges. She knew what was happening and first dismissed the idea, then found herself returning to it again and again. She threw the notes away, then went back an hour later to retrieve them from the trash bin. She had even gone so far as to ride to Basin Street, only to turn around and ride back home without crossing over. Now, without thinking about it any further, she waited calmly until another hack and a motor wagon passed by, and stepped into the street.

Valentin woke up to the noon whistle. He rolled over and sat up slowly, feeling the kinks in his bones from sleeping too long in one position. His head was groggy, like he had a hangover.

He dawdled and drowsed for another quarter hour, then stood up and stretched. He pulled on trousers and shuffled into the kitchen. Justine had gone out somewhere and hadn't left him anything, no coffee on the stove, nothing in the oven, no note.

He went out the back door and down the creaky wooden stairs to the privy. When he came back inside, he ran water for a bath and munched on an apple while he waited for the tub to fill. By the time he got out, she still hadn't come back, and he wondered idly if she had stayed so long at church because she had extra sins to confess.

He got dressed and walked over to Poydras Street to find a café where he could linger over breakfast and a newspaper.

With the long overdue bill in hand, the desk clerk knocked and called out Lacombe's name. There was no answer, so he called again, then used his passkey. He found the Negro lying on the floor, as rigid as wood, his eyes and mouth open in a ghastly mockery of shock. A telltale scribble of dried blood trailed down his forearm and a syringe hung there in the graying flesh like a brass leech.

The clerk wasn't shocked at all. He'd seen it a dozen times before. He spent a quick half minute going through the musician's pockets; if he didn't, the first copper on the scene surely would. He came up with nothing of value. No surprise there, either. He saw the clarinet case on the end of the bed and decided it would be worth at least something at a pawnshop. Lacombe wasn't going to need it anymore.

The clerk put the case under his arm, locked the door behind him, and went back downstairs to call the precinct to send a wagon.

Valentin came back to find Justine in the kitchen in one of her cotton frocks, fussing over a simmering pot. When she greeted him, he caught a flicker in her eyes that came and went in the space of a second. She was in one of her distracted moods, acting all nervous and not meeting his gaze.

He sat down in the front room and pretended to be busy rereading his *Picayune*. She left her pot to simmer and went into the bedroom to lie down, murmuring of another headache. She left her purse open when she dug out her prescription, and he noticed that the three pink envelopes that had been resting there for so many weeks had disappeared.

He thought over what that might mean, then abruptly decided that he didn't want to be there when she woke up. He had some work to do anyway.

He went down the stairs and along Magazine Street, then walked all the way through the Quarter to the corner of Conti, then around the white walls of St. Louis Cemetery No. 1 and through Eclipse Alley to St. Louis Street. Four blocks north, he found the first address.

The talk of policemen extorting money that Tom Anderson had passed on was odd business. Everyone from the commissioner to the patrolmen on the beat shared in the graft that was collected from the houses. The donations from the madams were made in an organized way, weekly, usually through the precinct sergeant, who then passed the money up and down the line. It had worked that way for decades and few ever bucked it. In the rare instance when someone did, the response was direct. Some lucky souls escaped with a brutal beating. The bodies of

others who misbehaved were fished out of the muddy Mississippi days later. So anyone who knew Storyville would understand that it would be insane to step outside the bounds and risk
Anderson's ire as these characters had.

Valentin stepped up to the facade of the house, a run-down
two-story brick building near the corner of Robertson Street. He
wasn't familiar with the address, so along the way, he picked up
a copy of *The Blue Book,* the pocket-sized volume that listed
almost every sporting girl in the District, by race, by religion in
the case of the Jew Quarter, and by certain specialties. The ladies
at No. 1604 St. Louis Street were of course billed as graduates
of an unnamed academy of amorous arts in Europe—even
though it was unlikely that any of them had ever traveled any
closer to that continent than the Georgia state line.

He knocked on the door and was greeted by the madam herself, a fat, surly-eyed woman named Carrie Butler. She was in
her stocking feet and a worn Mother Hubbard. When he stated
his business, she muttered gruffly and waved him inside.

The house was filthy, reeking from one room to the next of
mildewed wood, stale cigar smoke, and close sweat. The plaster on the walls showed islands of stain and the floor was buckling on a crumbling foundation. It looked like it hadn't seen a
good cleaning in years, and there hadn't even been an effort to
mask the grime that had soaked into the carpets and curtains.

Miss Butler led him to the back of the house and into the
kitchen. She sat down heavily at the table and grunted for him
to take the opposite chair. He told her he preferred to stand.

The women who passed in and out while they talked were
a sorry lot. Without the blessings of rouge and mascara, their
faces were dry and drawn, like they suffered from unknown ailments. Girls who couldn't have been more than twenty looked
twice that age in the hard light. Each one of them appeared hungover and wrung dry from the night before, and not one even

pretended to smile as she checked him up and down with cold fish eyes.

Though the establishment was advertised in the *Blue Book* as a French house, the truth was that these women, working the bottom rungs of the Storyville ladder, would do almost anything for money. They were coarse and ugly and a few small steps away from one of the cribs on Robertson Street that rented for ten cents a day. For all that, they were as much a part of the District as the denizens of the grand mansions on Basin Street.

Of course the madam understood this, because she began complaining to him the moment her vast bottom hit the chair. "You tell Mr. Tom Anderson something," she groused. "We ain't next door to his damn Café, but this is still Storyville. You tell him that." She rapped her knuckles on the table. "Ain't like we don't pay the goddamn coppers enough as it is! I hand over my envelope every Monday evening. I got chits in a jar over there that say I paid. Then these two show up at the door."

Valentin said, "When was this?"

"Wednesday, around suppertime. They said they was police. The one pulls out a badge, tells me I got to give him twenty dollars. Said it's a special fee or he's gonna shut me down. What the hell was I gonna do? He had a badge. So I give him the twenty dollars."

She pulled a soiled handkerchief from her sleeve and blew her nose, a wet, noisy snort.

"That ain't all," she went on. "I ask him for a chit to show I paid, he says, 'We don't give no goddamn chits.' Tells me to shut up about it. But they still ain't finished. One of my girls come down the stairs to see what the fuss is about, and this fellow takes ahold of her. He pushed her into the closet under the stairwell and makes her give him French right there. Then the partner takes his turn. When she's finished, they don't give her a dime."

"Then what?"

"Then what?" Her mouth twisted. "Then they left. Said they was gonna come back next week to collect again. Said if we tell anyone, there'd be hell to pay." She clenched both her hands into fists. "He grabs hold of me again, says, 'And you know what I mean!' When they walked out the door, they was laughing."

"Can you describe them?"

What she offered didn't help much. They were of average height, the partner slightly heavier than the one who did the talking. They both had medium brown hair, slicked with cheap-smelling pomades. She remembered that the one who showed the badge had a long nose and that his teeth were yellow. She'd never seen either one of them before.

"The fat one had a pistol on him," the madam said. "Mary, that's the girl he took under the stairs, she saw it in his trousers."

"What kind of pistol?"

"I don't know. A regular revolver, I guess."

"Was there anything else?"

"That's all." She gave him a snide look. "Now what are you going to do about it?"

"It sounds like a single incident," Valentin said. "Couple tramps passing through."

"What about the badge?"

He shrugged. "Fake."

The madam said, "It wasn't no damn fake! I seen enough New Orleans badges to know."

He wasn't about to argue with her. He told her he would be looking into it and that she should send word immediately if anyone saw either of the men again. She gave a grudging nod and got up to see him to the door.

Valentin visited a second house, an even shabbier affair a block away, and got a similar story. This visit had come about an hour after they were reported at Miss Butler's. The same de-mand for twenty dollars was made. The men didn't force anything on any of the girls, but the madam said that they were clearly drunk.

Valentin guessed that they had collected at Carrie Butler's, then visited the first saloon they happened upon to spend their booty. Once into their cups and with the money gone, they realized how easy the pickings had been and went out to find another likely house. They had no doubt caroused with the money they had collected there, too, and would have been throwing cash around like sailors all up and down St. Louis Street.

He spent the next two hours visiting the saloons and sporting houses, covering three blocks south and west. The two impostors were identified at three establishments, though no one knew who they were. Then the leads dried up. The pair wouldn't have dared to venture much farther. At that point, they would be on tonier streets with finer sporting houses and better restaurants and music halls, the kind of places that kept hired toughs on the premises to deal with such problems. They'd be lucky to get past the front door.

Valentin thought briefly about the badges and wondered if they might be rogue coppers, then dismissed the notion. It didn't make sense for a policeman to go off on his own. No, these fellows had come into the possession of a fake badge or a real one that had been stolen or lost. They would have been better off throwing it in the river. Instead, they saw a ticket and got greedy. They had gotten away with it the first time around. If they came back for more, Valentin would be waiting.

Lieutenant J. Picot, short and thick, his skin yellowish and his dark hair oiled, slammed the telephone into its cradle and then banged his fist down with such force that it sent his stack of papers flying into the air like startled birds. With a loud grunt of irritation, he called for one of the junior patrolmen to come in and clean up the mess, then stood up and stalked to the window.

The lieutenant had thought that St. Cyr was done poking his nose into police matters. After that Black Rose business, he had all but disappeared from sight. Now he was at it again, snooping around the east end of the District.

No one was more incensed than J. Picot that Tom Anderson, the most powerful man in the city, one of the most powerful in the state of Louisiana, had no faith that those sworn to uphold the peace could do so. At least, that was the way Picot saw it.

St. Cyr in particular exasperated him. For Anderson to keep a few thugs around to crack heads was one thing. Some of those fellows were off-duty coppers. Employing a private detective was something else entirely. St. Cyr wasn't even a Pinkerton. It was not just a professional slight; it was personal, too. He didn't like the Creole and never trusted what was going on behind those flat gray eyes. Just the thought of it made his blood percolate.

He spent a moment calming himself, then gave orders to two of his men to go to St. Louis Street and deal with the problem over there.

He turned away from the window to pace up and down while the patrolman who was trying to collect the papers dodged his steps like a clumsy pup. He knew it was his own fault. He had played the wrong hand during what the papers called the Black Rose murders. St. Cyr could have had him thrown off the force or even brought up on charges over that mess. He didn't, though he just walked away, as if Picot wasn't worth the trouble of an arrest. It left the lieutenant baffled and scared.

After that, they had managed to stay out of each other's affairs. And now a niggling matter of crude extortion on St. Louis Street seemed to have occurred for the sole purpose of putting St. Cyr in the lieutenant's path, and Picot in his place.

He stopped his pacing and sat down at his desk once more, thinking that crossing swords with St. Cyr again might not be such a bad thing after all. There was talk going around that the

Creole detective had fallen into some kind of funk and had lost his edge. If it was true, then the lieutenant just might get a chance to even the score and put things back where they belonged.

It was also a busy weekend at the City Morgue, and it was not until the late afternoon that one of the attendants got around to the body of Terrence Lacombe. There was a note pinned to the deceased's shirt, noting that he was twenty-five years old, had died of an apparent overdose of morphine, and that he was a "musician" by occupation. He received his toe tag forthwith, and his body was wrapped in gauze and placed on one of the shelves in the cooler. In three days, if no family or officials claimed him, he would be dropped in a wooden box that would then be loaded into a boxcar, carried off, and buried unceremoniously in an unmarked backwoods grave, erasing Terrence Lacombe from the earth as if by a stroke of God's own thumb.

FIVE

A few minutes after ten o'clock that evening, the front doors of the Café opened to admit two out-of-town drummers with familiar giddy looks that announced they possessed more money than sense. Valentin could almost hear predatory eyeballs shift in every corner of the room. Right behind these two came Beansoup, his gap-toothed face bobbing, a balloon on a string. His wide eyes got wider at the bright lights and happy noise that had the big room all aglitter and vibrating like a machine.

"Are you on your way to St. Mary's?" Valentin said pointedly. The kid's attention came back around, his mouth setting in a pout. He made a rough gesture that was half a shrug, half a nod.

"So if I send somebody over to Miss Burt's in a half hour, you won't be on the premises?"

"No, I won't be on the goddamn premises!" Beansoup crabbed. He pointed at the bar. "How about a drink? It's a long walk."

"You can have root beer or a Chero-Cola," Valentin said, and went into one of his pockets for a Liberty quarter. "Then you can walk or ride. A car will be by in a few minutes."

Beansoup accepted the coin with an absent frown. He decided against a drink, given the way the detective was eyeing him. He started for the door, then turned around, his moon face brightening. "Did you see Miss Justine?"

"Excuse me?"

"Miss Justine…did she come to see you?"

"When?"

"Tonight. I saw her…" He blinked rapidly and his voice trailed off.

"You saw her where?" Valentin said.

The kid swallowed, his Adam's apple bobbing. "I think… it was…maybe it wasn't her."

"Where did you see her?" Valentin's voice was even.

"Out front of Antonia Gonzales's." Beansoup's face flushed and his eyes skittered away. "But maybe it wasn't her."

Valentin said, "You better be on your way."

A few blocks back-of-town, a six-piece band was working hard, churning out one frenetic jass tune after another. The throng that filled Abadie's on Marais Street to the rafters couldn't get enough. They drank and danced, and the more they drank, the wilder they danced, until the floor looked like a stormy sea of flailing arms, juking legs, and bobbing heads.

It was an odd gumbo of a crowd: black, Creole, Italian, white, and a sampling of in-betweens. There was the usual number of rounders and whores, working their trades. The players at the card games upstairs had to raise their voices to be heard over the braying horns and stomping feet.

The jass the band was playing had only crossed over Canal Street within the year. Before then, it would have been heard only in low-down dives and dance halls out on Rampart Street. That was where Bolden and his gang had started it all, grabbing up gutbucket, ragtime, church music, cakewalks, and anything else they could find, mixing it up, and shoving it through the bells of their loud horns. It was something no one had ever heard before, raw and raucous, noisy and fast. First the Negroes went wild for it, then it was the Creoles, and then the American New Orleans got the fever. Bolden was gone, but there was no stopping the trouble he'd started, and jass rolled across Canal Street. Now, every night of the week, a half-dozen bands were rattling windows and shaking walls.

The band at Abadie's was among the best. Out in front was Anthony Cimonelli, a short, fat Sicilian blowing a trumpet. He puffed his cheeks and all but came off his feet with each mighty breath. To his left was Willie Cornish, a big man, over six feet tall and as wide as a freight train, swinging his valve trombone back and forth over the heads of the gyrating dancers and leading the band with nothing more than nods of his thick brow and flicks of a free finger. A freckle-faced Creole called Little Red tootled a clarinet in crazy loops as a skinny stick of a Negro named Vedre thumped a bass fiddle and Danny Dooley, a tough-looking Irish kid who couldn't have been more than fifteen, snapped a snare drum and crashed a cymbal. Jeff Mumford, the guitar player, sat on a café chair, his legs spread as he flailed an arch-topped Kalamazoo. His head turned from one side of the room to the other in a lazy arc as his right hand smacked the strings, laying down a solid, chugging rhythm for the horns, and his left hand did a four-fingered dance of shifting chords up and down the neck.

The back-of-town women liked Jeff. At twenty-two, he had smooth caramel-colored skin, piercing black eyes, and a ready smile of even white teeth beneath a sharp mustache. His body looked solid, too, not like one of those sports already worn down on hop, cocaine, whiskey, or all three. He looked like a fellow who could go the distance. The girls fancied that, too.

Tonight, like every other night lately, he took their steamy glances and tucked them away. There was a time when he was on the game, but it would be a rare one who could hold a candle to what he had waiting at home.

Not five minutes later, he was stunned to lay his eyes on exactly that. He looked at the woman, glanced away, looked again. Their stares met and locked over thirty feet of smoky space; then, as abruptly as she had appeared, she slipped back out of the light and out of sight. As they ran down the remainder of their set, Jeff kept looking at the spot where she had been. She didn't reappear. He shook his head to clear it, thinking it must have been some kind of illusion of shadow and light.

When they stopped for a break, he went looking, just to make sure. All he found was the usual assembly of sporting girls either working the crowd or out for some pleasure after an evening serving gentlemen in one of the houses, the sports at their usual hustles, and the young white men with nice suits and faces all shiny who had left the American side of town to hear some wild, foot-stomping jass.

Jeff was sure he had imagined the whole thing and gave up. He was turning around to head to the bar for a drink when she appeared suddenly out of one of the shadowy recesses between the furnace stacks. He took a step back. When she stared directly into his eyes, he had a startling notion that he knew her from somewhere, though he knew that couldn't be.

She was wearing a simple walking dress. That was all she had in common with the strumpets who were wandering or staggering around the saloon, looking to earn some quick Liberty dollars. She was watching his face from beneath a hat with a low brim that partially shaded her features. He was nervous trying to think of something to say when she leaned closer and in a throaty whisper murmured, "What's your name?"

"Jefferson. Jeff. Mumford."

"Jeff Mumford." Her eyes settled coolly. "Well, I'd like to get a breath of air, Jeff Mumford."

Outside, she led him through the crowd, down the banquette to the next corner. She kept her head down and they didn't look at each other, like two strangers who just happened to be going the same direction. They turned onto Villere Street and she steered him along the block some twenty paces to an alleyway that ran between two storefronts, just wide enough to permit a hack to pass. She slowed her steps and looked back over her shoulder, inviting him with her eyes. "In here," she said in her low voice.

Jeff followed her into the dark space, still not quite believing what was happening. A glimmer in a corner of his mind told him that he was being played for a sucker and some roughneck was about to appear with a knife or a pistol to rob or murder him on the spot. He'd heard of such things.

She kept watching him in a way that was oddly familiar and another warning bell sounded from far in the back of his head. There was something not quite right about her eyes. Still, she looked ready and willing. He was ready to put his qualms aside and see what she was good for, when from the street he heard Cornish yell, "Jeff Mumford!"

The woman's cool eyes slid off him and she frowned in the direction of the voice.

Jeff said, "*Damn* him!"

Cornish called his name again, drawing closer. The woman's gaze came back. First she looked angry; then she gave him a smile that he read in an instant. He almost called out to Cornish to go fuck his fat self, because he had something to attend to.

The trombone player wasn't going to let it be. "Jeff Mumford!" he called, now even closer.

"Jesus Christ! I've gotta go play," Jeff said.

"Later, then," the woman said. "I'll wait for you."

Still, he hesitated. One like her didn't come along often—or ever.

"Go on," she murmured. "I'll come find you after."

Jeff gave her a smile and a wink and slipped out of the alley. Cornish was standing on the corner, looking his way. As Jeff hurried to join him, he saw the big man gazing dazedly past him toward the alley, his mouth half open. He glanced back in time to see the woman turn away down the banquette, her skirts trailing behind, a pretty witch in flight. It was such a vision that Cornish stood staring until the guitar player yelled at him to come along.

When an hour passed and she didn't reappear, he began to wonder if he really had imagined the whole thing. He knew that voodoo women talked about haints that took the form of women who came to men in their beds. Maybe they came to jass players in music halls, too. He never believed that sort of thing; now he wasn't so sure.

No, something had happened; he could tell by the way Cornish kept glancing over at him. And he still could not shake the baffling notion that the woman was somehow familiar. Another hour went by and the cramped room got stickier with the heat of all the sweating bodies shoved together. A cloud of tobacco smoke hung thick and gray near the ceiling. The band played louder and faster and the dancing got wilder. There was a fight, with shouts and some shoving that was taken outdoors. The door swung open and closed as the sports and the sporting girls and the others, black, white, and every shade in-between, milled in and out. Jeff kept looking, but she was not among them. If she'd ever been there, she was gone now.

Justine sat on the couch with her feet up, looking out at the dark street. One of Valentin's books lay open on her lap. She had been trying to read, but the words just blurred. The St. Boniface bells had just struck two thirty, tolling with a gloom that fit her mood so perfectly that it almost made her laugh.

The madam had divined something from their passing encounter at the French Market a month or so ago. When the first invitation to visit arrived a week later, Justine guessed what it was about. She didn't respond. She stood before the mirror and told herself that she wasn't ready, not yet. It wasn't as if Valentin got drunk and beat her, or ran with street whores, or gambled away their money on the turn of a dirty card. That would have made it easy.

A second invitation came, then the third, both unerringly polite. She kept them tucked away in her purse, taking them out now and again. She couldn't think of a reason why she should go. Then she couldn't think of a reason why she shouldn't. She was confused, her regular state of mind lately. She didn't know what she was doing anymore.

Then that morning found her standing on Basin Street and a few minutes later on Miss Antonia's gallery. Afterward, she went back home and fidgeted until she could calm herself enough for a nap. When she woke up, she fidgeted some more, until she was sure Valentin wasn't coming back but going directly to work at the Café. She took a long bath and laid out one of her finer dresses and a new hat. Though she didn't like them, she wore a corset that cinched her waist and raised and plumped her bust. Then a shirtwaist that accentuated her figure all the more. The hat, a flowered affair, had a veil to hide her features.

She slipped outside in the falling darkness, hoping that Mr. Gaspare wouldn't see her and call out. She went around the block to Poydras Street and got on the St. Charles Line car. She spent the ride enjoying the admiring glances of the male passengers. Now she felt like a schoolgirl off on some innocent mischief.

One of the men tipped his hat and offered her a hand down at the corner of Rampart Street. She walked up one block, then crossed quickly over Basin Street, and went up the steps to the gallery.

She rang the merry bell and Miss Antonia herself appeared to whisk her inside. They spent an idle hour gossiping in the madam's private sitting room. Justine had been away from the

District for a long time and there was much to discuss. She did not mention Valentin and Miss Antonia did not ask after him, even though they both knew that at that very moment he was working just down the street. The madam served glasses of champagne and Justine got a little tipsy. It was like old times, when it was slow because of the weather or just a quiet night, and the girls would sit around talking and drinking until they got sleepy. There were no men demanding their attentions or favors. They were simply young again, and for a little while the drink washed away their heartbroken histories.

Miss Antonia excused herself and when she returned she brought a gentleman, a slender, well-dressed Frenchman whom she introduced as Paul Baudel. Mr. Baudel bowed politely, his Gallic eye sweeping Justine's face and body with a modest though clearly appraising glance. They chatted about nothing of importance for a few moments. Then the madam escorted him back into the front parlor, where his friends were waiting.

Miss Antonia returned and poured more champagne. She mentioned in passing that Baudel was a gentleman of considerable means, having married into one of New Orleans' most prominent old French families, the Sartains, their fortune coming from thousands of acres of rice plantations on the Delta to the north. Sadly, she said, the family had this generation produced three daughters and one drunken fool of a son, and so Paul, the arranged groom of their eldest daughter, was picked to replace the ailing father and manage the company. He made a success, enriching the family's coffers, and was much respected in the business community and in New Orleans social circles, known to give to the Opera House on the one hand and the Colored Waif's Home on the other. He had a sterling reputation and was a devout member of St. Michael's Church.

Though all this information was delivered in a casual way, as if it was just more idle chatter, Justine understood perfectly that she was being courted. There was nothing more said about it, and when the clock on the mantel chimed ten, she took her leave. That's when it happened.

Miss Antonia called for a carriage to carry her home, then stood on the gallery, waving a good-bye. Justine lifted her skirt and went down the steps and across the banquette. The driver offered her a hand up. She had just stepped on the running board when she sensed something and turned her head to see Beansoup standing there, staring at her, his face twisted up in bafflement, as if he couldn't quite grasp the picture before him. She realized that she had forgotten to lower the veil.

She stopped with one foot up as their gazes locked. His mouth opened and he raised a hand to greet her. She could tell that he still wasn't sure if it was her. He had seen her in the morning in her nightshirt and kimono with her hair all undone. He had seen her in one of her simple cotton shifts. He had never beheld her in the kind of finery that was intended to catch a man's eye.

He had to be wondering what she was doing there. For an instant, she felt like calling to him, asking what he was doing out at that late hour. Hadn't Valentin given instructions that he was to be off the streets after dark?

She caught herself and stepped the rest of the way into the surrey. The driver jumped up into the front seat and snapped the reins. As they pulled into the street, she peeked over her shoulder to see Beansoup standing there, his hand still raised and mouth still half open, watching the carriage roll away. She felt her stomach sink like it was full of lead. It was bad luck, terrible luck. Within a matter of minutes, she had gone from being eyed like a prize by a wealthy Frenchman to ducking her head and hiding in shame from a dirty thirteen-year-old street urchin.

The bells struck three-quarters and she let out a sigh of dismay. She knew that Beansoup had more than likely scampered into the Café to tell Valentin what he had seen. He was just too much the busy bee. So she had been caught out, and she had no doubt that she was going to pay for it.

She put the book aside, got up, and went into the bedroom. She sat down on the edge of the bed, realizing that there was another possibility: Valentin might hear the news and not say a word about it, because he didn't care what she did anymore.

Willie Cornish lifted his valve trombone and held one last long middle G until it filled the room to its grimy walls, then ran the scale like he was scurrying up a ladder. It was a good try, but he couldn't reach the top, and the run died in a weak gasp. With a tired chop of his hand, he brought the song to an end. He dropped the horn to his side and croaked, "G'night'chall."

Mumford flexed his aching fingers, sat forward in the chair to stretch his stiff back, then drew a handkerchief from his pocket to dab his brow. He took a moment to wipe the side of his guitar where the sweat from under his arm had already begun to blur the finish, then laid it gently in its case. It was exhausting business vying with noisy horns, and every night he had to beat so much hell out of the fragile box of wood and wire that Mr. Orville Gibson of Kalamazoo, Michigan, would likely drop dead if he saw the punishment Jeff had visited upon the fine instrument that his workmen had crafted.

There were a few claps, hoots, and calls for more, though they didn't carry much vigor. Jeff stood and made a small bow, for what little it mattered. The rest of the fellows had already packed up their horns and left the stage. He looked around the room, saw only the usual stragglers, the bartender, and one stranger who was slumped against the back wall with a slouch hat pulled low over his eyes—no doubt one of those determined drunkards who searched high and low for the last open saloon so that he might have a final round before the thick New Orleans darkness was broken by the hard morning light.

The woman who had appeared so mysteriously to lead him

into the alley and then evaporate was not in sight. Jeff wondered frankly if he had lost his mind or had indeed been visited by a haint.

He packed up his guitar, said his good-nights, and walked across the filthy sawdust floor and out onto the banquette. He could feel the sweat drying to a salty film over every inch of his body, and his ears were still ringing from the hours of loud brass, shrieking clarinet, and thumping bass fiddle.

After all that raucous jass, Marais Street was like a cemetery. Nothing was moving. Not a single sot staggered along the gutter and not one sporting girl screeched a curse into the failing night. It was one of those strange hollow pockets that came but once a night and usually in the minutes before dawn. He felt like he could hear a cat slinking.

He passed the alley, looked into the shadows. It seemed unreal, something that happened a long time ago. At least it was going to make a hell of a story. He yawned and rubbed his face and continued west, going home, almost shuffling, his guitar case banging the side of his leg. He would have paid a Liberty dollar for a streetcar ride, or even a leg up on the back of a hack, but nothing was moving at this hour. So he shuffled on.

As he passed another alleyway, this one between Fourth and Third streets, he heard a voice mutter. He glanced over, expecting to see a man with a woman either on her knees or bent over with her hands splayed against the wall and her petticoats hiked. It was a common enough sight in these parts. It always amused him that these couples never stopped their exertions, but simply glared with reproof until the intruder went on his way.

There was no busy pair this time. Instead, it was the stranger who had been lurking by the door in the dance hall. Jeff heard his name called and saw a flash of white teeth, beckoning him closer, and figured that he was going to be offered to share a hop pipe, a card of cocaine, or at the very least something from a bottle. People did that for the players sometimes as a way of thanking them for the music. A year or two ago, a fellow who played jass was about as low-down as you could get, no better than a pimp or drunkard or hopeless hophead. Now people wanted to buy his drinks.

It was exactly that. From beneath the brim of the hat, white teeth gleamed again and a hand came up, holding a flask of burnished silver. It was a fine piece of work, with filigree tooled into a crest. It looked like a rich man's possession, not often seen in these parts. Its owner was either brave or a fool, because a sneak thief would cut a fellow's throat for such a rare item.

Jeff accepted the flask, turned it over in his hand, feeling the satiny finish, then pulled out the stopper, a cork set in a silver cap and attached to the body of the vessel by a tiny silver chain. The lack of a screw top told him he was holding an antique. Whatever liquor was inside had an antiquated smell, too: he caught a whiff of something like old wood. He thought absinthe, a rare blend, or something just as exotic. He was in for a treat.

The stranger gave another encouraging nod of his head, the features of the face still indistinct. Jeff tipped the flask and drank, not bothering to wipe the lip. The liquid rolled over his tongue, warm and verdant. Absinthe, to be sure, but a blend he'd never tasted before. The stranger waved a hand for him to help himself to another sip. Now the heat filled up his mouth and moved deep into his throat.

He lowered the flask, smiling his thanks as he handed it back. With a single motion, the stranger replaced the cap, took a step backward, and raised his chin so that the night's light could play across his face. Jeff felt the eyes now fixed on him with a hard glint and he had a sudden startling rush of fear. Just as suddenly, a sharp spasm rocked his guts, his throat contracted, and he staggered, dropping his guitar case to the dirt.

He lurched into the brick wall, then tried to make for the street, but his legs wouldn't obey, wobbling like they'd been broken. He felt a stabbing pain and a sudden spout of blood erupted from his mouth. His guts were on fire and he fell to the ground, vomiting another spout of blood. Now he tried to crawl, but his arms had no strength and he collapsed, his body curling as the acid heat roared through his guts. His eyes rolled up and he saw the stranger looking down at him, muttering between clenched teeth. The pain was tearing him in half, and with one long, whimpering groan, he threw himself forward in a last try for the street. Then he stopped moving, his body twisted grotesquely.

The stranger stepped around the body and bent down to spit in the dead face, then strode away, kicking at the guitar case. It flipped over and broke open and the instrument tumbled out. The edges of the cobbles gouged the polished mahogany and snapped the high strings. The stranger stalked out of the alley and hurried down Marais Street, moving through the shadows on quick legs, head bent and shoulders hunched, another weary wisp of the night, creaking away home.

SIX

Jelly Roll Morton had not nearly gotten his sleep out when someone came pounding on his St. Charles Avenue door. The dove lying stretched out next to him just let out a soft groan and burrowed under the pillow as he jerked upright, his brain going off on a jagged jaunt, picturing the police coming to arrest him for some unnamed evil deed.

The pounding continued and he heard a voice that didn't belong to any copper. It was higher, almost girlish, thin with excitement. The dove who has holding the pillow over her head muttered in annoyance and kicked a brown foot. The one who was splayed across the foot of the bed didn't make a sound, dead to the world. Morton got up and went out of the room in a woozy stagger. He threw the door wide to find Beansoup, all pink faced, sweating and gasping for air. Behind him was his shadow, the Negro boy named Louis, huffing like a little black steam engine. "What do you want?" the piano man snapped.

The kid whispered a few words. Morton's eyes went wide. He cried, "Jesus and Mary!" and told them to run to Mr. St. Cyr's.

Valentin was standing on the tiny balcony, watching the quiet Sunday morning street. He had only slept a few restless hours, and when he woke up Justine was gone, probably to early Mass. Now he saw her, approaching from the corner of Common Street. She was walking slowly, her hands folded before her as if she was still at prayer. He went back inside.

Their eyes met when she came through the door and she hesitated, wondering if he would say anything. She amused herself for a vacant moment by imagining him raging like a husband who had caught his wife dallying. She tried to picture him in a fit like that, stomping up and down the floorboards, his face red and sweating and his voice all hoarse from shouting. She couldn't do it, though, because Valentin never went in for such dramatics. She tried to recall the times that he'd allowed her a peek behind his mask. Surely she could count them on a hand. It didn't matter; she couldn't think of any now.

And he wouldn't be adding to the tally this morning. He was silent, treating her the same way he would any other suspicious person, watching and waiting for telltale signs. She decided to try to disarm him. "You missed Mass," she said, keeping her voice light. It was a small joke. He never went to church.

He gave her a vague look. "And how was it?"

"The same as always."

"Did you go to confession?"

She heard the catch in his voice and saw something behind his eyes, swimming just below the surface. She hesitated, wishing she'd never brought it up. Then she nodded.

"And do you feel better now?" he said.

When she didn't answer, he seemed to take a step back, though he didn't move an inch. She had a sudden glimmer of understanding. He thought that she had betrayed him, first by going to Basin Street, and then by not falling on her knees to beg his forgiveness over it.

Now she wanted to say something, to confess to *him* if that's what he demanded, but she couldn't think of any words that might soften the eyes that now judged and found her wanting. God might have forgiven her trespass. Valentin wasn't about to. She felt her blood rising and bit her tongue to keep from cursing right back at him for being so heartless.

She moved past him and into the bedroom to change, half hoping that he'd follow her. He stayed where he was, though, and the silence from the front room was thick, almost eerie. She undressed slowly, down to her camisole, then put on a cotton housedress.

When she stepped out into the front room again, he was gone. She went onto the balcony and looked down Magazine Street in time to see him disappear into Bechamin's.

She felt a clutch in her gut and there was a strange dry taste in her mouth. He knew about Basin Street. And what else? Miss Antonia's? Paul Baudel? And yet he still wouldn't accuse her. The thought of it made her breath come short and for a moment she imagined the look on his face if he came back through the door and found her waiting for him with one of the big kitchen knives. Maybe that would loosen his tongue.

She let the moment pass, catching her breath, slowing her pounding heart, and holding back the tears that were about to brim. She stepped back inside, closed the door behind her. She had an unsettling sense that something had just happened completely out of her sight, a battle fought and finished without a single shot being fired.

She sat down at the kitchen table with a glass of water and the amber bottle that held her prescription. The doctor had told her two drops, but he didn't know her, so she drew three, no, four, and watched them drip into the clear water. The potion became a snake the color of old blood, twisting and slithering downward. Then the liquids blended into faint reddish brown. She drank it down in three swallows and closed her eyes while it went to work.

Time passed, minutes or an hour, and her anger faded into a dull gray hum. More minutes went by, and she heard footsteps on the stairwell. The front door opened and closed, and he came into the kitchen with a tin of coffee and a paper sack in his hands. It occurred to her dimly that she had forgotten to leave him anything for breakfast. She thought about getting up, but she stayed where she was.

Valentin, crossing to the sideboard, saw Justine's cheeks flush crimson as she rose from her chair just a little unsteadily, then sat back down. He opened the sack, took a bite of the egg sandwich that Mr. Bechamin had fixed for him, and sipped from his coffee tin.

She pushed her chair out, grabbed the edge of the table, got up, and walked out into the front room. Valentin took another bite and decided that he wasn't hungry anymore. He heard the loose board under the rug squeak with her passing steps. He went to the doorway and watched her pace, her gaze fixed on the braided rug beneath her feet. She looked troubled, like she had dropped something and was searching the floor in distress.

He cleared his throat and said, "Justine?"

She was surprised that his voice had come out so soft and unsure, and she stopped, her brow stitching. Though he seemed to be watching her from far away, his eyes weren't so hard now. She wanted to say something to him and was working her mind to compose the right words when the street door banged. Rapid shoes came slapping up the stairwell and then a hand rapped staccato on the door.

Valentin opened it and found Louis standing there. The shy boy with the twinkling eyes and ready smile now looked all grave as he spoke a few hushed words. The detective stared at him, then nodded. He turned to Justine. She knew the look. Something had happened. Someone was dead.

"I need to…" He made a weary gesture. "I need to go out."

"All right, then," she said, and held his gaze until he turned away.

Valentin and Mr. Jelly Roll left the two boys in the cobbled alley that ran behind City Hall and went through the door. The Colored Section of the New Orleans City Morgue was one floor down, befittingly underground. The corridor of damp stone was narrow and dark. There was a light glowing farther along, and when they got to the open door of the large room, they found it brightly lit, almost cheerful by contrast. The electric lamps overhead reflected off surfaces of white enamel and polished steel. The shelves that lined the side walls were filled with vessels containing various organs, floating in murky liquids, like undersea creatures from some Jules Verne fiction. A thick door on the back wall opened into the cooler. The air was chilly and the thick, stinging odor of formaldehyde saturated every corner.

Four gurneys were lined up along one wall, and on each was a body covered with a sheet, black feet and pink soles protruding. A mulatto attendant was running water over his hands at the sink in the corner. He looked around when they walked in and said, "Gentlemen?"

Morton didn't speak up, so Valentin said, "Jefferson Mumford."

"Uh-huh." The attendant flicked the rest of the water from his fingers as he went over to the gurneys and started checking the tags that were affixed to the protruding big toes. Valentin recognized the man. The attendant remembered him, too; he kept glancing over his shoulder with a cloying familiarity.

When he reached the third body, he pulled the gurney away from the wall to the center of the room. "Jefferson Mumford, at your service," he quipped, and drew the sheet down halfway. He looked at the two men to see if his humor had registered. They ignored him and he grunted and moved away.

At the sight of the dead face, Morton let out a soft groan, then crossed himself and whispered something under his breath. Valentin hesitated, standing back. Hadn't he seen enough corpses to last a lifetime? Beginning with his younger brother and sister in their little coffins, their tiny lives taken by Bronze John, the yellow fever epidemic of the 1880s. After that it was his father, murdered on the banks of Lake Pontchartrain. Then this sport and that sporting girl, dozens, all told, lying dead on a Storyville street or in a room in a Storyville house. There was Eddie McTier, the one cadaver he had created, with the help of his Iver Johnson pistol. Finally, there were the victims of the Black Rose Killer. It was a ghastly parade and he had to wonder what kind of career it was that collected so many carcasses. There was no escaping the fact that he and the dirty mulatto with the grinning yellow teeth had in common their firsthand knowledge with the dead.

He looked down at Mumford, taking a moment to remember him as he had been. Then, gradually, he pushed his mind away from all that and began a clinical examination of the remains. In his experience, the departed mostly looked peaceful in repose, their torments having evaporated with their final breaths. He noticed that Mumford's handsome face was instead reshaped into a strange mask, though, as if he was in the midst of a grimace when the bell tolled for him. He could see, as well, no wounds on the head or torso.

"What was the poison?" he inquired.

"Who said it was poison?" Then a yawn. "Strychnine."

The too-quick answer was no surprise. No one would even bother examining a Negro musician, magician, or mortician. An autopsy was out of the question. So strychnine it was.

There was nothing more to see. Valentin looked over the body once more, then pulled the sheet up and turned away.

"What happens now?" Morton said quietly.

The attendant spoke up. "Investigation's over. They're done with him."

"What investigation?" Valentin said.

The mulatto gave a greasy smile. "That's what I said." He looked between the visitors. "Is one of you gentlemen claiming the body?"

Valentin said, "No, I..." He glanced at Morton, who shrugged his indecision. "We'll see about it, I suppose."

"Because if he ain't claimed in another forty-eight hours, they take and bury him outside the city," the mulatto said.

"A pauper's grave," Valentin murmured.

"That's right." The attendant's yellow smile was ghastly in the light of the bare lamp. "Hell, he don't care. I swear I ain't ever heard a one of them complain."

They walked out into a midday that was under a bank of low clouds. Valentin half expected Morton to shake a finger and start railing about how he had warned him that this was going to happen. He didn't, though, and Valentin saw that his face had gone gray with melancholy that made him look years older. The piano man had known Mumford well, and there was real grief in those green eyes.

Valentin was anguished, too. Though he hadn't known Mumford as well as Morton had, he liked him, admired his talent, thought him a young man with much promise. He was a good-natured sort, not at all troublesome. And yet he'd been brutally murdered in a back-of-town alley.

"Maybe that woman of his will claim the body," Morton murmured absently.

"What?" Valentin said, coming out of his reflections. "What woman?"

"He had a woman living with him," the piano man said. "I can find out about his family. Cornish or one of those other fellows will know. If someone don't come collect his body, I'll take care of it."

"And do what?"

"Give him a proper place." He sighed and shook his head.

"Poor Jeff," he said. "It never should have happened." There was no recrimination, only weariness. He walked away. The Creole detective watched vaguely as he ambled a dozen paces in the direction of the street, then stopped and came back to stand before him.

The piano man's brow furrowed. "They played together," he said in an odd, distant voice.

"What's that?"

"Mumford and Noiret. They played together a few years back. In the Union Hall Brass Band. I thought you'd want to know that." He turned around and walked away again, and this time he kept going, passing by Beansoup and Louis, who stood waiting on the corner of the street.

Valentin dropped his gaze to the dusty cobbles, his thoughts in a jumble. He had discounted Morton's claim that there was something amiss, brushing Antoine Noiret's murder aside as everyday violence. From all accounts, the man had been a no-good rounder who'd probably gotten what he deserved. Now it didn't seem so clear. Seeing Mumford had rattled Valentin to his bones. The news that Morton had delivered sent another tremor up his spine.

Standing there in the narrow alley, Valentin felt something stirring. For eighteen months, beginning in the wake of the Black Rose murders, he had managed to muffle his instincts, his sixth sense, his detective's eye, or whatever it was that defined his skill.

Now, the combination of looking upon Mumford's dead face and hearing Jelly Roll Morton's muttered words was shattering the wall he had constructed, piece by piece.

Two musicians, both Negro, both playing in Storyville, both of whom had played together at one time, had died by violence within days of each other. There was no suspect in either case. Maybe it was a coincidence, and maybe it wasn't. It didn't signify. The murders deserved attention, if only because Mumford had died in Storyville. That made it Valentin St. Cyr's business. He needed to go to work.

He called to Beansoup and Louis to wait and went back to the side door and down to the basement.

The mulatto attendant was leaning against the doorjamb, puffing a cigarette. He cocked his head in lazy surprise when the Creole came down the corridor. "Forget somethin'?" he said.

"There was another Negro murdered, out on Philip Street, on Wednesday night," Valentin said. "Antoine Noiret."

"What about him?"

"Is the body still here?"

The attendant spat out a shred of tobacco. "What was that name?"

Valentin didn't have the time to waste. He went into his vest pocket for a Liberty half and shot it off with a snap of his thumb.

The mulatto flinched and snatched it out of the air before it hit him in the face. He sniffed, and then his smile returned. "Noiret? Yessir. I believe that citizen is still with us."

"I want to see him."

The attendant pursed his lips and examined the coin, holding it up before his eyes and flipping it around.

"There's another one when I see the body," the detective said. The attendant winked, tossed what was left of the cigarette, and jerked his head. Valentin followed him inside and to the cooler on the back wall. The mulatto grabbed an empty gurney and swung the heavy door open. "He can't walk out, so you're gonna have to come on in."

Valentin stepped into the cold room, lit only by four bare electric lamps that hung from the ceiling. There was an aisle down the middle and shelves on both sides, six feet deep and stacked with corpses that were wrapped in broad swaths of linen. Each shelf was no more than sixteen inches high, enough to accommodate all but the fattest of the departed. Those ladies and gentlemen were on the middle shelves, where they could be handled most easily. The lower shelves were the more average individuals.

It was a macabre collection that made Valentin's skin crawl a little. He couldn't wait to leave. The attendant seemed quite at home, a worm who spent his days underground with the rotting dead.

The worm went through a few more toe tags. "Noiret," he said. "Here he is." He pulled a gurney over and let out a loud grunt as he dragged the body on to the cooling board. In a quick minute and a flurry of busy dirty hands, the linens were gone and everything from the sternum up was exposed. Valentin stepped closer.

Noiret's face, a broad triangular affair, was like black wax in death. He was thick bodied, heavy in the shoulders, a brawler. His mouth was slightly open in a rictus smile. Below it, on the neck, was the fatal wound, trussed crudely.

Valentin reached up to grab the nearest electric lamp and swung it to one side so he could see better. From the look of the gash, Noiret's final moments had been about as horrid as Mumford's. The knife wound hadn't come from some fight in the heat of passion. It was too precisely placed. Someone had planned it, catching the victim sleeping, just as someone had gone to the trouble of poisoning the guitar player. Which meant, hard as it was to admit, Jelly Roll Morton could be right. Though Valentin couldn't believe it was over some Negroes playing with white men. The question remained, then. What was it all about?

Beansoup and Louis both came to attention when Valentin reappeared in the alleyway. When he went digging into his pocket for change, they responded like dogs hearing a whistle, hurrying to stand before him, their eyes and ears perked. Except that Beansoup hung back just a step or two, looking abashed, and Valentin realized that he was upset about Justine and Basin

Street. It had to be the reason he had sent Louis to fetch Valentin that morning.

He gave them each a Liberty quarter and said, "Go find Mr. Anderson. He should be back from church by now. He might be at the Café. Or at Miss Burt's or Miss Arlington's. If he's—"

"Okay, okay," Beansoup cut in, now all business. "We'll find him. What then?"

"Tell him I need to speak to him as soon as possible."

"You goin' to be home?"

"Yes, I'll—" He caught himself and looked around. There was a workman's diner across Carondelet. He realized that except for two bites of the egg sandwich from Bechamin's, he hadn't eaten anything since the night before. He pointed. "I'll wait for you over there."

The kid was giving him a searching look that made him appear in that moment wise beyond his years.

"Well?" Valentin said.

The two boys turned and ran away, all full of purpose, leaving the detective standing in the shadow of the building.

An hour later, he had finished a midday breakfast of boudin and eggs and was sitting over coffee and the Sunday *Sun*, staring at the page without absorbing any of the text, when the two boys came through the door and hurried to his table.

"Mr. Anderson's at Miss Burt's," Beansoup reported breathlessly. "He said he'll be there for a while if you want to come around." Valentin folded his paper and went into his pocket for money to pay his check. He glanced up to see that Beansoup had taken a step closer to the table. Louis stood back, his pop-eyed gaze wandering toward the ceiling.

Beansoup regarded the detective with a serious expression. "I didn't want to start no trouble," he said in a pronounced whisper. "Thing is, I don't know for a fact that that was Miss Justine I seen last night."

"Oh...it's all right," Valentin said.

"It coulda been anyone. There's lots of women on Basin Street. It was dark."

The kid's earnest intent was almost comical, and Valentin nodded seriously in response. "I'll go see Mr. Anderson now," he said.

"You want us to come, too?" Beansoup said, still fretting.

They escorted him down Magazine to Canal Street, where they all climbed on a car, riding in back out of consideration for Louis. It brought stares from some of the passengers, but Valentin was used to it. People assumed that he was one of those odd types who either didn't know any better than to ride behind the Colored line with the niggers or didn't care about the proper order of things. Occasionally, some ill-advised citizen, usually a drunk, would accost him about it. He met these accusers with a hard gaze that sent them back to their seats in the front of the car, muttering about what the world was coming to.

Valentin looked at the two boys. They were a funny pair. Beansoup, all pale faced and gangly, his hair like wheat straw, and Louis, a short little fellow, his eyes and smile wide and white against his chocolate skin. It was still permissible that they were friends, though it couldn't last much longer. Beansoup was getting too old; one day soon he would have to walk away from his small companion, and their days running the streets together would become a hazy memory.

As they pulled away from Burgundy Street, Valentin caught a glimpse of chimney stacks poking up from roofs along Basin Street. The clouds coming around from the southwest were getting darker, more animated. He watched them for a while, thinking about how he was going to present the matter of the deaths of the two jass men to Tom Anderson.

———

When they got off the car, he went into his pocket and dropped another Liberty quarter into each boy's palm. Beansoup gave him a searching look, then shrugged and jerked his head. The two of them sauntered off to find some likely place to spend their rewards.

Valentin crossed the quiet street, climbed the steps to Hilma Burt's gallery, and rang the bell. He was ushered inside by a Negro maid, who then led him to a sitting room with a sofa and two chairs of French design. While she went off to fetch Mr. Tom, Valentin went to the window, pushed the curtain aside, and looked out on Basin Street.

He only had to wait a few minutes before Anderson stepped through the door. The King of Storyville had been to church and was wearing a fine Sunday suit, complete with vest and watch and chain. It was part of his political genius to check his critics with sanctimonious displays, attending a different service every week, plus the occasional temple visit on Saturday. It also provided him an opportunity to spend a few private minutes with the priest, minister, or rabbi and offer assistance with the inevitable problems that came up in a sector where sin rubbed shoulders with piety.

It benefited both sides. On the King of Storyville's orders, Valentin had corralled parishioners who had left their wives and children to chase after a floozy. Or made sure that the erring son of a prominent church elder couldn't buy a card of hop anywhere in the city. Or saw that two young ladies who were developing what the parents thought was an unnatural interest in each other were kept apart. Most importantly, he regularly checked on the churches' real estate holdings in and around the red-light district, of which there were many, including some of the fanciest bordellos.

Anderson waved the Creole detective to one of the chairs and settled himself in the other. He reached into his pocket for one of his favored Cuban cigars, went digging for a lucifer, and blew a mighty plume of smoke. He took another moment to un- button the pockets of his vest and tug his tight collar away from his florid neck. With a sigh of relief, he sat back and raised his eyebrows, a signal.

"Thank you for taking time to see me," Valentin said.

"Is this about the fellow they found dead last night? What was his name? Mumford?"

The detective was surprised. "That's right."

"He was in Bolden's band, if I recall correctly."

"He was."

"What about it?"

Valentin said, "I think there could be something to it."

Anderson raised a polite eyebrow. "Oh? Why's that?"

"Because another musician was murdered, just a few days ago."

Anderson held his cigar in the air. "Where?"

"On Philip Street."

"Philip Street!"

"But he was playing over here," Valentin said quickly. "At Tournier's."

Anderson cocked his head, looking vexed. "Yes, and?"

"I just...I'm just thinking that there might be a connection between the two."

"Is this what you came all the way up here to tell me? That a couple of musicians died?" Anderson shook his head in an- noyance. "The one was stabbed in some damn boardinghouse? And the other one drank who knows what up on Marais Street. Do I have that right?"

Valentin's face flushed a little.

The King of Storyville puffed his Cuban. "We have enough trouble around here and we don't need to manufacture more. Speaking of which...did you go to St. Louis Street like I asked you?"

"I did," the Creole detective said. "There's been no sign of those fellows, whoever they were. I believe they're gone."

Anderson nodded, mollified. "Well, keep an eye on it anyway."

Valentin heard the dismissal in his tone and rose to leave.

"Wait a minute," Anderson said. He smoked for a quiet moment, his eyes wandering off with discomfort. "Have you got trouble at home?"

"Have I..." Valentin was flustered, wondering how the man knew. "It's...it's nothing," he stuttered. "I can take care of it."

"Very well, then." Anderson waved his cigar, showing him the door. "I wish you a pleasant afternoon."

On the way back to Magazine Street, Valentin stewed over the visit. He had been overtaken by his feelings going to the morgue and seeing Mumford and had let it get the best of his reason. Tom Anderson had officially deemed it a waste of time. It didn't explain how or why Anderson knew the details of both murders. Valentin was used to that; the King of Storyville knew almost everything about everything. Finally, he revisited Anderson's question about Justine. He was willing to bet money that he already knew about her being on Basin Street, too.

He stepped down at Magazine Street, not knowing what to expect when he got home. He wondered if he was the only person in New Orleans who didn't know what Justine Mancarre was doing.

He unlocked and opened the door. From the other side of the front room, she raised a hand to stop him from coming any farther. She had rolled the rugs and pushed them to the walls and was mopping the floor. The lemon soap she had poured into her bucket of water made the hardwood glow with an oily sheen and sent up a fruity scent. She worked the mop, her hair tied back with a few wet strands hanging down as she sweated right through her thin cotton housedress.

He leaned in the doorway to watch and wait. The balcony

door was open and the arched windows were pushed wide, so that the afternoon air was already drying the moisture on the floor. She worked on, intent on the task, as if he wasn't there, as if nothing existed outside the old mop and the floor she was attacking. She huffed with effort and he looked to see if there was some stubborn stain before her. The floor was fine, spotless and shiny. Still, she went at it, her eyes blazing and arms pumping.

She finished the last bit that took her up to the bedroom door and leaned the mop against the wall. She took a moment to study her handiwork. Then, with a wave of her fingers, she gestured for him to make his way around the street side of the room, where the floor was all but dry. As he got closer, she cocked her head and gave him a kittenish smile. It was a look he knew well, though he hadn't seen it in a while, and he did his best to hide his astonishment.

She backed into the bedroom and with each step she undid a button on her dress, so by the time she got to the side of the bed, it was loose all the way down the front. She was wearing nothing underneath. He came up on her and reached out with slow fingers. The dress dropped in a swirl to the floor. He rested his palms on her bare shoulders and she dropped down on the mattress.

Afterward, they lay together in silence, letting the air dry the sweat off their bodies. They didn't speak at all. Justine twirled one of her curls and gazed up at the ceiling, as if she had forgotten that he was there.

It had come to her suddenly, in the midst of their frolic. She knew him well enough to understand that there were times when the mix of blood in his veins distilled out and one or another of his histories would stand out in stark relief. This was one of those moments.

He had his mother's gray eyes, but it was his father's proud will that had lit them up. That was what she saw: a look of contempt mixed with anger and injury. Giving herself to him like that was a small gesture, something to appease his injured Sicilian pride, a token of apology and obeisance. And yet it wasn't near enough. She had shamed and insulted him before all of Basin Street, and no quick dalliance on a Sunday afternoon was going to change that.

When more quiet moments went by, she shifted a few inches away and slipped down a private path. A pall descended over the bed and she felt a soft blow in her gut, an odd sensation that something had just broken between them. Like a boat that had lost its mooring, she drifted off.

The sun was down when Valentin locked the door behind him and descended the stairs to the street. He stood on the banquette for a long minute. Nothing was moving. It was a cloudy night and the only light on the street was the golden glow of electric lamps through the windows of the Banks' Arcade.

He passed back over Common Street. He didn't stop when he got to the river, but kept on, heading west along Decatur Street, keeping a steady pace and gradually leaving the downtown lights behind. The moon hid, then peeked out from the silver strands of cloud, casting intermittent shadows. His profile stretched out long and thin at his side. He didn't have any idea where he was going, as he let his steps carry him away.

Four pairs of tracks came out of Union Station and followed the course of the river, turning north to Baton Rouge. Standing near the sweeping curve of rails, he heard the chugging engine long before it emerged from the darkness. He could tell from the sluggish huffing sound that it was moving slowly, still building up steam. It would still be at a slow creep when it got to him. A quick trot would bring him alongside the tracks and it would take nothing to pull himself into the first empty car, and just like that, he could leave it all behind like discarded clothes:

Justine, Anderson, Morton, Mumford, Storyville, all of it. Just like that.

The headlamp pierced the night. Then came the rhythm of the steel wheels, and the long, low moan of the whistle. Valentin stood watching it go by, a freight with no coaches, rolling iron, long and dark. He could see empty cars with doors standing open. It would be so easy: a few long strides, a quick hop, and he'd be on his way.

It was five minutes before he saw the lights of the caboose. The train went by, one red light and one blue blinking into tiny dots as the clacking and rumbling faded into the night. It was a long minute before the last small echo died away.

Justine had breathed a sigh of relief when, after an hour of discomfiting silence, Valentin put his clothes back on, gathered his things, and went out the door, mumbling something about needing a walk. It sounded like he was talking to himself.

She lay thinking for a long time. She got up to look at the clock once and found that it was evening. The next time she looked, night had fallen like a dark drape, and somehow she knew that he wasn't coming back for a good long while, and when he did, he probably wouldn't want to see her there. With that thought in mind, she put on a frock and went downstairs to knock on Mr. Bechamin's door to ask to use the telephone so she could call Miss Antonia Gonzales.

She went back upstairs, took a dose of her prescription, and fell into a slumber that was traversed by vagrant shreds of dreams, shadows that rose, took shape, then dissolved into darkness again.

Valentin started up the western edge of the city at an even-paced ramble with only the most general direction in mind. He saw few pedestrians at this hour, mostly low-down types skulking along the streets like furtive rodents. A police wagon went by and the two coppers treated him to narrow-eyed stares. The moon had gone away and the streets were so blankly dark that he wondered if they would ever see the light of day again. He drew a vague picture of himself walking around the city through a darkness that never lifted, like a blind man. He thought it would not be too bad a way to live. Then he thought how foolish he was to let his mind wander so.

He turned south again, walking along Conti Street until he reached the walls of St. Louis No. 2. He roused the night caretaker and asked to be let in. The old Negro refused until Valentin identified himself. He remembered; the Creole had been there before. He turned the key in the heavy lock and held the iron gate open.

Valentin located the biers of his younger brother and sister. He read the names and the dates on the bier and tried to recall their faces, but he couldn't conjure anything. Next to them was his father's larger bier, stalwart as the man himself. That face he remembered too well, olive dark, with dancing black eyes and wide white teeth capped by an expansive black mustache that he had always waxed with care.

Valentin felt the silence engulf him like a dark hand. As he stood there, the moon came out to wash the city of the dead in silver. He heard footsteps from the shadows and wondered if now, at long last, he was going to get a visit from a ghost. Who would it be, among so many candidates? It was only the caretaker, though, coming to see if he was all right. The old man escorted him back to the front gate. It closed with a soft metallic creak.

He walked through the night, barely noticing where his steps took him, except that he stayed on the darker sides of the streets, away from the lamps. A little before dawn, he came upon a café owner standing on the banquette as he sent his son off to the French Market. Valentin imposed on him for an early tin of coffee. With a grudging sigh, the gentleman poured from his own percolator.

Valentin was walking along, sipping the bitter coffee, when the first clap of thunder sounded. Some minutes passed and there was another, like the echo from a distant cannon. The wind kicked up, smelling heavy and fetid, as if the cloud that lingered over the bayous was moving in, bringing the smell of green decay with it. There was more thunder and then lightning crackled in a green morning sky. The day arrived with the first sheet of rain that crossed the river and swept along the city streets.

Valentin started trotting, his head bent down as the rain soaked his clothes, until he found the welcome light of a café that was open early. He went inside and ordered more coffee. The girl brought him some thick slices of bread with pots of butter and honey.

He ate and drank, then went into the privy and stood before the cracked and dirty mirror. Even in that dim light, he could see that his skin was pale and drawn and his eyes were all bloodshot. There was a shadow of beard appearing on his jaw and over his lip. He was tired and he looked it. Actually, he looked about a half step from one of the derelicts that wandered the uptown streets like shabby buzzards.

He tried to imagine what Justine was doing at that moment and had a vision of her standing by a window, looking out at the rain, and wondering in turn if he might be gone for good.

He splashed some water on his face and then went back to his table to wait out the rain or the morning, whichever ended first.

SEVEN

Justine stood in the middle of the room in her best walking dress. The French doors were standing open and the autumn breeze, still wet with the morning's rain, was like a gentle hand caressing her face.

It was very quiet. The morning traffic had come and gone, and the stillness of the street made it seem like she could be anywhere. Though the rain had passed, the eaves went on dripping, making a pattering kind of music, like someone tapping on bamboo.

She felt like she was in one of her half dreams, aware that she was dreaming but unable to break the spell and come out of it. There were images, fleeting little snippets, at the edge of her vision. It happened this way sometimes: Tiny pieces of memory would swirl around her like windblown rags, then begin to form into pictures. The grays and reds and whites of the city gave way to the deep, moist green of the bayou where she had grown up. The sun was never clear; it was always dappled through the tall oaks and cypresses. There was the squalid shack, tilting on the poles that supported it, the room caving in at one part, the small windows covered over with burlap so that no one could see inside. It all reeked of wet decay.

She knew that all she had to do was open her eyes again and it would all go away. She kept them shut tight, though, and now the picture broadened until she could see the entire clearing, and the children, filthy and ragged, running this way and that. Only the occasional sweet peal of laughter broke the grim quiet.

She heard footsteps. Someone was coming. Her breath got short as a shadow blocked the sun. Then a key rattled in the lock and the vision in her mind melted away, taking all the details with it, as the four white walls of the living room rose up again.

Valentin stepped inside wearing a strange face, his dark gray eyes spiked with hard light. It startled her back to the day they had first met, when he pushed into the room where the fellow from the traveling show had trapped her. She was in the corner, a sheet pulled up to cover her, a knife in her hand that she was ready to use.

Valentin had resolved the mess by knocking the man cold with an offhand violence that frightened and excited her. Afterward, he told her to come to his room if she wanted, and that's where it all began. She hadn't forgotten the look on his face that day, like he saw nothing and everything in the same instant, and now there it was again.

Some moments passed. "There's a hack waiting downstairs," he said, sounding ruminative, as if he was mulling this bit of news for himself.

That finally brought her out of it. She knew where she was and what she was doing. She felt her heart sliding into her gut and she wanted to say something, but there was nothing she could think of that wouldn't sound empty or foolish, so she stayed silent. She couldn't meet his gaze, either, and dropped her eyes.

"He's waiting," he said gently, and moved one step to the side, out of her path, then out of her line of sight.

She gathered herself and made for the door. She still didn't look at him, didn't offer him any words of farewell. He watched her go by. She closed the door behind her and went down the stairs.

The Negro driver had been standing on the banquette, enjoying a smoke. When he saw her, he tossed the butt into the gutter, straightened his cap, and offered her a hand up. He pulled
himself into the seat and snapped the reins. The hack rolled into
the cobbled street, the nags giving out little snorts and the
wheels clattering in the still afternoon. Justine sat very straight
in the seat. Though she felt him watching from the balcony, she
kept her eyes fixed dead ahead. She was afraid if she looked up
and met his gaze, she'd go back and then she'd never get away
from him.

As they turned the corner onto Common Street, she entertained a vague pang of guilt about Beansoup. She could just
imagine the look on that elfin face when he realized that she had
left. He might think it was all his fault. She was sorry she hadn't
taken the time to find him and try to explain that there was no
way she could stay on Magazine Street anymore.

Valentin stood in the doorway that led onto the balcony and
watched the hack move off down Magazine and turn the corner,
heading north onto Common Street. He went into the bedroom,
took off his shoes, and stretched out on the bed. It was very
quiet. Though he was bone tired, he didn't fall asleep right away.
He held the image of the hack rolling away down the street. She
hadn't looked back at all.

The hours passed into the evening. Every now and then, he
thought he heard footfalls. She didn't appear, though. No one
did. Magazine Street was quiet. More rain came, this time a
slow and steady drizzle that cast a soft mist over the entire city,
downtown and up.

By eleven o'clock, he'd had enough. He dressed and walked
down to Canal Street to catch a car heading north. He walked
through Storyville, right past Antonia Gonzales's mansion. He
wondered if she was already entertaining a gentleman and

thought what a shout it would cause if he was to walk inside and catch her in the act.

He thought better of it. It was too rainy anyway, and there was almost no one about. If she was behind those lamp-lit curtains, she was most likely sipping brandy and telling Miss Antonia her woes with the Creole detective who had run her off.

He turned onto Bienville and made his way to the French-man's on the corner of Villere Street. It was closed Mondays, but the door was unlocked, and when he ducked inside, he was not surprised to find a group of musicians there, including some of the best in the city, with Morton at their center, also not a surprise. When the piano man saw Valentin, he stopped in midsentence, his hand lofted.

He said, "Well, now. Speak of the devil."

Valentin took a quick glance at the brown and olive faces, recognizing about half of them. Buddy Carter and Freddie Kep-pard were there. Frankie Dusen and Anthony Cimonelli. A few others he recognized vaguely. A fellow serving as bartender. Two whores who had closed their cribs and wandered by slouched at the end of the bar.

Those he knew recalled his friendship with Bolden and the part he had played in that business. They always treated him with a certain deference and now nodded their heads in greeting. The rest just stared. He pulled up a chair, feeling two dozen cu-rious eyes fixing on him.

"We were just now talking about Jeff," Morton said as he sat down.

The gazes that had shifted from the piano player went back to the detective, who didn't speak. Frankie Dusen said, "It was a goddamn shame what happened, Mr. Valentin. Him, of all people."

Valentin guessed that Morton had been bending their ears when he walked in, probably announcing to one and all that it appeared Mr. St. Cyr couldn't be bothered investigating the murder of the likes of Jefferson Mumford. The small cloud of accusation that was closing in around him made him think about standing up, offering a good-night, and heading back out the door. *Speak of the devil,* indeed.

Instead of making an exit, though, he settled in a chair. Someone passed a signal, a clean glass appeared, a cork popped, and he was handed a short tumbler of Raleigh Rye, the uptown beverage of choice. He nodded a thank-you and took a short sip. The musicians continued to watch him carefully.

No matter what Mr. Jelly Roll said, he probably owed these fellows something. "I don't suppose there's anything going around about what happened to him," he asked momentarily.

Now glances were exchanged, but no one spoke up. For once even Morton exhibited the sense to keep his mouth shut.

Finally, Freddie Keppard cleared his throat. He always acted a little uncomfortable around Valentin, as if he thought the detective held him to blame for the bad business with the Bolden Band. He shrugged his round shoulders and said, "None of us here knows nothin'."

"He wasn't having any trouble?"

"Everything seemed to be good with him," Anthony Cimonelli said. "We was working regular. He had plenty of money."

"What about at home?"

"He kept a nice little house," the Sicilian went on. "And his woman... You ever seen that woman of his?"

Valentin shook his head.

"He was doing *fine,*" Cimonelli said, bringing a gurgle of quiet laughter.

"What about trouble with anyone on the street?" the detective said.

Frankie Dusen spoke up. "Jeff got along with everybody." The others in the room murmured assent.

"Any gambling debts?" Valentin went on. "Problems with

dope?" The questions met with denials. "Then maybe it was just a random crime. Like a robbery that went bad."

"He had everything left on him," Morton reminded him quietly. "Every dime was still in his pockets."

"Sounds like a regular angel, all right," the detective said. He took another sip of his whiskey. It was so quiet he could hear the rain falling on the cobblestones outside. "He had a problem with someone, didn't he?" he said, now looking from face to face. "Or he'd be sitting in this room right now."

The line had been delivered in his detective's voice, clipped and cool, the one he used when he was working an investigation. The men were watching him and perking their ears, trying to mask their expectancy. He sat back and folded his arms.

This was not what he had come for. He had been looking only for some relief from his thoughts and had stumbled into a trap. He glanced at Morton, imagining the self-satisfied smirk that was lurking beneath his innocent expression. The other men in the room were as sober as judges, though not one of them was exactly meeting his eyes. They all wanted the same thing, for him to speak up for them, to be their lance. In other words, for him to give in and do their bidding. He decided to hang on to a shred of his dignity and wait them out. For a distracted moment, he wondered if any of them knew about Justine. It wouldn't take long until they did. Then he thought about waking up in the morning to face empty rooms.

Freddie Keppard said, "So what now, Mr. Valentin?"

"What now?"

They all knew what was going on. He wanted someone to say it.

"You think you can find out what happened to Jeff?" Keppard's voice was hushed.

He let the silence hang for a moment. "You all understand that the trail is cold. When a murder case doesn't get solved quickly, it's more than likely that it doesn't get solved at all." No one said a word, as if they had nothing to do but wait for the next words to drip from his tongue. As it was, he held out until the last second. "I'll see what I can find out," he offered grudgingly.

There was a murmur and the air in the room seemed to lighten in a collective sigh. One of the fellows reached out with the bottle to top off his drink. He looked over the rim of the glass to see Morton watching him. Then the piano man broke the gaze, swung around abruptly on the little stool, flexed his fingers, and began hammering out a raggedy blues on the stained and chipped keys. After a short introduction, he began to sing, his mouth curling around the lyrics.

Mama bought a chicken, yeah, and mama bought a duck
Put 'em on the table just to see if they would fuck...

There were hoots of laughter as the other men put their glasses down and picked up their horns. By the tenth bar, they were riding the train, blowing raw and funky.

The two whores who had been hanging at the end of the bar and cursing musicians and their worthless yancies came staggering over and started to dance. One was pale white and ugly, with stringy black hair, sunken eyes, and a witch's hooked nose. She was too far into the bottle to do much but stumble around and push her bony pelvis against the nearest solid object, human or otherwise. Her scarlet sister was a fair-looking and young mulatto, chubby and bright eyed, with heavy hips and melon breasts that heaved so mightily under her thin cotton shirtwaist that fellows had to duck every time she shifted her weight.

Valentin stretched his feet out and took it all in. This was the way it had been since aught-one. These middle-of-the-night joints where the musicians got to put down the music they played and the masks they wore for white audiences and for the folks back in the neighborhood. Here they could unwind and blow off all the steam they wanted to. It must have been something like this in Africa, where his mother's descendants had lived for untold centuries, raising a raucous noise to get the attention of the gods. It was what Bolden and a few other lesser lights had created, in these same low-down saloons and worse.

There were nights that he thought the band was going to blow the building right off its pilings, they played so fast and so loud, to the sheer besotted delight of the sports and rounders and whores and drunks who came to see them. That was at first. No one could contain that much excitement, though, and it wasn't long before more respectable Negroes and Creoles were wandering down Rampart Street. The music and the men who played it were cursed roundly by preachers and politicians, which of course made it all the more enticing. So some brave white folks, college boys mostly, had to find out what it was all about.

That caused some trouble. A bunch of no-account niggers and dirty wops raising hell from dusk until dawn was one thing. If white sons went chasing these rude pied pipers, could their fair sisters be far behind? The saving grace was that all the sober heads agreed that it couldn't last and that sanity—and decent music—would soon prevail.

They called it nothing at first. Then they started calling it "jass." Some said it was from *jaser,* French for "chatter," which a newspaperman had used in an article. Others swore it wasn't that at all and that it had come from *jasi,* or "party," in the Mandingo language of West Africa.

The name stuck and the music stayed. It was more than a passing fancy, as if it had slithered north from Rampart Street and jumped Canal into Storyville, and not just at saloons like Nancy Hanks's and Joe Lala's on the back end of the District anymore. Lately, jass was stirring up half-a-dozen establishments, edging ever closer to Basin Street. These rough Joshuas blew their horns and the walls were tumbling down. If you believed Jelly Roll Morton, someone was taking exception to that and making their point with the blade of a knife and a vial of poison. Valentin wondered if anyone would really go that far over some no-account musicians.

He didn't believe it, even though he had to admit that more than a few people who'd see colored and white playing together would wonder where would the niggers show up next. The churches? The schools? The sporting teams? It was melodramatic to believe that these players that now surrounded him were starting something that large, but even to Valentin it was not so far-fetched as to be impossible.

It was coming up on dawn when they stopped and put down their horns. Valentin stood, stretched, and headed out the door. He ambled south to Canal Street in the company of the first of the laborers on their way to work. He caught a car and hopped off at Magazine Street as the bells of St. Boniface tolled six.

The players at the Frenchman's went home. Morton wanted to leave with Valentin, but he sensed that the detective would just as soon do without him and lingered. Singly or in pairs, they headed off for their flats, their shotgun homes, their dingy hotel rooms. By the time the morning sunlight was haloing the rooftops, the last one had gone out and the bartender had crept up the steps to find his cot. The white sporting girl wandered away as if she had somewhere to go, leaving the chubby mulatto, who had fallen asleep at one of the tables, her head drooping upon one of her substantial breasts.

Some minutes passed and the door creaked open again. A figure, huddled in a long coat, crossed the sawdust floor and stood over the sleeping woman. A finger prodded her soft flesh until her groggy head came up, and she blinked at a face that seemed to be out of focus.

After a dead second, a voice that was soft yet stern said, "Start talking."

EIGHT

Valentin was not fully awake and yet he sensed the difference, like there was a quiet pocket in the air of the room. He had known Justine for almost three years and she had shared his rooms for almost two. Now she was gone, and from the hollow space that lingered about the bed, it appeared she had left a ghost or at least a bit of a shadow behind.

Rather than lay there and brood on it, he got up and moving. He fumbled getting his coffee and a midday breakfast of Italian bread toasted on the stove and buttered, a chunk of provolone that was getting hard at the edges, and some mortadella that was turning gray, along with a piece of melon that she had left wrapped in waxed paper. When he was finished, he cleaned the table and washed his dish. It was all very precise and mechanical, and he took some satisfaction in completing the task.

He sat back down at the table to finish his coffee. The twenty-four hours came back to him like a series of pictures. He pushed his mind past the images of Justine walking out and disappearing down Magazine Street and arrived at the late-night scene at the Frenchman's and the faces, black, brown, and olive, watching him.

If his recollection was accurate, he had announced to one and all that he was going to investigate the murder of Jefferson Mumford, though the details of how he had reached that point, and why, were hidden in some corner of his brain. It had something to do with an unspoken rebuke in the air, the seeds ably planted by Jelly Roll Morton. There was something else hovering, too: a sense of alarm that was stirring up among the players. Who would be next?

He grumbled over giving in like that, and in public. He could have worked the case quietly, privately. It was most likely all smoke anyway. Of course, he could do nothing, and sit around his rooms and see the pictures and listen to the echoes over and over again. As he finished his coffee and headed off to the bathroom, he uttered a small word of thanks that on this of all days, he had something to occupy his mind.

Lieutenant J. Picot was standing at his second-floor window, watching the early afternoon traffic on Royal Street when he saw St. Cyr step to the corner of Conti, glance left and right, then cross over, heading directly for the building. He stared down at the Creole detective for another startled second, then came away from the window with a rough gesture for his desk sergeant to follow him into the corridor.

The two coppers were planted like sentinels at the top of the marble stairs when the Creole detective appeared.

"Well, well, well." The lieutenant had his hands on his hips and was wearing a thin smile as he looked down at his visitor. "If it ain't Valentin St. Cyr, the famous private detective. New Orleans' own damn Sherlock Holmes." His eyes, dirty pennies, slid sideways. "Sergeant, did you know that this here fellow used to be a police officer? That's right. Didn't stay with us very long, though. And he's the one cracked that Black Rose murder case." Though there was much venom mixed with this honey, the detective kept his expression placid. Which of course irritated Picot all the more. "What's your business here?" he snapped.

The detective stopped on the third step. "I'm looking into the killings of Jefferson Mumford and Antoine Noiret."

Picot said, "Who?"

"Two men who died in the past week," Valentin said evenly. "Noiret was murdered in a rooming house on Philip Street. Mumford was found in an alley off Marais on Sunday morning."

Picot's expression said, *So?*

"Are you investigating either one?" the detective asked.

The lieutenant's jaw clenched. "And just what the hell do you care about a couple of dead nigger jass players?" His lips twisted. "Oh, yes, I forgot. They're all friends of yours, ain't they?" He made it sound like it was a crime.

Valentin ignored the taunt. "I wanted to extend you the courtesy," he said, and turned around and continued down the remaining steps.

"St. Cyr!" Beneath Picot's sharp tone, Valentin heard something else, the slightest tense note. He stopped and waited. With a flip of his hand, the lieutenant sent his sergeant back to the squad room. Then he jerked his head for St. Cyr to follow him.

They found a quiet place at the far end of the second-floor corridor, in the broad recess of the arched window that looked down on Conti Street, and took up opposite positions like boxers waiting for the bell to begin the first round. After a moment's grudging silence, Picot said, "We found this fellow Mumford's body, but it ain't been established that he was a homicide."

Valentin stifled a smile of his own. "The man was poisoned."

"It could have been an accident," the copper said, his face flushing red. "These sons of bitches will drink any goddamn thing, and you know it."

Valentin thought to mention that Mumford was not the type to throw down whatever was put in his hand. He didn't, though.

"That other one," Picot said. "What was his name again?"

"Noiret."

"And he was where?"

"Philip Street. He was murdered in bed. His throat was cut."

The lieutenant grimaced. "Philip Street ain't our precinct. And it's way out of your territory. So what the hell?" His eyelids came down to narrow slits. "I thought you was keepin' out of police matters. I thought you learned your lesson."

Valentin wasn't quite sure what lesson Picot was talking about. Probably something having to do with the murders of the year before. In any case, he wasn't about to give up any more than he had to. "Both victims were playing in bands in Storyville," he said.

"Tell me something," the lieutenant said with another spike of irritation. "If Tom Anderson wants somebody investigating these damn crimes, how come he don't call the police?"

"Maybe he doesn't want to spend the taxpayers' money," Valentin replied.

He had almost said "waste," and Picot was sharp enough to catch it. His face darkened. "Well, then...," he said tightly. "There ain't much I can say, is there? This is Storyville. He can do anything he wants." He crossed his arms and turned to stare out the window.

"I'd like to see the report on Mumford, if I may," Valentin said, keeping his voice even.

Picot gave him a cold look, then walked away abruptly, without a word.

Valentin stood by the window for twenty minutes, watching the traffic moving in jerky eddies on the street below. For all he knew, Picot had gone on to other business and had left him standing there like a perfect dunce. He was thinking about how much longer he would wait when the lieutenant reappeared, carrying a police file in his hand. He snapped it at the detective and resumed his position on the opposite side of the recess.

Valentin opened the folder and began to read. There wasn't much to the report, and he covered it in a matter of minutes. He had forgotten his notebook, so he could only make mental notes of the sparse entries and commit the sketch of the position of the victim's body to memory. The whole time, he felt Picot's icy stare resting on him.

According to the scribbled comments, Mumford had ingested a toxic substance, an acidic that went down and caused internal hemorrhaging. It also caused sudden nerve paralysis, leading to lung failure and asphyxiation. Or so whoever had written the notes opined. There was something about the scrawl that suggested it was done by rote, and Valentin wondered if a doctor had reviewed the case at all.

With just enough information to meet the minimum requirements, it was obvious how little effort had been invested in Mumford's file. A Negro musician who turned up dead in a Storyville alley in the middle of the night was a minor problem to be dispatched, and the quicker the better.

Valentin closed the folder, handed it back. "Thank you for your assistance, Lieutenant," he said, and started moving away.

"St. Cyr!" Valentin stopped again, but whatever Picot had on the tip of his tongue stayed there. He waved the folder like he was swatting at an insect. "You know the way out," he muttered. "Use it," and stalked back to his office.

The lieutenant was at his window when St. Cyr stepped out onto the banquette below. As soon as he saw the detective turn north, he knew where he was going. He cast a quiet curse, then called two of his men, telling one of them to hurry downstairs and throw a tail on St. Cyr and the other to get Chief O'Connor's office on the telephone right away.

A half hour later, Valentin stepped to the mouth of the alley that cut from Marais Street through to Villere, the very one in which

Jeff Mumford had coughed out the last bloody drops of his young life.

Now, in the hazy light of the New Orleans afternoon, the detective stopped to consider that it was not too late to stop. No one was paying him a dime, and he didn't owe the bunch at the Frenchman's a damn thing, Morton in particular. No matter what he had said in that smoky saloon in the middle of the night, he could quite easily stroll to Canal Street, catch the next car rolling south, and be done with it.

Then he thought about walking away only to find out that there was something to it after all. Unlikely, but anything was possible in Storyville. After another few moments, he imagined going back to his empty rooms and spending long hours waiting for night to fall.

As he gazed blankly at the dusty floor of the alley, these thoughts gave way to the image of Mumford laid out on the cooling board, his handsome face twisted into that awful grimace, his eyes blind and half lidded in death. He saw Noiret with that obscene wound like a red and festering mouth. Two musicians who had played in the same band dead in the space of five days. Tom Anderson was right; it didn't add up to much. Still . . .

He hesitated for another moment, then stepped off the banquette. Marais and Villere streets were producing the usual bustle of city noise, the clamor of carriages and automobiles mixing with human shouts and the neighs of horses. All of it faded away as Valentin fixed his attention on the plot of dirt before him, eight feet wide and twenty feet deep. He let his gaze roam vaguely over the space, searching for any bit that was out of place. As he expected, there was nothing to find. The coppers had swept the alley clean.

He made his usual intense inspection anyway, from one side to the other and ten paces back from the banquette. He remembered the sketch of the location of the body and pictured it there. After ten minutes, he saw nothing more of value, save for a slight discoloration in the dirt, a last stain of blood that told him where Jeff had fallen in his death throes.

There were no signs of a scuffle, no scrabble of footprints in the dust, no shreds of torn clothing. That pointed to a careful execution, with the victim drawn in and then surprised. That was really all he could say, since officers of the New Orleans Police Department had been diligent in cleaning the alleyway of anything that might benefit a private detective who might come along later.

With no evidence to collect, he leaned against one of the walls and imagined the scene that night. The killer would have been lurking in the shadow beyond the light from the streetlamp. He wondered why Mumford had stepped into such a dark cove. Perhaps he recognized the party calling to him. Or maybe it was some woman, beckoning like a Siren, a street whore looking to make a last dollar or some floozy too drunk to care who lifted her skirts.

Would Jeff Mumford, a handsome sport with a good-looking woman waiting at home, fall prey to such a crude temptation? Not likely. If it wasn't a woman, then who or what had drawn him to the killing floor? Only the killer and the victim knew.

It added up to exactly the kind of puzzle that no one else, certainly no police detective and no Pinkerton, was likely to crack. They'd take one look, give up, and walk away. Because they didn't possess Valentin's combination of sharp wits, knowledge of the streets, and gut instinct about the way people behaved. And because they wouldn't care about a dead nigger jass player in the first place.

The detective took one last survey of the space. Then he stepped out of the alley and back onto the banquette to cast an idle eye up and down Marais Street.

He caught sight of the fellow standing in the doorway of the apothecary a few doors down on the opposite side of the street. He was small and thin and nervous, and he gave himself away by turning his head too quickly when Valentin's gaze found him. The detective smiled quietly; he would have been frankly surprised if Picot hadn't sent a man. He headed down to Basin Street, and ten minutes later was stepping onto a streetcar heading west.

As the car rumbled away from downtown and into the darker reaches of the city, the scenery changed. From his seat by the window, he viewed Black Storyville, a shadow of the legal District, a four-block square of narrow brick sporting houses, starting at Freret and Gravier streets, and serving a mulatto and Negro clientele. The next few blocks beyond were crowded with cafés, saloons, barbering parlors, and corner stores, mostly of a seedy sort, with dark-skinned men in cheap suits lounging around their doors. The storefronts gave way to a stretch of wood-framed shotgun doubles that showed the sagging, peeling, and rotting of poor construction in a damp climate.

When the car stopped at the corner of Fourth Street, he hopped down and walked the four blocks to the Philip Street rooming house where Antoine Noiret had died.

He found a two-story structure of gray clapboard that listed a bit to one side where the foundation was sinking in the soggy Louisiana earth. The windows were yellowed with grime, and the boards of the gallery bowed and creaked under his feet. A FOR SALE sign was nailed to a stake in the patch of dirt next to the gallery steps. Another sign announcing ROOMS TO LET, but almost weathered to invisibility, was nailed to a gallery post.

The door swung open with a slap, and a homely, thick-bodied mulatto woman with a face cut by thick lines into lumps like blocks of dark clay stood glaring at him. She was wearing a frumpy Mother Hubbard and her woolly hair was tied back under a checked chignon.

"Whatchu lookin' fo'?" she demanded roughly.

"Are you the landlady?"

"For one more fuckin' day, I am. I'm leavin' out tomorrow."

"Because of the murder?"

Her face tightened. "Thas right. Because of the murder."

"My name's St. Cyr," he said. "I'm a private detective."

"So?"

"And your name is?"

She hesitated, then snapped, "Cora Jarrell. Whatchu want here?"

"What can you tell me about Mr. Noiret?"

"I can tell you someone come in and cut his goddamn throat."

"Do you—"

"I knowed this was gonna happen!" she cried suddenly, and threw a cursing hand in the air. "I knowed this would happen if I kept lettin' rooms to these no-good jass players! The bastards! This is what I get. A dead body. And I'm out on the street. I'm lucky I don't have to go work in some damn *crib*."

"What—"

"God*damn*it!" she yelled again, and stomped her foot furiously. "I run a decent house!"

Valentin gave her a moment to calm down, then said, "What about Noiret?"

She glared. "What about him? He took a room here now and then." She crossed her arms.

Valentin shifted to a comfortable slouch, as if he was ready to wait there all day.

"You hear what I said? I didn't see nothin' and I didn't hear nothin', so I don't *know* nothin'." Her voice went to a hoarse whine, and she raked him with a hard glance that might have worked, except for the sliver of anxious, telling light that was lurking behind it.

"What about Noiret?" he repeated quietly.

She held the stare for another few seconds, and then her shoulders sagged into a shrug. "He played horn in a band. He drank plenty, but they all do. He toted a razor, 'cause I seen it onst. That's it. I didn't hardly know him at all."

"Did he have a woman here?"

"This is a house for gentlemen!" she half shouted. "Women ain't allowed in the rooms!"

Valentin let out a quick laugh. He knew if he checked with the local police precinct, they'd tell him the rooms were used regularly for assignations and that Cora Jarrell was a well-known procurer with an impressive record of arrests. She had that look. Still, she kept the righteous front, her thick chin jutting. She was a tough customer. She would have to be to run a house outside the District. She'd no doubt seen and dispatched her share of trouble, including murders.

Indeed, he saw the angry way she was eyeing him, all but putting up her dukes. He countered by locking his best stony gaze on hers. "You don't want the kind of trouble I can cause you," he said.

She drew back, finally getting the message. "They was one in there with him," she said in a low voice. "I heard 'em."

"Heard them what?"

"Raisin' holy hell, that's what." She came up with a dirty smirk. "First I thought they was fuckin'. You know how some women do. But that wa'nt it. She was mad about somethin'. They wasn't fuckin'; they was fussin'. Least, she was. The fellow let the next room was poundin' on the wall, yellin' for her to shut up. It got quiet for a little bit. Then she started up again, cussin' him out. I heard the room door slam and the front door after that. And that was all."

"Was this a sporting girl?"

"I don't know what she was," she muttered.

"Can you describe her?"

"No, I can't describe her. 'Cause I didn't see her."

He knew the moment that the words crossed her lips that she was lying. He didn't push it, though. She was already backing up, her eyes shifting away. He didn't want to lose her, so he let it go and asked instead to have a look at the room. This time she hedged only a few seconds before waving him inside.

She led him down the dim hallway to the last door on the right. Her hand went into her Mother Hubbard and came up with a ring of keys, and she unlocked the door and pushed it open. She stayed right where she was as he stepped over the threshold into a cramped box of a room.

It was low ceilinged, the usual for that type of structure. There was no window, which meant the door was the only way in or out. He dug in his pocket for a lucifer to light the gas jet on the near wall. With the room bathed in a murky yellow glow, he made out the washstand that stood in one corner and the closet door hanging open. Patches of plaster had flaked off the walls and leaking water had stained the ceiling. It was close, with a mixed odor of sweat, musk, and unwashed linens.

The bed had been stripped down to a rusting iron frame. Of course, superstition dictated that the mattress and sheets would have been taken out and burned. There were dark splotches on the floor next to the bed where Noiret's blood had run down and soaked in.

"You keep the door locked?" he asked her.

"In this here neighborhood? All the damn time."

She cringed and fidgeted as he wandered about the tainted space. "Was it you who found him?" he said.

She nodded grimly. "It was checkout time. Check out or pay. I knocked. Wa'nt no answer. I got that fellow next door to come rouse him. Man still didn't answer. I went and unlocked it. And there he was. Cut open like that. They was blood all over the bed." She stared at the stain on the floor and wrung her hands. "Look at it! They ain't ever gonna get it out. They gonna have to tear up the damn boards." There was nothing false in her voice or her look of distress.

The detective took a last glance around, then walked out. He stopped and tilted his head at the door of the next room.

"So who was this fellow?" he asked.

The landlady looked askance; giving names was dicey business in this part of town.

"I know you keep a book," Valentin went on. "Perhaps I could see it."

He had guessed that she had been skimming and wouldn't want anyone inspecting the ledger until she was long gone. He was right.

"Lacombe," she said, too quickly. "Negro. Plays clarinet in some band."

Something about the way she spoke the name bothered him, a sharp blurt accompanied by shifting eyes. "He left out," she went on. "Nobody gon' stay in a house like this. Man's ghost is all back in there."

"He was the only other one here?"

"They was people in and out, them ones that took a room for an hour or so. He was the only other one stayed. The only one here when the two of them was."

"You know where I can find him?"

She shrugged her thick shoulders and turned her face away. "He's somewhere back-of-town, I guess." Another lie; or at least an evasion.

"Anything else you can tell me?"

She shook her head resolutely in one quick jerk. "No. I tole you all of it."

They reached the front door and Valentin opened it and stepped out onto the gallery. A welcome breeze stirred along the street. He was about to thank the woman for her trouble when she said, "Whatchu doin' here? Coppers come by, said it's over and done and they ain't ever gonna find who did it. So what the fuck are you lookin' fo'?"

He didn't see any harm in telling her. It might even raise a reaction. "Another musician was murdered just a few days ago."

She gave him a sharp glance, then broke out another cold smile. It was not a pretty sight. "Mister," she said. "You are wastin' your damn time." She let out a raw laugh and closed the door.

He walked away from the house, more annoyed with every step about the way he'd handled her. If he'd been on his game, he would have pried loose everything she knew about the woman and Noiret, along with the tiniest details of what happened that night. He would have taken the time to scour the room inch by inch for evidence. Then he would have visited the houses on either side to ask if anyone had heard or seen anything. He would not have told her why he was there. In other words, he would have handled it like a professional detective. He didn't though, and he would have done about as well beating her with a club. He'd give it some time and then come back to pick up the pieces he'd missed.

Walking on, his head bent to the banquette, he wondered if the wags who were whispering that he had lost his notorious skills were correct.

He rounded the corner at Liberty Street and stopped at the first saloon he came upon. He peered through the grimy window to find the establishment midafternoon quiet, without a single customer inside. It looked like a good place to disappear and ponder his mistakes for a while.

About the time he was stepping into the beer hall, Justine was standing in the bedroom of the second-floor apartment on Girod Street, putting the last of her things into a chest of drawers that smelled of cedar.

She closed the drawer and turned to survey the room. Curtains of white linen rose and fell in the afternoon breeze like waving hands. The brocaded wallpaper beneath the wainscoting had rich red swirls around pale blue crests. The eggshell walls above boasted a series of framed paintings, portraits and gentle landscapes. A fine Persian rug covered the floor. The furniture was finely crafted of old hardwood, oak and walnut.

She paused to glance at the bed, a wide four-postered affair covered with a thick off-white quilt. It looked quite sturdy.

She had been in grand hotels a few times, and this was at least as fine as any of them. The room was spotless. She could almost smell the money that had soaked into every surface, and she wondered frankly what she was doing there. She felt ill at ease, like a servant waiting anxiously to please her master.

Running an idle hand over the polished moldings, she wandered into the front room, where a love seat and single mission rocker were arranged around another Persian rug, this one a red and black design. She crossed to the French door and opened it to the afternoon. There was no balcony, just an ornate wrought-iron railing. She stood there for a long time, looking down on Girod Street, musing on what she had done.

She had strayed to Basin Street and was introduced to a man who was shopping for a comely woman of color to be his mistress. Valentin had caught her in the betrayal, and not only was he refusing to forgive her, he wouldn't even talk to her about it. So she took her anger and went downstairs to ask Mr. Gaspare to call for a hack to come collect her and her things. The tobacconist gave her a curious stare, then made the call. She went back upstairs, took a long bath, and put on her walking dress. It took no time at all to collect her things. She went into the front room, and when the hack came clopping to the perron, she went out to the balcony and called down to the driver. The teamster, a burly Negro, climbed the steps, collected her few satchels of clothes, and carried them to his rig. She told him to stand ready and went back inside to wait.

She didn't know how long she had been standing there, adrift in her thoughts, when Valentin finally showed up, looking like he had been dragged through the streets. He had been gone most of the night and half of the day. He didn't smell like a saloon or a music hall and there was no scent of a woman on him. She wondered where he had been.

It was his last chance to tell her to stop. He didn't say a word, though, and his expression didn't change at all when she walked out the door, got in the hack, and rode off to the rooms that a wealthy Frenchman had secured for her. The details had all been addressed by Miss Antonia.

She was glad that Mr. Paul hadn't been there when she arrived. She needed time to drag her mind away from Magazine Street and get it fixed on her new duties. She went down a list in her mind, reminding herself of the expectations from there on. She would be displayed on the Frenchman's arm for certain functions. She would be expected to dress well, fetching and demure, while still revealing just enough of herself to draw men's attentions. In public, she would not speak unless invited to, and then only to fill a silence. No one would care what she thought anyway.

In private, she would do whatever he demanded on that fine bed, with the skills to keep him happy. If she performed well, they might keep the arrangement for years. It happened. If he decided he wanted her to carry children, she would be set for life. She would never again have to worry about a roof over her head or the source of her next meal. She would never have to sell her favors to strangers. She would be the possession of a rich man and so could hold her head up in public. Her life would be a dream that would pass in loneliness that was as cloistered as a nun's.

The prospect of all of it drew her into a pit of sadness that made her think of throwing herself over the railing and ending it right there. She didn't want this rich Frenchman and his fine apartment. She didn't want to be his companion and lover, and she surely didn't want to bear his children. She wanted to go home.

She stopped and got hold of herself. It was too late. She had cast her lot and that was that. It didn't mean she had to be miserable. She turned away from the window and went looking for the bag that held her prescription.

There was another person in the saloon after all, a sot who huddled over the table in the far corner, a muttering lump in an oversized coat that was too heavy for the close room.

When the bartender brought his mug of beer, Valentin asked after some of the characters from the neighborhood. The barkeep gave only gruff one-word answers: "Gone. Jail. Dead." And so on. The detective understood. He could be a private copper, a jealous husband, a creditor, or some other someone on unpleasant business. At the mention of a clarinet player named Lacombe, the barkeep gave him a cool smile, like he was hearing a poor joke, and moved away.

Valentin finished a second glass of beer, dropped a Liberty dollar, and thanked the bartender, who coughed and spit into a towel. The drunkard at the corner table did not comment.

Valentin walked out of the saloon with one bit of useful news: Nate Joseph's barbershop had moved from First and Liberty to Jackson near Rampart Street, a busier part of town with more traffic. He headed off that way.

The best place in the Crescent City to find information or a bit of action was always the nearest barbershop, shaving emporium, or tonsorial parlor. If a fellow wanted to place a bet, pick up a card of hop or an envelope of cocaine, find a particular sort of woman, or secure a quick loan to get him through the week, New Orleans' barbers could provide.

Nate Joseph's shop offered all these services while also serving as a sort of union hall for the local horn players, guitarists, and drummers. A musician looking for a night's work would find the wooden frames around Nate's long mirrors festooned with scraps of paper announcing who was hiring for this job or that.

Cornetist, one might read. *For two nights' engagement at Longshoreman's Hall. Reading musician only. Call M. Durand.—4461.*

Nate and his barbers maintained a clean shop, unlike many of his competitors. The glass was always polished, the hardwood floor swept and mopped shiny, the chairs saddle-soaped to keep the leather supple. All the potions and tonics that lined the shelves combined to give off a heady aroma.

The men who congregated there ran the gamut from upstanding citizen to low-down criminal. As long as they made a good appearance and did not cause trouble, Nate welcomed one and all, along with the Liberty dollars they carried in their trousers. Though it could be a raucous place, with loud arguments over women, money, and ponies, no one ever took advantage of the straight razors that lay gleaming wickedly on every surface. Nate wouldn't tolerate it. Pistols were checked at the door.

The establishment was known for the best haircuts and closest shaves in uptown New Orleans. Nate kept a fellow for manicures and a Negro boy to shine shoes. Valentin's father had brought him there as a child, and it was one of the few places back-of-town that still felt like home.

He walked in the door to find Willie Cornish with a towel wrapped about his face, leaving just enough space for him to see the eyes widen and the brows arch in surprise when the barber swung the chair around. It was a quiet afternoon and at the moment Willie was the only paying customer. Two rounders sat in chairs in the corner, bickering over the merits of a certain nag. Nate and the other barber were not on the premises.

"Mr. Valentin." Cornish's voice was a rumble that came from deep in his chest. "What brings you out this way?"

Valentin said. "Can you spare a minute or two?"

The Negro was agreeable, though there was something guarded in his expression as he plucked off the towel and draped it over one thick shoulder. The barber closed the pearl-handled razor and moved away.

Willie sat up. He was big all over, six foot three and well past three hundred pounds. His skin was the color of teak and his face was broad, with a wide African nose, thick cheekbones, heavy jowls. When he was on a stage, his valve trombone looked like a child's toy in his grasp. He had led a series of conglomerations, the most recent being the Crescent City Band. Valentin knew that Willie felt bad about the way things had ended with the Bolden Band; and now they had lost Mumford, too.

"I thought I might see you at the Frenchman's last night," Valentin said as he leaned against the second chair. "Everyone was there."

"Oh, no, not me," Cornish said with a nervous laugh. "My woman wouldn't 'low it. We ain't got a show, I got to stay home with her and the childrens." He glanced over at the barber, who was busy cleaning instruments at the basin in the corner, then turned wary eyes back to the Creole detective. "What can I help you with, Mr. Valentin?"

Valentin said, "It's about Jeff."

Willie shifted in the chair and his face grew somber. "Poor Jeff. I still ain't believin' he's gone. He was a decent fellow."

"Good guitar player, too."

"He was that," Cornish said, jumping to familiar ground with an emphatic nod. "Anybody could play behind King Bolden had to have somethin', yessir! Had to have somethin' is right. He done good with us, too."

A motorcar rattled over the Jackson Street cobbles. It wasn't that often one appeared in this part of town, and they all stopped to look out the wide window. The machine, a Model N with a bad exhaust, turned the next corner and the racket subsided. The barber went to humming a tune as he cleaned his razors. The rounders changed their bickering to the subject of sporting ladies.

Valentin said, "Have you heard anyone else talking about what happened to him?"

"No, sir," Cornish said. "Not a thing." He paused. "I guess he just got into somethin' that went bad for him." There was the smallest note of strain in that rumbling voice, the sound of a speaker skirting something.

Valentin lowered his voice. "You played that night. Was there anything unusual going on?"

"Nothin' I could tell," the big man said, pursing his lips. "We done five, six hours, from before ten till after three. When it was over, we packed up and went on home. Jeff left out by hisself." He stopped and sighed again, ruminatively. "It musta happened just after that..."

"Was he having any trouble lately?"

Cornish blinked and his brow furrowed. "No," he said, "no trouble." He repeated, "He was a good sort, didn't drink much and didn't gamble, kept his mind on his music and even practiced on his off days. He was even known to attend church now and—"

"What about this woman of his?" the detective broke in.

"Yessir?" Willie said carefully.

"Who is she?"

"Ethiopian gal name of...Dominique. That's it. She's off of some island somewhere." His wide eyes got wider and he stretched out his arms. "Fine-lookin' gal. Darker than me, though. We talkin' a *black* girl, now."

"They stayed together?"

"They did, yessir. A little house right up on Freret. Just past Jackson. I believe she's still there."

"Any others he might have been going around with?"

Cornish's thick lips pursed and Valentin could tell he was watching his words again. "I don't know 'bout none of that," he said. "I'll tell you, though, if they was any, then he was a fool.

You oughta see this here Dominique." His shook his head in admiration.

"She the kind men would fight over?"

"Maybe so, if she was on the street. It wa'nt like that. She's just a young girl and she ain't been here long. She stayed at home. I don't think he had no trouble with her."

Willie looked over at the barber as if to beckon him, but the fellow had his back turned as he worked at the sink. There was no doubt about it; the Negro wanted out from under the detective's attention.

"You know he's the second musician died in the past week," Valentin said.

Cornish looked startled for a second. "Oh...who...you mean Noiret?" His face fell into a grimace of disgust. "Now, that wa'nt no surprise at all. He wasn't no damn good. I'm surprised it didn't happen sooner."

"He and Mumford played in a band together at one time."

"Yessir, that's right." He shifted in the chair. "That was a while back, though. Couple years. Hell, you know how it is round here. Sooner or later, everybody play with everybody else."

Valentin hesitated for a second, then said, "Morton and some of the others think both of them were killed because they were playing in Storyville. With white men."

Cornish rolled his big eyes. "Oh, yeah, I heard some of that."

"And you don't believe it."

"Why the hell would anyone care?" he said. "Enough to go killin' somebody over it, I mean. Don't make no damn sense at all."

"That's what I thought, too."

The big man came up with a wry grin. "It ain't like we high society, Mr. Valentin. Once you blow a horn on Rampart Street, you just another nigger, no matter who you are."

They shared a short laugh and then Valentin said, "Do you know a fellow named Lacombe? Plays clarinet?" The laugh died as quickly as it had begun and Cornish came up with an odd look. Valentin said, "What is it?"

"You mean Terrence Lacombe?"

"If that's the name, yes. Why?"

"That boy dead," the barber said. He'd been listening after all. Valentin stared at him. "Dead how?"

"Dope," the barber said, mimicking an injection. "He took a needle. Took it one time too many. They found him dead on the floor of his room."

"When did this happen?"

"It was, when?" He looked at Cornish. "Friday night? Saturday?"

The big man nodded somberly, then settled back and motioned to the barber, who came up on the chair with a glinting razor in one hand and a cup and brush in the other.

Valentin stood aside while Cornish got his thick cheeks slathered with foam. "Is there going to be a funeral for Jeff?" he inquired.

"We gonna have a little parade for him tomorrow," Cornish said. "Won't have no body. I heard they carryin' him back to Arkansas to bury him there. But I think he'd appreciate it if we do somethin'. You'd be welcome."

Valentin thanked Willie for his time, then took a moment to ask after his family. "How many now?"

"Eight of 'em." Willie grinned, relieved to be off the subject. "'Well, a nickel is a nickel and a dime's a dime, got a house full of children, ain't none of 'em mine.'" It was a line from a gutbucket tune that had been going around. Valentin smiled, gave a wave of farewell, and went out the door.

He was almost to Rampart Street and mulling how much—or how little—he had collected so far when he sensed a heavy presence bearing down on him from behind and turned around.

Most of the shaving soap had been wiped from Cornish's broad jowls. The barber's towel was still draped over his shoulder and he used it to mop his brow before he spoke. "Somethin' I need to tell you, Mr. Valentin," he said, and then looked back the way he came.

Valentin veered to a grocer's clapboard storefront and gestured for Cornish to follow. He leaned against the rough boards, crossed his arms, and said, "What is it, Willie?"

The big man looked around again before dropping his voice to a whisper. "This was on Saturday night, the same night Jeff died. We took us a break and when it was time for us to start up again, he wasn't around so I went outside to look for him." His eyebrows peaked. "And he was in the alley out there. With a woman."

"Who was she?"

"I don't know."

"A sporting girl?"

"I didn't get a real good look at her." There was a tight note in his voice, as if he was biting down on something. "Then afterward, I wasn't even sure I saw what I saw." He stole one more glance up the street while Valentin digested this information. "One more thing," he said. "Why was you askin' about Lacombe?"

"Someone gave me his name. Why?"

"'Cause he played in the Union Hall band with Mumford and Noiret, too." He held up three thick black fingers and folded them, one by one. "Noiret, Mumford, Lacombe. They all played together, Mr. Valentin. And now they all dead. Ain't that some odd business?"

The street lost its shadows as new rain clouds had come in from the Gulf, throwing a peculiar metallic gray cast over the city.

Valentin took a cigarillo from his pocket, struck a lucifer on the brick facade of a building, and smoked as he walked east on

Liberty Street. He worked to keep his mind clear, because Cornish's parting words had sent a tingle up his backbone.

Three men who had once played in the same jass band dying in the space of less than a week pushed the bounds of coincidence, even in a shifting fraternity of back-of-town musicians, with almost everyone playing with everyone else at one time or another.

There was more. He had gone to ask the landlady about one of the victims and she had used another's name. It couldn't be another happenstance. He thought about turning around and marching back to brace her about it, then decided it could wait. He didn't want to spook her. He could still catch her before she left town and find out what kind of game she was playing.

He had smoked the cigarillo halfway down. It tasted bitter, and he tossed the butt into the gutter. At the next corner, he saw Picot's man again, drawing attention to himself with his clumsy attempts to remain invisible. Valentin snickered faintly; if the lieutenant had any idea how badly he was mangling the case so far, he would have saved himself the trouble.

Two girls came to fetch the madam in her upstairs room in the house on Robertson Street just as she was settling down with her hop pipe. A minute later she would have been off on a carefree cloud of gray smoke. Instead, she was drawn away by the two doves, both jabbering at the same time about a couple of rough-looking fellows who were at the door, demanding money.

With a grunt of displeasure, she marched down the hall and down the creaking stairs to the front door. Two men stood there, roughnecks, with the same doughy faces and dull eyes.

"What's this about?" she crabbed.

The one on the right produced a New Orleans Police badge. "We're collectin'," he said.

"We paid," the madam said. "Yesterday like always. What the hell is this?"

"Special tax," the copper said. "We need twenty dollars." He yawned, bored by the whole business.

The madam began to demand to see the precinct captain. She never got it out, though, because the second fellow suddenly lost all patience with the argument and punched her flush on the mouth, so hard that it knocked her back onto the dirty carpet of the foyer. Her skull banged the floor and her eyes went wide with shock as her gums spurted blood. The two doves, veterans of male violence, turned into statuettes.

"Now get the goddamn money," the first fellow ordered in the same flat voice.

When Valentin got to the intersection of Jackson and Freret, he looked around until he spied a house with a wreath that was affixed to a door, stark black against the white clapboards. There were no banquettes on these poor streets, just gravel pathways, and he walked to the shotgun double, trailing little swirls of dust.

He stepped onto the perron and knocked, once, twice, before he heard footsteps padding across the floor. The door opened and he was staring up at a young woman's striking face, dark, oval shaped, with high cheekbones and a perfect round nose. Her eyes were also round, black as ink, long lashed, and slightly lidded, making her appear a little sleepy. There was a gap between her ivory-white front teeth and a girlish pucker to her full lips. He guessed her to be not much past twenty. Her black hair was straight and woven in back into one long braid. Her figure was full in the bust and hips, her smooth skin a shade between cocoa and ebony. She gave off an earthy, florid scent, as if the perfume of flowers was wafting from every one of her pores.

She was wearing a loose cotton frock of pale blue pastel that hung below her knees, as common as a servant's. Her feet were bare and around her left ankle a Liberty dime hung by a thong. Standing there, she looked like a painting of an island girl posed in the doorway of a little grass hut. The only thing missing was a palm tree.

The voice was right as well. "Suh?" she said with a soft lilt that had started British then turned into something else.

"Are you Dominique?" Valentin asked.

"Yes, suh. Dominique Godet."

"My name's Valentin St. Cyr. I knew Jeff."

"Oh . . ." She let out a long sigh and her dark eyes drooped. Then, remembering her manners, she stepped back, holding the door. "Come inside, please, suh."

He moved past her and into the house, making an effort to hold his thoughts straight. She was even prettier up close, her face a dark flower. Though he had never been one to lose his wits over a woman's looks, Valentin believed this one could pull a fellow dangerously close to the edge. She was that fine. Cornish was right: if Jeff Mumford had strayed, either the girl in the alley was beautiful beyond belief or the guitar player had gone blind or insane.

He told himself to keep his mind on business as he stepped into her front room. It was furnished sparsely, with two upright chairs against one wall and a long table of pine against the other. A crucifix was affixed on the wall above the table. The only other adornment was an unframed picture that appeared to have been clipped from a magazine, a Caribbean panorama in muted pastels. A packing crate and two satchels had been pushed into the corner.

Dominique looked wearied, as if she wasn't really in the mood for the guest in the house. She pulled the two chairs away from the wall and set them in the center of the floor, facing each other, doing her best to be courteous.

She turned a pink palm upward. "Sit down, please," she said. "I'm sorry, but I ain't got much to offer you. Jeff's friends come by yesterday and they ate up and drank every't'ing we had. Ain't nothin' left."

Valentin took a seat. "It's all right," he said.

She sat down in the other chair and placed her hands on her knees. Even though her black eyes were motionless, with a flat calm, he got a sense she was studying him.

"I'm a private investigator," he began. "And I want to talk to you about Jeff's death."

It didn't move her. She didn't ask why he was investigating or on whose behalf. She just continued to watch him with that odd blank gaze.

"Will that be all right with you?" he said.

She let out a small sigh and said, "Yes, all right, suh." She blinked once, slowly, gathering her thoughts. "That night...he left out of here to go play over in Storyville. I went off to bed. The next thing I know, it's morning, and the police is at the door, asking can I come identify his body." Her voice broke on the last word; she let out a short breath and her eyes swam, forming black pools, and her body seemed to go liquid with grief. She collected herself. "I went with them to the station and they took me down in the basement and there he was...They had him all laid out." She swallowed and her lip trembled. "They said they found him dead in some alley over there. They said he drank some kind of poison." She bent her head to dab her eye on the sleeve of her frock.

He allowed a respectful pause. "Do you know if he was having trouble with anyone?"

"He didn't say so. He never said much of nothin', though."

"Was he drinking?" He kept his voice matter-of-fact. "Using hop?"

Dominique shook her head. "Oh, no, suh. He didn't mess with none of that. Maybe a little glass of whiskey now and then."

"What about gambling?"

She didn't respond to the question. Instead, she fixed her gaze on him again, holding it for a long moment. He returned the stare, a guilty pleasure. She raised one hand from her lap and touched a gentle finger to her lower lip. It was an odd, fetching gesture that distracted him, whether she meant it to or not. "I don't believe he cared for gambling," she said finally.

Now she slumped in her chair and crossed her bare feet, looking even more drained. And yet he got the notion that she would sit there for as long as he wished, politely answering his questions. He also guessed that she couldn't tell him much more than she already had.

He looked around the room and his eyes came to rest on the crate and satchels in the corner. "So, are you leaving now?"

"I want to go home." It sounded like a child's petulant plaint.

"Where's that?"

"Tobago. I can't go right away, though. I ain't got the money."

"It looks like you're all packed."

"Yes, suh, 'cause I got to leave out of this place pretty soon. Most of that's Jeff's t'ings. His clothes and his watch and chain. His guitar and all. There's a man comin' to collect it and send it on. His family wired back a little bit of money to have his body carried home, too."

Valentin tilted his head. "Would you mind if I had a look?"

"I don't mind, no, suh," she said.

He got up, went to the corner, knelt down, and lifted the lid of the crate. Along with the guitar case, it was filled with men's clothes, folded neatly, every piece of good quality and nicely tailored. "He certainly cared about his wardrobe," he commented.

"Oh, yes, he liked to look good, all right. He always liked to look good for the ladies." He caught the tiniest chill in her words.

Valentin straightened and turned around. "Was there anyone in particular?"

She blinked up at him. "What's that?"

"I asked if there was a particular woman Jeff was friendly with."

Her face closed and her soft mouth drew out to a pout. "I ain't got no idea." She leaned forward, one hand on either side of the chair and hunched forward in a lazy posture, not realizing or caring that the movement had loosened her frock to permit him a glance at her upper anatomy. A golden chain gleamed against the dark swell of her bosom. When he managed to pull his gaze away, he met hers and was startled to see a curiously sly light there.

He felt his face getting warm and stammered, "What, uh... what did you say you were going to do now?"

Her gaze shifted away. "I got to get a little bit of money together," she said. "I don't know how, though. Jeff paid for everything here. He wanted it that way." She pondered. "Guess I'll go downtown and see if I can find some work for now." She came up with a dim smile that held a shade of mischief. "Or I could go to Perdido Street. A madam down there told me I could come around anytime."

It gave him a startled pause and sent his thoughts into a spin. There was no doubt about that; she could get a room in a house in Black Storyville that very day. Once the word got around, the sports and well-to-do Negro citizens would come running. She might at first be distraught at having to use her body that way. No matter; there was always hop or morphine or rye whiskey to cure that, not to mention the cash and the gifts. She could easily earn in two nights what a shopgirl took home in a week. She might become some rounder's mainstay and live the life of a kept woman.

She would do well, and she'd have the money to go home in a matter of weeks, a month at most. But he had seen it too many times to count: a girl who went into a house just to make some quick cash ended up spending her life there. It was a trap, as sticky as a spider's web. A year or two of hard fucking would start wearing on her and she wouldn't be quite as pretty. Lines would break her satiny complexion and her firm body would start to sag. She would be drinking or doping more and more as the rigors of the life wore her down. Before she knew it, she would be thirty and on her way down a sad road that led only one direction. She might never get back to her island. She might never get out of New Orleans at all.

"Somet'ing wrong, suh?" She was watching him curiously.

"Don't do it," he said.

"Suh?"

"You'll be sorry if you go to Perdido Street," he said.

She laughed quietly. "Oh, no, I wouldn't never do that. I don't believe I could. I did get invited, though." She reached over the collar of her frock and pulled on the chain. The gold cross gleamed with a tiny diamond at its center. "Ain't like I'm all alone," she murmured.

It was time to go. He asked her to try and think of anything that might help him with his investigation. He wrote down his address on a piece of paper, along with the telephone number at Gaspare's, where she could leave a message for him.

She studied the paper. He thanked her for her time and offered his condolences. She saw him to the door and stood watching him walk away.

He turned for home, his steps suddenly slowing, as if he was dragging a weight. It had been a good while since he had questioned so many people in the space of an afternoon, and he had forgotten how exhausting it was, listening and watching for the telltale sounds and looks that revealed dodges, lies, slips, and slides. There was no doubt he was off his game.

He made his way south to Franklin Street. This was the edge of his old neighborhood, the place where he was born and had lived until he was sixteen, and at any intersection, he need only turn his head to see landmarks that would stir memories. He might catch a glimpse of St. Francis de Sales School for Colored, where he had first met and befriended Buddy Bolden. Not far from there was the house where he had been born and raised. It had long since fallen into disrepair, a run-down, deserted hovel. By now it may have collapsed to the ground. There were more such places all around, the houses, storefronts, and street corners he had known so well, the deserted lots where he had played as a happy child.

It was all that close by, and yet he had no desire to revisit any part of it. He kept on, arriving at the corner in time to pick up a South Peters Line car back downtown. As he rode along, he felt a welcome pang in his stomach that told him he was hungry. He took it as a good sign and guessed that it had much to do with having gone without anything since noon, and perhaps just a bit to do with Dominique Godet. For that little while, she had pushed Justine from his mind.

He could keep it that way. When he got home, he'd busy himself getting ready for work. He'd stop for dinner along the way and after that he'd be occupied with the main room of the Café, attending to the security of that piece of Tom Anderson's empire.

The telephone chattered just as the King of Storyville was stepping out of his office for a private visit with Josie Arlington, his most recent paramour. He was of a mind to ignore it. Then it occurred to him it might be Josie herself, warning him to stay away, because Hilma Burt was on the prowl. It had happened before. Once, Hilma had come banging on Miss Arlington's front door just as he and the madam had conjoined upon the plush Louis Quinze divan in her upstairs parlor. Josie was delighted, thinking it the height of pleasure to be serviced so admirably by the King of Storyville, even as his mistress stood waiting like a beggar at her front door.

It had quite the opposite effect on him. To her dismay, he jumped away, pulled up his britches, and slipped out the back way, as guilty as a dog.

Josie still got her moment. She called down to allow Miss Burt in, then went to the top of the stairs and stood there, her dress undone and wearing a smile that was full with a meaning that couldn't be denied.

"Why, he just left," she cooed.

Hilma had never let him forget it and with the sting of her tongue in mind, he snatched up the earphone and leaned down into the bell. "Yes?"

The voice on the other end was neither Josie's nor Miss Burt's. It was distinctly male, distinctly clipped and officious, and he recognized it immediately. "Chief O'Connor," he said.

The voice said, "Tom, I think we've got a problem."

Three minutes later, the King of Storyville put the phone down. He spent some moments staring out at the night sky over Basin Street. Only when his telephone jangled again did he remember that he was expected at the Arlington.

Justine took a long bath and put on one of her best dresses in preparation for Mr. Paul's arrival. It was the first time she would greet him as his mistress, the opening scene in a play that was being staged outside her body and mind, or so it seemed. She felt as if she was not taking part in it, but standing in the doorway to watch.

At seven o'clock she heard an automobile come to a rackety stop on the street and arranged herself prettily on the love seat.

His steps came lightly up the stairs. Curiously, he knocked and then waited for her to invite him in, as a nervous suitor. He stepped gingerly into the room, took off his hat, and held it before him as if trying to hide behind it. With that bit of business, it began to dawn on her that he might not be what she had expected at all. He had yet to display one bit of backbone.

Now seeing him more closely, she noticed more signs of a weak man about him. His beard and mustache hid a shallow chin and a nervous thin-lipped mouth. His nostrils twitched like someone was tickling his nose, and his pale eyes were skittish.

And when she motioned him to join her on the love seat, he looked like he was ready to jump back through the door and run away. In another man, all this might have come off as boyish charm. From him, it was just irritating and she fought a sudden urge to slap his face and get him to stop his jittering.

The impulse passed. She remembered what she was doing there and embarked on her duties by offering to serve him some refreshment. He smiled and mumbled something about a glass of sherry.

She got up and went to the cabinet for the bottle and a glass with a surge of cunning that all but washed away her melancholy. Maybe she could play this feckless rich man as she could never have played Valentin St. Cyr, and have the upper hand. Maybe she could be in charge for once.

She turned around to face him with the false smile of the serpent that was coiling in her breast.

Treau Martín walked out the door of the church on Fourth Street, feeling very much sanctified. It had been a good sermon.

Treau went to church every evening. He went every morning, too, if he could find a service to attend. He spent a good bit of his time in church, working to battle the devil that was chasing after his soul.

His given name was Charles, but everyone back-of-town called him "Treau," a collapsed version of *taureau,* or "bull." They had begun calling him that when he was sixteen, they called him that all the time he was playing music, and there were still too many people around from those days who were used to it for him to shed it now. Though of late he did his best to avoid that crowd.

To be sure, it seemed an odd moniker for him, because Charles Martín had not been like a bull as a boy and was not so as a man. He was of medium height and build. He was in fact medium from any angle, a middle-brown Negro with even brown eyes and a plain brown face. His hair was cut short and parted neatly on one side. He was not remarkable in any way.

At least not in any way that anyone would notice at first glance. The nickname had been donned on a special occasion years ago, the first time the young Charles visited a sporting house back-of-town. This was something of a rite for boys his age in uptown New Orleans, and young Charles was all too ready when his turn came.

It was when he unbuttoned his trousers that the sporting girl, a veteran of Basin Street, gaped in astonishment and cried out, "God in heaven! We got us a *petit taureau* here!" She went to the door and called down the hall for the other girls to come see. Young Charles stood there, on display and mortified as the girls viewed his yancy in stunned wonder. They murmured amongst themselves. The verdict was unanimous, and so Charles became Taureau, then T'reau, then simply Treau.

This feature had been an embarrassment when he was growing up. Then he realized that he had been blessed in a particular way and went about making the most of it. Being a musician gave him ample opportunity. The word got around until all the back-of-town girls knew about him and would call out his nickname and make the crudest gestures when he was onstage. The joke was that he chose to play bass fiddle as a sort of advertisement; a guitar would have been too small for a man with such an unusual gift. It got to be quite the thing for the whores to bring him around when a new dove arrived at a house, a sort of initiation. So he often got for free what every other rounder on the street had to pay for.

Those were wild times. King Bolden drew so much attention that the other back-of-town jass players got some of the adoration, too, including Treau. He spent long nights playing the saloons and dance halls along Rampart Street and the pavilions out on the lake in the warm months, carrying on like a crazy man. He drank his share and more, hit a pipe now and then, and dallied with the prettiest of the sporting girls. Since this didn't leave much time to hone his musical skills, it was just as well that he played a simple bass fiddle. All he had to do was to lay down a solid thump for the guitar players to ride and the horn players to dance around, and he could apply his energies making mayhem in other ways. He had been just about the happiest young jass man on Rampart Street. He had been the devil's child.

Then came the moment it all ended, a nightmare of drink and hop and wet flesh that was drawn out hour after hour, through one night, the next day, and then another night. When that second dawn came around, Treau reeled out onto First Street and, like Paul on the road to Damascus, fell under a light that struck him deaf, dumb, and blind. He knew in that instant that he was evil, the worst kind of sinner, bound for hell unless he found salvation.

He stumbled into the nearest church and went down on bended knees. Later that day, he took an axe and smashed his bass fiddle to pieces. Then he found another church and stayed there, praying, until the preacher put him out. From that moment on, he never took another drink, never again touched pill or powder. He went about turning his life around completely. Though he had been born and raised a Catholic, he found the Baptists harsher on evil, and one fine morning he got himself dunked in the muddy Mississippi and so was saved.

It didn't mean he didn't face temptation. The devil was a busy fellow, especially jealous of those who were snatched from his malignant clutches. Treau saw painted faces smiling at him from the windows of French houses, saw the thumbs sucked in a crude mimic of the girls' specialty. He smelled rye whiskey wafting out the open doors of the saloons and sweet smoke drifting from opium dens. Most of all, he heard the siren call of jass, the horns echoing inside his head as the rhythms shook his guts. He remembered all the crazy nights and could almost taste those wicked pleasures again. Now and then, when a girl recognized him and called out his nickname, he would feel the blood stirring below his belt.

It was Satan, of course, tempting him. The devil, always there to test his resolve, had lately grown more insistent. Like this evening, walking down a quiet Fourth Street, he sensed something dark and ominous dogging his steps, peering out from shadows, breathing down his neck. Though when he turned his head, there was of course no one there; clever fellow.

No matter; he was saved. Whatever it was, and whenever it came for him, "Treau" Martín stood ready.

NINE

"M r. St. Cyr! Hello! Mr. Valentin!" It was a woman's voice, foreign to his ear, yet somehow familiar, coming from the street. "Mr. Valentin?"

He opened his eyes. The sun coming over the rooftops told him it was around eight o'clock. It took him a few seconds to come awake enough to sit up and swing his legs over the side of the couch. He was still in the clothes that he'd worn to the Café the evening before. A book lay on the floor, splayed open, the spine broken.

When the voice called again, he got up, stumbled to the French doors, and stepped out on the balcony. Dominique was standing on the banquette, looking up at him, wearing a shy white smile.

"Good morning, suh," she said.

Valentin stared down at her, still dazed with sleep and befuddlement.

"May I come in, please?"

She was wearing a day dress, plain blue with a pinafore that was stark white against her dark skin, and a brimmed hat that she took off and placed next to her on the couch. She had twisted her hair into two long braids that draped over her dress in front, making her look even younger.

"I'm sorry," she said once she was settled. "I didn't mean to be disturbing you."

Valentin rested one hand on the back of the morris chair as he worked to chase away the cobwebs. His brain wouldn't quite engage and he still didn't understand what she was doing there.

"I don't want to be botherin' anybody," she said. "I needed to come see you, suh. I got me a problem."

"A problem . . ."

"Yes, suh. The landlord come around last evening. He asked for back rent. But I don't know nothin' about it. Jeff paid all the bills."

He nodded, trying to fathom what all this had to do with him.

She came up with a tight smile. "He said I could work it off. You want to know what kind of work he wants me to do?"

"I can guess," Valentin said, beginning to catch up. He'd seen this sort of low-down swindle before. Most likely, there was no back rent owed at all; and even if there was, the tally would be beyond what the helpless woman could afford. At the same time, she might be flattered to be considered worth so much, and the combination of fear and flattery might just get her out of her bloomers.

"He want twenty-two dollars," she told him. "I ain't got but three or four left. He say I got to pay up one way or another or leave right now. Today."

"I thought you wanted to go home anyway."

"I do, yessuh. I just ain't got the money yet. Jeff didn't leave me nothin'. I don't know what I'm gonna do."

"Do you want me to talk to this fellow?"

"Thank you, but no," she said. "I don't want to have nothin' to do with him. I know men like that. You talk to him and as soon as you go away, he's gonna be back after me again."

She was probably right about that. Of course, he could do more than talk to her landlord, but that was another matter. Why would he? He didn't know the girl at all.

"Is there someone here who can help you?" he asked her.

"They all back home," she said. "I come up alone. I been alone, except for Jeff Mumford."

Her eyes wandered past him and around the rooms, as if she was looking for something or someone. Valentin watched her, entertaining a sudden notion of what she might be up to. Then he decided that his mind was playing tricks and shoved the thought aside. Still, he could tell that she was waiting for something.

He considered for another moment. "Maybe I can help you," he said.

She gave him a hopeful look. "Yessuh?"

"Suppose I give you enough money to get a room."

"Oh...well..." Her gaze slipped away and her mouth dipped. "For how long would that be?"

"For a couple days. Then we'll see. Maybe I can find you a situation."

She hesitated, then nodded. "All right, suh. Only 'cause I don't know what else to do." She gave him her shy, pretty smile. "I appreciate it, your kindness."

She waited while he went into the kitchen, opened the icebox, and dipped into the coffee can where he kept his money. He came back into the front room to find her standing at the balcony door with her eyes closed and the sun on her face, an image as pretty as a painting.

When he spoke her name, she turned around and smiled. He handed her a Liberty ten-dollar gold piece. She looked at the coin. "This is too much."

"You can pay me back later," he said.

She murmured another thank-you that was followed by an awkward silence. "I guess I need to go ahead and go," she said.

"I do have some business to attend to," he told her.

"Is it about Jeff?"

"That's right."

She stopped, her brow furrowing. "Why you doin' that?"

"Because, some of his friends, I mean those fellows he played with, they asked me to look into it. They just want to know what happened to him."

She gave a vague shrug. "What happened was somebody didn't like him poisoned him and he died."

She took a little shuddering breath. Valentin allowed a pause, then said, "You can catch the Canal Line car at the corner. Take it to the corner of Commerce Street. There's a hotel there that accepts unescorted women. It's called the Savoy. You can tell them I sent you."

"And then what?"

"Then...I'll come and check in on you."

"When?"

"This afternoon or tomorrow, I suppose. As soon as I can."

That seemed to satisfy her. She picked up her hat, put it on, and tied the ribbon in a bow beneath her chin. He escorted her out the door, down the steps to the street, and along the two blocks to the corner of Canal. He waited with her until the streetcar arrived and helped her aboard. She waved good-bye and kept her eyes on him as the car rolled away.

Cora Jarrell had her bags packed and sitting by the door, ready to go. She wanted to make one more round to see if there was anything of value that she hadn't already carried off and pawned. She checked her own room first. All that was left were the bare sticks of her furniture and the white envelope that was propped against a candleholder on her mantelpiece. In it was a single sheet of paper with a message that she had composed in a labored hand after the detective St. Cyr had walked away from her door. As soon as she got to Union Station, she would find a street urchin and have him locate the detective and turn it over to him. Let him do what he could with it. She didn't want another murder and the hoodoo that went with it hanging over her, and she wasn't about to tell the coppers, because then she'd have them all in her business and she'd never get out of town. She planned to take the Southern Crescent running east, leaving everything behind for more profitable points. She'd heard that there were chickens to be plucked in Mobile.

She went down the hall, pushing the room doors open and taking a quick glance inside each, avoiding only the one where that son of a bitch Noiret had gone and got himself murdered. There was nothing left in that haunted space anyway.

She had just finished her inspection and was heading back to her room when she heard a creak. It was nothing, the slightest squeak, and at any other time it wouldn't have caught her ear. It was most likely one of the horde of rats that scrabbled about beneath the floors, day and night. That's what she told herself as she hurried along, feeling a cold shiver on the back of her neck, as if one of those filthy critters was crawling on her.

She was all too glad to be quitting those premises for good. She was especially pleased to be escaping from the owner of the house. She had kept the man at bay and out of her business only by giving him French once a week, a regular part of his visit to collect the room rents. And him a married man.

As she stepped through her room door for the last time, she heard another creak, this one louder and closer, and she was just turning her head in surprise when an explosion went off at the soft point just below the back of her skull. She felt a hot blast of pain as her legs buckled and she tumbled to the floor.

Her eyes rolled up as the bits of her life scattered like startled birds and came to rest on the ivory envelope that was propped on the mantelpiece.

It was just before noon when Valentin walked into Frank Mangetta's Saloon and Grocery on the north end of Marais Street.

The saloon, with its bar, tables, booths, and low stage all crowded together, took up the front half of the building. Through an archway halfway back and accessible from Bienville Street was a grocery in the best Italian fashion, with imported meats, cheeses, and other specialties so dear to the palates of New Orleans' southern Italian community, large and growing larger.

Frank Mangetta was a padrone to the musicians in uptown New Orleans. An artiste himself (though he admitted that he played a poor violin), his establishment offered regular entertainment at night and was a second home to the uptown's floating population of musicians at all hours.

When Valentin asked to see the proprietor, the bartender told him that he had stepped out but would be back directly. He ordered a short beer and spent a few idle moments considering the morning visit from Dominique. It puzzled him; she was like some marvel of nature, an exotic jungle creature, and he didn't quite know what to make of her, especially her showing up so close in the wake of Jeff's passing and Justine's leaving. He was actually relieved when he put her on the streetcar and could go back to his day. Maybe it was all a game to cadge ten dollars, but he didn't think so. He wondered if he'd ever see her again.

He sipped his beer and took a look around the room. There were only a half-dozen early customers on the premises, two at the bar and another four at a booth in the far corner, among them one mulatto and two Negroes, and for once the dark-skinned men weren't serving the light. A strange sight, anywhere but there; Mangetta had been the first to ignore the color line when it came to music. Anyone who could blow a decent horn or pound the ivories with some skill was welcome. The Sicilian just did it and no one had thought to stop him. Things were different, any way he looked at it.

So, Mangetta was helping to change Storyville's chemistry. And it wasn't just the makeup of bands that was changing; it was their music, too. Was it only three years ago that Buddy Bolden's horn was considered a scurrilous plague on New Orleans' tender youth? They called what he played *jass* and claimed it was the Devil's music to be sure, a gumbo of raucous noise that was so loud and fast that the proper reading musicians and their polite white audiences didn't know what to make of it, except to throw up their hands in horror and call for someone to stamp it out before it spread.

It did spread, though, and the sedate waltzes and precise rags were shoved rudely aside by crazy inventions in rollicking 4/4 time, a rhythm that made people want to dance, and not in the stilted, precise postures of schottisches and cakewalks, either. The lyrics that went with the music were dirty and sinful and should rightly have been made illegal, except that almost nothing was illegal in this bizarre corner of the world. As the bands played on, then it was the audiences that were changing.

Negroes, Creoles of every stripe, then Italian and Irish workers, and finally Americans from the Garden District came carousing down dark and dangerous back-of-town streets, all wild to hear Bolden and the others that he and his crazy horn dragged along. For a short while, he was the maniac Pied Piper of New Orleans. Then it was over, and when he went away he took the best and the worst of it with him.

It happened so fast that even some of those who were there weren't sure what they saw and heard; and within an even shorter span of time, jass was being played all over uptown New Orleans.

Then Mangetta's and Nancy Hanks's saloon, both on the north side of Canal Street, opened their doors. Crowds flocked and more music halls sprang up, a half dozen in the past year, most of them along Villere and Marais streets, though wide-awake Basin Street madams like Lulu White saw a coming thing and were talking about hiring jass bands, too.

At the same time, it dawned on musicians who had worked all the low-rent dives along Rampart Street what the hard life did to Bolden and the others and they gave up their wild ways and began to behave themselves. The days when jass player equaled drunk or hophead or whoremonger were over. Things were calmer now.

Or maybe not, Valentin mused as he stared bleakly out the window onto Marais Street.

After all the bloody drama of the Black Rose murders, he had been grateful for the long dry spell. It couldn't last, though, and now he had a case that was all smoke and paid nothing to boot. He had gone traipsing into his old neighborhood, kicking up the dust from memories that were best left buried. People were lying to him and he found himself standing over dead bodies. It was familiar terrain that he had vaguely hoped to escape for a while longer.

To cap it all, Justine had gone away, and no sooner had she vacated the premises than a black beauty of a girl had shown up to drop her passel of troubles on his doorstep.

He turned his brooding thoughts back to the murders. While he didn't mind so much going after Mumford's killer, it irked him that he was working the death of Antoine Noiret, a man he hadn't known and wouldn't have liked if he had. And now this fellow Terrence Lacombe was gone. There was no way around it. All three men had played in the same jass band, and that made it a mystery.

When Frank Mangetta came in off the street and spied Valentin, he stopped cold and threw out his arms in greeting.

He told the detective to wait and stepped behind the bar to mutter some instructions to his day man and pour himself a quick glass of wine. He waved for Valentin to follow him to the table that was tucked in the little alcove next to the door, right up against the front window.

Frank could have played the part of the Italian peasant at the Opera House. He was short and as broad as a barrel, with oily black hair and a luxurious mustache planted on a round and swarthy face. He was a passionate man, known to cry out in joy or weep like a woman when the feeling came upon him. At the same time, he had a sharp eye when it came to matters of commerce and his scrutiny of the characters who peopled Storyville's strange pageant.

He'd known Valentin's father from the old country and so had kept a paternal eye on the detective in the wake of that tragedy. He was of course delighted when Valentin came back to work in Storyville, first as a copper, then as Anderson's right-hand man. Mangetta had benefited, winning certain business favors.

He always enjoyed a chat in Sicilian dialect, but as the years passed, Valentin came to recall less and less of the language: a greeting, some common words, a few everyday phrases, and little else.

"I haven't seen you in six months," Mangetta said. He frowned and stretched a dramatic hand. "You live ten blocks away, you work four blocks away, and you can't show your face more'n that? *Come va? Tu sei un straniero.*"

Valentin smiled and blushed a little. *"E vero."* He said haltingly, *"Ma...ma..."*

"But what?"

"But I've been keeping to myself."

"So what brings you out today?"

"Jeff Mumford."

Mangetta's face would have been comic in its geometry but for the sincere sadness in the eyes. "Poor Jeff. He was a good fellow, eh? I never had any trouble with him. He wasn't a braggart like some of these rascals. And he sure could play that guitar. To end up like that..." He shook his head, as melancholy as Pagliacci.

"I'm investigating his murder." There, he had said it. "His and Noiret's."

The saloon keeper regarded him shrewdly. "Why? Because of Morton and that bunch at the Frenchman's?"

Valentin said, "You know about that?"

Mangetta's eyes went wide with fervor and his black eyebrows hitched. "Morton thinks someone's after musicians who play on this side of Canal? If that was true, I'd be out of business." He snickered richly. "You know as well as me that them fellows died over money or a woman. Ain't it always? I'd put my money on the woman." He lowered his voice. "There's been rumors going round."

"What kind of rumors?"

"Some woman shows up late, picks a fellow, and takes him somewhere to fuck all night, then disappears again like a ghost. And nobody ever sees her again."

Valentin sat back. What Mangetta related was a twist on a story that surfaced every few years. The phantom woman comes out of nowhere to select one lucky candidate, works him until his yancy is about to fall off, then slips back into the night. The tale went around, getting all tangled up with voodoo, and eventually fell apart under the weight of exaggeration. The woman became a gorgeous octoroon; she could wind for six hours, eight, twelve, without missing a beat; she made strong men cry and sent weak men to the infirmary, broken into pieces. In reality, it was just a special Storyville version of a haint, more hoodoo fiction for the gullible. They had been telling the same stories for fifty years, going back to epics about legendary bawds like America Williams and Mary Duffy.

Mangetta saw the expression on the detective's face and raised his hands. "I'm just telling you what I heard," he said. "Anyway, I believe Jeff had a woman. A sweet looker, from what I heard."

"She is."

"You've seen her?" Valentin nodded, working to keep a straight face. Mangetta smiled slyly. "Well, what do you think, maybe it was her? Maybe she caught him with someone else and made him pay for it? She seem like the type that could kill a man?"

"Everybody's the type," the detective said. "So anyone could have done it. It's not going to be that easy." Out of habit, he took a glance around to see if any parties were listening too closely. Then he said, "Do you know Terrence Lacombe?"

Mangetta's brow furrowed. "Plays clarinet?"

"Played," Valentin said. "He's dead. He had an overdose."

The saloon keeper's eyes widened. "And he was in the band with . . ."

"That's right."

Mangetta counted down his fingers, murmuring. "Mumford, Noiret, Lacombe . . ." Then: "Treau Martín. Played bass fiddle."

"Is he—"

"Yeah, he's still around. Don't play music no more. Got religion and gave it up."

"Who else?"

Mangetta hesitated briefly, then bent his head to whisper a name. Valentin stared at him. The saloon keeper nodded slowly, with much drama.

"Damn!" he said. "And him? Is he...?"

"Alive, as far as I know." Valentin looked troubled by the news and Mangetta eyed him speculatively. "You ain't had a case to work on for a while, eh?"

"Nothing like this."

Mangetta lifted his glass in a small toast. "Well, then, *buona fortuna, paisan.*"

Valentin raised his glass as well, though it was only out of courtesy.

He took a car to Philip Street and walked along the dirt path. As soon as he rounded the corner and saw the New Orleans Police wagon standing in the street in front of the rooming house, he knew he was too late. He felt his stomach drop as he realized that it was starting all over again.

There were two coppers leaning against the side of the rig, smoking cigarillos. They were both young rookie patrolmen, their faces shiny with the flush of youth, with wispy mustaches and thin beards. They looked Valentin up and down as he approached, and the taller of the two straightened up from his slouch.

Valentin said, "What happened here?"

"Who's askin'?" the partner said.

"My name's St. Cyr. I work for Tom Anderson."

The two patrolmen exchanged a glance. The partner tossed his butt away, hitched his trousers, and climbed the gallery steps to disappear through the open door. The taller copper made a point of ignoring him, concentrating instead on his smoke. A few moments went by and Valentin was startled to see Lieutenant Picot appear in the doorway, his suit buttoned tight around his thick middle and his derby perched high on his round head. He was sporting his usual cool and narrow-eyed glare. He waved the patrolmen away and beckoned St. Cyr closer.

Valentin came to the bottom of the steps. Picot regarded him with a notable lack of surprise. "What do you want here?" he inquired.

"Is it the landlady?" Picot didn't reply. "What happened?"

"Somebody bashed her a good one in the back of the head," the copper said.

"Is she dead?"

"I'd say so."

"Can I have a look?"

"No, you can't have a *look*," Picot snapped. "Look at what? You think we don't know the difference between dead and alive? There ain't nothin' to see in there no how. Place is clean. Looks like she was about to leave out."

"She was," Valentin said.

Picot cocked an eyebrow. "Oh? And how would you know that?"

"I talked to her. Yesterday."

"Is that right?" Now the copper produced a wolfish grin. "Well, then, we could wrap this case up in a hurry if you want to go ahead and confess." The leer faded. "You came back today why?"

"To...ask her something."

"About?"

The detective returned the favor, keeping his face stony and his mouth shut.

"Well, it don't matter, because she ain't available for questioning," the lieutenant said. "So you might as well go home." He put his hands in the pockets of his jacket, making a show of blocking the doorway.

Valentin got the message. The subject was closed. The detective thought about mentioning Noiret, or Mumford or Terrence Lacombe, for that matter, just to see Picot's reaction. Then he realized it would get him nothing but another blank look so he turned to leave.

The copper wasn't quite finished. "Goddamn, St. Cyr, you're some kind of curse, ain't you?" he said in a snide tone. "You come back to work and right away the bodies start piling up. It's a damn wonder anyone comes near you." He couldn't hide his amusement.

Valentin walked away without asking the other obvious question: what was the lieutenant doing so far afield when his precinct stopped one block south of Canal Street? He wouldn't get an answer to that one, either. At least not there.

He turned the corner at Second Street and went wandering aimlessly up and down the adjoining blocks, his hands clasped behind him and his gaze fixed on the banquette.

His guess was the landlady had been murdered because of Noiret. And perhaps because she had spoken to a detective, using a sly lie that of course he would uncover and then come back to resolve. Why didn't she just come out and tell him, then? He mulled that one. It had to be because she wanted to get out of town before he showed up again. Which led to the possibility she had left something for him, a clue or message of some sort. Then he wondered if the crude, homely woman was that clever. She might have been smart, but she wasn't smart enough and with Valentin's help she was dead.

It was true. Just like that, he had cracked a door on someone's dirty little secret. Just like that, he had played an unwitting role in a plot to keep it that way. Just like that, a murder had been committed and he was in the thick of it.

Circling back to Philip Street now would be a waste of time. Picot wouldn't leave a speck of evidence behind for him. They were back where they belonged, butting heads, doing battle.

Lieutenant Picot waited around for them to load the woman's body in the wagon and cart it off to join Noiret and Mumford at the morgue, another worthless piece of back-of-town trash disposed of. The lieutenant sometimes thought it would be a very good thing if every person residing south of Canal and east of Basin could be dispatched so efficiently.

He stepped onto the gallery and stood watching until the hack became a small dot far down Philip Street, then took a moment to look up and down the block, just in case St. Cyr had gotten it in his head to sneak back around for a look at the crime scene. Not that he really expected it; the poor fool had looked beaten as he skulked away along the dirt path. It was no wonder. In the space of forty-eight hours, he had lost his woman, saddled himself with a case that went nowhere, and left a corpse in his wake.

He hadn't even had the nerve to ask what a precinct lieutenant from the other side of town was doing there, though Picot could see in his eyes that he wanted to. He had an answer ready, a "favor for a fellow officer," or something like that. He didn't care if St. Cyr believed it or not. It was none of his damned business what any New Orleans policeman did.

When he was sure that neither the detective nor any other prying eyes were about, he went into his pocket and drew out the white envelope that had been found on the mantelpiece. It was a stroke of luck that it had not been snatched away before he got to it. Someone was in too much of a hurry or too dim to realize that it could be evidence. Now the lieutenant tore open one end, drew out the single sheet of paper, and read the words that were scrawled there.

The handwriting was rough and he read slowly, his lips moving and his brow stitching as if he was translating from a foreign tongue. When he got to the end, he stood without moving for a half minute. Then he went into his vest pocket for a lucifer, struck it on the gallery post, and put it to the corner of the page. When the flame crawled up to lick his fingers, he let the breeze take the ashes and scatter them like black snowflakes over the packed dirt street.

Valentin walked all the way home, twenty long blocks. He locked the door behind him, took off his jacket, and draped it over the morris chair. He sat down on the couch and unbuttoned his shirt with slow fingers. His feet were aching from all the walking, so he took his shoes off, too. He put his head back and stared up at the cracks in the ceiling, trying to make sense out of what he knew.

It wasn't much; not yet. All he had were pieces. Three musicians who had played in a band together had died in the space of a week. The landlady at the house where one of them had been murdered was also dead. Picot was lurking, doing his best to keep him at bay. It seemed that if there was a connection, it would be obvious, and yet he couldn't see it.

After tossing it this way and that, he closed his eyes and dozed off. Odd images slipped through his half-awake mind.

Justine was standing in the middle of the room. She was telling him something, but she was speaking too low or he had gone deaf, because he couldn't catch a word of it. The door opened, letting in a rush of wind, and she was gone. She walked away down Magazine Street, looking back over her shoulder, her face cold and accusing. He knew he should go after her and tried to make his legs move, only to find them as stiff as wood....

A sudden hard rapping brought him out of the dream. His head felt foggy and his mouth was dry. He stood up, took three stumbling steps, and opened the door to find Beansoup standing there, regarding him with quizzical eyes.

Valentin rubbed his face. "What is it?"

"Mr. Anderson wants you to come in early this evening," the kid said, looking him up and down.

"What time is it now?"

Beansoup grinned. "What time is it?" he chortled. "Round four o'clock."

Valentin let out a little grunt of disgust. He'd been asleep for over two hours. "All right, then."

The kid was making an effort to peer past him and so he moved away, leaving the door open. Beansoup took the invitation and stepped inside. He followed the detective into the kitchen and watched him down a glass of water from the spigot. He fidgeted for a few seconds, then screwed up his courage and in a hushed voice said, "Miss Justine ain't here no more?"

Valentin shook his head. He saw the crestfallen look on the kid's face and decided to have mercy on him. "It wasn't your fault," he said gently. "She would have gone anyway. She wanted to get away from here."

Beansoup nodded gravely. "Where did she go?"

Valentin shrugged. "I guess she found herself a situation."

"You don't know for sure?"

"I don't know for sure, no."

Beansoup frowned, troubled by the news.

"What's Mr. Tom want me for?" Valentin asked him.

"Didn't say. Just that he wants you in early."

"Then I need to get dressed."

Beansoup backed away to let him pass. The detective went into the bedroom and began putting out his things for the evening at work. After a few quiet minutes, he heard the front door close. Beansoup had left without a word.

By the time Justine finished her errands and the driver deposited her and her packages at the apartment, her head was pounding. She hurried into the toilet to draw some of her medicine, then came out into the front room to wait for it to take hold. She sat down on the love seat and gazed vacantly at the bags that Mr. Paul's driver had left inside the door.

Like a dutiful mistress, she had made market and then went to Mayerof's to purchase other items for the household, using money that the driver provided. Soon she would get up, unpack them, and get on with her other duties in the service of her benefactor.

She had slept fitfully and woke up in a dark mood. For the first time in over two years, she was a bought woman again, a piece of merchandise. She had gotten past the hardest part, though, and had to admit it could have been worse.

When the moment came, he had stuttered, hedged, and flitted about, never quite getting to the point of a demand. It was no surprise. Even with her mind addled by her medicine, she was already figuring him out. She went about performing the seduction, which was also part of her duties.

She had poured another drink to relax him, then took his arm and guided him into the bedroom. He sat down on the bed, looking all the more unnerved. She turned her back and asked him to undo the hooks of her dress. He obliged, though it took him so much time that she started to get bored. When he finally got her undone, she made a languid show of drawing herself out of the sleeves and then letting the top drop away. She raised her eyes and caught her reflection in the tall mirror on the wall. Without a rib-crunching corset, it was a pretty picture, her flesh tawny against the white lace edge of her camisole. Most any man with a pulse would have snapped to attention at the mere sight of her. When she glanced over her shoulder at Mr. Paul, though, she saw him looking embarrassed, as if he had seen something shameful.

She asked him to finish with the hooks that went over her rump. He did a little better this time. She stepped out of her dress and let it swirl around her and fall to the floor. She stood before him, posing in her silk camisole. He didn't move, barely batted an eye. She slipped down beside him on the edge of the bed and murmured something about helping him with his clothes. She unbuttoned his shirt, then reached to undo the buttons on his trousers.

Without warning, he pounced, and for a moment, she thought perhaps he was a lover after all. He wasn't, though; with flailing hands, he pushed her onto her back and got busy, first stripping off her camisole, then pushing his trousers down around his knees. He lay on her, his weight crushing her into the soft mattress, and huffed away.

It was over in less than a minute. He immediately rolled off her and went about pulling up his trousers. He buttoned his shirt shakily. He did not look at her, as flustered as a schoolboy on his first frolic. She was pondering this when he mumbled about having to go home. And just like that, he was out the door. She heard the motorcar cough to life on the street below, then putter away.

She thought about what had happened. Though in truth she had barely felt him, for the first time in almost two years, she had allowed a man inside her who was not Valentin. She felt a part of her heart shatter like thin glass and hot tears brimmed in her eyes, then rolled off her cheeks and onto the soft pillow. Behind this came a rush of anger at Valentin for putting her there in the first place.

It would have been better if Mr. Paul had been all ferocious and had gone digging for China, working her until she turned to jelly inside. At least that might have erased thoughts of Valentin from her mind, if only for a moment. Instead she discovered a boy in a man's body and realized that if she had been looking to get revenge, she had chosen the wrong fellow.

Valentin stopped for dinner on the way to work. He got to the Café as dusk was descending and went up to the second-floor office, to find the King of Storyville behind his desk, muttering into his telephone set. He raised one eyebrow in greeting and pointed to one of the chairs. Valentin sat down to wait and marvel idly at the man's inexhaustible energies.

Day and night, he seemed never to stop. As a Louisiana state senator, now in his third term, he was required to attend to the many needs of his New Orleans Parish. Louisiana politics was a turgid business, like the soil upon which the lower half of the state was planted, thriving with life and fetid with decay. New Orleans, especially rich and wet, spawned a particular breed of parasitic life-form that found a haven in various local and state offices. So Anderson spent long days and longer nights rubbing shoulders with corrupt louts and honorable statesmen alike.

He also had the mundane day-to-day concerns of Storyville to mind. He was too protective of his power to share much of it; and so he fussed regularly with the most trifling matters. The benefit being that little went on around those streets without his knowledge and blessing.

He was up late most nights at the Café. There was always some dignitary, sports figure, or renowned artiste in town, someone who demanded a visit to Anderson to prove his own prestige.

After which the totsy gentleman would head down the line to have his whims sated by one of the District's able sporting women. Just hosting these individuals meant that Anderson's presence was expected on Basin Street six nights out of seven.

From what Valentin could tell, it was Café business that was keeping Anderson on the telephone at that moment, a dispute about the wholesale price of certain liqueurs. He listened for another half minute, drumming his fingers, then spoke a few clipped words, dropped the handpiece into its cradle, and pushed the ornate box aside.

"You might consider getting yourself one of these contraptions," he said, nodding brusquely to his telephone set. "Half the homes and most of the businesses in New Orleans have one. It would save me having to send some street Arab every time I need you."

Valentin was about to explain why he didn't want a telephone, but Anderson waved the subject closed with a sharp hand.

"Never mind, never mind," he said. "My telephone rang this afternoon. It was Chief O'Connor. He called to inform me that a madam of a house on Robertson Street was assaulted by two men who came to the door, said they were coppers, and asked for money. They knocked the woman down and made off with twenty dollars." He glowered. "I thought you took care of that."

Valentin was surprised. "I thought so, too."

Anderson's glare and tone grew sharper. "The chief also wanted to ask why I didn't extend him the courtesy of telling him I had a man investigating the death of this fellow Mumford and some other... What was his name?"

Valentin said, "Noiret."

"Noiret. Yes. I'm sure you can understand my confusion. I didn't know I had a man investigating anything." He delivered the last line with wide eyes and upturned palms, as if innocently baffled, belying the flush of anger that was reddening his cheeks.

"I never said that," Valentin told him.

"You never said what?"

"That you sent me. Picot assumed."

"And you didn't bother to explain."

"I didn't, no."

"I told you to leave this alone."

"You told me it wasn't worth the trouble." Anderson glared again and the detective spoke up quickly, "It's not just those two anymore. There's another fellow who died of an overdose of dope. And all three of them played in the same band."

The King of Storyville's face twisted into a frown. Valentin plunged on. "And a woman has turned up dead in a house on Philip Street. The same house where Noiret was mur—"

"All right, that's enough!" Anderson slapped his hand down on the desk. "What are you talking about? Some jass players turned up dead? And an old whore in a house on Philip Street? Good god, what a surprise! You think there's something to it?" He came up with a crude mask of concentration. "Let's see if I have this correct. One of these musicians drank poison. Another took an overdose of dope. The only one who you know was murdered was a no-good piece of shit, and it happened so far back-of-town it's halfway to east Texas. Is that correct?"

"I'm—"

"Is that correct?" Anderson barked.

"It is," Valentin admitted.

"Of course, it is." The white man pointed an accusing finger. "You went poking into something without my permission and this is what happens. Now you've got the police in a fit and I've got O'Connor calling to complain."

Valentin wanted to ask *why* the chief was calling to complain, but he knew better than to say a word. He waited for the storm to pass. The King of Storyville stared at him for another moment, his mouth a grim line below the gray mustache. He dropped the scolding hand and settled back with a sigh of frustration, as if baffled at his failure to communicate. He swiveled in his chair to gaze out the window, following the progress of a train leaving the station and letting the tension in the room ebb away.

"Does this have anything to do with King Bolden?" Anderson asked. Valentin, startled, said no, then the King of Storyville went to musing. "You were some kind of a hero after those Black Rose murders. You were right and everyone else was wrong. And now it's a year and a half later, and you've got nothing. Less than nothing."

The last wisps of smoke from the departing train drifted back over the roof of the station and disappeared into the blue evening sky. Anderson turned slightly in his chair.

"What about your girl?" Anderson said. "I heard that she's no longer staying with you."

Apparently, there was nothing wrong with Anderson's network of spies. Valentin said, "She isn't, no."

The King of Storyville shifted his weight and the old chair squeaked. "I understand she's taken up with a gentleman. His name is Paul Baudel. He married into the Sartain family. Very prominent. They own rice plantations." He looked at the Creole, saw only a morose stare. "So she's being well cared for," he went on quietly. "He'll see to her ne—"

"It's getting busy downstairs," Valentin interrupted.

Anderson came the rest of the way around in his chair, frowning at the insolence. "All right, then, we're through," he said. "You can go."

Valentin went down the stairwell, walked along the back hall, and pushed through the doors into the big room to begin his evening rounds. It wasn't very busy at all; he had just wanted to get away from Anderson.

He made his first slow circuit, reflecting on the conversation in the room upstairs. First came the news about Robertson Street. He thought it was fixed. Now he'd have to go back. Anderson berated him about investigating the deaths, announcing that the police were "in a fit" over it. And why was that? Was it just Picot's sensitive feelings or something more? Anderson himself was acting strange, angry with him over the case, abruptly gentle and solicitous when it came to the subject of Justine. Now Valentin knew that she had found a situation. She was going to become the downtown mistress to a man of means. She must have been plotting it all along. The betrayal was complete.

Through the night and into the small hours of morning, he went over the pieces of the case again. He needed something to occupy his thoughts. Along the way, it dawned on him that even with the scolding, the King of Storyville had never ordered him to drop the case. Which he could have done at any time.

He managed to keep his mind off Justine, except for when a quadroon passed by on the arm of some well-dressed fellow, on her way to being parked in the ladies' salon. Once he thought it was her and felt a dizzying blow in the pit of his stomach that didn't let up even when he got a closer look and saw it was only a woman of her same size and shape. He stepped to the end of the bar and asked for a short glass of brandy. The head bartender hiked an eyebrow in surprise, then went for the bottle. Valentin downed the drink in a quick swallow and went back to his rounds.

The customers had all shuffled out the door and the only sound was the scraping of the chairs as they were dragged off to make way for the cleaning crew. Valentin leaned at the end of the bar, watching them work, his mind miles away. Some minutes passed and he could sense someone inching closer and looked up. A woman was standing there, a mulatto with broad features and a heavy bosom. She wore a tawdry evening dress and a hat missing half its artificial flowers. Except for the lateness of the hour, she would have never been allowed through the front door.

"Mr. St. Cyr?" she said. "I was at the Frenchman's this week, that night y'all come over and stayed till the morning. Mr. Jelly Roll and Frankie Dusen and all them. You remember?"

"I remember," Valentin said. "Can I help you?"

"I heard you was lookin' into what happened to them fellows what died. Jeff Mumford and Noiret."

Valentin grimaced with annoyance that his business was on the street. "What about it?" he said.

"Well, I wanted to tell you what happened after y'all left that night." She looked around for a second, then said, "I was asleep in there. And I felt somebody pokin' at me to wake up. It was light out. I thought it was the nigger that cleans up, but it wasn't. A fellow was standin' there, said he wanted to know what y'all had been talking about. Specially wanted to know about you."

"Is that right?"

"Yessir."

"Who was it?"

"I ain't sure I should say. I don't want no trouble."

"It's all right."

"It was a copper. Not no patrolman neither. He wore a suit and all. I seen him around."

"Was it Lieutenant Picot?"

She nodded. "Yes, sir, it was."

Valentin found himself not the least bit surprised. He said, "Who told you to come here?"

"Mr. Jelly Roll. I told him about it, and he said to go tell Mr. St. Cyr at the Café."

Valentin thanked the woman, handed her a Liberty dollar, and sent her on her way.

He waited for the last solitary soul to depart, for all the bartenders and waiters to finish and leave, and for the cleaning crew
to arrive before starting his long walk home. He wanted to make
sure it was too late for Beansoup, too late for Morton, too late
for anyone he knew to be out and about. So late that by the time
he got to Magazine Street, dawn would be breaking. Then he
wouldn't have to face dark and empty rooms, and could sleep.

TEN

In the first gray light of day, he was startled by the sight of Dominique standing on the banquette between Gaspare's storefront and the street door to his rooms. His surprise gave way to a rush of nervous pleasure, which gave way to a spike of suspicion, the curse of his trade. For her part, she produced a timid smile, her chin tucked shyly downward.

This morning she was wearing a simple walking dress, pale green and soft with wear, along with a straw boater with a ribbon around it that draped down her back. She presented such a picture in the misty morning light that he felt his pulse rising. He stopped to catch his breath.

"Good morning, suh," she said, nervous in kind.

"Dominique...what are you doing here?"

"I couldn't stay at that hotel," she said. "There was men bothering me all evening."

He didn't understand. They were usually good about watching out for single women there. Perhaps she was simply too much of an exotic to be left alone. He could imagine fellows tripping over each other to assist her, banging on her door all hours of the day and night to offer courtesies.

Down the banquette, a door opened. Mr. Bechamin stepped

out with his broom and began sweeping his threshold. The old man saw the Creole detective and the black-skinned young lady and stopped to regard them with frank interest.

"Would you like some coffee?" Valentin said quickly, and went into his pocket for the key.

If Valentin had taken a last look around before he swept Dominique inside, he would have caught sight of Beansoup strolling along the banquette on the other side of the street.

The kid came to a startled stop when he saw the detective and the Ethiopian girl disappear through the doorway. He could see even at that distance that she was pretty for a Negro, full in the hips and chest, one of those who made a fellow look and then look again. Dark as she was, she was high-toned, too, at least from the way she dressed, like a lady instead of a whore. She was a sight, all right, and after the door closed behind them, Beansoup moved a few paces along the banquette to see if he could catch a glimpse of anything through the second-floor windows.

He had come by Magazine Street to say hello to the detective and take the opportunity to drop a bit of news about Miss Justine. He felt like it was his fault she left, no matter what Mr. Valentin said, so he got busy trying to find out where she had gone. One of the maids out of Miss Antonia Gonzales's told him that the madam had made an arrangement for Miss Justine with a rich Frenchman and she was now staying in rooms he kept on Girod Street.

Beansoup talked to some street characters he knew. One led him to another and he soon located the building. He stood vigil through the evening, until he saw her figure pass a window. Sometime later the Frenchman, a slight sort, arrived in a dark green Oldsmobile cabriolet chauffeured by a colored man in livery.

That was all Beansoup needed to see. He was proud of his detective work and got up early the next morning to hurry and report to Mr. Valentin, only to find the Creole not brooding his loss and hungry for any word about Miss Justine, but in the very act of squiring a comely black girl into his rooms.

Valentin got Dominique settled on his couch, then carried a pail to Bechamin's and had it filled with chicory latte. The shop-keeper gave him a quizzical look but kept his questions to himself. When Valentin got back upstairs, he went for cups, poured them full, and carried them to the front room. Dominique thanked him, blew over the steaming cup, took a small sip.

He sensed that in his absence she had been up and about, poking around. It was the way the quiet air was stirred up. She'd been wandering through his rooms, looking for something.

They drank their coffee and talked about this and that, edging around each other. He was frankly delighted to have her there. It was lifting his spirits in an odd spiral. At the same time, he couldn't quite quell his misgivings about what she wanted from him. And yet he found her face quite open, without guile, and he could not detect anything devious lurking there. She looked nothing so much as relieved to be under his roof. He let it go at that.

She asked how long he had taken his rooms, and he told her that he had been at his Magazine Street address for eight years, since he had first gone to work for Mr. Anderson. He didn't bother to explain that Anderson owned the building and so he got to stay in a part of the city that he could not have afforded otherwise. When he went on to tell her about his work at the Café and the mansions on Basin Street, he noticed that she looked distracted.

"What am I gonna do now?" she finally broke in, all fret-ful. "I ain't got the money to go home. I can't stay at that hotel. What am I gonna do?"

He sat back. He knew, and she probably knew as well, that there were other places in New Orleans that could offer safe lodging to a single woman. There was something else going on here. He began to surmise what she had on her mind and waited to see if she'd say it.

She fidgeted some more, then shifted her position on the couch, tilted her head to one side, and said, "Is she comin' back?"

He gave her a questioning look.

"Your woman," she said. "She just left out of here, didn't she?"

"How did you know that?"

She shrugged vaguely. "Is it true?"

"Yes, she just left. On Monday."

"And you t'ink she's comin' back?"

"I don't know," he said. "Not anytime soon, I guess."

"Then I could stay with you, if it's all right," she said.

She was forcing herself to be brave, and it took an effort for him to keep his face composed.

"I'll do whatever she did around here," she went on hurriedly. "I don't mind workin'. I'll take care of cleaning and all. Cook for you." When he still didn't speak up, her eyes widened into a beseeching gaze. "I ain't got nowhere else to go, suh."

Valentin said, "I don't need a maid, Dominique. I can't afford one."

"I wouldn't be no *maid*," she said, now sounding peeved. "And you wouldn't have to pay me nothing. Your woman's gone and you need someone to take care of t'ings. I ain't got nowhere to stay. That's all."

"I don't have much room," he said.

"I don't need much. I'll make a pallet on the floor."

"You know people will talk."

"I don't care what people do," she said sharply. "Ain't nobody cares about me around here anyway."

He rested his chin in his hand as if soberly considering the proposition, as his true thoughts went vaulting ahead. Surely, she had somewhere else she could stay. She was up to something, though he couldn't imagine what it might be. Or maybe his suspicious nature was getting the best of him and she was what she said, a young lady with no place to go. She was alone in her shock and grief over Jeff's sudden passing, and if what she said was true, she had no one to turn to.

She sat up and straightened her shoulders, making as if to go. "I'm sorry, suh. If you don't want—"

"No," he said decisively. "It's fine. You can stay."

She looked a little discomfited. "I don't want to cause you no trouble."

"It's all right, Dominique."

"Well…thank you." She let out a relieved breath that made her chest heave provocatively, and Valentin stifled a smile. She sat there all tense for another moment, then cast an eye about. "You have your breakfast this mornin'?"

"I haven't, no," he said.

She stood up and gestured toward the kitchen. "Do you mind?"

She made do with what she found in the cupboards, eggs and boudin and a half loaf of French bread. She told him she would make market later to find some things to "fix you up a proper *Trini* breakfast."

They both avoided each other's eyes for the most part and made only small talk. After they finished eating, she cleaned the dishes. "You been up all night," she said. "Don't you need to go on and get some sleep?"

"I do, yes."

"Then I'm gonna go back and get my t'ings at the hotel."

Valentin said, "I'll leave the door open."

She gave him another of her shy smiles and said, "Thank you for helping me this way. You're very kind."

She put her hat on prettily and went out the door and down the stairs.

———

Beansoup was hanging around Bechamin's, talking the poor old shopkeeper's ear off with preposterous stories and meanwhile trying to pry loose information about the girl who was visiting Mr. Valentin's rooms. Mr. Bechamin claimed he knew nothing about it, and it wasn't his business anyway.

Beansoup was gazing out at the street, working up a plan to surveil the detective, when he saw the black girl pass the window. He yelled a good-bye and ran outside. He gave her a lead to Common Street, then sauntered off on her trail.

Brother Martín spent two hours on the corner of First and La Salle, testifying. He had chosen for his scripture the Book of Ezekiel, and the words poured forth with the same rumbling mellow resonance that he had one brought to his bass violin, deep, sweet, and rhythmic all at once.

"For the land is full of bloody crimes!" he began, rolling out the text. "The city is full of violence!" And off he went, calling God's judgment on the wicked.

He stood there, a rock in a stream of humanity, his back straight and his voice steady as the bodies swirled past. A few people stopped, listened, exclaimed, "Praise God, brother!" and moved on. Some kids came by to taunt him like he was a madman. Most of the citizens just ignored him, too busy in their petty lives to pay heed and understand that the city they traversed was so full of sin that the earth beneath their very feet was liable to open up and swallow the whole mess down into damnation.

"Disaster comes upon disaster!" he called in a soaring voice. "And rumor upon rumor!"

Who knew better than the former Treau Martín about the wages of sin? He spoke with an echo of experience in every blessed word. And yet they still wouldn't listen.

"The king shall mourn and the prince shall be wrapped in despair!" he cried. "And the hands of the people shall tremble!"

As he looked around at those lost sheep who were the citizens of New Orleans, he got a sudden prickly sense that someone was studying him. He dropped his eyes to the page, read a passage, then looked up, but saw no one watching. Then, as he closed his Bible and made ready to go home, he was startled to see a familiar face. Standing there, ten feet away, staring directly at him. He heard a word whispered—a name. Then an automobile came rattling into the gutter, making a racket and a splash, and he turned his head. When he turned back, the face was gone.

Brother Martín walked away, glancing over his shoulder and murmuring a prayer for God to deliver him from evil.

Valentin woke to the sound of banging in the kitchen. He sat up, rubbing his face, and caught the rich aroma of chicoried coffee that mingled with something baking, smells that had him bewildered for a few seconds. Then he remembered: Dominique.

His vest was hanging on the bedpost and he pulled out his pocket watch. It was after two o'clock. He had slept a good bit of the day away. He pulled on trousers and went out into the front room, where the afternoon sun had cast the walls with a reddish glow. Her two satchels were pushed into the corner. Still foggy from sleep, he went to stand in the kitchen doorway.

She was kneeling to open his old oven with its spindly cast-iron legs and peer inside. She had traded her walking dress for the simple shift she had been wearing on Freret Street. She smiled up at him and he felt an errant twinge of pleasure that carried with it another spike of suspicion, though she seemed quite at ease and quite harmless. There was fresh coffee brewing in the percolator.

"Something smells good," he said.

"It's oven bread," she said as she drew a round dark loaf from the oven. "From Tobago. Only down there we make it outside, in clay ovens." There were two plates, a little tin of butter, and a small pot of honey on the table. All shy again and eager to please, like a servant—or a new wife—she said, "Sit down, please, suh."

She poured coffee and cut the bread. Over the midafternoon breakfast, he asked about her home and family. "I growed up in this little town called Batteaux Bay. It's on the water down there. I got three sisters and two brothers, they all still there. I went to school and then I went over to Trinidad to find some work. I didn't want to stay there, so I saved my money and got papers and come to New Orleans. That was last year, right about this time. I wasn't here but two weeks and I...I met Jeff Mumford." The light in her face dimmed and her gaze turned melancholy and dropped away. She told him that Jeff had courted her like she was a lady and not some sporting girl. She agreed to come stay with him in his little house. She had been mostly happy with him, though at the end it wasn't the same.

"Wasn't the same how?"

"He was just different. I t'ink maybe he was getting tired of me. I don't know. And then he was gone."

He allowed a moment's respectful silence and then said, "Can you think of anything else about what happened to him?"

Now a cloud came over her features, bringing with it a resentful glint to her eyes. "I t'ink it was a woman," she said in a low voice.

"You think a woman murdered him?"

"I t'ink a woman was mixed up in it."

"Why do you say that?"

"Why?" She drew herself up. "'Cause I know about these t'ings. I believe he was witched, suh. Where I come from, we know all about that. What we got down home make your voodoo here look like somethin' for little children. So I know. Some woman got claws on him and that was the end."

Valentin had to make an effort to keep a sober face. He'd noticed the dime on the thong around her ankle that first day, and was disappointed to learn that it wasn't just an ornament.

Uptown New Orleans was awash with voodoo and all its trappings. It was, in fact, this girl's ancestors who had carried it from their islands to New Orleans over a century of migrations. It had spread through every corner of the city, until it stood with the Catholic and the Baptist faiths. While there were no magnificent churches, no sonorous sermons, and no golden collection plates, it was hard to find anyone in the blocks north and west of Rampart Street who didn't give voodoo or hoodoo at least a passing respect. Most made it part of their daily lives. Valentin, in his disdain for it, was a definite minority.

"He died of poisoning," he reminded her.

"I don't care what he died of," Dominique said stubbornly. "He was witched, and it was a woman done it to him. It was *voudun*."

He didn't bother to argue with her.

"I should have seen it comin'," she went on, her voice now breaking a little. "I could have done somethin'."

"You couldn't have known," Valentin said.

She sighed, calming herself. "Don't matter now, does it? He's gone."

Valentin finished the last slice of his bread and honey, drank off his coffee, and stood up. "I'm going to work," he said.

She sat back. "Now?"

"I've got to see about a problem in Storyville. After that I'll go to the Café. I'll be there all night. It's my usual schedule." He wondered why he felt the need to explain his movements.

He also wondered why he soon found himself taking extra care with his clothes for the night. When he came out of the bedroom, she was sitting on the couch, her hands folded in her lap. She gave him a modest glance up and down and said, "You look nice, suh."

He smiled. "You know, you don't have to call me that."

"Sorry. It's a habit, you know."

He gathered his keys and went to the door.

"When will you come back?" she said.

"It could be four o'clock or so." He nodded to the bedroom door. "You go ahead and take the bed."

"Oh, no, suh. I couldn't do that."

"It's fine." She gave him an uncertain look. "It's all right, Dominique. It's easier that way."

She dropped her eyes. "I can wait up, if you like."

"No, don't do that. It will be late when I get back. I mean early."

"I don't mind."

"It's really not necessary," he said.

"I'm sorry," she said. "That wasn't polite, was it?"

"It's fine. You go ahead and take the bed," he said, and went out the door.

Beansoup rounded the corner of Girod Street, as nonchalant as could be, and this time he got it right. Miss Justine, just stepping onto the banquette, couldn't help but notice him.

Justine glanced around, saw him, and knew right away that it was no happenstance. When their eyes met, he feigned surprise and stopped in his tracks. She wondered if he had come with a message from Valentin and wondered what she'd do if he had.

"Miss Justine..." He took a moment to survey the facade of the house. "Is this where you stay now?"

"That's right." She gave him a glance of bemused affection. "I'm making market," she said. "Will you walk with me for a while?"

"Oh, sure, that'll be just fine," he said, and they started off.

She asked how things were at St. Mary's and if he was paying attention to the nuns. After a few minutes of idle banter, she sensed him growing impatient and gave him what he had come for. "How is Mr. Valentin?" she inquired.

Beansoup slowed his steps. "Who? Oh, him? Oh, yeah, I guess he's all right. You know he's working again." He nodded knowingly. "Some musicians died and it looks like something's wrong about it. So he's working on that now."

They walked on for a few paces more. She sensed something more on the tip of the boy's tongue, so she said, "And what else?"

"Ummm...I don't know if I should say."

"What is it?" She saw the way Beansoup's gaze wandered away. "What? Does he have company over there?"

The kid shrugged. "I seen him with a girl. Real black-skinned lady. They was at his rooms."

Justine felt her mind go into a dizzy tilt. "How well for him," she said, with a catch in her voice.

"Sorry," Beansoup said. "Maybe I shouldn't have said nothin'. She just showed up after...you know..." He jammed his hands in his pockets, and they walked on without speaking for a minute. "What about you?" he said presently.

"What about me?"

"You doin' all right with yourself?"

"I'm doing well, yes."

That brought another look of pouty displeasure as Beansoup saw his short career as a cupid coming to an end. This wasn't going at all the way he'd expected. They stopped across from the French Market. Justine was touched by the hurt look on his face. He was taking this all to heart. She was about to say something comforting when he suddenly turned around and said, "I believe there's going to be some trouble."

"What trouble?" she said. "When?"

"I don't know. Soon. I just got a feeling." He threw a hand up in farewell and ran away.

Valentin knocked on the door of the house on Robertson Street. Across the street was that whitewashed wall of St. Louis Cemetery No. 2.

The door was opened by a thin woman with red hair and splotched cheeks on her pale, puffy face.

She looked ill, but then many of the women in that part of town were walking germ colonies. He stated his business and she invited him inside.

He stepped over the threshold with an effort. He didn't want to be there. It was particularly irksome because he thought this business was over and done. The word was on the street. Who would be so foolish as to defy Tom Anderson?

The madam of the house appeared, interrupting his brooding. She was a white woman with a face that, except for the split lip, was flat and wooden, defining one of those types who came off hardscrabble land and into the city to find a different kind of slavery. She might have been fairly attractive as a young sporting girl. Now she was growing old and mean. Valentin had seen them by the dozen, and at some point, they all looked the same: dry, grim, and pinched, like the witches in fairy tales.

He listened to her story. It sounded much like the incident of the week before. He did not bother to question the two doves who were on the scene that day. Because what had happened there followed the pattern too closely: The two characters had come to the door, made a demand, then got rough when the victim didn't snap to. It didn't make sense. It felt like someone had gone to the trouble of putting on a crude farce.

He thanked the madam, told her he would be looking into the matter, and left her with her pinched and crabby sneer in place. On the way back to St. Louis Street, he glanced around, but saw no sign of Picot's tail. Either he'd lost him or this one was better at his job. He hoped it was the latter, because he'd decided that it was time to stop fooling around and bait a trap.

A half hour later, he was stepping down before City Hall. He went around to the alleyway in back, passed through the door, down the steps, and along the dank corridor.

The mulatto attendant was in the tiny office that adjoined the autopsy room, dozing in his chair. He came awake with a start when Valentin rapped his knuckles on the desk. His eyes fluttered and he used one hand to wipe a dribble of saliva from his chin.

He recognized the visitor. "What the fuck's this?" he gurgled. "Whatchu doin' here?"

"I need some information," Valentin said.

"Need what?" The man was still half asleep.

"Information," the detective said in a harder voice.

Now the attendant began to come around. "What are you talkin' about?" There was stale liquor on his breath. "What information?"

"From your files."

"Them's all confidential. It's city business."

Valentin took a casual look around. "Where do you keep the records?"

"You need to leave," the mulatto said, swaying to his feet. "And I got to go back to work." He made a shooing gesture with one hand.

"I could tell your superiors that you've been stealing from the corpses," Valentin said.

The hand stopped its motion. The mulatto blinked quickly three times and he swallowed. "I...what?"

"You know what I'm talking about."

The attendant twisted nervous fingers. "I said you need to leave. Who the fuck are you, anyway?"

"Don't play coy. You know who I am." He cocked his head. "I'm betting that if I go out on the street and find the closest pawnshop, they'll tell me that you do business there all the time. They probably have some of your most recent pieces on hand. The kind that could be traced back to their original owners. And I'll bet I can find the jeweler who buys the gold teeth you bring around. At best, you'd be out of a job and out of business. You might even end up in a cell across the street. And if they find out you stole from anyone important, you'll be there for a long god-damn time. Understand?"

As Valentin wound his way through this speech, the mulatto sagged back down into his chair. Now he looked sick, his face going paler by degrees. When the detective finished, he croaked, "What do you want?"

"I want to know if any other musicians have turned up here in the past month."

"Any other what?"

"You go through the records," the detective explained patiently. "Pick out the ones with 'musician' on the line next to Occupation. Copy their names down. I'll be back tomorrow to see them."

"Tomorrow!"

"In the morning. So have the information ready."

"I can't do it!" the attendant moaned. "If I get caught, I lose the job."

Valentin said, "Then don't get caught."

He went out the door and down the hall, leaving the attendant with his mouth hanging open in a half-formed moan of protest.

The evening sun was going down as Treau Martín waited for the ferry to Algiers. It was a glorious sight to see, the sun turning from gold to orange, and the high clouds spreading the rays out like separate pathways to heaven. The warm and gentle breeze was like a caressing hand on his brow.

He looked across the muddy water. On the other side was a small church. He pictured a steepled wood frame, a few benches for congregants, a table that served as an altar, some rough boards nailed together as a pulpit. The flock was small, a mere handful, but they were pious souls and in need of someone to guide them through this world of woe to the other side of Jordan.

Treau's sermon this night would be in the manner of an audition. If he passed, the church would be his. He could leave New Orleans, that sewer of sin. He could forsake his past and with time forget what he had been and what he had done in his darkest hours. As one washed in the blood of the lamb, he would be renewed, reborn.

The ferry was running late and though he could see the dark shape chugging closer, he was anxious to go. There were a dozen other folks waiting. They huddled in little packs, except for one lone character who hung back in a black duster that was too long for the September weather.

The flat-bottomed boat pulled up to the dock with a wet creak and disgorged its few passengers. The waiting dozen filed on. The Reverend Martín—he did like the sound of that—tipped his hat to the ladies and then made his way down the gangplank to board.

The roof of the cabin of the craft had been extended back to provide cover for crossings in bad weather. It was a pleasant evening, though, and the passengers stayed outside to relax along the railing and watch the stirring wake and the city lights recede into twinkling stars.

Treau paid heed as the sun bid a glorious farewell to the day and then sank down over the Gulf of Mexico. He heard the rough churning of the engine and the sloppy splash of the prow cutting the water. He saw the evening's first blinking lights from the other shore. They were halfway there. A small welcoming party of elders and sisters would be waiting for him on the other side.

As he stretched to see, he caught something in the corner of his eyes. Shuffling up the rail toward him was the passenger in the long coat.

Treau sensed something wrong and looked around. All the other passengers were on the port side, watching the sunset. He turned back to greet the stranger with a kind word. Before he got it out, an arm shot out with something that cracked his temple. He let out a grunt as a wild light flashed across his brain. He started to collapse, but before he could tumble to the deck, hands grabbed his shoulders, and with a hard burst of strength, lifted him off his feet. He was toppling over the railing and then the frothing water swallowed him. He sunk into the Mississippi, the wake of the ferry churning him down into the brown darkness.

Justine did her dutiful best to be patient while Paul worked himself into a lather, worrying her pelvis like one of those eager little dogs that got sudden urges and went for the nearest available leg. He didn't seem to get this fucking business at all. His clumsy efforts made her suspicious that he would have preferred another person, maybe one of his own sex. Or maybe he had just never learned what to do. She knew that a taste of a quadroon was something of a ritual for rich white boys coming of age. She had entertained a few herself. She hoped those young men had improved their amorous skills more than the fellow who was currently installed between her thighs.

She stifled a yawn and mused on these things as he banged away at her. Finally, he let out a little hiccup of a gasp, collapsed, and rolled off. He reached immediately for the white hand towel that was draped over the headboard and attended fussily to his private parts, as if to wipe every trace of her from his pink and flaccid self. She noticed the look of relief on his face, as if he had completed an unpleasant task.

When he went to soak in the bathtub, she began pulling on her clothes. When he got out, he would spend an hour or so dressing and drinking coffee and then call for the car to carry him to his family's offices on Carondelet. He had something to do with managing rice plantations that she didn't understand. It really didn't matter what he did, now or later. It had only been two days and she knew that she was not going to be staying with him. She didn't really like him. She thought him a fool and a weakling, and she could not be the mistress of such a man for life. She could not bear his colored children. She could not live in a prison on Girod Street for his pleasure and her wealth. Let someone else accept that sentence.

For the moment, though, there was nowhere else to go. She wasn't about to run back to Magazine Street. So she would stay where she was until she could escape with something other than her satchel of clothes.

It was a generally slow night at the Café. Valentin saw Tom Anderson as he made his usual rounds. When the King of Storyville came down from his office, he didn't have a word to say. He simply glanced, nodded, and moved on. By now, his spies would have told him that the detective had paid a visit to Robertson Street. He would be satisfied with that.

Valentin took a seat at the end of the bar and listened to the band. Later, when they stopped for the night, the detective ambled over to talk to them. He asked if anyone had heard any talk about the jass players who had died recently.

A saxophone player named Raymond DeVille was the only one who had.

"It doesn't bother you?" Valentin said.

The Negro shook his head absently. "Why should it? When your time's up, you're gone."

Valentin left him and the others to pack up for the night. DeVille wasn't finished, though. He called, "Mr. Valentin!" Then gestured for him to wait.

They stood at an empty spot in the middle of the floor and DeVille bent his head confidentially. "I did hear that a copper's been poking around, bracing fellows, asking about Mumford and Noiret and all."

"Picot?"

"That's him." He leaned closer. "He's been askin' about you, too."

Valentin was putting the key into his lock as the bells tolled four. When he got upstairs, he crept into the bedroom, went to the closet to pull down the blanket Beansoup always used, and carried it to the couch. He was aware of Dominique on the bed but didn't look at her. He could sense that she was awake, her eyes open, watching him as he walked in and out.

He went back into the front room and settled on the couch, wrapping the blanket around him. He heard the bedsprings squeak once as she moved and then no more.

Later, it was light out when he came half awake to find her standing next to the couch, completely still, watching him. He gave a start and she said, "Sorry, suh," and moved away. He pulled the blanket over his head and dropped down again.

ELEVEN

Picot's man was a corporal named Tyler, a nervous little drunkard who could not decide whether he was a New Orleans police officer or a Pinkerton agent, stumbling back and forth between the two careers on something like a yearly schedule. He had been lost in the shuffle some time ago, and so the lieutenant could use him without having to account for his time.

This morning Picot fidgeted as the corporal reported on the Creole detective's movements from the sporting house on Robertson Street to his visit to the morgue.

Tyler blinked his rheumy eyes and ducked his head up and down like a pecking shorebird. "I went in after he left and talked to the mulatto that works there. He said St. Cyr wanted to know about what all musicians had turned up dead. Don't make no sense, but that's what he said."

Picot nodded, sorting the information. There was no telling whether or not St. Cyr had learned anything about the thugs who had visited Robertson Street. He had gone to the morgue and threatened or bribed the attendant to gather the information. The lieutenant knew he could call him on it, but that would only show his hand. With a grunt of frustration, and a warning to stay sober, he sent Tyler back to work.

Dominique was all ready with breakfast and coffee when Valentin woke up. She had gone out early and bought a copy of the *Picayune* and laid it next to his plate. When he sat down, she moved about him in gentle circles, then hovered as he worked his way through his eggs and coffee. She kept watching his face, then jumping to his every need and generally making him nervous. He hurried to finish eating and escape into the bathroom.

He took his bath, got dressed, and slipped out the door with a quick explanation of business to attend to. She waved a good-bye from the balcony. It was all very sweet and too much for his taste.

As he made his way along the banquette, he tried to reassemble the exact sequence of her coming to his door. It had happened so quickly. Wasn't she Jeff Mumford's woman less than a week ago? Why wasn't she grieving? What did she want from him? His thoughts jumped to Justine and what she was doing in her new home with her Frenchman. He pushed the images away as he went through Bechamin's door. He had more pressing matters at hand.

It was Friday, his day for rounds. He started off for Basin Street, then changed his mind. For some reason, he felt oddly apart from Storyville. The banquette seemed to be shifting under his feet. It was an alien place, the streets familiar and yet different. Even the money he took from there seemed tainted in a strange way, and on this morning he didn't want to walk from house to house like some beggar.

He didn't want to face Lulu White and her prying, snooping questions. He didn't want to go to the Café and spar with Tom Anderson. So he just dismissed that entire piece of his day. He had not done a thing all week at any of the houses, anyway. He hadn't even paid them a visit. He could collect his pay envelope from Anderson when he went to work that evening. As for the others, they could pay him, if they wanted and when they wanted. He had a spice can full of Liberty dollars that would carry him for a while.

As he glanced at his reflection in a storefront he passed, it occurred to him that he was developing a bad attitude of late. It was a relief. It meant he was getting his skills back, too.

Something had begun forming in the back of his mind, the beginnings of a pattern. A year ago, or two, the random pieces would have already fallen into place and he would be seeing the construction of the murders of at least two musicians, more likely all three and the landlady. He came to the rueful realization that he had been away so long that his sharp mind was operating more like a rusty old pump.

The mulatto attendant was standing just inside the alley door, smoking a Straight Cut that was all but turning into tatters in his nervous fingers.

"Fellow come by from the police," he stuttered by way of greeting. "Askin' what you wanted."

Valentin was neither surprised nor very interested. "Did you tell him?"

"No, goddamnit! I lied! To a copper, yet!"

The detective knew that the mulatto had told the copper exactly what he was up to. He had expected it. "Do you have the information?" he asked.

"I can't be doin' this kind of thing." The attendant was almost moaning again.

Valentin extended his hand, palm up. The mulatto made a show of refusing, then let out a grunt and went into his pocket for a folded sheet of paper. "They's all on there," he said. "All right, then? Just take it and go. I ain't doin' this no damn more. So don't ask."

Valentin looked at the paper, then slipped it into his pocket. "You won't see me again," he said, and turned away, hoping that it was true.

———

By early in the afternoon, Justine found that she couldn't get her mind off the news about Valentin that Beansoup had delivered. It danced around every thought in her head, replete with images. The kid's last strange words about trouble brewing had her worried, too, and she wanted to see about that as well.

She caught a streetcar down to Magazine Street. On the way, she thought that would be just her luck of late to run up on him. Then what would she say? There could be no other reason for her to be there. She decided to take the chance anyway. She had to see for herself what the kid had described.

Once she arrived, though, she wished that she hadn't. She walked down the opposite side of the street, hoping to avoid any neighbors who might report her appearance to Valentin. As she came close, she saw a black-skinned woman in the act of sweeping the little balcony. Justine stopped, staring, nursing a throb of jealous rage. That was *her* balcony and *her* broom; it was *her* dust from the floors of *her* rooms. Of course, none of it was correct; she had been replaced, and in a matter of days.

Valentin had never paid too much attention to younger girls; he preferred women who knew the ways of the world. Or so she had thought; this one didn't appear to be much beyond twenty. The heavy breasts and hips would be to his taste, though. She looked like she was built for hard work in the bedroom and for childbearing, too. Maybe that was it; he had decided that at twenty-four, she was too old and too used up by the sporting life to please him.

The thought made her stomach churn so sourly that she had to stop and lean in the space between two storefronts for a moment.

She wanted to run away and yet at the same time she was tempted to cross over for a closer look. For one crazy moment, she imagined banging through the street door, running up the steps, grabbing the bitch by the hair, and dragging her down to the street. She felt her blood begin to race as she pictured the scene. Then she let out a grim laugh: she wouldn't do any such thing. She wasn't some common whore, after all. Anyway, the girl on the balcony could probably handle herself. Worse than starting a tussle would be starting one and then losing and having to skulk off in shame.

Her heart stopped aching long enough for her to ponder how Valentin had captured the girl so quickly. The same way he had trapped her, she guessed: by staying still and drawing her in like a snake waiting motionless for its prey.

Whatever happened, she was out and the black-skinned girl was in. There was nothing she could do about it now, except to turn tail and go back to her Girod Street rooms and her rich weakling of a Frenchman. On her way to Canal Street, she took one last glance over her shoulder and saw that the girl was now gazing her way, the eyes as dark and still as stones. She walked on.

At the same moment she was lifting her skirt to mount the back step of the Canal Line car, Valentin was getting off the front. She didn't see him, nor did he see her. She was lost in her thoughts and his eyes were fixed on the banquette. And so they passed each other.

Two boys who decided to go fishing instead of to school saw the body in the water near one of the bridge pilings. At first they thought it was just some old clothes that had gotten caught up. Then a wave from the wake of one of the heavy freighters came through, and they found themselves looking down at a bloated black face. They dropped their bamboo poles as one and went screaming up the bank.

Dominique had a midday meal waiting for him when Valentin came in, chicken, yams, corn, and the rest of her island bread. Though he didn't eat very much, he made a point of telling her it was very good. His mind seemed to be miles away as he finished his meal and sat sipping a glass of water.

After she cleared the plates, she sat down again. She studied his face anxiously, watching for signs, wondering if he had already changed his mind and was trying to think of a way to put her back on the street. Or maybe his quadroon girl had gotten to him out of her sight.

"What's wrong?" she said when she couldn't stand it anymore.

He looked at her, blinking, like he was surprised to find her sitting there. "Nothing...It's just...I'm thinking."

"About me?"

"About you?" He gave her a vague look. "No, about this case I'm working on. The murders of Jeff and those others."

She sat back and crossed her arms in a posture he knew all too well. He saw suspicion tinged with worry in her eyes. "What is it?"

"She was here."

"Who?"

"Your woman. What's her name? *Justine.* I saw her."

"She was where?"

She tilted her head toward the front of the house. "I was on the balcony and I saw a woman come walkin' along real slow. She stopped when she got right across the street. She was watchin' me, I could tell. And I knew right away it was her."

"Are you sure?" He described her, taking pains not to speak too highly of her features.

"It was her, all right." She stiffened and stuck out her chin. "What's she doin' round here? I thought she took her t'ings and left out."

"She did."

"Then what's she want?"

"She does know other people in the neighborhood."

She shook her head. "No, she was spyin'. She's up to somethin'. Now what if she wants back in?"

"That's not going to happen," he told her. "Don't worry about it."

She sulked for another moment, then got up to do the

dishes. Valentin's vacant gaze rested on her back as he thought through this news. Somehow Justine had found out that there was a girl on the premises and, just like Dominique said, had come spying. She would be thinking how little time he had wasted in bringing another woman to his bed. To her bed.

The whole thing was a crazy mess, like one of those stage comedies where one misstep led to a next. The whole thing was preposterous. Justine had no sooner left out than Dominique had shown up and talked her way inside. So a beautiful island girl began by cleaning house and cooking his meals and was now staking out her territory, looking ready to do battle over it. It was completely ridiculous. He couldn't help himself and let out a cracked laugh.

Dominique looked over her shoulder at him. "What's funny?"

"This." He spread his arms to take in the whole tableau. "All of this. Me. You."

"You t'ink I'm funny?"

"I think this is all so odd." He laughed again.

When she realized that he meant well, her frown changed into a smile that began as grateful, lingered, and then turned smoky.

He said, "What?"

She pulled her hands from under the water tap, turned around, and drew her palms down the front of her dress, leaving wet prints. The water soaked through the thin cotton and he saw that she was wearing nothing underneath.

She came away from the sideboard and pressed herself against him.

"I been feelin' so bad, suh," she whispered.

"It's all right," he said.

"Please, I been feelin' so bad. I don't know what's gonna happen to me…"

He could feel her heart thumping close to his ear, and when

he reached down to lift the hem of her skirt, she shivered and let out a soft sigh.

An hour later she was sprawled across the mattress, her arms and legs splayed like they had no bones. Her eyes were soft, half-lidded.

He got up and lurched through the front room, where he saw the trail of clothing they'd left behind. He went into the kitchen, took down the bottle of brandy from the cupboard, poured two glasses, and carried them into the bedroom.

She took a sip and fixed him with her black sleepy eyes. "I was wonderin' about you," she said. "I thought maybe you didn't like me this way."

"I didn't know if you..."

She smiled drowsily. "No, it's all right, suh."

"Can't you call me Valentin?"

"Yes, suh. I mean yes, *Valentin*." She settled back, holding her glass in the hollow of her stomach. "Valentin," she said it again. "So you one of them French Creoles."

"That and some other things, too."

"What other things?" she said, and lay back with her arm crooked behind her head, watching him with interest.

He knew he would have to tell her at least a little bit of his history. He had just spent an hour frolicking with her, after all, and she wasn't some back-of-town dove who had spread her thighs just for a Liberty dollar.

He remembered that when he had told Justine the story, he had drawn out all the details and then felt poorly for days afterward. It was too much, a purging that he didn't care to repeat. So he related it to Dominique in an abbreviated form.

He had been born in New Orleans, near First and Liberty streets, to a Creole mother and a Sicilian father. He had lost a younger brother and sister to Bronze John, the yellow fever.

There were few families in that time and place that hadn't buried at least one child.

Then came the troubles of the early 1890s, when white hatred for Italians was at a fever pitch, with certain American factions fomenting violence out of jealousy over the Sicilians' control of the produce business on the docks. There had been rioting in the streets that ended horribly in the framing and the mass lynching of eleven innocent Sicilians inside Parish Prison. As the violence raged on, his father had avenged an insult and was abducted and murdered as well, hung from an oak tree on the banks of Lake Pontchartrain.

His mother had sent him away and then descended slowly into madness—or so he had been told. When he came back to New Orleans, she was gone and no one could say where. He searched for her, throughout the city and then far beyond, but she hadn't left a trail. He joined the police force in hopes of tracking her and finding clues to his father's killers. He had failed on both counts. His career as a police officer was mercifully short and he found himself in the employ of Tom Anderson, the King of Storyville, where he had remained for the past eight years.

He did not tell her about any of his cases. He did not talk about the Black Rose murders or King Bolden. It would have been too much.

She listened without moving or making a sound. Her eyes were so dark it was hard to read anything there. The only reaction he could discern was the slightest little breath of pity, a near-silent sigh. "That's so sad," she said after he had finished. "About your family, I mean."

"Lots of people have sad stories," he said.

She nodded. It was now true for her, too. She was quiet for another little while. Then she said, "And what about her?"

"Who?"

"Justine." All the vitriol was gone, and the question came out in a vague way, as if she was satisfying some small curiosity.

He shrugged. "She's taken up with a rich Frenchman."

"And you don't care?"

"He's a man of means. She's lucky. She's in no danger." He realized that was more than he could say for the time she'd spent under his roof.

"I wonder what she wanted here," Dominique murmured, her eyes drooping.

"Who knows?" he said, and smiled at her. "You look like you're ready to go to sleep."

She smiled back at him, a sweet bowing of her full lips. "Maybe just for a little while." She closed her eyes and pulled the sheet around her. "You won't have to stay on the couch tonight," she whispered. A half minute later, she had dropped off. He watched her for a few moments, then got up to dress for work.

Just before he left, there was a knock on the door. One of Mr. Gaspare's young clerks from downstairs had a message from Frank Mangetta, requesting that the detective come by his establishment as soon as possible.

Lieutenant J. Picot stood by the window, watching a line of heavy gray clouds roll in from the west. There would be rain by afternoon, and heavy, by the looks of it. The *Picayune* said it was going to last for days.

In Picot's hand were two pieces of paper. One was the report of the recovering of a body from the river, one Charles Martín, a former musician. Though it had just come in, the news would soon be all over town, including in the ear of Valentin St. Cyr.

How foolish he had been to imagine that Valentin would stay off the game. He had been an idiot, sending those thugs to Robertson Street. They had overdone their task by assaulting the madam and their ruse hadn't fooled the Creole detective one bit. Now he was getting busy, peeking through cracks and turning over rocks. In no time, he would turn over one too many, and there'd be real trouble.

It galled Picot that people dropped dead all over town, but somehow St. Cyr never got a scratch, even though he planted himself right in the middle of all sorts of mayhem. It was like he wore some kind of armor. It was one of the reasons Tom Anderson used him.

The Creole had already begun to unwind the first strands of the case, and Picot had felt powerless to do anything about it. He knew that St. Cyr would eventually figure out why those musicians had turned up dead and again embarrass the New Orleans Police Department. It was bad news for the department. It was worse news for Picot for a whole other reason.

With a growing sense of panic, the lieutenant had gone looking for something that would stop St. Cyr. The man's entire family was gone, so there was no angle there. The woman who had stayed with him for the last two years had just packed up and left him—another dead end. Picot knew about the island girl who had been with Jefferson Mumford and was now staying in St. Cyr's rooms. Though it was strange business, it was nothing he could use. The girl had only been in the city for a year and had behaved herself. St. Cyr was just that lucky. No one like her had ever shown up on J. Picot's doorstep.

The lieutenant went back to the first girl, Justine Mancarre, and realized that he knew nothing about her, which was a mistake any way he looked at it. He went to work fixing that. He sent one of his people to speak to Antonia Gonzales, as the girl had rented a room from the Basin Street madam when she first arrived in the city. Miss Antonia couldn't say much, only that Justine had been on the road in traveling shows for some time. It was a common tale and it led nowhere. Then one of the other girls mentioned in passing that she had spoken once or twice about Evangeline Parish.

It was a start. Picot was aware of the fact that a decent portion of the denizens of uptown New Orleans were either running
or hiding from something. Over a period of twenty-four hours,
telegrams flew and telephone calls crept back and forth between
his precinct and the parish. The information came in bits and
pieces; soon enough, it began to add up. Picot got excited. The
name Mancarre had struck a chord with someone in the sheriff's
office. The final bit arrived in the form of a telegram, the other
paper that he held in his hand.

He could barely contain himself. Suddenly everything had
changed around, and it was his turn to run the game and set
things right. He was a police officer. He, not some damned Creole detective, was the authority and the power in those parts. It
was time to settle that business once and for all.

Picot moved away from the window and went to his desk.
He snatched up the handpiece of the telephone set, then hesitated for a moment. When St. Cyr found out what he was doing,
there would be hell to pay. The detective might even come looking to kill him. Picot knew the man could do violence. He knew
about McTier the Georgia gambler and others who had crossed
him. He knew what a risk he was taking. It didn't matter; there
was no other way. He had only one hand to play.

He picked up the phone and asked the operator to connect
him to the police commissioner's office.

Valentin found Frank Mangetta behind the bar, muttering furiously because his day man had gotten drunk at Groshell's Dance
Hall the night before and could not be roused from his bed.
Valentin received a curt nod of greeting as he settled down to
wait. Mangetta careened between the saloon and the grocery to
the cadence of a vile string of English and Italian curses.

After about twenty minutes, there was a break in business
and the saloon keeper stepped over to lay an elbow on the bar.
He got down to business before it got noisy again.

"I don't know if you heard this or not..."

The saloon keeper gave a look that sent a chill running up Valentin's spine. "Heard what?"

"They pulled Treau Martín's body out of the river this morning."

"Jesus! What happened?"

"He was crossing on the ferry and he went in. He drowned. I guess it could have been an accident."

"It wasn't any accident, Frank." He shook his head grimly. "Now there's only the one left."

"Ain't anybody seen him in a long time," Mangetta said. "He might already be gone."

Neither man spoke a name. There was no need. Even a cynical type like Valentin saw no need to tempt fate that carelessly.

Justine heard a familiar piping voice calling from the banquette and in her half drowse, imagined that she was on Magazine Street. She told herself she was dreaming. Then the voice called again, this time louder and accompanied by a sharp whistle. She got up from the couch where she had fallen asleep and pushed one of the street windows open.

Beansoup was back, standing on the banquette below, this time with his friend Louis from the Waif's Home at his side. He lifted a dirty hand and waved the envelope he held there. "I got a message for you," he called up.

Through the fog in her head, she felt a tiny tingle of excitement. If it was Beansoup calling, the message could be from Valentin. She waved for the boys to come inside, and a minute later there was a knock.

Beansoup led Louis into the apartment and stopped to survey the fine furnishings. Then he turned his attention to Miss Justine. She didn't look so good. Her hair was frowsy; her face was a bit gray; her eyes were too wet and seemed unable to fix on anything. She was wearing a kimono and didn't seem to care that it was hanging open, revealing her thin camisole. Beansoup was embarrassed, but kept staring, too. After a short glance, Louis wouldn't look at her at all.

She cleared her throat and said, "Well?"

Beansoup handed over the envelope. When she opened it and took out the folded sheet, she discovered that it was not from Valentin at all. Her dismay was mixed with her astonishment that it was a missive from Tom Anderson, the King of Storyville himself.

The note, on fine cream-colored paper, requested her presence at the Arlington on Saturday at two o'clock in the afternoon "on a matter of some importance." Anderson had apparently penned it himself. The script was thick and sloppy, the scrawl of a man of substance in a hurry.

She looked at the two boys. They were both keeping their eyes averted, and she realized that they were embarrassed that she looked such a mess. She put the envelope and paper between her teeth and fumbled about tying the sash of her kimono. She took the papers out of her mouth and ran the fingers of her free hand through the hopeless mess of her hair. She cleared her throat again. "I don't understand," she said. "What's this about?"

Beansoup shrugged. "I don't know. He said bring it to you, that's all."

She went to get her purse and handed each boy a Liberty quarter. "Tell Mr. Anderson I'll be there," she said.

Beansoup held the coin in his palm, absently, as if there was something else on his mind. Then he jerked his head once and led Louis out the door and down the steps. The street door banged and they were gone.

Justine sat down on the divan and looked at the note again. It was very strange. She had no idea what Tom Anderson could want with her. It was true that he was Valentin's employer. He was probably familiar with Paul Baudel, too. Still, he'd never paid attention to her before. Whatever it was, she'd find out soon enough. Even if she wasn't curious about it, there was no way she could have refused an invitation from the King of Storyville.

Valentin spent another half hour at Mangetta's. The day bartender didn't show his face and there was another rush of business, so the saloon keeper left him alone with his thoughts. It was just as well that the Sicilian was busy and not refilling his empty glass. He did not want the habit of drinking during the day to add to his troubles.

It started to rain and he gazed out the window for some long minutes. Then he turned around and laid the sheet of paper on the bar, took his fountain pen from his pocket, and started to scribble, names and shapes and lines in random patterns.

Every one of the players in a single jass band save one was dead, each one most likely murdered. It could not be coincidence. Four men—each a musician, each colored, and all having played together in one small band, along with a woman connected to at least one of them—dying in the space of two weeks led to only one conclusion. The question wasn't "if" anymore, but "why?" What had they done, what had they seen, or what did they know that had made them targets for murder?

And so quickly that Valentin couldn't catch up. Two were gone before he had lifted a finger. Two more had died while he was trying to make up his mind whether or not to investigate. The landlady on Philip Street had passed him a hint that he never got to use, dying before he could get back to her.

There was only one member of that band left. Maybe. No one knew what happened to the man whom neither Valentin nor Frank Mangetta wanted to name.

Valentin drank the last drops of his brandy, nodded a thank-you to the flustered Sicilian, and went outside to stand on the banquette, smoke one of his cigarillos, and watch the afternoon traffic creep through the rain. After a few puffs, he tossed the butt into the gutter swollen with water, garbage, and horse manure. He pulled his collar up, bent his head, and strode off.

He was fairly soaked by the time he got to the building on St. Charles where Jelly Roll Morton kept his rooms. He climbed the three flights of stairs and spent a good five minutes rapping on the door and calling out before he finally heard the sounds of life from inside. Morton, looking like a train wreck, opened the door. He glared, then waved him inside with a growl of irritation. "What?"

"I'll only be a minute," Valentin said. "Then you can go back to bed."

"What's wrong now? Is somebody else dead?"

"Yes," the detective said. "Somebody else is dead."

Morton started to come awake. "Jesus!"

Valentin sat down on a café chair. Morton planted himself on his couch, a fine overstuffed affair of walnut and brocade.

"Treau Martín," Valentin said. "The bass fiddle player in the Union Hall band."

He allowed a moment for the news to sink in, glancing over Morton's shoulder and through the bedroom door. He saw dark limbs tangled in the sheets atop the four-poster bed. The woman was coffee colored, just like Justine, and for the briefest instant, he felt his heart thump and his stomach clutch; then he saw the long, thick hair and relaxed.

Morton snapped his fingers to bring his attention back. "So what the hell is going on?"

"All those fellows who played in that band are dead, except for one."

As hard as Morton tried to keep his face blank, his eyes flicked, giving him away.

Valentin said, "I need to find him, Jelly."

The piano man was quiet for long seconds as the rain rattled the windowpanes. Then he said, "You better go see my godmother."

As she went about tidying herself and the apartment in preparation for Paul's appearance, Justine picked up Tom Anderson's note a half-dozen times, then put it down again. Her curiosity was quickly turning into unease. What did the King of Storyville want with her? It had to do with Valentin, of course. There was no other connection. Unless...

She brushed the thought away, but the unsettling feeling remained. There was something about Mr. Anderson, the way he seemed to know everything about everyone. Valentin had told her once that the man was like God, lording over Storyville and its denizens. It had never occurred to her that he might know things about her, too. She was a nobody, another back-of-town sporting girl, one out of the thousands. Now she realized that she was different because of Valentin St. Cyr, Anderson's right-hand man. Maybe, like God, he kept a ledger and her name was on it, along with an accounting of her sins.

That drove her mind on a jag and sent her rushing to the bathroom, where she brought up what little was in her stomach. She was glad that the apartment had a new flush toilet and she didn't have to clean a mess. She wiped her mouth and drank some water from the tap. Then she opened the cabinet over the sink and took down the amber-colored bottle that held her prescription. This time she put a full dose and then some into the glass of water. She knew her mind wouldn't be right when it took hold, but it didn't matter. Paul wouldn't care. He was already beginning to ignore her, and his interest in frolicking with her was a sham. She could guess what was coming next: he would ask only for French and Greek, because he didn't want her as a woman at all. He was just playing his part in the farce that his position in New Orleans society demanded. She'd seen it before.

She studied her face in the mirror as she drank the medicine down. She saw lines creeping from her eyes. Twenty-four and there were lines from her eyes.

She put the dropper back in the bottle and then held it up to the light. She had just visited the apothecary and it was almost full. It occurred to her that all she had to do was drink the contents in one quick swallow and her troubles would be over. There would be no broken heart over Valentin St. Cyr. There would be no disgust over what she had to do with Paul Baudel. There would be no facing Tom Anderson tomorrow. There would be no past, no history of a dirty, broken-down, foul-smelling shack along the bayou north of Ville Platte haunting her. There would be nothing, only a blessed darkness.

She regarded her face more seriously, looking into her own eyes to see a light that made her smile. No, not that; not today and not ever. Though sporting girls did it all the time, her life was too precious to end. She wouldn't let Valentin or Paul or Mr. Tom Anderson or any of the other men who passed through with such arrogance drive her that far down. Never.

She put the bottle back in the cabinet and left the bathroom, turning out the light.

It was a noisy, busy night at the Café. Some dignitaries from out of town, rich business types, had appeared without notice, and there was a scramble to make sure their every whim was sated. They took over two of the best tables and ordered champagne all around. The band played tunes at their request. The gamblers sniffed the air, then got up to welcome the gentlemen and ask if they might perhaps like to join in a game of cards.

Valentin did not see Tom Anderson all evening. The King of Storyville was on the premises; the detective could tell from the bottle of the best Scotch whiskey that was hustled from the bar through the back hall to the office upstairs. When Valentin asked the head bartender who was visiting, the response was a blank shake of the head. He cornered the waiter who had been serving Anderson and learned that there were two men in the office, and one of them was Chief O'Connor. The other, he believed, was a city official, perhaps an alderman. Whatever was going on was a solemn affair, the waiter whispered, and on a Friday night yet.

Valentin had a prickling sense that what was being discussed upstairs had something to do with him and the dead musicians. Maybe it was finally dawning on someone that there was something brewing.

He thought about creating an excuse to knock on Anderson's door, then realized that it would be too much of a ruse. The King of Storyville would know exactly what he was doing and chase him off. So he waited for some trouble or problem that would give him good reason to break in on the little party and at least catch a glimpse of these mysterious guests and overhear a snippet of their conversation. Nothing happened, though; the gentlemen behaved like angels for once, and everyone was having a marvelous time, drinking, gambling, eyeing the pretty octoroons, and dancing to the music from the six-piece band.

Later, when Valentin inquired again, he was told that Anderson and his guests had departed, their destinations unknown.

Dominique tried to sleep, got up, lay down again, stared at the wall. She couldn't stay still. There were too many ghosts about, too many sounds in the night that told her spirits were getting restless. Or maybe it wasn't spirits at all. Maybe it was that woman. Justine. She might well be the one who had been lurking about, stirring up the air as she put some kind of juju around the door, as a way to witching her replacement into leaving out. Dominique had been hearing footsteps and the creaking of the hinges of the street door, had seen the slips of shadow that disappeared around a corner just as she got to the balcony.

Enough was enough, she decided. In the morning she would visit a shop and buy some things of her own to put around the door. At least she could put something out when Valentin was gone. He didn't believe, wouldn't stand for it. She'd do it anyway. They both needed the help.

She hadn't meant to carry whatever had got on Jeff Mumford to Mr. Valentin's rooms. She had only been looking for a place to hide from fear and get relief from her loneliness at having her man taken away. The Creole detective, so quiet and respectful, seemed like a safe choice in a city full of men with nothing but bad intentions.

He was a gentleman. Still, Jeff or no Jeff, grief or no grief, she was ready almost right away for him to come to the bed. Something about him made her want to grab hold and not let go. She understood why Justine would want back in.

That quadroon wasn't going to go without a fight, even though she was the one who had left him. Now she was sneaking around, worrying their door, laying who knew what kind of charms about. Dominique was ready for anything Justine could bring. She would fight back with her own hoodoo. She wasn't going anywhere.

It was late, almost midnight, and Lieutenant Picot waited on the dark street corner. The collar of his overcoat was turned up and his derby pulled down low. He kept his hands in his pockets and his back turned to the street, lest anyone who might recognize him happen by. The wind was blowing through the treetops, shaking more rain down on the streets and banquettes.

Aside from the faint hissing of the drizzle, it was quiet on the corner. Up and down the streets in four directions, the stately homes of white Americans of means stood in elegant silence. Through tall windows, he spied chandeliers all aglow and, beneath them, figures moving in ballets of wealth and position. If he went closer, he would hear their mellow voices and rich laughter, the low whispers of servants, and the music from Victrolas.

He'd been waiting and he wondered what he would do if she didn't appear. Then, moments later, she was there, as stealthily as if one of the shadows had materialized into human form. She was wearing a long coat and a shawl that she had drawn up over her head like a fascinator, so he could barely make out her features.

Picot didn't speak for a long moment; he couldn't. Each time he tried, something caught in his throat and he had to turn his face away.

She grew impatient. "Well?"

"There are five people dead," the lieutenant said, sounding grim.

"Five?" She seemed impressed by the number. "Is that right?"

"I can't keep it hidden."

"You're a police officer," she said brusquely. "You can do anything you want. You've kept all sorts of things hidden. You're quite good at it." The voice was almost teasing, but with an edge like a sharp blade, a sound he never got used to.

"This is no comedy!" he hissed at her. "Crimes have been committed!"

"Be calm, now," she warned him, softening her tone.

He took a breath, settled himself. "Five dead. I'd say that evens the score. More than evens it."

She shook her head. "Not yet."

"There's someone who can stop it now," he warned her.

"And who would that be?"

"That one I told you about. Tom Anderson's man. The Creole detective St. Cyr."

"Don't worry about him. Or anyone else, either."

"He's no fool."

"We'll see who's a fool and who isn't," she murmured.

"I can't help you."

"I didn't ask you to," she said petulantly, with a schoolgirl's lilt. She looked back along the street, fixing her eyes on the facade of a Victorian house that was halfway down the block on the other side. A streetlamp stood before it, casting a glow of amber over the sculptured front garden. She turned back to him, smiling deliberately. "Is that all you have to say?"

"This is goin' to end bad," Picot said. "I got a feeling."

She laid a familiar hand on his arm. "You were always so superstitious," she said. She took the hand away, drew the shawl farther over her head until it almost shrouded her eyes. She made a wave, a common little motion, and then drifted off, back into the shadows of the quiet street.

TWELVE

Saturday dawned with a sun that was first pale yellow then hazy white as it cut through the chill of the autumn morning. The rain had stopped sometime in the middle of the night, leaving the streets shiny wet. The sun rose high enough to poke through windows and chase the shadows away. It wasn't yet warm enough to burn off the puddles, so water stood in tiny ponds among the cobblestones and glistened when the rays struck them, making some streets look like they were paved with diamonds.

It was market day and the wagons clattered into the city from the Delta farms. It was also a day for enjoying the city's earthier delights, and trains chugged into Union Station and unloaded hundreds of men and boys who were lucky enough to be off work.

One such citizen, fresh out of the fields, with his face scrubbed, his hair oiled and parted, and his week's pay heavy in his pockets, stepped onto the platform, as wide-eyed and giddy as a schoolboy.

As he crossed Basin Street for his first look at Storyville, he saw a comely quadroon, startlingly pretty even with her face partially hidden by a thin veil. Other men along the banquette stopped and turned as she went by. Winks and whispers lapped in her wake. Just because none of them could ever afford such a prize, there was no law that said they couldn't look.

Later, after the young man's day was done, after he had tasted rye whiskey and a sporting woman, after he had spent his last dime and climbed aboard the train that would carry him off to the tedium of his backwoods home, he would recall the first image that greeted him, a woman the color of latte with doe eyes and a curving figure that made promises, a walking mystery that he would never fathom.

Justine arrived on the gallery of Josie Arlington's mansion a few minutes before the specified time of two o'clock.

She was alert for once, having gone to bed early and slept through the night. Paul had shown up at his usual time and they had chatted over brandy. At least she thought so; she didn't really remember. She did recall the way he watched her, with pointed frowns and little mutters of annoyance. Abruptly, he drained his glass, mumbled something about a society obligation, got up, and left. She took off the fancy dress she had put on for him and went to bed. She was still a little groggy when she woke, and it took the better part of the morning for her head to clear. She thought about taking another small dose of her medicine to brace herself for the appointment, then decided against it. She didn't want to miss anything because her mind was dull.

This day she wore a broad-brimmed rose-colored hat with a crimson veil to conceal her features. When she got to Basin Street, she passed through the crowd of men who had just crossed over from Union Station, caught their stares, and heard their whispers. She hurried to the door of the Arlington, thinking that all she needed was for Beansoup—or, god forbid, Valentin—to spot her.

One of Miss Josie's girls came to the door, ushered her inside, up the staircase, and down the long hallway. For just a moment, she entertained the bizarre notion that Mr. Anderson was going to be waiting in one of the doves' rooms, intending to make use of the appointments and of her.

However, the door at the end of the hall upon which the girl knocked opened into a cozy sitting room. Justine stepped inside. A couch and two armchairs were arranged about a fine Turkish carpet. A linen bureau was against one wall with a mirror in a walnut frame over it. On the top was a tray with a decanter of brandy and four crystal glasses. A chandelier glittered overhead. The street window was draped in lacy curtains that fluttered in the afternoon breeze.

Tom Anderson rose from one of the armchairs, so broad and solid that he gave an impression of taking up a good portion of the room. His blue eyes were kind as he waved her to the sofa and waited for her to sit down, take off her hat, and place it on the cushion next to her.

"If those things get any bigger, you ladies are going to have to hire someone to wear them for you," he said, with a wry smile. "Would you like some refreshment?" he asked her, gesturing toward the brandy.

She shook her head. "No, thank you, Mr. Anderson."

He waved his hand again, and the girl, who had been waiting, stepped back into the hall and closed the door. Justine was relieved that he hadn't invited her to address him with more familiarity—"Mr. Tom," for instance. There was something unnerving about the way he watched her. Her instinct told her to keep a distance from this man, who just happened to be the most powerful person in the city of New Orleans. She felt like she was at the mouth of a trap and would get snatched and gobbled up if she wasn't careful.

The King of Storyville, on the other hand, seemed quite at ease as he settled into the chair and picked up the cigar that had been smoking in the glass ashtray on the stand at his elbow. The clattering of wagon wheels, the occasional sputtering automobile engine, and the loud breaths of engines puffing out of the station drifted inside through the open window.

Through the strings of smoke, Tom Anderson regarded Justine frankly. She truly was a pretty dove, and he had a moment's regret that he had never visited her when she first arrived at Miss Antonia's. She had a fine body, too, lithe as a cat. St. Cyr was a lucky fellow. That was her surface. He turned a sharp eye to what was going on underneath her skin and sensed a tension there. He knew about her visits to the apothecary, knew she was walking along an edge with a steep drop on the other side. He wondered if Paul Baudel had seen it yet and if he was going to put up with it.

He noticed her watching him in return, with faint suspicion rising in her eyes, and spoke up promptly. "It must have been a surprise to get my message."

"Yes, sir, it was," she said.

"How are things?" he inquired. "Are you satisfied with your arrangement with Mr. Baudel?"

"It's only been these few days," she said. "He's a kind man, though."

Hearing a false note in her voice, Anderson said, "Do you plan to stay with him?"

Justine nodded, even more baffled. He was talking to her as if he assumed she would divulge her private affairs, though this was only the third time she had spoken to him, the first two having consisted of the words "hello" and "good-bye" after being introduced by Valentin.

In fact, the King of Storyville had kept an eye on her since she first took the room with Antonia Gonzales. He had heard the story about St. Cyr saving her from the brute that had her cornered in another house. When he learned that the detective had developed a special interest in her, he put out some feelers. Those who visited her claimed she was very capable, always clean, and quite energetic. She did not drink to excess, did not dabble in hop or whiff cocaine. She knew how to read and write and could keep up a conversation. She was too young and pretty to be bought and sold by the minute, and spent most of her time in the company of men of means and rounders who were flush for a few days or weeks. He was more intrigued when he learned that she became the only sporting woman that Valentin visited and that they socialized on the weekends, going for walks in the park and to band concerts out on the lake, like a courting couple.

When the Black Rose murders began and sporting girls were dying one after another, Valentin took her out of the house and into his own rooms. She stayed there, giving up the life for him. There were even whispers that they might get married at some point.

That never happened. In the wake of the murders, St. Cyr went into a long funk that had now reached the point of driving her out the door and into the bed of another man. At the same time, Anderson's spies reported that she had been acting strangely. Even now, he had a sense of something not quite right about her. Her dark eyes flicked this way and that, as if she was looking for something that had gone missing.

He let out what he hoped was a paternal sigh and said, "The truth is, I brought you here to talk to you about Valentin."

"Yessir?"

"You were with him for a long time."

"But I'm not anymore, sir," she said, too sharply. "Someone else is."

He nodded deliberately. "Oh, yes, the black girl." He tapped the ash from his cigar. "I think that might just be a matter of him licking his wounds. We'll see soon enough, I suppose."

This was all delivered in that oddly familiar way, and it puzzled her even more. What was she doing there? She had always heard what a clever man Anderson was. She had also heard the gossip about his appetites for women, and she wondered again if this was all a ruse to get his hands on her. She couldn't fail to notice how his eyes glittered as they navigated her face and body. He might well think that with Valentin out of the picture, he could move in on her. For all she knew, he had been admiring her all along and now saw his chance. She knew men well enough to understand what lengths they would travel just to get between a girl's legs. And yet that didn't quite make sense, either. The King of Storyville could have any woman, or as many women as he fancied, with the wink of one eye.

All this went through her mind in the space of a few seconds. She didn't know what else to do, so she decided to play just a little slow and see if he would voice his true intentions.

"He's been in my employ for a good while," Anderson was saying. "I don't want to see him landing in trouble."

Justine said, "Oh, he handles himself quite well."

"Yes, he does," the King of Storyville agreed. "That's why I've kept him around. But you know better than anyone that he's changed. Look what happened last year. Things could have gone much worse. For him and for you."

Her face flushed. "It turned out all right in the end," she said in a low voice.

"And it's fortunate that it did," Anderson said matter-of-factly. "It might not be the same next time."

"I don't under—"

"He's about to get into water over his head," the white man told her, his voice hardening. "I know you want to help him. And help yourself, too."

Justine gazed at him, frankly puzzled. There seemed to be a whole different conversation going on than the one she was hearing, like someone was speaking in the next room. She wasn't skilled enough at this sort of scheming, and when she didn't pick up the hints he was dangling, he let out a little sigh of impatience. She thought, *Too bad; let him come out and say what was on his mind.*

"You know, everybody has secrets," he stated, and gave her a piercing look.

A small light came glimmering along the edge of her thoughts and she was suddenly alert. "Yessir," she said carefully. "I suppose that's true."

"And everyone should be allowed to keep their secrets to themselves. Don't you agree?"

She nodded slowly. The way he kept staring at her with those cool eyes was making her nervous. She felt her heart begin to race.

Anderson paused again, puffed his cigar, let out a long trail of smoke. Then he said, "Valentin doesn't know about Ville Platte, does he?"

The room went black for a second and she felt like she was falling into a dark pit. She grabbed on to the arms of the chair and shook her head slowly and stiffly.

"Well, he doesn't have to," Anderson murmured. "No one has to know. That's what I mean by keeping secrets." He paused. "But I need your help."

Now Justine's mind jumped forward in frantic leaps. It was all too much. How did he *know*? After a moment, she began, "I don't..." She swallowed tensely. "I don't understand what you're asking, Mr. Anderson."

He settled back. "It would be better for everyone if Valentin just stopped what he was doing and got back to his regular work around the District."

She gave him a baffled look.

"What I want is for him to drop this investigation he's been working."

"I can't make him do anything," she said. "I'm not with him anymore. And he works for you."

Anderson's face got severe. "I wish it was that simple. Maybe a year ago, it was. Now if I order him to stop, he'll tell me to go fuck myself and then walk out on me. He's changed,

Justine. He doesn't listen to anyone anymore. Of course, you already know that."

She did know. And yet it was absurd to think she could do any better with him than the man now fuming in the armchair, the King of Storyville himself.

He apparently thought otherwise. "He has to know how badly it could go for you if certain information gets into the wrong hands," he went on, giving his words an even harsher edge. "Like the name you've been using and your current whereabouts."

She stopped cold, feeling the blood drain from her face as the room closed in on her even more. Her face broke out in a sweat, and for a few seconds she thought she was going to be sick.

The nausea passed and she realized with a sense of deep dread what was on the table. That feeling gave way to a rush of anger and she felt like lunging at him. Then she had to fight an urge to bolt for the door, run out into the cool of the autumn afternoon, and keep going until New Orleans and Tom Anderson and Valentin St. Cyr were all far behind and forgotten.

"So you need to talk to him," Anderson finished.

"I can't..."

"All that time you were with him counts for something. You can make him listen."

She sat silently. She didn't know what to say.

"Just talk to him and explain the situation," he said, more calmly. "Tell him what's at risk if he doesn't stop. That's all. Can you do that?"

She thought about it for a few anguished seconds. "Yes, sir, I suppose so."

"Good. That's all I ask." He stood up and she followed suit. "Now, is there anything I can do for you? Anything you need that I can provide?"

She understood. He was now offering payment for the deceit of plotting behind Valentin's back. She shook her head. "No, sir, nothing."

"Well, then…" He stepped around her and opened the door. Miss Arlington's girl was waiting in the hall to escort her out.

"My car will take you home," Tom Anderson said. He put one of his big hands on her shoulder to gently guide her along. "Thank you for your time."

She took a last glance into his eyes, to see if she could catch something there. It was no use; he was too good of an actor and his face, though pleasant, was closed, revealing nothing. She arranged her broad-brimmed hat and took a moment to get the veil set right.

Anderson's Winton automobile was waiting outside. As she descended the gallery steps, the driver hopped down. She waved him off and instead went to the corner, crossed over Basin Street, and walked out of the sun and into the cool darkness of Union Station.

She went to the wall where the schedules were posted and stopped to study the destinations. She didn't want to think about what had just happened. She remembered when she was small, she loved visiting the station and reading the schedules with the names of all the faraway places that a person could go. She once promised herself that she would visit every one. Now, all these years later, she stood reading the signs and feeling an old impulse to move. She had money in her purse to buy a ticket. She didn't have any idea of which of the destinations she would choose. It didn't really matter. She could turn up anywhere on earth and make a living, she reflected grimly, just by lying on her back and lifting her skirts.

She read down the slats of white wood with the names of cities painted on them, conjuring vague pictures in her head: Houston, St. Louis, Memphis, Chicago, Atlanta, New York. Then there were the smaller destinations: Lafayette, Bayou Breaux, Villiere, and others that she recalled some from when she had traveled with the tent shows and carnivals.

Once she left home, she had made her way to Houston,

where she landed herself a job dancing in a traveling show that was just heading out on a summer tour. There was no need for any training in the balletic arts. The routines were simple. The prime requirements were a good figure and a willingness to show it off in a skimpy dress.

With her latte skin, eyes with the slightest Chinee slant, and tight and slender body, she was a sight up on a plank stage. Right away, she was courted by members of the shifting company of musicians, comics, and patent medicine drummers. Though she didn't care much for having a regular man humping away between her legs, she understood what she had to do to get by. At least she had the choice of who she lay down with and when. She played them like clowns and took their gifts and their coins.

She thought the money she was collecting was decent, until one of the other dancers took her aside and explained exactly where the real cash was made. She began entertaining men in the towns they visited, rich farmers and local businessmen who couldn't risk getting caught patronizing local women. Not to mention that in the backwoods, clean doves were few and far between. Most were dirty, unschooled, good-for-nothing drunkards who had neither the looks, the skills, nor the ambition for the outside world. So Justine had stayed busy in the evenings after the shows were over. The best part was that the next morning she was gone again, on to the next town and the next eager fellow.

Her eyes settled for a moment on the name Ville Platte. She fixed on the two words for a long moment, then turned away and sat down on one of the hard oak benches. She stared out through the wide, tall windows at the trains, long and dark, blowing steam and soot as they rolled in and out. Eddies of passengers, their faces white, brown, and deep black, swirled before her eyes.

She had stayed out with the last circuit of shows for two years. The one called the Flying Horses brought her to the fairgrounds in New Orleans. She had gone with the new manager one time as a payment for keeping her on. When he demanded more, she quit the show and tried to lose herself in the city. Then he found her in the upstairs room in a house on Basin Street and tried to force himself on her. Valentin St. Cyr, who happened to be on the premises, stepped through the door and into her life.

That had happened almost three years ago. Now it was over and she was staring at the placards on the wall in a train station, realizing that there were so many places she could go and get lost, leaving Valentin St. Cyr and Mr. Tom Anderson to fend for themselves. She could escape and become a whole new person. Again.

Valentin passed not fifty feet behind her as she stood staring at the wall. So intent were they both on their thoughts that they didn't notice each other.

The detective bought a ticket on "Smoky Mary," the small gauge rail that ran from downtown to Lake Pontchartrain. In the spring and summer, the train would be full of those traveling to enjoy the concerts, fairs, carnivals, and other amusements that kept the lakeside communities lively. Now, with the concessions closed for the winter, there were only a handful of passengers in each car. Valentin sat by the window, watching the scenery change from the buildings and bustling traffic downtown, to the neighborhoods of single homes on the north side, and into the sparsely populated flats beyond the fairgrounds.

He got off at the Spanish Fort Station and walked along the sand and gravel road that edged the lake. Most of the attractions were shuttered. The dance halls that stood on pilings out over the water looked particularly forlorn. During the warmer months, the revelry was so loud that people swore you could hear the shouts, laughter, and especially the music all the way downtown. Now they looked like pieces of flotsam adrift on the gray water.

The road narrowed and there were houses on each side, small frame structures, also built up on pilings, with wide galleries. Some were residences used only part of the time for those who wished to escape the murderous heat of the summers in the city. Others served as year-round homes.

Though Valentin hadn't paid a visit to Eulalie Echo in almost two years, he remembered her house right away. It stood out brightly among the drab clapboards up and down the road, painted a bright white, the gallery overrun with all sorts of plants and festooned with carvings and sculptures of wood and metal that harkened back to Africa.

The house was fitted with a Dutch door, and before Valentin could call out a greeting, Miss Echo appeared in the open upper half.

"Well, well," she said, clapping her hands lightly. "There's a face I haven't seen in some time. Must be trouble in Storyville."

The tall Creole woman was related to the LeMenthes and had been named Ferdinand's godmother. She was a midwife, a seer, a healer, and a good voodoo queen, as compared to those foul witches who sold their talents to do harm. Some years ago she had moved out of the city and into this tidy house on the banks of the lake and had since dwelled there among her herbs and flowers. She had many regular customers who visited for her advice, for help with problems, for herbs and spices. She also traveled into New Orleans several times a week to deliver her goods and services. Believers swore her cures and potions never failed, so she stayed busy. Valentin was lucky to find her at home and alone.

She invited him into her kitchen and to a seat at the heavy old table of pale oak. She took down a jug of her home-brewed whiskey and poured them both a short glass. She took a moment to ask after her godson and question him about the goings-on around Basin Street.

"And what about your young lady? Justine, is it?"

"She's gone," he said.

"Oh...I'm sorry to hear that."

He shrugged and sipped his whiskey.

"So, Valentin," Miss Echo said. "Were you just passing by this afternoon? Or do we have business?" Her eyes brightened with mischief. "I know! You finally decided that there's true power to the *voudun* and you need some help from me. Is this it?"

He took the teasing with a smile, pleased that Miss Echo never took offense that he dismissed voodoo as foolishness. "I wish it was that," he said.

"What, then?"

"I've got something on my hands," he said. "There was a jass band a few years back. Played quite a bit on Rampart Street. The Union Hall Brass Band. And four of the five members of the band have turned up dead in the last two weeks. Along with the landlady at the house where one of them died."

She put her glass down. "Dead, how?"

"Two of them could have been accidents, but I don't think so. I think all of them were murdered."

"And you don't know why."

"No."

"And, what, you need my help?"

"That's right."

"But not for *voudun*."

"No, ma'am. Not exactly."

"What, then?" She watched him steadily for a moment. Then her brow furrowed. "You said, except one?"

"That's right."

"And who was that one?"

"It was Prince John, Miss Echo."

"Good lord!" Her eyes swung around to him and she drew back with revulsion. "You come to ask me about *him*?"

"I need to find—"

She raised one finger, shushing him, then turned her face away to look out her kitchen window at her back gallery and the flat scrub beyond. Her mouth set in a tight line, and when her eyes came around again, they were black blades.

"That man...," she said. "That man and them other ones like him, they gave *voudun* a bad name. I don't even know that he ever had any powers, but if he did, he used them in the worst way. He brought at least one poor woman down. Turned her into an animal. You know that story?"

"I've heard it, yes."

"He was never no goddamn good."

"I still need to find him. He's the only one left."

She was quiet for a moment, calming herself. "How you know he ain't dead?" she asked him.

"I don't."

The voodoo woman sipped her whiskey. "Christ in heaven, Valentin, he ain't ever been anything but trouble for anyone who come near him," she said. "Just so you know. Even if you'd let me, I couldn't do much to help you with that."

"I understand," Valentin said gently. "If you can tell me where he is, I'd be grateful."

"I don't know where he is," Miss Echo said. "But...I know where he was."

"Where?" Valentin said.

Eulalie Echo gave him a searching look. "Do you got any idea what you're 'bout to do?"

Dominique left the balcony door open, and every few minutes she would lean out and look off down Magazine Street in hopes of catching sight of him when he came around the corner. She was eager to surprise him, to greet him with caresses and then see what happened. She sensed her parts tingling and her heart

beat a little faster just thinking about it. That made her feel a
bit guilty about Jeff. What she was doing would have him spinning in his grave.

It had just gone dark when she finally saw his figure pass beneath the streetlamp on the corner of Canal. She began to unbut-
ton her dress. She got it all undone and leaned out to check his
progress before she slipped out of it entirely, just in time to see
two figures move away in the direction of Gravier Street. One was
Valentin. She felt her heart begin to pound with anger when she
realized who the other shape belonged to.

Justine had been waiting a few doors down, across the street
from Bechamin's. Somehow, Valentin wasn't all that surprised to
see her there.

He stopped when he was still five paces away. "Did you forget something?" he asked her, keeping his voice even.

"I need to talk to you," she said.

He hesitated for a moment, then stepped forward and offered his arm. She was touched by the unexpected courtesy, and
it took an effort to steady herself again as they turned around
and walked back toward Common Street.

For his part, Valentin kept his gaze fixed on the banquette,
as if he didn't want to face her directly and deal with the confusion. She glanced at him, saw the same perturbed look that
she had seen so many times when something he didn't care for
was dropped in his lap. It didn't matter. She had to do this.

She looked back over her shoulder and saw a distinct profile framed in the balcony doorway. She couldn't quite make out
the features, only that the girl was looking their way.

"I see you already have a guest," she said, trying to keep her
tone light.

Valentin's eyes switched at her, then went back to the banquette. He was wondering if she had come all the way to
Magazine Street to start an argument about Dominique. "What

did you want to talk about?" he said. It came out sharper than he had intended, and she didn't say a word for a few paces, as she reconsidered the wisdom of the visit. Valentin was getting impatient. "What do you—"

"I went to see Mr. Anderson," she said.

Valentin stopped. "What for?"

"Because he sent me a note and asked me to."

He stared at her and she proceeded to recount the conversation at the Arlington. Valentin listened, his thoughts running in busy circles. There was something wrong about it. Why would Anderson try to get to him through her? She knew nothing about his business. And they weren't even together anymore. It didn't make sense. He did know that she was letting herself in for trouble by going behind Anderson's back to alert him. The King of Storyville would be furious, and when that white man got angry, people found their lives changing for the worse.

He turned another corner. What if Anderson knew perfectly well that she would run to him as soon as she got out the door? It could be part of the game or a way of sending him a message. Which brought him back to why the man cared whether or not he chased down the murderer of four of the five members of the Union Hall Brass Band.

She remained silent while he puzzled. They reached the corner of Camp Street and started west. He couldn't see his way through it. All he knew for sure was that Anderson was pulling strings behind the scenes and that there could be traps at every turn. It annoyed him that the man whom he had served so ably could so complicate his life.

"What am I supposed to do?" Justine said, breaking into his thoughts.

"Don't do anything."

"He's expecting an answer."

"You don't work for him," he said curtly.

"I thought everyone worked for him. You said that."

He grunted softly. He had said it, and it was true.

"He's going to make things go bad for me, too," she blurted. "He said he would."

He heard the fearful note in her voice and stopped again to stare at her. "What are you talking about? Make things bad for you how?"

"I don't know!" she cried. "He can do anything he wants to anyone he wants. You said that, too!"

He looked at her, saw the light dancing in her dark eyes, and knew in that moment she was hiding something. "What is it?" he asked her. She shook her head, her face paling beneath the streetlamps, and he began to discern something looming ominously, something she had kept from him for the entire two years that she had shared his bed.

"Whatever it is, you're going to have to tell me."

She stayed quiet for so long that he wasn't sure he had heard her. He was about to repeat it when she said, abruptly, "I don't know why I came here. I don't have to talk to you anymore." Her tone was cold, almost accusing, as if whatever was tormenting her was his fault.

"Does it have anything to do with your Frenchman?"

It caught her by surprise. She turned slowly. "What did you say?"

"I asked you if it has something to do with the Frenchman?" There was no mistaking the lurking anger.

"No," she said, biting down on her own words. "It doesn't."

"Then what—"

"What do you think he'd do if he found out I came here like this?" she cried, her voice taking on a frantic edge.

"It's all right," Valentin said, trying to calm her. "No one will know you came here."

"You know. I know." She made a furious gesture back toward his flat. "Your damn black girl knows."

With that, her voice cracked and wavered like the air had gone out of her. Looking lost, she took his arm again, as if she now needed the support.

They stepped to the corner of Magazine and Gravier. After another few seconds' silence, Justine sighed, released his arm resignedly, and nodded in the direction of his rooms.

"You need to get back," she said. "She's waiting for you." When he didn't move, she hardened her voice and said, "Go."

"What about your—"

"Don't worry about it," she told him. "Just go."

Valentin hesitated for a few seconds, then walked away from her. As he moved off, Justine heard the woman's voice coming down from the balcony, sounding hollow, wounded. Valentin murmured something in response. The street door opened, casting his profile for a second as he stepped inside. Then it closed, leaving darkness.

The woman—Dominique—lingered on the balcony. It gave Justine a moment's sad pause, and she felt like weeping as she recalled all the evenings she had stood there, waiting for him to turn the corner. Then feeling him drawing closer before he actually stepped into view. She would hurry inside to greet him home. There was a little period of time, just after she had come to stay with him, when she all but lived for such moments, and would fairly swoon like a schoolgirl at his approach, as if she might topple over the railing and onto the cobbled street in a delirious, broken heap. That had ended, of course. The Black Rose murders had changed all that. She stopped waiting on the balcony or by the window when it rained. There came a point when it didn't seem to matter anymore. She tried to remember who had given up first.

The crackling of wires interrupted these dark thoughts as the Magazine Line car came grinding toward her. She held up her skirts and crossed over to the other corner, where she could step on. As the streetcar rolled away, she caught a glance of Valentin's woman, still on the balcony, again peering her way. There was something about the way she stood there, with her chin and heavy bosom thrust out, her hands on her solid hips, her eyes and claws no doubt sharpened, lurking over the street like a bird of prey defending her nest. As the tableau grew smaller in the back window, Justine wondered why she had brought her problem to Valentin at all. It looked like he was going to have plenty on his own.

Valentin spent a troubled night. As soon as he came inside, Dominique treated him to a reproachful stare that was followed by a long string of questions, which he deflected as best he could. She finally gave up and took her hurt feelings back into the kitchen.

She had prepared a nice meal, but he ate so little that she asked him if he was feeling poorly. Afterward, he sat on the couch, with a book that he did not read open on his lap. Dominique fretted, pestering him until he spoke sharply to her. When it got late, she changed into her nightgown and made it clear by her longing looks that she was ready for a repeat of the night before. He told her to go to bed, that he would be in later.

She pouted, her soft lip curling. "It's her, ain't it?"

"It's not what you think."

"No? What then?" She gave him an accusing look. "You ain't got no appetite. You ain't got two words to say to me. Now you sendin' me off to bed without you. What's wrong?"

"She's in trouble."

Dominique said, "She's in trouble all right."

She saw the look Valentin was giving her and closed her mouth.

"She didn't say anything about coming back," he told her firmly. "That's not what she wanted. She's with that Frenchman. So you don't need to be fretting about it."

She watched his face for signs of deceit, saw none. Maybe he was that able a liar, but she didn't think so. "She needs to have some respect, that's all," she said. "I'm the one in your bed now, ain't that right?"

"Yes, that's right," he said. "She's in trouble, that's all. And it's probably because of me."

Dominique frowned darkly and muttered something he couldn't catch, then went off to the bedroom to wait for him.

When he didn't come to bed by midnight, she gave up and drifted off. At one point, she came awake when the front door creaked open and then closed. She drowsily wondered where he had gone, if he had run off to meet Justine under the cover of night. Maybe he was just another false-hearted rounder like Jeff Mumford after all, one of those who would take pleasure in her body and then steal away to enjoy another. If he was, she'd know what to do about it. She had learned a long time ago, at her mother's knee, how to deal with evil men, or anyone else who crossed her.

Gradually, she let go of her bloodthirsty thoughts and fell back to sleep. She rose partway out of her slumber a second time to the sound of footsteps on the landing. She dreamed then that he would come in, slip through the shadows, undress, and love her. But there was no more sound, he didn't appear, and she dropped off once more.

Valentin walked to the river and stood on the levee, watching the freighters and barges slide through the inky darkness as he tried to make some sense of the jumble that he now had on his plate.

Morton had been correct that someone had stalked musicians and eliminated them. He was wrong about the reason. Now, just as he got closer to finding out what it might be, Tom Anderson wanted the investigation over. When Valentin wouldn't bend to his will, he pulled some dire secret Justine was holding as his trump card. Lurking at every corner was Lieutenant Picot. Why the copper was so determined to have him out of the way was another mystery that was thickening the stew. It had to be more than personal dislike. It had to be more than the competition with the police department. He wondered if and how Anderson and Picot were in it together.

He was confounded by the realization that Justine had hidden something from him that was worth her life. He wondered what she had done that was so terrible that Anderson could hold it over both of them like a bloody sword. He was convinced that it was somehow tied in with the murders of the jass players; he just couldn't see how. He would find out, though.

He thought about going back home, then sat down on the levee instead. Dominique was another dilemma for him to wrangle. She was such a wonder that he felt like he could spend half his waking hours exploring the uncharted territory of her lush body. It wasn't going to be like that. He had won her without lifting a finger, but her strange island ways, her demands for attention, and her jealousy over Justine were already driving him to distraction. She was alone and frightened and clinging to him like a child. She seemed to have forgotten her plans to go home to Tobago. She hadn't mentioned it once since he'd allowed her to stay. He suspected that, having found a sanctuary, she had decided that she wasn't about to give it up.

Valentin sat for a while longer, mulling this web of troubles, sensing shadows closing in around him. Then a freighter's horn moaned, a chilling sound from a ghostly vessel far down the river. He gave a start, feeling suddenly uneasy. Justine would be safe in her Frenchman's rooms. At the same time, Dominique slept alone and unguarded in his bed on Magazine Street. The door had been breached before.

He hurried down from the levee and walked at a fast clip back to his rooms. Twice he swore that he heard footsteps behind him, only to turn and find an empty banquette as far as he could see. By the time he turned the key and stepped inside, his curls were wet with sweat and he was panting like a dog.

All was well. He found Dominique deep in sleep, her full body stretched along his mattress. He undressed without making a sound, but when he came to bed, she opened her eyes, smiled, and reached for him.

"Come here, Valentin, suh," she murmured in a voice as soft and sweet as the night breeze. "For a minute there, I thought I lost you."

THIRTEEN

Tom Anderson was enjoying an after-church luncheon at Germaine's on Ursulines in the company of Father Cassidy of St. Ignatius, city of New Orleans alderman Alphonse Badel, and Billy Struve, the busy-bee publisher of *The Blue Book* guides to the Tenderloin, a gossipmonger of superior skills, and one of the King of Storyville's most able spies.

They were talking over a problem in the Jew Quarter when the front door opened and Valentin St. Cyr strode in.

Struve nudged the King of Storyville and tilted his head. As soon as Anderson laid eyes on the Creole detective's face, he knew that he had made a rare miscalculation. For the past week he'd had a sense of losing some of his legendary control, and now it looked like there was going to be trouble. He gave nothing away, though, and kept his expression neutral as he excused himself, stood up, and ambled around the back of the dining room and through the archway to the bar. Struve followed a few paces behind. St. Cyr started across the floor, weaving around tables crowded with church-dressed Americans.

The state of Louisiana was officially dry on Sundays. This was New Orleans, though, and Germaine's bar stayed open. At the moment there were only two customers, huddled together over glasses of Raleigh Rye. Anderson waited while one of the Mississippi toughs who were always lurking somewhere nearby stepped over to whisper to the pair. They listened, then turned their heads in unison to see the King of Storyville standing there. Without a word, they took their feet off the brass rail and walked out, leaving their drinks. After another few hushed words from the roughneck, the bartender realized he had forgotten something in the storeroom and promptly evaporated.

The King of Storyville took off his spectacles and laid them atop the bar, as if getting ready for fisticuffs. It had been awhile, but he had been a brawling youth and could still put up a fight, or so he believed.

When Valentin came through the archway, his face was such a cold mask that the roughneck straightened like a hound going on point. Then he caught Anderson's gesture, a mere flick of a finger, that told him to stand down and let the detective pass. He relaxed, though he never took his eyes off the Creole. Struve glanced between the two men and decided it was his turn to back out of the line of fire. He took refuge at the far end of the bar, still close enough to hear if they raised their voices.

Tom Anderson lifted his chin in a posture of regal aplomb. When Valentin met his stare, it was like two sabers clashing. There was no need for niceties. "What are you holding on Justine?" the detective demanded.

"You don't take that tone of voice with me, sir." Anderson drummed his fingers on the bar. "Your concern for her is very touching. You weren't so concerned when she walked out on you. You weren't concerned enough to stop her from taking up with that Frenchman. You weren't so concerned that it kept you from bringing someone else to your bed."

Valentin forced his voice steady. "I want to know what you have on her."

The King of Storyville cut the air with one hand. "It's up to her to tell you. If she trusts you, that is."

Valentin understood perfectly that this was a ploy to knock him off balance. And it did deflect him, though only for a second. "You're using her to keep me from going after whoever murdered those jass players," he said. "It's blackmail."

Anderson folded his arms across his chest and shook his head. "It's not blackmail, my friend. It's persuasion. And if I can't persuade you, I'm going to take you off the table. I don't pay you to make trouble. I pay you to fix it."

"What trouble?" the detective said, and now the King of Storyville looked like he wished he had bitten his tongue.

It didn't matter; Valentin wasn't going to win the exchange. He had spent the morning nursing his anger and now he'd let it get the best of him and walked into a trap. He had given away Justine's deceit and now she was in deeper trouble. He silently cursed Anderson's cunning and his own stupidity.

"I'll save you the trouble of firing me this time," he said.

Anderson cocked his head to one side. His hard frown went away and he grinned indulgently, as if listening to a child's bragging. "You want to quit on me? And what will that accomplish?"

Valentin, his face flushing, wanted to say, *I'll be out from under your heel,* but he kept quiet.

Anderson's smile turned chilly. "You better think about what you're saying. You quit on me, and you won't be able to earn a damn dime. You'll have to move so far back-of-town just to find a place to hang your hat, you'll be halfway to St. Louis. You'll be finished."

"Then I'll be finished," Valentin said, and walked out. As he reached the archway, he turned around and said, "But I'm going to find out who did those murders."

A gust of wind came swirling along the banquette and up his back, as if to lift and propel him away. He was a block over on

St. Philip Street, when it dawned on him what had transpired in Germaine's bar.

Not only had he defied the King of Storyville; he had done it in front of witnesses that included the gossipmonger Billy Struve. He was going to pay a price. He didn't know what it would be, only that it would be painful. There would be more trouble for Justine. Anderson might even decide to come after Dominique. He could do anything he wanted to.

Valentin looked over his shoulder. For all he knew, the King of Storyville had already dispatched his roughnecks to chase him down, beat him to a bloody heap, and drag him back.

He crossed over into the District at Bienville Street, ducked into the alleyway behind Frank Toro's Saloon and leaned against the back wall of the building. He patted his pockets for a smoke, found none. He closed his eyes, listening to the jostle of the street.

An alien blade of fear poked through his gut. He wasn't worried about anything Anderson's man might do. He had handled rougher sorts. He was afraid that he had done exactly what the King of Storyville said, which was to quite efficiently cut his own throat. It had been stupid, because he could now end up disgraced and shoved so far away that he'd never break the very case that had brought him there.

His mind went calm, something he could have used with Anderson at Germaine's. Like a fool, he had let his true feelings rise up and pour out in a rush. He saw Anderson's face again, in anger and then derision. He had blundered with the threat of quitting and the bluster of the promise to close the case. The King of Storyville could relax. Valentin posed no threat to whomever or whatever he was protecting.

He suddenly recalled a story Struve once told him. Some years in the past, a successful pimp who generally behaved himself one day decided to put two sisters on the street who were too young for Tom Anderson's comfort. Anderson sent a polite request that the pimp send the girls back home, wherever that was. The request was ignored; the sisters were already turning a nice profit. Then Anderson sent a message that the pimp had twenty-four hours to get out of Storyville. The fellow sent word back for Anderson to mind his own business, that he wasn't going anywhere and neither were the girls. By daybreak he was gone, as completely as if he had been turned to dust and blown away, and was never seen or heard from again. The sisters were cleaned up and put on a train back to their family in Ohio.

When Valentin asked if Anderson had the man killed, Struve laughed and said that he doubted it. More likely, the King of Storyville simply had someone explain to the fellow that by sundown he and his various broken limbs would be occupying a bed in Charity Hospital, and when he could walk again, he would be locked away in Parish Prison and would not see the light of day for a very long time.

Valentin himself had been an arm of the authority that Anderson wielded in those parts. If you crossed him, your next stop was the ticket window at Union Station, if you were lucky. Now the tables were turned and the detective spent an idle moment thinking about where he would go if he had to choose.

In any case, he was not about to crawl back to beg for his job. It was too late. Maybe it was time for a change. He had been on a slow descent, and he needed more than anything to break that spiral and fix what was wrong. Though it was also possible that one of Anderson's men was at that moment purchasing him a ticket to parts unknown.

When he got back to Magazine Street, he found that he couldn't sit still and told Dominique to put on a walking dress. She hurried to get ready, delighted for a chance to get out of the house. She snatched up a hat and a coverlet to lay on the ground.

On the streetcar across town, they got odd looks from the other passengers, and it dawned on Valentin that this was the first time the two of them had been out in public. It was one thing for him to be squiring a quadroon like Justine around town. It was quite another to be escorting someone like Dominique. There was no getting around her dark mahogany skin and darker ebony eyes.

He didn't care; indeed, he was in a mood to stare back. Dominique saw the looks and thought how different it was on Tobago. There, no one cared whether she was with a man who was as pink as a seashell or the blackest nigger on the island.

Not so in downtown New Orleans, though once they crossed Basin Street, she relaxed. The puzzled and resentful stares were now fixed on him and came from the colored passengers showing their resentment at someone who appeared to be a white man bedding one of their own.

They transferred to the Esplanade Belt and rode four blocks west to Dumaine Street. The car was crowded, and as they drew near the stop, they saw gaggles of pedestrians crossing over the tracks and into the park, a sea of parasols and derby hats. It was a pretty fall day, with high, puffy clouds and a cool breeze off the Gulf.

A wagon had been pulled onto the grass, and Valentin got in line to buy them both a boudin wrapped in waxed paper and a bottle of Chero-Cola. Dominique laid the coverlet on the grass, and they sat down to eat and watch the swelling crowd. When they finished, they got up, folded the blanket, and strolled closer to the bandstand. The crowd changed, shifting by degrees to take in more whites and Creoles. So Dominique was now one of only a few darker faces.

They came upon a row of large tents that had been erected along one of the pathways, staffed by Negro waiters pouring libations and offering light snacks. These were private areas, cordoned by long ribbons that were tied to wooden stakes. They were passing near one of the tents when Valentin glanced over to see Justine standing with a gentleman who could only be her Frenchman. They were outside the tent, just on the other side of the cordon. She was wearing a demure cotton walking dress and held a parasol over her shoulder. She looked lovely, like the daughter of some well-off Creole family, and yet there was something wrong about her appearance that Valentin couldn't put his finger on.

She must have sensed his stare, because she turned her head. Dominique noticed, too, and he felt her tense beside him. Justine looked from him to the black girl and the women's gazes met in midair. Though Dominique was bristling, Justine stared back at her with a blank wonder.

Paul Baudel turned around to say something to Justine and saw the three of them standing there, frozen, like cats in an alley. He looked Valentin up and down, then glanced at the pretty young black-skinned girl. He looked sidelong at Justine and saw that she had gone into another of her dazes. With a sigh of annoyance, he touched her arm and hissed something quick and biting. The spell was broken. She blinked, then nodded and turned away obediently. The Frenchman led her into the shade of the tent, where other white men with their dusky companions drank and talked.

Dominique watched them walk off. "What's she doin' out here?" she blurted.

"The same thing we are," Valentin said, placatingly. "She can go anywhere she wants."

"She just better stay in there where she belongs," Dominique said.

Valentin let out a sudden laugh. It caught her by surprise and her anger went away. He offered his arm, and as they started moving off, he glanced back over his shoulder. "So that's her fellow," he murmured.

Dominique said, "He dresses right well."

Valentin found this comment funny as well, and his mouth crooked gently.

Dominique smiled up at him, then pointed off toward the bandstand. "Maybe we could find us a place over there," she said. "I mean *way* over there."

They got back home late in the afternoon. Though he didn't see them again, he had thought about Justine and the Frenchman throughout the day. He didn't know what to make of it. It was the first time he had seen her in daylight since the morning she had walked out. That one close look told him that she did look different, like someone he had met somewhere but couldn't quite place.

He followed Dominique up the stairs, feeling wearier with every step. As he opened the door, he paused to consider that Anderson was not likely to let him keep the rooms. The down-town flat had been offered years ago, as part of their original arrangement. There was no reason that he should be allowed to stay there. For tonight, though, he still had a home.

When they got inside, Dominique took off her hat and placed it on the arm of the couch. She stood in profile in the afternoon light that was coming through the window and just beginning to turn gold. He was startled in that moment at how beautiful she looked and was humbled that she had come to him. It was still a mystery to him why she had done it, but he decided that pondering that could wait until tomorrow, too.

She looked at him, saw the odd, dreamy expression on his face, and said, "Suh?"

He studied her face for a moment, then stepped behind her and began undoing the hooks down the back of her dress, slowly, revealing her dark skin inches at a time. She closed her eyes and bent her head forward. When his fingertips touched her flesh, she caught her breath. Once the hooks were undone to her waist, he took the dress in his fingers and pushed it off her shoulders. She was wearing a ribbed vest of soft cotton underneath. With the same slow movements, he undid the hooks on the back of her skirt. He opened the last one, and the skirt dropped to the floor around her feet.

She turned to face him. He brought his hands up, held her face, kissed her mouth. She sighed softly, the tiniest breath, tasting of cinnamon. He put his hands on her shoulders and moved the straps of her vest down over her arms. She smiled at him and he saw the coy look in her eyes. He pushed her gently down onto the couch.

Afterward, they curled for a long time, not speaking at all, as the sun dropped, turned deeper gold, then a dark, bloody orange.

She started to get up once. He held her there. She murmured something about dinner. He told her it could wait.

They were quiet for more minutes. Then she said, "She ain't at all happy, suh."

"Who?"

"Justine. Who else? And she's goin' to try to come back."

"You think so?"

"I t'ink so, yes. No, I know it."

"Why? That Frenchman's rich. She's got what every woman wants."

Dominique shook her head. "No, suh, not every woman. Not her. Not me."

They were quiet for a while longer. Then she roused herself. "I want to make you a good dinner tonight," she whispered. "I believe you earned it. It's going to take me a bit of time, though."

"How much time?"

"Couple hours, I t'ink."

She kissed him, stretched her arms and legs, and stood up.

He reached out and slipped a hand inside her thigh. "Don't you start, or you gonna starve to death," she said, and backed away from him. He laid there thinking as he watched the sun disappear over the rooftops, then sat up and pulled his trousers on. With all that had happened that afternoon, now the cloud was back.

He walked into the kitchen to find Dominique hard at work. "I'm going out for a little while."

She stopped working and looked at him. "Out where?"

"Basin Street."

"Whatchu wanna go there for?"

"I need to close some business."

"Tonight?"

"If I don't go now, by tomorrow morning there's going to be talk all over the street."

"So?"

"So I need to be the one who puts it there first."

She gave him a searching look. "You're comin' back, though."

"Oh, yes. I'm coming back."

"All right, then."

After he finished dressing, he went to the kitchen and kissed her cheek. She smiled and her eyes softened. When he got to the door, he looked back through the doorway and saw her watching him, her face composed in a sweet calm. She knew he'd be coming back.

The truth was he didn't want to have to explain his plan to Dominique. It wouldn't make sense to her. His first stop would be Countess Willie Piazza's mansion, where he would inform the madam that she should expect Mr. Anderson to demand his firing by the Basin Street madams. He was saving her the trouble by quitting. From there he would work his way down the line. They could believe anything they wanted about what was happening. At least, they would hear it from him and not Tom Anderson.

It didn't work out that way. When he came upon Countess Piazza's mansion, he found a gaggle of boys standing outside, listening to piano that was tinkling through a half-opened window. He stopped to lend an ear, then climbed the steps to the gallery and knocked on the door. A maid appeared and ushered him inside.

He found Professor Tony Jackson at the piano. The professor, small, trim, and as homely as could be, was dressed in light tan trousers and a white collarless shirt. His suspenders were dangling and he was in his stocking feet as he worked his way through a stately ragtime number. He glanced around when Valentin walked in and stopped playing.

"Mr. Valentin." His soft voice belied his surprise. "What are you doing here?"

"I was...I was passing by." Valentin nodded toward the window. "Do you know you have an audience out there?"

Jackson rose a few inches from the bench to peek out. "Oh, them. Yes, they come around all the time. They all gonna be professors one day. Or so they say. They don't know no better."

He sat back down and let his fingers roll over the keys. In an instant, the tangled knot in Valentin's head was washed away in the lush trickle of notes.

Jelly Roll Morton had been known to mutter that Professor Jackson got his skills by way of some private magic. Valentin knew that it wasn't magic at all. It was these hours spent on off days and nights, laboring away, worrying a single passage until it was perfect. While Morton was still sleeping off last night's fete, Tony Jackson would be sweating over the ivories in an empty Basin Street parlor.

Valentin stood by while the professor played the same eight bars a half-dozen times. It sounded flawless to the detective's ear, but Jackson kept shaking his head, sighing and frowning. Finally, he closed his eyes and played the passage twice more.

Only then did he stop. He sat back, straightened his spine, flexed his fingers.

"You ever miss a day?" Valentin asked him.

"Not many." He eyed the detective speculatively. "You ain't just passing by, are you, Mr. Valentin?"

The detective sat down heavily in one of the tufted café chairs. "I came up here to tell the Countess that I'm not going to be working for her anymore." He could hear the way his own voice sounded, tired and hollow. "I'm not going to be working on Basin Street at all. I quit from Mr. Anderson's employment."

"Yes, I heard."

"You did?"

"People talk," the professor murmured.

"And what do they say?"

"That you aren't doing well at all," the professor replied frankly. "Your woman left you. You're causing mischief about those fellows who died. Then just this afternoon, I heard that you quit Mr. Tom."

Valentin closed his eyes and said, "Billy Struve."

"Yessir, I believe that was who said it."

The detective wondered what he had been thinking. Of course, Struve would waste no time putting such racy news on the street. It would probably turn up in the *Mascot*, the local penny newspaper, too. Anderson wouldn't mind at all; it meant his side of the story was the one everyone heard. Valentin let out a sigh of frustration and ran a hand over his face. While he was dawdling in the park and then frolicking on the couch with Dominique, the word was going out that a bumbling and ungrateful Valentin St. Cyr had left Tom Anderson's employ.

"I want you to know that I've always thought well of you, Mr. Valentin," Professor Jackson said, keeping his eyes shyly averted. "You've always been fair to me. And I'm sorry for whatever strife you're having."

Valentin bowed his head slightly, grateful for the kind words. The professor went back to playing, a peaceful cascade of round notes. Valentin thought about leaving, since his trip there was a waste of time. Then he decided he would rather just sit in that chair and be carried away by the music. If Tony Jackson's playing couldn't offer a balm for what ailed him, nothing could.

A few minutes later, Jackson came to the end of the melody and began fiddling about with his sheet music. "So what do you think happened to them?" he said casually.

Valentin opened his eyes. "To who? Those musicians?"

"Yessir."

"I think..." He hesitated, wanting to get it right. Before he could begin to explain, though, there was a clamor outside the window, a babble of excited voices. Professor Jackson got up from the bench and went to see what it was all about.

The professor said, "My word, look at that."

"What is it?"

"Mr. Anderson's out there. He's passing around dimes to those kids."

Valentin knew instantly that it was no coincidence. Anderson had obviously sent the word down the line for any sightings of the detective St. Cyr. Though it had taken all day for Valentin to show up, just that quickly someone passed the word that he was in Countess Piazza's parlor. And just that quickly, Tom Anderson was making a rare appearance on the Basin Street banquette on a Sunday night.

Surely enough, the professor had just come back to the piano again when the front door opened with a jingle. There was some muted conversation in the foyer, and a moment later Anderson stepped into the doorway. At that moment, Valentin wished that he had ducked out the second Professor Jackson announced that the King of Storyville was outside. Now he was trapped. He'd look like a coward if he tried to run.

Anderson strolled over to stand next to the piano. He was wearing one of his fine suits, though it appeared in some disarray, as if he hadn't had time to put himself together properly. He chatted with Professor Jackson about music for a few moments. He did not look at or speak to Valentin. Presently, though, he asked the professor if he would excuse the two of them. Jackson threw an apologetic glance at Valentin, then got up, gathered his sheet music and his shoes, and made a quick exit to the back of the house.

Anderson waited until he padded away before taking a seat in one of the plush armchairs. He placed his derby on his knee and regarded the Creole detective with an expression of frank curiosity.

"Some people would say it's unwise to quit me," he said. Valentin stayed silent. Anderson made a thoughtful steeple of his fingers. "What exactly did you think you would do, now that you're a free man?"

Valentin said, "Leave, I suppose." He paused deliberately. "That's once I've settled this business with the murders."

"Oh? You think you can do that?"

"I do."

"Do you have any idea at all what happened? Or are you still guessing?"

Valentin hesitated. *Let the man go begging,* he thought. He did not have to give him a thing. Then he considered how his hot head had already gotten him in trouble. And he could not ignore Anderson's reasonable tone. The man was being solicitous, though as usual there was something else lurking behind the quiet words. At least they weren't crossing swords.

"I'm guessing," Valentin admitted. "But I'm getting closer. I just need more time." He smiled thinly. "And now I have some."

Anderson studied him, his heavy brow stitching. "So you're serious about this quitting business?"

"I am."

"I believe you are," Anderson said after a moment. "Well, then...it seems we're at an impasse, doesn't it?" Valentin waited. The white man sat forward in his chair. "I want you to consider an offer," he said. "You stop your investigation and you can continue to work in Storyville. Whether or not you work for me is your decision. As to your disrespect for me at Germaine's this morning...I'll call it the heat of the moment."

Valentin had begun to shake his head. "I'm not finished," Anderson said, with a brittle edge on his voice. "You get Justine's life, as well."

"What's that mean?"

"It means that if you don't cooperate, her fortunes will take a turn for the worse. Along with yours." He saw the look of mistrust and resentment in the Creole's eyes. "You think I'm making an empty threat?" he said snappishly. "Well, that's a chance you'll have to take. Are you willing to do that? Are you willing to risk her just so that you can chase after these murders, which might come to nothing in the end anyway? You can't have both. You go on with the case, or you get to save the girl." He smiled icily. "I guess you'll be a hero, either way."

"Can you tell me what you've got on her?"

Anderson shook his head. "I told you. I'll leave it to her, if she chooses."

"How bad is it? Can you tell me that?"

"Bad enough that you don't want that to happen. If you care for her at all."

Valentin was one of a handful of people who knew when the King of Storyville was not putting on his well-honed act. He now recognized a rare stark moment when the mask was lifted and the true face of the actor revealed. Whatever he had on Justine was dead serious.

"Why is it so important that I drop the investigation?" he inquired.

"I'm not answering any more questions," Anderson said, with gruff impatience. "What will it be?" When Valentin didn't respond right away, Anderson let out a huff of annoyance and said, "Are you really going to gamble with her life?"

"This is wrong," the detective muttered. He raised a hand as if in protest, then dropped it. He was cornered and he knew it. Anderson remained silent, staring grimly and waiting. "All right, then," he said at last.

"You're doing the right thing," the King of Storyville said. "Now everyone can go on with their lives. No one will be bothered. I guarantee it." When Valentin didn't say anything, he stood up. "We're finished here. Tomorrow is Monday, and you'll be back to work." He stopped on his way to the door. "Tell the professor I said he's playing better than ever," he said, and walked out.

Valentin wandered onto Basin Street. He was at first of a mind to go home and take the brandy bottle to the couch to think about his total surrender to Anderson. He didn't even know what he had gotten in the deal. He might never know, if Justine didn't want to tell him. Though perhaps now she'd do him the service of explaining exactly what he had saved her from.

He knew that if he went home now, in his mood, Dominique would read it the wrong way and get all suspicious again. He didn't have an appetite anymore and that would only add to her mistrust. He decided instead that he wanted to be alone just a little while longer. A half hour, no more, and he'd go home to her. They could eat dinner and go to bed and he wouldn't have to think about any of it.

He walked down the block to Fewclothes Cabaret, a wild dance hall throughout the week but a quiet saloon come Sunday night. He stepped inside and found it empty except for a table of sporting girls taking the evening off and a few sots drinking more pieces of their livers away at the long bar. He ordered himself a glass of rye and carried it to the table in the farthest corner, where it was dark and no one could see him.

He drank three whiskeys, enough to ease the pressure in his mind. He left his money on the table and went out onto Basin Street. It was a pleasant enough night for a walk. He knew Dominique would be waiting, probably getting anxious, and he picked up his pace. Fifteen minutes later he was crossing Canal Street and stepping onto Magazine.

Dominique didn't hear any footsteps on the stairwell and was surprised by the hand rapping on the door. First she thought Valentin had forgotten his key. Then she remembered that he had locked up on the way out.

She went to the door to ask who it was. The voice was indistinct. She couldn't even tell if it was a man or a woman. The only words she caught were "Mr. St. Cyr" or at least something that sounded like it.

When she said, "Who is it?" the reply was another string of muffled words.

It had to be Justine, back to have it out over her rights to Valentin and the rooms. Dominique set her chin, twisted the key, and turned the knob.

The door flew open, the edge cracking into her forehead and knocking her backward. Her heel caught on the braided rug and she tumbled to the floor, momentarily stunned. The door slammed, shaking the walls, and a dark shape passed over her. Or maybe it was two. There was noise from the back of the house, the sound of furniture being tossed around. She couldn't move, couldn't find her voice.

The dark shape was back, bending over her, the mouth snarling something. When she couldn't answer, a hard slap knocked her head to one side and made her ears ring louder. Fingers like claws grabbed at the neckline of her shift and ripped it right down the middle. That brought her out of her shock, and she kicked with one furious foot and threw a clumsy punch with her right hand. Both collided with something solid.

She saw the face, saw the dead look in the eyes, the lips stretched over grinding teeth. She couldn't move, couldn't cry out as the hard hands fastened on her throat.

Dominique was not on the balcony, and when he opened the street door and started up the stairs, she did not come to the landing to greet him. There was nothing but an echoing silence from above. At the landing, he discovered the door thrown wide. He called her name again. There was no answer.

Like a fool, he had gone out with neither his pistol nor his stiletto, so he grabbed his whalebone sap from his back pocket.

"Dominique?" Still no answer. He pushed the door open the rest of the way. "Dominique!"

She was lying a few feet inside. The shift was torn jaggedly in two, something white oozed at the corners of her mouth, and her dead eyes stared at the ceiling.

Valentin let out a cry of rage, then raced down the steps, tripping and falling, righting himself and limping to Bechamin's to pound on the door and yell for the storekeeper to call for an ambulance.

They had covered her body with a sheet. A patrolman had appeared, then another, then a police detective. Inevitably, Picot's heavy steps rose to the landing.

He came inside and crossed over to lift the sheet from the dead girl's face. He asked quietly if there was any worthwhile evidence about. His officers shook their heads. He dropped the sheet back and looked up at the police detective, who nodded in the direction of the kitchen.

Picot stood in the doorway. St. Cyr sat at the table, looking at nothing, his face unreadable. The lieutenant stepped into the room, pulled out a chair, and sat down. "Are you responsible?" he asked. Valentin didn't bother to answer. "You hear me? I asked if you're—"

"Yes, I'm responsible," Valentin said, startling the copper. "But if you're asking if I committed a murder, the answer is no."

"Who did it then?"

"Do your own police work, Picot," Valentin said dully.

The lieutenant settled back. "You know, you ain't nothin' but trouble. I believe I could have a fair to middling career just following you around. Now I need to know if you have any idea who committed this crime. Yes or no?"

"I don't," Valentin said, and raised his eyes. "Do you?"

The copper look surprised. His face went red and he pointed an angry finger. "You better get yourself straight. You're in the middle of this."

"It's this case," Valentin told him. "Somebody got worried. Somebody who came looking for me. She got in the way. And that's what they did to her."

Picot let out a grunt of irritation, as if frustrated at the way things had turned out. Once again, someone was dead and St. Cyr was still alive. It was a bit of grim comedy, and Valentin came up with a smile that folded as quickly as it had appeared.

Picot caught it, though. "What's so goddamn funny?" he demanded, his voice sliding higher. He was about to start up again when one of the coppers stepped to the doorway to tell him that they were finished with the body and ready to quit the scene.

Picot got up from the chair. "You be where I can find you," he told the Creole detective, and stood up to leave.

FOURTEEN

The news of the girl's death raced through uptown New Orleans, and by noon on Monday everyone in Storyville north and west had heard about the tragedy.

The juicy word that the victim had just replaced Justine Mancarre in St. Cyr's bed raised eyebrows and stirred gossip all over the streets. The girl was murdered in the very rooms kept by Tom Anderson's private detective! Even the *Mascot* sent a scribbler out to sniff around, for it was just the kind of spicy, bloody drama that Storyville readers devoured. The mystery made it all the more delectable. Who was Dominique Godet and what had she done to deserve such a gruesome fate? The whispers sizzled from the mansions of Basin Street to the Robertson Street cribs.

Tom Anderson was so stunned when he heard the news that he went to his office and closed the door. Within the hour he had spoken to the police department and knew as much as anyone else. The girl had been surprised, beaten, and strangled to death. Though her clothes had been torn, there was not yet word about a sexual attack. There were no clues pointing to a guilty party. Lieutenant Picot, who was in charge of the investigation, had been heard to mutter vaguely about St. Cyr himself, though no one seriously considered the Creole detective a suspect.

So it was either a random crime, the girl had trouble no one knew about, or she had gotten in the way of someone who had come after St. Cyr. The word on the street leaned toward the latter, since the Creole detective had enemies. Poor Dominique Godet had simply picked the wrong man and had lost her life.

Anderson's spies reported that St. Cyr sat in a daze while Lieutenant Picot's officers tore his rooms apart looking for clues. They had left without finding anything of value. When Picot questioned him, the subject had answered in a voice that was dead with shock.

That Dominique was such a vague presence only stoked the fires of gossip. She hadn't been in New Orleans very long, and Mumford had kept her away from the sharp eyes and quick hands of the back-of-town rounders. She was alone, and no family or friends had yet come forward on her behalf. Anderson sent word that he was to be notified regarding the disposition of the body, which had been carried off to the morgue for a preliminary autopsy. He offered to pay the freight back to her island if no one else appeared to take responsibility for her.

That done, he left instructions that he was not to be disturbed and huddled in his office with his bottle of brandy. He sat and drank, sensing that matters were once again tilting out of control. He had corralled St. Cyr, fixed the problem, settled things. Or so he thought; now another murder had occurred and there would be worse trouble brewing.

Running Storyville was a balancing act that Tom Anderson performed with a delicacy that belied his lumbering size, yet he had stumbled like some common oaf. He hadn't counted down all the factors with his customary keen eye and had badly misplayed his hand. Instead of trusting St. Cyr, he had deferred to the judgments of others. He had made the betrayal worse by using Justine Mancarre and her dark secret for leverage. It had been one mistake, one miscalculation piled atop another, and now he had a mess on his hands that he didn't know how to fix. He felt weakened and full of anxiety about what he'd done. He was all too aware that the one person who could have come to his rescue had just been shattered.

He drained his glass, refilled it. He took a moment to remind himself that he was the King of Storyville, then settled down to figure a way to save himself.

That very night, Jelly Roll Morton and his cronies at the Frenchman's set their tongues to wagging, already starting the rumor that it was somehow connected to the murder of Jeff Mumford and the other musicians. And so the word spread.

Anderson had his people watching for St. Cyr. He wasn't surprised when the detective didn't appear at all on Monday. He would be devastated, probably stumbling around half crazy. It would be a horrible blow, even though he had known the girl only a matter of days. No doubt he would believe that it was his fault. And maybe it was.

When Tuesday brought no sightings of the detective, the King of Storyville sent the Basin Street Arab called Beansoup and his little tagalong Negro friend with the big eyes to sniff around. The boys reported back that there didn't seem to be anyone home at the Magazine Street address. The windows were dark, the curtains drawn. They had climbed the steps, knocked, and called St. Cyr's name. There was no sound of movement from inside. Beansoup had the presence of mind to go back downstairs and step into Gaspare's to ask after the Creole detective. Mr. Gaspare said he had seen him and thought to add vague condolences about the terrible tragedy. They asked down the street at Bechamin's, too, and got the same response.

Anderson put out more feelers and was surprised to learn that the detective may have been at one or more of the low-rent dives far out on Rampart Street, though no one would swear it was him. This fellow, whoever he was, bought glasses of Raleigh Rye that he drank at a corner table. Then he got up and left, only to appear at another saloon down the way, where he repeated the performance.

The King of Storyville grew more uneasy. St. Cyr brooding in his rooms was one thing. Having him stalking uptown haunts and seething over the poor girl's death was quite another. Who knew what kind of trouble he might stir up?

When Wednesday came around and the detective still hadn't shown his face, Anderson began to wonder if something was seriously amiss. Maybe he had left town. Maybe he had fallen into misadventure and had ended up at Charity Hospital or was lying dead in an alley somewhere. He even entertained the thought of St. Cyr taking his own life, then dismissed it. He wouldn't do it. No, Anderson's gut sense told him that he was out in the city somewhere, prowling like a wounded animal.

When evening rolled around with no more word, Anderson sent one of his toughs in his Winton motorcar to St. Charles Avenue to collect Jelly Roll Morton with orders to drive to Magazine Street and break the door off its hinges, if need be, in order to locate St. Cyr or produce a clue to this whereabouts.

Morton had forgotten his silk scarf and pulled his suit coat tight around his throat as the motorcar rattled and bounced through the cool October night. He was not looking forward to the end of the ride. Anderson was plenty worried, or they wouldn't be going to these lengths. He had to be thinking that St. Cyr had gone crazy over the killing of the girl and was fearful of what he might do.

Valentin didn't seem like the type to go berserk, but what if he had come apart? He had lost Justine to the Frenchman and then Mumford's girl had suffered a terrible attack in his own rooms. And what about the four musicians and the landlady on Philip Street? All this mad violence going on, and he couldn't stop it. Who knew what he might do now?

They banged into the rut of a missing cobble. The thought of the detective all distraught like some character in a tragic opera made Morton snicker grimly and the driver, one of Tom Anderson's Mississippi toughs, gave him a dull glance. Though the fellow was a lout, Jelly Roll was glad he had company on this errand. The whole mess was giving him a morbid feeling, and he wondered if he just should have kept his mouth shut in the beginning and saved everyone a lot of woe.

As anxious as he was, when they got to Magazine Street, he insisted on going up alone. He was worried about what Valentin might do if Anderson's man started taking down the door. The roughneck shrugged, folded his thick arms, and leaned on the fender of the Winton to wait.

Morton went upstairs and started knocking and calling. He announced that he wasn't leaving and that Anderson's henchman was waiting to break in. He cajoled and pleaded. He finally announced that in thirty seconds the fellow downstairs would be taking over. He felt like a fool, realizing all the while that he might be talking to empty rooms.

He was about to give up when he heard movement from inside, a slight shuffling of feet. The door opened. Morton caught a glimpse of a man's back as he moved away.

"Shut it behind you," a voice muttered.

Morton went inside and closed the door. He could just make out the detective standing in the shadows on the other side of the room. "Can I turn on a light?" he asked, and before Valentin could answer, he switched on the lamp that was on the stand next to the door.

He was shocked by what he saw. Valentin looked like one of the derelicts that peopled the streets of the District, day and night, human scarecrows. He was wearing a white shirt that had a yellow dinge to it and was stained with brown splotches of drink. His curling hair was more than unkempt. He hadn't shaved and the beginnings of a beard stubbled his cheeks, chin, and upper lip. He was wearing gray cotton trousers, also stained. His feet were bare and looked dirty. The only thing Morton could think to say was, "Jesus, look at you!"

Valentin waved a curt hand. He went over to the French doors that opened onto the balcony, pulled the curtain back an inch, and looked outside. "You brought Anderson's car," he said. His voice was low and raspy, like he had an ague.

"He sent me," Morton told him. "That's one of his roughnecks down there."

"You can send him on." He stepped back.

Morton went to the door and out onto the landing, catching a whiff of something unpleasant. He leaned over the railing and called down for Anderson's man to go to the Café with the message that all was well. He went back inside the apartment as the Winton's engine gurgled to life. The car rattled away.

Morton sat down on the couch. Valentin was moving between the bedroom and kitchen like a creature submerged in muddy water. The air in the room was close and held an odd mix of odors, sweat, tobacco smoke, whiskey, and another scent. Someone had been at a hop pipe.

He didn't know what to make of any of it. He had never seen Valentin this way, though he had been around long enough to know that rounders were rounders and fell prey to bad habits. The only surprise was that he hadn't done it sooner.

Morton knew that for the eighteen months since the end of the Black Rose murders, the detective had been holding his breath. Maybe it was a good thing that he had let it out before he exploded. It was awful that it had taken the vicious murder of a young girl to bring it on. Of course, there was also the possibility that he was taking the first step in the direction of the gutter. Morton had seen it more times than he could count and it started out just like this.

No; even now, Valentin was trying to regain some order. He disappeared into the bathroom and there was the sound of water splashing. When he reappeared, he said, "I lost my watch. What time is it?"

When Morton looked at his own watch and told him the hour, Valentin was silent for a long breath. Then he cleared his throat and said, "What day?"

"Wednesday. Almost Thursday."

"You don't have to go to work?"

"Mr. Anderson took care of it."

Valentin blinked. An odd look crept across his face. "Any bodies turn up lately?"

"Not that I heard," Morton told him.

He was quiet again. "Why did Anderson send you?" he asked presently.

"He was concerned."

The Creole detective let out a rough grunt of a laugh, then slouched down into the morris chair. He rubbed his face with his hands, then left them over his eyes.

"Where have you been?" Morton said.

After the crime scene had been gone over and the last of the coppers departed, Valentin closed the door, pulled the shades, and tumbled headfirst down into a tunnel of despair. Once again, his blind arrogance had brought on a tragedy. This time around it was worse. He had only the vaguest claim to the case, or what there was of it. No one save a handful of musicians cared and he could have left it alone, a mystery that would become another chapter in Storyville's thick book of sordid legends. Now, because of him, an innocent young girl had lost her life, and he still hadn't found the first clue that might lead to a solution to the mystery.

He sank deeper into darkness. At one point, there was a knock on the door. He thought it might be Justine, coming to console him. He didn't answer and whoever it was went away.

He related these bare facts to Morton. What he didn't describe was the arc of his anguish over poor Dominique. She had come to him, scared, alone, and in need of assistance. She had shown him kindness and affection, she had offered him her lush body, and now she was dead. He had seen her that last time before they dropped the sheet over her and she looked beautiful even in death, her face sweet and her flesh as vibrant as if it was still bursting with life.

After uncounted hours went by, he had suddenly roused himself and, in a baffled rage, went out on the street with bad intentions in mind. His first stop was a Rampart Street saloon, where he had some quick drinks. Then he went to the apothecary on the corner of First Street. The druggist had been a source of information over the years and had often provided the Creole detective with whatever potion might loosen an informant's tongue.

He filled Valentin's request without blinking an eye, even though he'd just come from his warm bed. The detective tucked the envelope in his vest pocket with a muttered word of thanks. His next stop was a tiny shop with Chinee characters on the door. He was in and out in a matter of minutes with a round pill wrapped in gold paper that he tucked away. Then he went home.

The next forty-eight hours were lost in a haze. He drank and smoked and sniffed. Numbing his brain with rye whiskey, burning it with coca, and then soothing it with hop. He did not remember sleeping or eating. He stayed in the dark, save for the light of a few flickering candles. The daylight barely passed the drawn curtains.

"And that's all?" Morton asked him.

Valentin shrugged. He did not want to explain the dark cave he had entered in the thrall of the liquor, opium, and cocaine. He did not want to revisit the haunting visions of his father and mother and sister and brother, Bolden, Justine, and Dominique as they paraded through his mind and then surrounded him with their accusing eyes.

He did not want to describe the awful dark thing that grew in the pit of his gut, a terrible shape, like some serpent rising up to devour him. It was a fearful beast without form or dimension, and he had the dim sense that if freed, it would turn back and swallow him whole. Such were the insane thoughts that went rushing through his head.

But it was all too much. At one point, at the bottom of the worst hour, he burst onto Magazine Street and staggered south to the river. He stayed there under the first glimmer of dawn, aware of the ships passing, but seeing little and feeling less. He let the muddy water, deep and roiling, calm him. Then he ambled back home just before daybreak and, finally, was able to sleep. That was all, until Morton's knock on the door.

"What happened to... What did they do with Dominique?" he asked.

"I believe she's at Gasquet's," Morton said. "Mr. Anderson's taking care of that. Gonna send her back home."

"To Tobago."

"I believe so, yes."

Valentin nodded slowly and then fell silent. Morton remained quiet, too. He didn't know what to say about any of it. So he just watched and waited, and for a brief, strange instant, something came across the detective's face that he had never seen before, a dark shadow that could only be grief. Morton had heard about his family and knew firsthand about Bolden. Now an innocent girl had been taken. The piano man saw all of it in those gray eyes, and for one small moment he thought something was about to break. Then, just as quickly, it was gone. Valentin's back straightened, his gaze hardened, and he let out a long breath.

Morton sat back, relieved that it hadn't gone any further. Valentin turned his head and met the piano man's worried face.

"It's all right, Ferd," he said. "You did what he asked. Now you need to get away from it. Just don't say anything more."

"I feel like it's my fault."

"It's not your fault," Valentin said flatly. "If I would have been paying attention, we'd have the killer. And Dominique would be alive."

The piano man brooded for another moment. "What happens now?" he said.

"You can tell Mr. Anderson that I've been ill, but that I'm recovering."

Morton stood up. He reached out to place a hand on St. Cyr's shoulder, then thought better of it and slipped to the door and opened it.

"Ferd?" Morton stopped. "You can tell him something else. Tell him I'm going to finish what I started."

FIFTEEN

No one around uptown New Orleans ever learned his true name. He first went by the moniker "Brother John." He was small of stature, hard muscled, with skin a burned bronze color, with long straight hair that he sometimes tied back Indian style and eyes a dazzling, hypnotic shade of green. No one knew where he came from, either; he just appeared back-of-town one day in aught-five, a battered horn in hand, looking for work in a band. It turned out that he was a player of meager skills and, when he couldn't find anyone to hire him on (this was New Orleans, after all), he decided that voodoo might be a more promising career.

It certainly came easier. All a fellow needed was a good act, babbling gibberish while fussing with roots and bones, and the superstitious types would come flocking. Brother John worked a Negro and Creole clientele, helping himself to their hard-earned dollars and taking his pleasure with the young women.

It was through some of the colored maids that he first came to the attention of white ladies of a superstitious bent, the type who adored the Ouija, numerology, table-tapping, and ghosts, and found himself invited into American parlors on the wealthy side of New Orleans.

The trouble began when one woman in particular fell under his spell in a dramatic way. Like the spider to the fly, he drew her out of her brick antebellum mansion to his low-down digs, a bare, roach-infested room along an alleyway off Franklin Street, not much bigger than a crib, with just enough space for the iron bed that they proceeded to press into near-constant service.

Brother John believed that his ship had come in, that he had captured a goose that would lay him a golden egg, for the woman was married to a rich Irish Channel doctor. John went about servicing her insatiable needs day after day and in every conceivable fashion, but his reward never came. The woman refused to do his bidding and bring him money, jewelry, or fine silver from her home, insisting that all the good fucking should be payment enough. At that point, it began to dawn on Brother John how deranged the woman was and what mortal danger he was inviting for nothing, save some jellyroll that was not all that sweet. So when she arrived the next day, she discovered that he had vacated his premises for parts unknown.

She was spotted wandering the Negro streets and the coppers collected her and carried her back to the Irish Channel. She didn't stay long. Now she did help herself to some of her husband's cash and threw it all over uptown New Orleans in an attempt to buy information about Brother John's current whereabouts. Most of the scoundrels who took her money didn't have the slightest idea where he'd gone, and those who did wouldn't say for fear of incurring one of his much-vaunted curses.

The crazy woman wasn't to be denied. She set up shop in the upstairs room of a saloon and took all comers. Her appetite was insatiable. There were estimates of a hundred partners in all, though this was probably a gross exaggeration. Whatever the number, the party ended when the word went out that there were Regulators on the way, their lynching ropes in hand, causing her amorous congregation to evaporate like so many puffs of smoke.

The Pinkertons her husband had hired later found her staggering around the alley off Franklin Street, a delirious mess. She was carted away, placed in a hospital somewhere far beyond the Mississippi, and was never seen or heard from again.

So Brother John escaped. Though in the beginning there were whispers that he had not been so lucky, but had been caught, strung up, his yancy sliced off like andouille, his body burned and what was left buried in an unmarked grave. Or so one rumor went around.

The fact was, no one knew how much of the tale was true. It was impossible to find anyone who could actually name the doctor's wife or point out the room where she had offered her entertainment, or to find a man who would admit to being one of the cars in the train she pulled that day. For all anyone knew, Brother John had started the talk himself just to have something so lurid attached to his name. The story swelled and made the rounds for a couple years afterward, then went up onto the shelves of Storyville's sordid lore. One thing was certain: Brother John was gone.

Most people forgot about him, too, until he showed up again in the high summer of '06, now as lean as a stick, his hair cropped short, carrying a shiny new trumpet and the new moniker *Prince* John.

He had heard about the King Bolden Band raging through uptown New Orleans, and became one of those who grabbed on to the tail of Bolden's comet for that brief period when anyone who could blow a scale got to share in the whiskey, the hop, and the willing women.

He put on an act that was a stage version of his voodoo routine, and all done up, was something to behold. Bolden saw him perform once or twice and stole a few of his more outlandish moves. That was all, though; the man didn't have anything else worth filching. He blew fast and loud to cover the fact that his skills hadn't advanced much. He was fortunate that he could put on a show and that the other players were good enough to make up for his poverty.

He landed in an ensemble that was thrown together from the pieces of other groups that went by the name Union Hall Brass Band.

They did fair business and then something happened. The rumor was it was trouble with some woman, with Prince John right in the middle of it. Whatever it was, he was there one day and gone the next. This time he didn't come back. The members of the Union Hall band drifted off to other employment and to their tragic fates.

So went the story of the notorious Prince John, the last member of the band who might still be alive.

Valentin slept another ten hours, then woke up late in the afternoon to find that the sun had gone away and clouds had come up over the Gulf. It looked like rain. He hoped so; he could use the cover for his evening's work. After he visited the privy in back, he filled the tub with hot water and soaked away the muck of his three nights and days on the back-of-town streets and holed up in a closed flat. He went to the washstand and labored to scrape the stubble from his cheeks.

He rummaged in the back of the bedroom closet for his work clothes, a pair of de Nimes cotton trousers, a thin jersey, heavy socks, and his ankle-high police brogans. From the hook on the wall, he grabbed an old railroad jacket that smelled so musty that it made him sneeze. Finally, he dug out his slouch hat. It was an outfit he kept for those rare times he had to wander off the city streets. He hadn't worn it in years.

Once he finished dressing, he spent a few minutes putting his rooms back into some kind of order. As he made ready to leave, he found a pill of hop, still wrapped in its silver paper. He thought about throwing it away, then decided it might be useful and put it in his pocket. He went out and locked the door. The city was draped in pale ocher light as the twilight sun dropped below the horizon and refracted through the rolling clouds.

He turned north on Common Street. A few blocks up, he came upon a diner he didn't know and went inside for a quick meal of fried chicken and potatoes. He ate, then ordered some more. He dawdled after he finished and was looking out the window as the first drops of evening rain tapped on the glass.

He thought about what he was doing, now that he had escaped from the nightmare of the past three days. Let Tom Anderson try to stop him if he wished, but he was going after Dominique's murderer, who had to be same person who had taken the lives of Mumford, Noiret, Lacombe, Martín, and the landlady Cora Jarrell.

He knew it would mean trouble and not just for him. Justine was going to have to fend for herself. He couldn't help that now. She had betrayed him by keeping her secret, whatever it was, then by going to Basin Street, finally by leaving him. Maybe he could have protected her before. Not now. He might have even given up on the murders of Mumford and the others, but he couldn't let Dominique's killer walk away. He was the one who had left her vulnerable. It was his fault she was dead. He at least owed her justice.

At Union Station he once again purchased a seat on the Smoky Mary and out of sheer contrariness sat in one of the "star cars" that were placed up front in the smoke and sparks from the engine and reserved for Negroes. There was only one other person on board, though, so no one bothered him over it. The train, the next to last of the day, rolled east and then north through the darkening city.

Valentin stared at his reflection in the window glass, listening to the rhythm of the wheels on the rail as he thought about the night to come and the man he was seeking out.

A half hour later, he stepped onto the station platform at Milneburg. He waited around for a few minutes to see if Anderson or Picot or whoever else took such an interest in his movements had sent another tail. The train pulled out and the last passenger disappeared. He walked through the station and turned east along the gravel road, rain dripping from the brim of his cap. When he reached the banks of the lake, he stopped again to make sure that he wasn't being followed. It was hard to tell with the steady drizzle hissing in his ears and making mist in the darkness. He would be just as hard for someone else to see as he slipped into the low brush off the side of the trail.

Following Eulalie Echo's directions, it took almost half the night to travel from the gravel road to the wagon trail that cut through the brush and trees, and then more miles of walking on the footpath that ran east along the lake. He stopped at regular intervals to rest, get his bearings, and check for a tail. If there was anyone following him, it had to be a ghost.

As he drew close, he began to think he had gotten lost, then suddenly found the site just as Miss Echo had described it, a stand of tall bamboo on two sides of a clearing and a grove of stunted willows and live oaks on the other. On the side that faced the lake, the ground was sopping and slick with mud and algae. It was inhospitable terrain that bordered shallows too stagnant for fish. It was no place for a human, in other words—unless it was a human who was looking to hide.

After five minutes of searching, he found the twisting path through the thick stalks of bamboo. When he emerged and stepped into the clearing, he was greeted by the sight of a building that tottered shakily three feet above the ground on wooden pilings. From the smell, it seemed the crawl space underneath was a combination garbage dump and latrine.

The rain had slowed to a light drizzle, lightening the night sky, and he could now see that the shack had been thrown together with clapboards that had been scavenged from the store, so the facade was a patchwork of varied colors and textures. The roof was rusty corrugated tin and a chimney pipe stuck up another four feet, wisping gray smoke. Next to the open door was one dirty window with a burlap sack hanging behind it as a curtain. The steps to the door were building stones crossed with rough lengths of plank. Valentin put his foot on the first one and peered inside. He saw only darkness.

"Whatchu want here?" a voice croaked, startling him.

"My name's Valentin St. Cyr. I need to talk to you."

"How'd you find this place?"

"I found it. Now I'm here."

There was a pause, then: "You need to go."

"I'm not going anywhere," Valentin said to the darkness.

"I said get away. I got me a pistol in here, goddamnit!"

"If I leave, I'll come back with the law."

There were sounds of movement. It could have been the man in the shack, some scrabbling rodent, or just the patter of rain. The voice croaked again. "Step inside."

Valentin climbed the two sagging steps. As he stood in the doorway, he was assailed by the pungency of strong herbs, gamy sweat, smoke, and something else all sour and fecund, saturating the close air and deep murk. His eyes adjusted and he began to discern details. The single room was low ceilinged and square, twelve feet by fifteen at the most. A cast-iron stove glowed weakly in one corner. The walls of unpainted wood planks were festooned with leaves and drying flowers and various parts of animals, the tail of a rabbit here, what looked like the skull of a nutria there. He could see gaps in the boards and feel wisps of breeze. The place would be an icebox come wintertime.

Among this clutter, he discerned a small man, copper brown and thin of bone, who was sitting on a pallet that had been pushed up against the back wall with a low table of rough pine boards and stacked bricks before him. The face was feral, like some swamp animal, and his hair stuck out at spiked angles where it wasn't knotted. The eyes, though half-lidded, still glowed a sharp green.

"Prince John," Valentin said by way of introduction.

"How you know my name?" The voice sounded like rattling gravel.

"You're famous."

Prince John let out a dry hack of a laugh. He got quiet then, as his eyes prodded his visitor's face. "You been running wild lately, aintcha?" he said. "Where was you at? Rampart Street?"

Valentin was startled at the man's intuition. "There and other places," he admitted.

Prince John produced a wolfish grin of sharp teeth. "I knowed it," he said. "I can still smell that place." A bony arm came up, pointing. "There's a chair. Sit."

Valentin made out the backless wooden chair against the wall to his right, pulled it out a few feet, and sat down.

Prince John's smile gave way to a blank frown as he fiddled about with something that he held at the tips of his fingers.

Valentin remembered seeing him at work once, years back, playing his horn at some carnival. He recalled the body of a circus acrobat and a handsome, sharp-featured face with those green eyes set against bronze skin, a gift of Cherokee grandparents. What he now beheld was a shrunken shadow of that striking man; the flesh was parched and drawn, the rickety bones jutting. Valentin got a sense of something broken inside, too. Then there was the voice, sounding as if he was being choked with every breath.

"I asked what you want here?"

"I'm conducting a murder investigation," Valentin said.

"Murder?" Prince John's eyes flicked. "You a copper?"

"Private security."

"Private..." The eyes narrowed, brightened. "I know you. You was friends with Bolden."

"That's right."

The man on the pallet gave out with another jagged laugh. "I thought I had me some tricks until he showed up," he said. "Man could play that horn. Goddamn, that's the truth! He had some *voudun* on him, too. Yessir. What happened to him? He dead?"

"He's...gone," Valentin said.

Prince John shifted on the pallet and the gamy smell from his clothes wafted across the room. Valentin was thankful that the door was open.

"How'd you find me?" Prince John said.

"I'm a detective," Valentin said, and realized that it had been some time since he had mouthed those words.

"Anyone else know you come?"

"No, no one."

"You gonna state your business?"

Valentin paused, letting the drama build. He wanted the man's full attention. "Every member of your band is dead," he said. "Everyone except you."

The Prince grunted. "Well, they was a wild bunch."

"I mean dead in the last three weeks, Prince. I think they were all murdered by the same person. Someone was out to get them."

A moment went by and then the green eyes came alive, blazing from the shadows. The Prince let out a long breath, more like a gasp. "Christ..." He drew back, hunching his thin shoulders.

Valentin said, "Do you know who might be committing the crimes? Or why?"

"There ain't nothin' I can tell you," the Prince said, his voice rising. "Not a goddamn thing. So you can leave now." When Valentin didn't move, he muttered, "I can make you go, if I want to."

The detective laughed shortly. "Go ahead, then."

Prince John stared, then turned away. "I ain't got nothin' to say."

Valentin made a show of digging into his pocket to pull out the pill of opium in its silver paper. Prince John's head came back around and his eyes went wide with hunger. "Talk first," the detective said. "And then it's yours."

Prince John licked his lips noisily. "It coulda been..." He coughed. "I mean, I don't know."

"What?"

"There was this one woman..."

"Is this the one from the Irish Channel?"

"You know about that?"

"I've heard the story."

"No, it wasn't her. This was another one. Later on."

"What was her name?"

"All I know was what she called herself."

"Which was what?"

"Emma. Emma Lee. I think."

"Emily?"

The Prince got snappish. "Not Emily. *Emma Lee.* Two words."

"So her last name was Lee?"

"I don't know no last name. All I remember is Emma Lee. That's what she went by."

"When was this?"

"What, right about two years ago? It was wintertime."

"So that's the winter of oh-six?"

"I believe that's right."

"And what happened?"

"What happened..." He took another raw breath, his vacant gaze fixed on the silver foil package, and Valentin could almost see his mind winding backward in time. "She showed up back-of-town one night," he rasped. "And she had that look."

"What look?"

"Like she was out for trouble, in the saloons like that. But them young gals, they used to love that jass. God almighty! They used to—"

"What about Emma Lee?"

"Oh. We run her off. But she come back the next week. Actin' crazier than before." He kept eyeing the pill of hop as if it might disappear. For a moment, he seemed ready to snatch it away and take his chances.

"Go ahead," Valentin prodded him.

"We was playin', uh...It was down to Longshoreman's Hall, and there she was again. All drunk and hopped up and wild as could be. You know how them women can get. They chased her out the front door, but she just come around the back. She was out there in the alley when we was done playin', so..." He made a vague wave of his hand.

"So?"

A wicked grin bowed his mouth. "So we took her back to my rooms."

"And?"

"And we all had at her."

"What?"

"I said we all had at her. You know what I mean. We all fucked her. The five of us." He laughed with raw humor. "Hell, she let us do any damn thing we wanted. She couldn't get enough. We just took turns. Sometimes two at onst. Jesus! We was all drunk as hell, and there was some dope around. What's that one fellow's name...Lacombe, that's it. He took a needle, but the rest of us was just smokin' some hop. We had us a hell of a time. Went on for the rest of the night, all the next day, and the next night, too. We kept her busy all that time. And she never missed a lick."

"Then what?"

"Then the mornin' come and I ran her off. What else?" He laughed again. "She was mad as hell. Said if we didn't let her back in, she was going to..." His eyes fastened on the package. "Now how about it?" he muttered.

"When we're done," Valentin said. "She was going to what?"

Prince John gave him a blank look.

"All right, so you put her on the street. Do you know what happened to her after that?"

His dark brow furrowed. "I think...I heard later on that she got put away in that hospital."

"What hospital?"

"It's called...uh...some retreat? Is that right?"

"You mean the Louisiana Retreat?" Valentin knew the place. "It's in New Orleans. On Henry Clay."

"I believe that's right. That's where they put her. She was crazy as hell..." He looked up at the detective for a moment as if some new thought had just wound through his brain. "All them fellows was all murdered?"

"I believe so, yes."

"Jesus Christ almighty!" he moaned suddenly. "Then she done got out!"

"I don't know if that's—"

"She's done got *out*!" he repeated, his eyes getting wild. "She done got out and went and murdered all of them!"

"Who says it's her?"

The rasping voice went up. "It's her! It's her! Who else would it be? Jesus and Mary!"

"Why?"

"Why? You got any idea what we did to her? We worked her like some goddamn field whore." His eyes skittered from side to side, then his panting slowed and his hard stare settled on Valentin. "I done what you asked. I need somethin' now, god-damnit. You gonna gimme that pill or do I gotta cut you?"

"You're not going to cut anybody," Valentin said, then tossed the package onto the table.

Prince John dropped the object he had been holding so tightly to snatch it up, and Valentin saw that it was a tiny doll, fashioned of bits of cloth, string, and sticks.

The dirty hands went scrabbling and produced a rough clay pipe. He tore into the silver paper, broke off a piece of the pill, tamped it into the bowl, and struck a light. As the flame bulged, Valentin was startled to see a raw gash that ran from the center of the Prince's throat up to his left ear, where a chunk of the lobe was missing. The black man gave him a shrewd look.

"You see how I am?" he said.

Valentin kept staring at the ghastly wound as the Prince puffed noisily on the pipe. "I should have got away from there, but I was stupid. One night my door got kicked in. There was two of them. They held me down...and they did this..." He made a rough gesture to the scar. "They thought I was dead. I would have been, too. 'Cept there was a conjure woman in a house back behind me. I got to her and she fixed me until I could get to a doctor. Ain't never been right, though." He stuck the pipe back in his mouth and fixed his eyes on his visitor's face. "But it still ain't over, is it? She's bound to get her revenge for what we did to her. You know she is..."

The pupils began to dilate and he nodded sleepily. Valentin sensed that he was losing him. "Prince?" The green eyes wandered away. "Prince John!"

"I hear you."

"You said the Louisiana Retreat."

"I did...Louisiana Retreat..."

"That's a white hospital."

Prince John studied the glowing embers in the pipe and a weird smile crept across his face.

Valentin said, "Emma Lee was *white?*"

"White as you," the Prince snickered, with another devilish flash of yellow teeth. Then his smile dropped away and the fearful look returned. "She's gonna be comin' for me?"

"She'd never find you."

"I got myself hid good, that's for sure," Prince John said, and sucked harder on the pipe, the scar rising again in the glow of the tiny fire.

Valentin got up and went to the door, where he stopped and said, "What about that other woman?"

The Prince didn't look up. "What other woman?"

"The first one. The doctor's wife. From the Irish Channel."

"Oh. What about her?"

"Is the story true or not?"

"True enough." He allowed a long sigh and a short silence. "Guess I should have learned my damn lesson, eh?" He struck another lucifer and held it over the bowl of the pipe. He didn't notice when Valentin backed out of the shack and disappeared into what remained of the night.

The detective got to Milneburg Station a half hour before the first train of the day. The platform was dark and silent. Only the faintest lingering mist of rain remained. He stood around the side of the building out of sight, thinking about Prince John and his shack and wondering if he had carried any of that awful stench away. He felt like something other than lake mud and sweat was clinging to him.

A wet, gray dawn crept in behind the starless night. When Valentin walked out of Union Station, he found the avenues eerily quiet. Nothing was moving. Then, as he made his way down Canal Street and onto Magazine, dark shapes wavered like phantoms out of the silver shadows to cross the intersections. The day's first workmen trundled along, on their way to the docks, their lunch pails banging against the predawn silence.

It was oddly calming to him, a sound and rhythm he recalled from when he was a young boy. His father had carried just such a lunch pail when he went off to work, and it was that crude music that announced his return home at the end of the long day.

Valentin trudged to his door, dirty, wet, and tired to the bone. He undressed in the middle of the bedroom floor, tossing his muddy clothes into the corner. Then he stretched out on the couch, wrapped himself in the blanket, and thought about the place he had visited, the foul-smelling shack hidden away near the lake and Prince John, once a proud rounder with a string of strumpets at his beck and call, now a skeleton, huddling in the shadows, half mad and taunted by demons.

And what of the young white girl named Emma Lee? According to the Prince, she had crossed Canal Street and arrived alone at a back-of-town Negro dance hall where jass was played and had ended up spending thirty-six hours being ravaged by five colored men, four of whom were now dead. Soon after, she was placed in a hospital for the insane. Or so said Prince John. She might still be there and she might be long gone. She might be in her grave. Wherever she was, she was casting a long shadow and, alive or dead, he would have to find her.

SIXTEEN

Valentin dozed and woke up through the morning and into the afternoon. He took a long bath and scrubbed his skin. He dropped down beneath the warm water and tilted his chin up until nothing but his nose and mouth protruded. The quiet soothed him. There were whole minutes in which he did not think about Dominique.

When he got out, he rummaged through the icebox and made himself a meal from the food that she had brought home. He ate steadily, lingering over eggs and ham and slices of her island bread, and washed it down with cups of coffee. Then he went to the bedroom to dress.

He selected his gray cassimere suit and a white collarless shirt and stood looking at his reflection in the mirror. Then he stepped away to collect his wet and muddy clothes from the night before and gather them into a ball.

He walked to the corner and turned west on Poydras Street. Halfway down the block was a Chinese laundry, where he dropped his dirty clothes and asked to have them back by evening. At the next corner, he caught the St. Charles Line car and rode away from downtown, past the Garden District, the

Audubon Zoo, and the universities. He stepped down at Henry Clay Avenue.

Seven blocks south he came upon a three-story brick building with a mansard roof, surrounded by a six-foot-tall stone wall. There was a brick kiosk for the guards at the front gate, and mounted on it was a small bronze plaque modestly announcing the Louisiana Retreat. Valentin knew that the name on all official documents was the Louisiana Retreat for the Insane.

It was a private sanitarium devoted to mental illnesses and nervous conditions and served a clientele of Americans of means and well-to-do French citizens, including members of some of New Orleans' best families who contended with disorders of the mind, addictions to drink and drugs, and other sorts of errant behaviors.

Valentin stepped through the gate and stated his business to the uniformed guard. He was directed along the sidewalk to the door of the main building. He walked up the flagstone path with purpose, all the while surveying the landscape with quick glances.

The building was in the shape of an E, with the center prong larger than the outer two. In the open spaces between the prongs were courtyards where staff and patients could take the air. The only obvious difference from any other hospital building was the upper-floor windows, which were heavily barred.

The guard who greeted him when he reached the lobby sent him on to an adjoining administrative office where a gentleman who said his name in such a clipped way that Valentin didn't catch it informed him that he could not be allowed to view any institution records without official permission, *which would require a statement of reason or reasons for the...*

Valentin stopped listening. He had expected this. He was using the visit as an excuse to case the site, and it was worth the off chance that he might happen upon an official who was not so *official*. He let the gentleman finish his recital, thanked him, and departed with a sheet of paper detailing in small print all the requirements for obtaining records. When asked for his name, he said, "John Doe," just to see if it would get any kind of rise. The man didn't even blink; "Deaux" was not such an uncommon name in that city.

In the lobby he stopped and pretended to be reading over the paper while he got a good look around the layout, making a mental note of the directory that was affixed to one of the heavy columns.

He pushed through the heavy doors and walked back down the pathway to the gate, where he nodded a thank-you to the guard. He strolled the seven blocks north to St. Charles and caught a car back to town.

The sun was going down when he arrived at Magazine Street. He got the brandy bottle out and took his drink back to the bedroom, where he untied the string around his laundered clothes and changed. Pulling open the top drawer of his dresser, he left his pistol and stiletto, but took out a leather case no bigger than his hand.

After his father's death, he had gone to Chicago, where he was enrolled in a school run by the nuns. It was his first experience passing for white. Despite the sisters' best efforts and his own hunger for books, he got a better education from his Italian and Polish classmates, who were, like him, the sons of immigrants. He learned the ropes from these young hoodlums and was on his way to becoming a true criminal when the beating death of one of his gang changed his outlook and sent him packing.

He did learn many interesting things along the way, one of which was how to pick a lock. It was simple if you had the right equipment and knew a few tricks. He had brought his little set of tools in their leather case from the Windy City, and he had kept it back in the drawer ever since. Until this night, he'd never had occasion to use it. Now he tucked it into an inside pocket and, after another brandy, headed out the door.

The downtown streets were falling quiet by nine o'clock. He wanted to avoid even the slightest chance of someone recognizing him on a streetcar and so he walked. He didn't care if Anderson, Picot, or both had someone watching him. Whoever it was, he'd lose them.

It was a little over five miles and he took his ease, strolling along at an even pace and stopping to rest when he reached Napoleon Avenue, about halfway. He used the time to think about what he was going to do. It had been years since he had used his skills to do something so far over the legal line, but he saw no other way to get the information he needed.

He arrived at the Louisiana Retreat a few minutes after eleven o'clock. He found a space in the shadows of a church down the block and spent a half hour observing the site. There was no movement in or out. He could see the immobile profile of the guard in his kiosk, which told him the man was probably dozing, always a good sign.

And why not? The Retreat cared for patients with less serious problems who were placed there voluntarily. The criminally insane were penned elsewhere. The bars on the upper-floor windows were there to protect those on the inside.

Valentin knew from arresting a fair number of sneak thieves that they were most often caught because they lingered too long and were spotted coming or going. Of course, most criminals weren't known for their feats of wit. The smarter strategy was to get to the target and either go inside or go away.

The detective made a slow circuit and then found a shadowed point on the north corner of the building. He took a quick look around, scaled the fence, and went over. When his feet hit the ground, he froze, listening. There were no shouts, no patter of running feet, so he didn't hesitate, crossing the lawn to the closest of the doors.

A cat burglar would bring a small crowbar to jimmy open any door that wouldn't give way. Valentin had decided against using anything that crude. He didn't want anyone knowing he had been there, in case he had to come back. He got out his kit and fumbled about getting used to the tiny tools again. It took him five minutes to pick the lock on the first door, only to find it barred from the inside. He hadn't thought of that. If they were all secured that way, he was finished before he even began.

Slipping around the building, he managed to crack the lock on the second door in less than a minute and was relieved when the knob turned and it fell open. He pushed it just enough to get his head through for a peek inside. If anyone was standing close by, he would have no choice but to run back to the fence and climb over.

He found himself peering along an empty corridor that was illuminated by a single electric lamp on the ceiling. He slipped in, closed the door behind him, and hugged the wall, his eyes and ears perked. He could make out recesses for doors down both sides of the corridor, all entrances into offices and examination rooms. He started down the hall, stepping lightly. That part of the building was completely silent.

Halfway along on one side he found a wider recess and double doors that led to a stairwell. From his glance at the lobby directory that afternoon, he knew that the Records room was in the basement. He took the stairs downward into the darkness. From above he heard some voices calling and doors squeaking and slamming.

When he reached the basement, he found another set of double doors that opened onto the middle of a corridor. An electric lamp burned at either end, casting faint yellow light. He stopped to listen for anything untoward. Then he stepped into the corridor and looked up and down. The door with RECORDS painted on the leaded glass was the second one on his left.

The lock was sturdier than the ones on the outside doors, and it took him five sweating minutes and four sweating attempts to finally get the tumblers to click. When the first one went, it echoed like a pistol shot. He wiped his face and palms with his handkerchief, wondering if there was some kind of electrical alarm hooked to the door. It could even be the silent type that sounded only in the guard's kiosk. It was too late to worry about that now.

He stepped into the dark room and closed the door behind him. There were file cabinets lining the right and left walls of the room, then a back-to-back row of cabinets in the middle of the floor. Three desks were pushed against the back wall, each one with a lamp overhead, for the convenience of the staff.

He waited and listened for another minute, just to be sure no one had detected him. He didn't know where to begin, so he spent the next forty-five minutes going from one file cabinet to the next and reading the labels affixed to each, burning up so many lucifers that the air fairly reeked of sulfur. He finally found the one he was looking for: Admissions Records from 1906. If Prince John's recollection was correct, this was when "Emma Lee" would have been admitted.

Now came the dicey part. There was no way he could examine the records by the light of lucifers. If he took the file and left, it could be discovered missing. Which could alert someone and then he might never find the woman. He would have to risk one of the electric lamps and hope that no one would happen by and notice. The desks were partially blocked from view by the file cabinets, but anyone passing by could still see the light.

He took half the files in the drawer, a twelve-inch stack, and went to the desk farthest from the door. He turned on the lamp and sat down. It took him about ten minutes to go through the stack. There was no one he recognized as Emma Lee. Most of those admitted were men, and of the half-dozen females with files, none was the right age. He went back for the other half and carried them to the desk, and after a quick shuffle, put the men's files aside. When he opened the fourth of the women's files, he found her.

The top sheet was a standard form, carefully noting the essential data for the subject, "Emma Lee Smith." She was twenty-three years old, five feet two inches tall, weight 110 pounds. She was described as in good health, though her appearance was "unkempt." Her date of birth, place of birth, and current domicile all were marked "Unk."

According to the notes scribbled in the file, Emma Lee Smith was brought to the hospital in a "state of extreme agitation" by two police officers, one detective and one patrolman, both unnamed. They reported that she had been acting wildly, and they believed she had a problem of a sexual nature, which took the form of "an addiction to promiscuous behaviors." It was also noted that she seemed to be "suffering from delusions."

Valentin was so engrossed that he did not hear the footsteps padding along the corridor. He almost jumped out of his chair when the door squeaked open.

A man's voice called, "Dr. Rose? Is that you?"

Without thinking about it, Valentin muttered, "Uh-huh," keeping his head down and his voice gruff.

There was a pause that seemed to last an hour, and then the man said, "All right, sir. Good night," and closed the door.

Valentin allowed a half minute to let his heart stop pounding, then went back to the file. He found a page in a doctor's scribble detailing her treatment. From what Valentin could tell, it consisted mostly of an administration of various drugs to control her mania. He noted morphine sulfate among them. The entries covered a period of fifteen days.

He flipped through some more pages that had little information other than short notations of examination results and medicine doses. As he closed the file, he found a Release Form attached to the back. According to the notation, the patient had been released into the custody of the New Orleans Police Department. No reason was provided. He skipped to the bottom of the page and the box for the signature of the party who had accepted custody of the patient. He let out a grunt of surprise. He stared at the box to assure himself that the name he was reading was that of Lieutenant J. Picot.

He replaced the files and used his picks to lock the doors again. He went out the way he had come in, carefully retracing and covering his exit at each step. He crept up the stairs without making a sound and hurried back down the first-floor corridor, heading for the door.

"You there!"

He stopped and turned around slowly, ready to fight or bolt. A woman in a nightgown stood ten paces behind him. She looked to be in her fifties, gray haired, thin as a rail, with wild eyes that glared into his face. Her hands were on her hips and she looked him up and down like he was a misbehaving schoolboy.

"You're not William!" her incensed voice brayed down the hall.

Valentin said, "No, ma'am."

"Where's William?" she demanded.

"He's...*upstairs*," Valentin whispered, lifting his thumb.

She tilted her head back and took one hand from her hip to wag a finger in the air. "Ah, of course, he is!" With a nod of dismissal, she turned around and marched off toward the lobby.

Valentin stopped when he reached the door. He heard voices far-off, one raised in surprise, the other the woman's, demanding to know "William's" whereabouts. He pushed the door open and lingered until he sensed a dead space in the night. Then he slipped out, trotted to the fence, and clambered back over. His bones creaked as he walked south on Henry Clay. He thought for a moment that he was getting too old for this kind of business.

As he made his way along Magazine Street, the detective went back to pondering, fixing on the scribbled signature on the bottom of the sheet. It shocked him. Why had Picot, of all people, signed for Emma Lee Smith's release? It could be simple coincidence, though Valentin's gut told him otherwise. The copper had been just a bit too close to this case all along. He had thrown up obstacles. It was probably Picot who had sent the thugs to Robertson Street to try and divert his attention. He didn't have any idea why, but Picot was in the thick of it.

It was almost 3 A.M. when he reached his door, exhausted by the trek. He suddenly recalled the morning when he had come up the street to find Dominique on his doorstep, her pretty, nervous face watching him, filled with hope that he could save her. He pushed the image away.

He unlocked the door, climbed the stairs. He went into the bedroom, and as he undressed, he glanced at the bed, then dug out the old blanket and carried it to the couch for another night.

SEVENTEEN

Lieutenant Picot came out the door of his office at eleven o'clock and saw St. Cyr standing at the sergeant's desk. The Creole detective didn't see him and he quickly stepped back.

Picot was galled. He couldn't believe St. Cyr was already on the streets and, no doubt, with his nose back into the killings of the musicians and the black girl. Any other man who was blighted with the terrible murder of a paramour, five other killings right under his nose, and his regular woman leaving him would have given up. Not Valentin St. Cyr, though; here he was with that same dogged look about him, his brow knit, eyes piercing, and shoulders set forward, like a fox on the scent of something.

The lieutenant realized that he had made another mistake by not keeping a tail on him. Though who would have thought St. Cyr could go right back to the case like that? But then what else would he do?

It didn't matter. Picot decided that he wasn't going to hide or run from the Creole detective. He came out the door, strolled over to the sergeant's desk, and produced his best lip-curled, lazy-eyed glare. "Now what?" he inquired.

"I want to check an arrest record," St. Cyr said. "A woman named Emma Lee Smith."

Picot's face tightened. "It's Saturday morning," he said.

"I thought you might do me the courtesy."

There was something lurking behind St. Cyr's impassive facade. He knew more than he was saying. Picot was sure of it.

The lieutenant glanced at his sergeant, who was regarding St. Cyr with a testy copper stare. He crooked a finger. "Let's go," he said, and led the detective back to his office. He went around and sat down at his desk, making a point of leaving his visitor standing. "All right, let's have it," he said.

"A woman was released from the Louisiana Retreat into your custody in December of 1906," Valentin said. "I want to find out what happened to her."

As soon as he started, Picot's brow knotted, though whether it was anger or something else, Valentin couldn't tell. The copper said, "What woman?"

"She went by Emma Lee Smith."

"And how do you know about her?"

"I saw the release form."

"You what? Who the hell—" Picot caught himself. "All right, so what about it?"

"It had your signature on it."

Picot picked up a pencil and began driving its point into his desk blotter, his jaw clenching.

"December of oh-six?" he said. "That was going on two years ago. You know how many people we put in and pull out of those places? I can't remember one damn woman."

"Then I'd like permission to go downstairs and see her card."

"I said it's Saturday and they're closed."

"Someone's got a key."

"And what if I say no?" Picot griped. "What are you going to do? Find a way to break in?" He snapped out an accusing finger. "That's what you did, didn't you? Went out there and broke in. I oughta goddamn arrest you right now!" Valentin didn't change his expression, and Picot gave him a furious look, then shrugged his thick shoulders. "I could go pull the damn card. But there ain't no point. I can tell you what it says."

"You remember her now?"

"Yeah, I remember her," Picot said, blustering. "And the reason is because she died in custody." He went back to tapping his pencil in a rapid staccato. "We picked her up and brought her in, me and one of the officers. We put her in a holding cell and she wasn't in there but a couple hours, and one of the matrons found her. She had torn up her petticoats and made a rope. She hung herself off the bars."

"Why did you take her out of there?"

"To testify in a court case."

"What kind of case?"

"She claimed she was molested by one of the attendants."

Valentin mulled the information. There had been no mention of anything like that in her records. "Do you know why she was in there in the first place?"

"I guess because she had a nervous condition."

"Did her family put her in there?"

"I don't know," Picot said sharply. "You're the one who saw her record."

"Is there a death certificate?"

"Of course there's a goddamn death certificate!" the copper groused. "You want to see that, too?"

Valentin did want to see it. He just didn't want to push the lieutenant any further. He was already on shaky ground. Picot was mixed up in this case in some way, and he was afraid of scaring him into doing something rash, like destroying evidence.

"You can go on up to St. Louis No. 2 and see her bier, if you don't believe me," Picot added. He dropped the pencil. "Now it's your turn. You ain't told me why you're interested in her."

"I heard a story," Valentin said.

"A story. Is that right? What story would that be?"

"You remember Prince John?"

Picot's stare went past the detective to the wall behind him.

"The story is that a couple years back, this woman went chasing after him," Valentin said. "And he and the other fellows in that band took advantage of her. They spent a day and a night using her like a whore and then put her—"

"So you spoke to Prince John," the copper broke in. "And here I thought that nigger bastard was dead."

Valentin stopped, now catching something raw in Picot's tone. "He's not," he said. "I talked to him. And he remembered this Emma Lee."

"I'll bet he did. So what?"

"I believe she's connected to the murders."

Picot smiled dimly. "And how exactly would that be? Seeing she's been dead, what, two years?"

"I don't know. That's why I wanted to see her records."

"I don't think so," the copper said, suddenly brusque. "I'm not showing you anything. You're not going to be meddling in any more police business. That's over. And if you think you can run to Tom Anderson and get him to lean on me, you'll want to think twice. 'Cause he won't do it. I know that for a fact." He stood up. "Emma Lee Smith was a madwoman who committed suicide. She's dead and gone. She's got nothing to do with any killing except her own." He jerked his head toward the door. "Now, why don't you leave, so we can get back to wasting the taxpayers' money?"

There was much that Tom Anderson loved about Storyville. Even the District's grimier corners were in a strange way dear to him. He lorded over its streets, grand and mean, and each of its denizens, from the highest-toned madam down to the dime-a-trick Robinson Street crib whore, with a benign eye. He truly did have everything a man could desire: wealth, power, respect, pleasure, and all in abundance. He had used his wits and worked hard, yet he knew that he had also been very lucky.

Except he also had to pay a grim price and had traded parts of his soul, his honor and dignity, to keep what he had. The image of the King of Storyville, like some monarch in a fairy tale, was made of whole cloth. He, like the neighborhood he governed, was something other than what appearance proclaimed. Behind the public facade was a much darker, bloodier, more tawdry face. It was the way of the world that he ruled.

He had started out modestly, selling penny newspapers. He parlayed talk he picked up on the streets by informing to the police, a common stool pigeon. When he went into business with a small café, he found his police contacts held him in good stead. He played both sides of the street. His hands, if not bloody, were certainly stained with corruption. It was the grim price he paid.

He indulged his mood for approximately one minute. Then he shoved it aside and went back to the message that the chief had delivered. Tom Anderson's ear was so attuned that as soon as O'Connor started talking, he knew that St. Cyr's name was going to come up. He marveled for a moment at his own antennae when it came to Storyville and wished at times that they weren't so sharp.

That was the easy part. What followed astounded him. The information that the chief passed on was startling enough. When he told Anderson what he wanted him to do with it, the King of Storyville had a rare moment of dislocation. For that one instant, his universe was turned on its head.

Automatically, the chief went on, all business. He laid out the facts and waited for a response. Anderson told him not to worry. He'd take care of it, as he always did. He would handle St. Cyr and the rest of the matter. They spent a moment in small talk, then he put down the phone. He sat for a long time wondering if once this blew over, things would ever be right again.

Valentin asked for Mr. Anderson and leaned against the end of the bar to wait. The Café was a different place in the daylight, the dusty streaks of sun through the window playing over the liquor bottles with their oak brown and amber gold contents. One of the janitors was down on his hands and knees, working his way along the bar with a can of paste and a rag, rubbing the rail to a high gloss. It was an odd, quiet time, a preamble to all the noise and motion of the night to come.

Tom Anderson sent a fellow Valentin didn't know with instructions to step upstairs. The detective found the King of Storyville standing by the window, looking down the line. He did not turn around when the detective stepped through the door, just kept gazing into the distance. Out over the Gulf, tall, dark clouds were rising. There had been much rain this autumn, even for New Orleans, and now more was on the way.

Valentin was alert. When Anderson did not immediately attack the business at hand, it meant that he was not to be pressed.

"I want you to know how sorry I am about the death of that young lady," he said without turning around. "It was a terrible tragedy."

Valentin said, "I understand that you took care of sending her body home."

"It was the least I could do for the poor girl. I made some contacts with government officials down there. They reached her family. They'll lay her to rest."

Anderson paused and gestured for Valentin to join him at the window. When the detective reached his side, he returned his idle gaze to the panorama beyond. "Sometimes I feel like I could stand here all day and just watch the street," he murmured. "It really is like seeing a play unfold. And sometimes I feel like I wrote the whole thing, that those people out there are just dancing at the end of the strings that I hold in my hands."

Valentin rolled his eyes. Anderson was getting dramatic, something he did on rare occasions. The detective wondered if he had been at the brandy bottle already. There was another half minute's silence and then the King of Storyville turned around and went to his desk. He settled himself, getting down to business. Valentin leaned against the window frame.

"Are you ever going to come back to work?" Anderson said.

"I don't know."

"Then what do we have to discuss?"

"Six deaths."

"What about them?"

"I'm not giving up the case."

"Yes, I heard."

"So I'd like to ask you some questions."

Anderson stiffened slightly. "Such as?"

"I want to know why you would do the bidding of a piece of shit like Picot. To the point of letting a killer go free."

Anderson's face flushed from pink to crimson. Valentin had spoken to him without respect, in the tone he used to brace street rodents when he wanted information and had no time to waste.

The white man swung around in his chair and pointed an angry finger. "Don't you talk to...," he sputtered. "You have no idea... You're on dangerous ground. You're forgetting that I can make one telephone call and Justine will be on her way to Evangeline Parish in chains."

Valentin shook his head. "No, sir, I don't think she will," he said, now letting a bit of deference color his tone. "Because then I would be digging even harder and you'd have to have me shot to get me off it."

"That's not out of the question," Anderson snapped. "You and I had an agreement."

"I broke it. Those musicians and the landlady were one thing. A young woman who had nothing to do with it was murdered."

After another tense moment, Tom Anderson relented, sagging back in his chair. He stayed silent, pondering. He should have known better to get involved in such business. He should have known that once St. Cyr latched on, he would never let it go, no matter what he said. There was nothing to do now but let it play out. He cleared his throat and saw the detective straighten, perking his ears.

"As I understand it, Lieutenant Picot did a favor for someone," he began. "It was one of our civic leaders. A city alderman."

Valentin knew he wouldn't divulge which alderman and didn't ask. "A large favor?"

"Yes, a large favor. I believe it had to do with making a body disappear. There was an unfortunate accident, you see..." He waved a hand. "Never mind, that part doesn't really matter. What happened was Picot came to the alderman and said he needed help with a problem of his own. Asking that the favor be returned, in other words. He made it very clear that he would divulge what he knew if he didn't get what he wanted. The alderman called Chief O'Connor. The chief called me."

"What problem did Picot have?"

"I don't know and I don't want to," Anderson said. "That's the truth. Whatever it is, he's taking a huge gamble over it. He's going way out on a limb and pushing some powerful people." He looked at the detective. "How much do you know about him? Other than he's a jackass."

"He's been in uptown as long as I've been here," Valentin said. "He's no dirtier than the rest of them. He doesn't like me and I don't like him. We've tangled a few times." There was more, but he wasn't about to share it now.

"Do you have anything you could use against him?" Anderson said.

Valentin shook his head. "Not anymore."

"Well, then, that's the situation. I'm caught in the middle of it and I don't like it, but for now that's the way it is." He sat back. "Now the question is, what are you going to do about it?"

"I'm going to find out who committed those murders. I think I'm getting close. I saw a—"

"Stop right there!" Anderson said. "I don't want to know any more about it. You better think about how far you're willing to go. You realize that I can still crush you like an insect. I can have you beaten to within an inch of your life. I can have you judged insane and locked up in Jackson. Since you already know your way around there." He stopped to allow the message to sink in. "You're so determined to get to the end of this matter, you're even willing to sacrifice Justine over it."

"I'll take care of her, too," Valentin said thickly.

"Will you? I hope so. Because now it's her life on the table. And you don't have anyone else, do you?"

He drew himself up and waved a heavy hand, dismissing him.

Valentin put the word out on Basin Street, and within an hour Beansoup showed up at Mangetta's and strolled over to the corner table, hands stuffed in his pockets, and looking all serious.

"Heard you wanted to see me."

"You know where on Girod Street Miss Justine stays now?"

"Umm...yessir, I do. It's up past Baronne."

"What's the number?"

"Can't remember exactly. I know the building, though."

Valentin drained his glass in a quick swallow and stood up. "Let's go," he said.

When they got to Girod Street, the kid pointed out the house, then whispered that the forest green Oldsmobile parked at the curb belonged to the Frenchman. That meant the owner was upstairs with Miss Justine at that moment, doing who knew what. He stole a glance at Mr. Valentin's face. It was unreadable.

Valentin sent him off with a Liberty quarter. Beansoup walked away, glancing over his shoulder, and when he got to O'Keefe, he stopped to peek around the corner. Something was about to happen. Maybe Mr. Valentin was going to call the Frenchman out. Maybe they'd have it out right there on the street. Whatever it was, he didn't want to miss it.

But Mr. Valentin found a doorway and settled in to wait.

In less than an hour, the Frenchman emerged. As soon as he stepped onto the banquette, his driver came trotting from his post in front of an apothecary. Baudel got into the automobile as the driver hurried to turn on the ignition, then bent to crank the engine. The car started on the first pull then rolled off in a puff of gray smoke.

Beansoup watched the car go by, feeling like he'd been cheated. Mr. Valentin hadn't done a thing. He'd just let the man who had stolen his girl walk away like it meant nothing at all. If it was him, he swore, there'd be a dead Frenchman lying in the street.

He figured there was nothing else to see and strolled off, heading back to the District. As long as Mr. Valentin was busy on Girod Street, he might find himself some action in Storyville.

Valentin reached the landing and stood in front of the door. He heard music from a gramophone. He knocked, lightly, then harder. The music stopped. There were footsteps from inside and Justine opened the door. She stared at him for a long few seconds. "Valentin...I heard. About the girl, I mean. I'm so sorry. I saw her that day, too."

She stood back and he stepped inside. She closed the door behind him. He paused to survey the fine furnishings. "You've done well," he commented. His voice was without inflection, as if he was a stranger offering an observation.

She made a vague gesture and came up with a tiny smile. "Are you sleeping in your clothes now?"

He looked down at his rumpled shirt and sagging trousers. "I've had a few hard days," he said.

"But you're all right?"

"I'm as good as I can be," he said, now peering closer. "What about you? You look..."

"Pale?" He nodded. "I stopped taking that medicine. It doesn't feel so good."

"I need to talk to you," he said.

Justine sat down heavy on the love seat. "Talk about what?"

"I need to know what Tom Anderson has on you."

"I'm so sorry, I—"

"What is it?" he demanded harshly. "Six people are dead in this city! Dominique was murdered because someone was trying to get to me. Tom Anderson's trying to stop me, too. And he's been using you and whatever it is you've got hidden."

She cringed. "What good will it do if I tell you?"

He took a breath to calm himself. "It's all tied up together, Justine. It's a piece of the puzzle. Because I have to know. Because I'm asking."

She knew the look on his face. He wasn't going to give up. And there was something else: he was trying to keep up the hard front, and yet she detected a glimmer of concern for her. She hadn't felt that in a long time. He was looking to protect her, too. She wished she had just gone ahead and confessed a long time ago and gotten it over with.

"I'll tell you," she said resignedly. "I'll tell you." She nodded to the armchair. "You'll want to sit down."

Valentin sat, staring at her face.

"Please, I...I'm..." She bowed her head and folded her hands before her. "All right...," she whispered. "All right."

She had done this a hundred times in her dreams. She had rehearsed the way she would tell him so that he would understand. She could never bring herself to do it. Now she didn't have a choice.

She began by going back miles and years, arriving at a clearing along the bayou outside the town of Ville Platte, and the dirt yard of the little shack with the rotting clapboards, leaking tin roof, and the smell of dead things moldering in the soggy earth.

It happened on a Saturday in August in the steaming height of summer. Her father stood in the doorway, barefoot, in a greasy shirt, his suspenders hanging down to his knees. He wore that look, the glowering, dull-witted grimace he saved for his children. He looked like he knew that they had been sent there to torment him and he was the one to make them pay.

She told Valentin that if the Regulators ever needed proof of what they said about the races mixing, they could point directly to her father. She had never solved the mystery of how her mother, her true mother, had ended up with such a black-hearted devil.

She glanced at Valentin, her mouth dipping. "Course I found out later just how stupid some women could be about their men," she said. "Even some who oughta know better."

Maybe, she said, he hadn't looked so bad courting, in his one good suit, his nut brown face scrubbed, his black hair oiled slick and shiny and parted down the middle, his mustache trimmed and waxed, his pale eyes sneakily shy. He must have been some picture, given what he became.

It was even more puzzling that she and her brothers and sisters—each one decent-looking and not without wits—had sprung from his loins. Maybe they hadn't; maybe they belonged to the man who plowed the next field over. That would explain a lot. It could have been what made this one who claimed to be her father so evil. Or maybe it was his wife, their stepmother, a weak stick of a woman, cold and angry when she wasn't sick in bed. Their true mother had died giving birth to a ninth child. Justine barely remembered her face.

She stopped for a moment and saw the way Valentin was watching her, cautiously, almost tense, as if he might jump up and run away at any second. She knew she could keep him there, though. Once she took him deeper into the story, he wouldn't budge. She knew that much about him. So she went back to it.

It was a bad day. There had been many of those, too many to count, but this one was the worst. As the hours had passed, the old man had revisited his still in back of the house and worked his way through his brood, finding an excuse to lay his razor strop to each one in turn. There had been bruises and red welts, shrieks and howls, sobs and tears.

Though Justine was the youngest girl, she tended to the others as best she could, with cool mud and embracing arms. Except for her brother James, two years her senior, she was the only one with any spirit left. The rest of them had been broken by the years of cruelties.

The sun went down and the old man got meaner by the minute. James would be next to face his wrath. Then it would be her turn. The old man would lay the strop aside to free his hands so he could grab her by the hair, drag her around back of the house and into the shed, where he would lift up her shift and have at her. He had done it before, and she knew it would be worse if she tried to fight him. She saw that raw, hungry look in his bloodshot eyes and knew he was already fixing on it for this night.

She looked at Valentin, saw his deep gray eyes staring.

"But this time, it didn't go like that," she told him.

"No?"

She shook her head.

Something was different that evening.

There was an alien weight in the already thick air, like the electricity before a storm. The riotous scent of the wildflowers that grew along the banks of the bayou mixed with the biting odor of ozone. Even the low light over the slow-moving water had shifted to an odd ancient green. The shadowy and haunting ether had the other children huddling and rolling their eyes in fear. All the while, Justine felt a sharply bitter taste rising from her gut.

James stood at the corner of the house, his face grim and rigid as he flexed his hands. Justine looked at him, sending a message, and he gave her the faintest nod.

"It was a signal," she murmured. "I had to get to the old man first."

Valentin said, "Get to him how?"

She had moved into his field of vision, turning his vile gaze away from James. He snorted, wiped the back of his hand across his nose in one direction, then the palm across his mouth in the other. His red, dirty eyes swam as he tried to focus.

She was wearing a cotton shift that doubled as a nightdress and clung to her supple body at every curve. She knew how she looked. When she was alone and in front of the tall mirror in the back room, she guessed that in the shift, with nothing on underneath, she could make a man slaver like a dog or rut like a pig. Especially a drunken cur like her father.

Now she saw Valentin draw back a little, like he didn't want to hear what was coming, and yet couldn't quite tear himself away.

The old man stood at the top of the gallery steps, watching her with those wet eyes, too drunk to see that it was a show. She gave him a small smile and moved off around the side of the house, her body swaying like a willow tree.

"I heard him come down off the gallery and I knew I had him," she said.

He laid the strop over his shoulder, hitched his pants, and descended the broken steps, stumbling and biting off a curse as the bottom one gave way. He walked past James as if he wasn't there, trailing Justine like he was in a trance.

She got around back of the house and slipped into the shade of the live oaks at the edge of the bayou. She stood by the stack of firewood he had bent her over time and again. It was one of his special places.

His mouth twisted into a vile excuse for a grin as he stepped closer, his fingers already beginning to fumble at the buttons of his trousers, thinking that she had finally gotten the idea and wasn't going to fight anymore.

He was so mesmerized that he didn't sense James coming up from behind to his side, two paces off his right shoulder. When he caught the movement in the corner of his vision, he stopped and swung his head to one side like a bull.

"Goddamn you," he growled at his son. "Get around front."

James stayed where he was.

"I said"—he reached up to grab the strop in his fist—"get back around front until I'm done here!"

James said, "You're done now," and brought up the knife that he had been holding at his side around, and with one long stride, planted it squarely in his father's barrel chest.

The old man's eyes bugged and his mouth dropped open in a soundless shout. Justine gaped as James jerked the knife out. Blood, bright red, bubbled and cascaded down her father's shirt and trousers. His hands flapped to the gaping chest wound, as if he could stanch the red fountain. With a keening groan, he took two staggering steps, dropped to his knees, and then pitched forward onto his face. He tried to crawl, clawing into the gray dirt, leaving a slug's trail of red. His mouth opened and closed like a swamp turtle's.

"Then James gave me the knife," Justine said.

Valentin watched her. "And what did you do?"

"What did I do?" Her face looked terrible, paling, almost ugly. "I said, 'Turn him over.' James grabbed hold of him by the shirt and put him on his back. I pulled the buttons off his trousers."

"Oh, god...," Valentin said.

"I'd had dreams about it," she said, her eyes glazing and her breath coming short. "Dreams that I had him like that. And I would turn him over, open his drawers, and cut him like a hog while he was still alive." Her hand was in a fist, as if she actually held the blade.

Then her grip relaxed. "I couldn't do it."

The old man was looking up at her in shock and horror, his

hands now pawing weakly at the seeping hole in his chest. She bent over him and held the knife poised for an endless second, then straightened and threw it into the bayou. She felt her stomach revolt and bent her head away to vomit. She was sick and dizzy and had to lean a hand on the woodpile for support. Her father was gasping something, a strangled prayer for Jesus to save him. He could barely move now, though his eyes were open and staring. He was soaked in red from his chest down.

Justine said, "James grabbed hold of him by his shirt and dragged him to the bank. The water was deep, maybe eight or ten feet. He stopped, like he was waiting for me. So I went and helped push him down the bank."

Grunting and cursing, they shoved the heavy body until it tumbled through the slick mud, over the exposed roots, and into the oily green water. He rolled one time, so that the last thing he saw before he went under was the pitiless eyes of his son and daughter staring down at him.

She sagged as if all the air had gone out of her. Her shoulders hunched and she clasped her hands. "So that's my secret. I took part in the murder of my father. I came this close to cutting off his yancy with a knife. Then I helped my brother push his body into the bayou while he was still breathing and I watched him die."

Valentin waited a few seconds. "What happened after that?" he said softly.

"My stepmama saw what was going on and she took the other children inside where they couldn't see. Later on that night, we got them all packed on the wagon and we rode into town."

They rode through the darkness toward Ville Platte. Justine remembered that the children did not speak at all and would not look at her or at James. They huddled numbly in the back as the wagon creaked along through mist as heavy as cotton. When they got to town, they said muted farewells and they all went their separate ways.

"Went where?" Valentin said.

"To Lafayette. We had kin over there to care for them. James went on. He took another name and moved to Atlanta."

"And what about you?"

"I ran off and joined up with a show. I took Mancarre for my name. That was my grandmama's family."

As she wound her story down, Valentin could not read anything from her face, only that she looked at once young and old.

"So this Lieutenant Picot, he knows all about it?" she asked him.

"Yes. And so does Tom Anderson. That's what they're using to tie my hands."

"I wonder how they found me," she said.

"A little bit of investigative work is all it would take," Valentin said. "You made a mistake when you took a family name. It connected you. Picot went looking to get something on me. When he couldn't find anything, he went after you and somehow he found out you came out of Evangeline Parish. He contacted the sheriff down there and got the story. Then he told Mr. Anderson."

"And why do they care about it?"

"Because Picot's trying to protect someone. He's using it to stop me before I find out who it is."

"And what happens if you don't?"

He looked at her. "Then most likely Picot will arrest you on suspicion and turn you over to Evangeline Parish. You'll be tried for murder. Maybe not in the first degree, but it would be murder." He paused, watching her face pale even more. "But...if I do stop, they'll leave you alone. Which would be fine, except the murderer of six people goes free." He stared vacantly past her. "Six people, including Dominique."

The clock chimed lightly the quarter hour. Justine's chin came up stubbornly and some of the color returned to her cheeks. "I don't expect you to do it, Valentin," she said in a measured voice. "You don't owe me nothing."

He stayed quiet, staring at the swirls on the carpet. She was wondering what else she could say that—

"The question is why," he blurted suddenly. "He's got Tom Anderson dancing to his tune. He's using this trouble from Ville Platte to keep me off the case." He stood up and started to pace. "Because he's protecting someone. A woman. I can't figure out why."

"What woman?"

"Her name's Emma Lee Smith."

Justine gave him a look. "Smith?"

He flipped his hand in the air and said, "I know, I know. That was the first thing I noticed. You'd think she could come up with something better. Anything."

"Who is she, then?"

"A white woman who went crazy back-of-town and got put away in the Louisiana Retreat. But then Picot went and took her out of there. She ended up killing herself in jail. So he said."

Before he realized the words were coming out of his mouth, he was telling her about finding Prince John and his tale about the woman, followed by his own adventure breaking into the Louisiana Retreat. It was like all the times he had come home and talked to her about his work. Though she had never finished school, she loved to read his books and was plenty sharp, with a natural cunning that matched the criminals. After a while, he was talking to her about all his cases. He found her a level-headed judge, and she enjoyed the gossip that often swirled around his work. It had been a long time since he'd done it, and he could see her whole bearing changing, like the weight on her was easing. It took her mind off her own troubles.

"She died while the coppers had her?" she said when he finished his story. "Maybe they killed her. And now they want to cover it up."

He considered, then shook his head. "I don't believe it. I think she's still alive. And I think she's mixed up in the murders.

"I wonder...," he began. "Picot said she's in St. Louis No. 2. But I wonder who's really in her bier. It could be some crib whore they collected off the street. Or from the morgue. Who would ever know?" He pictured the slimy mulatto attendant with his awful yellow teeth, leering. "It would be no trouble at all."

Justine saw the look on his face, taut with intent, his eyes sharp as blades and fixed on something invisible. His body had tensed and his breath came shorter as he walked up and down the Turkish rug. He stopped his pacing and stood there for a few moments, then started moving again, this time for the door, breaking the spell.

"Thank you for speaking to me," he said, the familiarity evaporated and the distance was back, stretching between them.

"Wait a minute," she said anxiously. "Now what? I mean what about me?"

"Don't talk to anyone," he told her. "Not to Anderson, not to Picot. No one. Not even your...friend here."

"I've never told him anything," she said in a muted voice.

Valentin fixed her with a look that lasted a second but seemed to cling to her. Then he opened the door and walked out. She listened to his footsteps going down the stairs in a quick patter, moving away, and yet the look in his eyes lingered behind.

EIGHTEEN

The sun was almost down when he arrived back in the District and walked through the Saturday evening crowd on Basin Street, catching the music and laughter from windows of the mansions and the raucous jass that was bubbling out from the open doors of the saloons. Along the way, he encountered no less than a dozen familiar faces, rounders for the most part. They gave him the wary, narrow-eyed looks he expected: They'd all heard about Dominique, of course, and probably his battle with Anderson. He was damaged property, to be sure, so they all nodded and moved on.

Frank Mangetta was installed at the end of the bar, regaling the regulars with a story of two whores who had drawn down on each other in the middle of Gallatin Street in a fight over a fancy man. Both missed their targets, as he related it, but the fellow who was so lucky to have two women doing battle over him was not quite lucky enough. He stepped into the path of one of their stray bullets and fell dead in the street, a smoking hole over his left ear. The two women swore off their dispute and at the cemetery bawled in each other's arms as the man they both loved so dearly was laid to rest.

The Sicilian was about to launch into another no doubt even taller tale when he saw Valentin sidle up to the bar. He gaped in surprise, then excused himself and hurried to serve the detective personally.

"You feel all right?" he murmured, his black eyes warm with concern.

"Yes, why?"

"Because you've been having a rough time. I heard about the girl. I couldn't—"

"I guess I'll live," Valentin cut him off curtly, and, to Mangetta's astonishment, downed his Raleigh Rye in one swallow and grabbed the bottle to pour another glassful.

A half hour later, he was two-thirds of the way through the bottle and three-quarters of the way to properly drunk.

Mangetta hovered nearby, watching worriedly. The detective seemed to be dissolving by degrees into the whiskey. The saloon keeper saw all the familiar signs of a sloppy drunk: wet and bleary eyes, clumsy fingers, head nodding all loose like his neck was broken. He heard the detective mutter, then laugh, then mutter some more, casting mean looks around the room, like he was looking for a fight.

The Sicilian finally couldn't stand it any longer and stepped up to him. "Valentino...*compare*...*basta,* eh?"

"Fuck *basta,*" Valentin said, his gray eyes all bloody.

"*Andi—*"

"Fuck it!" the detective snarled. "Fuck all of you. Motherfuckers!" Along the bar, heads started turning. He jabbed a bellicose finger at Mangetta. "Especially that fucking Picot. I got the goddamn goods on him, Frank. I'm gonna finish him and that damn woman, too!"

"What the hell are you talking about?" Mangetta hissed urgently. "Be quiet!"

Valentin snarled something and grabbed for the bottle. Mangetta was quicker. "That's enough!" he said, snatching it away. "You're drunk. Now, quiet down."

"Quiet down or what?" he barked.

"Or what?" The saloon keeper's olive face turned shades darker. "Or I'm gonna throw your *guappo* ass out on the street there."

Valentin pushed himself away from the bar and stood there, tilting one way and then the other, working to keep his glaring eyes fixed on the saloon keeper. "*Va'fottere,*" he said. "You and all the rest of them and especially that fucking *Picot!*"

He turned around and marched slowly and righteously to the door, banging his shoulder into the jamb as he passed outside. Mangetta came from behind the bar and went to stand in the doorway, watching him weave away. He thought about following him, then decided against it. He had never seen Valentin this way, and who knew what he'd do if challenged. So he let him go.

A voice behind him said, "What the hell's his problem?"

Valentin was coming up on Basin Street, taking careful steps as he tried to slow the spinning of his head. It had been a long time since he had downed so much so fast, and he was reeling all over the banquette. In his drunken state, he felt himself slipping toward an abyss, as images of Dominique, alive and then dead, came into his mind. He knew dimly that if he let it happen, it would ruin everything, and so he put his total intent on placing one foot in front of the other and making it to his destination.

By the time he reached the thoroughfare, he could walk with only stumbling, and he had put thoughts of poor Dominique aside. He cut down the alleyway and pushed through the back door of Fewclothes Cabaret. When the cooks saw who it was, they nodded and went back to work. He stepped to the porcelain sink and splashed cold water on his face. Then he drew himself a cup of coffee from the urn, carried it to the corner of the kitchen, and sat down on the sacks of rice that were stacked there.

He was into his third cup when Beansoup came bursting through the back door, his face all sweaty and his hair sticking up in clownish licks.

Valentin could now stand without swaying and got to his feet. "Well?" he said. "What happened?"

"He called for a hack," Beansoup reported. "After he left, I went inside. One of his coppers said he went to Prytania Street."

"Prytania Street?" Valentin said. "Are you sure?"

"Sure, I'm sure, goddamnit!"

"All right, all right," Valentin said. "Did you get—"

"Number twenty-six hundred twenty-three."

"Are you sure it was Prytania Street?"

Beansoup treated him to a scathing look.

"What about the car?"

"Waitin' on the corner," Beansoup said, all snappy in his efficiency.

Valentin carried his empty cup to the sideboard and splashed another handful of cold water on his face.

"All right," he said. "Let's go."

The car, a two-seater Model N with a bed for hauling attached to the chassis behind the seats, was parked across Iberville Street. Sitting behind the wheel was a former New Orleans patrolman named Whaley. He had wanted off the force and Valentin set him up with a job driving and running errands for one of the uptown ward bosses. He felt like he owed the detective and was always ready with a favor, like using his employer's car on personal business.

When he saw Valentin coming across the street, he jumped down and started twisting the crank. The engine hiccuped, coughed, and gurgled before settling down to a steady chug. Valentin pulled himself into the passenger seat. He offered Beansoup his hand, one professional to another. "Good work!" he said. The kid's elfin face broke wide open in a giddy smile and he waved happily as they drove off.

The automobile was light and as quick as a hornet, and they sped down Basin Street and then south on Canal, dodging around the streetcars. The cool wind was welcome, helping to clear his head some more. There was a light rain coming down when they got across town and it stung his face like needles. Whaley asked if he wanted him to stop and raise the canvas top. Valentin shook his head and told him to keep going.

They turned onto St. Charles for a few blocks, then headed down St. Mary Street toward the river. A right turn onto Prytania Street took them into the Garden District, the preserve of New Orleans' upper-class Americans. Old and heavy sycamore and live oaks spread their limbs over the small mansions and broad Victorians, all of them pristine and kept that way by the efforts of staffs of Negro help, some of whom were just now trudging home. Valentin wondered if Picot was somehow connected with one of the servants. He hoped to find out directly; that, and more.

The elaborate comedy of getting drunk and shouting vile threats had worked exactly as he had hoped it would. One of Picot's spies had rushed into the precinct to pass the word along. Valentin had stationed Beansoup close by, and as soon as the lieutenant bolted out the door, the kid strolled in. Picot had left word where he was headed, and it took Beansoup no time at all to pry the information loose.

It was on the money. When they reached the twenty-five hundred block, Valentin saw the police hack parked up ahead. He told Whaley to pull to the curb and shut off the engine.

He hit the banquette at a trot. The hack was on the other side of the street, a uniformed officer up on the seat huddled under an umbrella as the rain drizzled down. Valentin passed by unnoticed, then slowed his steps, trying to peer through the blue darkness and silver mist.

He heard them before he saw them. First was Picot's guttural voice, whispering urgently. The woman murmured an answer, low and calm. Valentin saw them then, picking Picot's short bulk and a woman in a walking dress out of the shadows. Picot held an umbrella in one hand and waved the other one about in agitation. The woman didn't move at all.

There was no way that Valentin could get close enough to hear them without being spotted. He could tell that Picot's utterances were getting shorter, until he was down to a couple words at a time. There was pronounced silence in the midst of the hissing rain. The woman moved away as lightly as if she was gliding on air. Picot watched her go, then turned around and started for the hack, walking slowly, his head bent. He pulled himself up and the driver snapped the reins. The slap and jangle of the harness faded away.

Valentin stopped across the street from No. 2623 just as the woman was lifting her skirts to mount the gallery steps. The door opened, but before she went in, she turned to look back down the street in the direction that Picot had gone. Valentin saw her face then; and the profile cast in the pale yellowish light from the foyer looked like a cameo. She wasn't any servant. She was white, handsome in a patrician way, with molded cheeks, an upturned nose, a full, bowed mouth. Her hair was rolled above her ears in the coiffure of the day. Her gaze lingered in the distance, and then she stepped inside. The door closed behind her and the light was gone.

Valentin looked up and down the street, then crossed the wet cobbles to the corner of the property. The house was stately, a Victorian with a wide gallery and leaded windows draped with lace curtains. It was bordered by a wrought-iron fence atop a brick footing. The lights were on inside and he could see figures moving about like a shadow box.

He took a quick glance over his shoulder, then vaulted over the fence, praying that the family didn't keep a dog around. He stood in the front garden among the azaleas and dogwoods, listening for anything unusual, then stepped out from the foliage and crept around to the side of the house. The branches of a poplar tree stretched overhead, sheltering him from some of the downpour. Still, anyone who was looking later would find his footprints in the soggy earth. There was nothing he could do about that now.

He came up on the window of leaded glass and peeked inside on the dining room. A man in a three-piece suit sat on the left side of a large table that was covered with white linen. He appeared to be in his fifties, slender, graying, not in the best of health, and yet he had that unmistakable look of wealth about him. His elegant hands rested on either side of a plate of untouched food. There was a full wineglass before him. Across the table was another place setting and an empty chair. It appeared that the woman had gotten up in the middle of her dinner and gone out in the rain to meet Lieutenant J. Picot. Valentin wondered what would drive her to do that.

Now the door on the other side of the room slid open. The man didn't look up as the woman took her place at the table. He used his napkin to dab his lips with an expression of distaste, then returned it to his lap.

Though the sheer curtains veiled his view, Valentin was closer now and could study her. She had a certain society presence, and yet there was something not quite right about the picture. After a moment, he realized that she looked somehow familiar, though he couldn't imagine that he'd ever met her. Still, there were features of her face that reminded him of someone. Her dark hair was done up just so. She wore a fine but simple day dress. The gold band on her finger glimmered in the light of the electric chandelier.

When she picked up her knife and fork to resume eating, the man started speaking in a measured voice that was too low for

Valentin to hear, but the detective could sense the tension. Between sentences, the ends of his mouth turned down in bitter curls and the cords in his neck went taut. The woman responded with a cold look, then abruptly pushed her plate aside and lifted her wineglass to her lips, staring at him over the crystal rim.

The wind came up, rustling leaves that scratched the window above Valentin's head, and the woman looked over. He stood still, holding his breath as her eyes appeared to move down and stop at his face. He knew she couldn't see him out there, and yet a smile, knowing and bemused, crossed her face for a few seconds. The man said something sharp and she turned back to him, her gaze going icy and her nostrils flaring. The man dabbed his thin lips once more.

She drank off what was left in her glass and stood up, looming over to mutter a harsh sentence. He drew away, treating her to a stare that was almost hateful. She went to the doors, threw both sides open, and made her exit. The man gazed at her empty chair with morose eyes.

The wind rose up again, shaking the branches, and Valentin used the cover to slip back along to the front of the house, over the fence, and onto the banquette. He went all the way around the two blocks, startling Whaley when he came up from behind.

"You see what you wanted to see?" the driver said.

"I saw who I wanted to see."

"You mean Picot?"

"I mean Emma Lee Smith."

Whaley's Irish brow furrowed. "Who?"

"Let's go home," Valentin said.

Lieutenant Picot had no sooner walked back into his office and taken off his dripping coat and hat than Tyler scurried in, looking more and more like a rodent every time he came into view. He reported that someone had told someone who told someone who told him that St. Cyr was seen riding in a tin lizzie that was being driven by an ex-copper named Whaley, just as the car turned off St. Mary Street onto St. Charles, heading downtown.

Picot turned away so that Tyler couldn't see his face. All he could think was that St. Cyr knew, goddamn him! He was getting closer and there would be no stopping him. It was as if two runaway trains were steaming toward each other and there was nothing he could do to keep them from crashing.

NINETEEN

The street door squeaked ever so slightly and footsteps came padding up the stairwell. Valentin thought he was dreaming. When a step creaked—the loose one, sixth from the top—he came fully awake and swung his legs off the couch.

From the light through the window and the noise from the street, he judged it to be around eight o'clock. Too early for visitors. He rubbed his face to get some blood flowing and perked an ear. There was no doubt, someone was coming up the stairs at a hesitant pace. He kept still and waited.

After Whaley left him at his door, he dragged himself upstairs and collapsed on the couch like a dead man, wearied to the bone by the days of strain and the lingering effects of the glasses of Raleigh Rye he had swilled at Mangetta's.

Blearily, he looked at the door and saw no key dangling. He had been so exhausted that he had forgotten to lock it. So whoever was now stepping onto the landing could simply turn the knob and walk right in. He couldn't remember ever doing that before and hissed out a curse at his stupidity—now of all times.

He got to his feet, willing his stiff legs to support him. At least he had taken his shoes off and could move without making a sound. Feeling around to his back pocket, he drew out his sap. If this visitor came bursting in with a gun or a blade, he'd be in trouble.

He sensed the body on the other side of the door, heard a soft sigh of movement. He held his breath and gripped the sap tighter. The silence lasted five seconds. Then the steps retreated down the stairs.

He jerked the door open and quickly moved onto the landing. Justine stood gazing up at him. She looked abashed, perhaps a little fearful, her eyes blinking nervously. She glanced at his hand and he realized that he was still gripping his sap at a right angle to his body, as if ready to swing it.

He put it back in his pocket. "What are you doing here?" he asked her. When she didn't answer, he said, "Won't you be missed on Girod Street?"

"I don't care," she said. "If he wants to put me out, I don't care." There was another silence, this one longer. "I'm sorry, I don't know why I came here." She turned to descend the stairs.

"Wait," he said.

He told her to have a seat while he got cleaned up.

She said, "I can make coffee. If you don't mind, I mean."

"All right, then."

She went into the kitchen, got the percolator going, and took down cups. It was a ritual she had repeated hundreds of times, and now she felt clumsy and out of place, as if she had been gone a year, rather than a handful of days. Where had she lost that time?

When she heard him come out of the bathroom, she poured two cups full and went about fixing his the way he liked it, with much cream and just a touch of sugar. She carried both cups into the front room. He sat down in the morris chair. She sat on the couch.

In the quiet moments that followed, she sensed something kinder in his bearing, if not forgiveness for her betrayal, at least respite from the cloud of blame that had been hanging over her.

She knew it was not in his nature to forswear a slight and was grateful for his small act of mercy.

"Did you find her?" she asked presently.

"What's that?"

"The woman you were looking for. Did you find her?"

"I did," he said, then went about recounting the hours since he had seen her last.

"I put on a show up at Mangetta's and got Picot to run to her. I followed him and saw her with him. Then I spied inside her house." He described the silent drama between husband and wife that played out on the other side of the glass.

Justine said, "Are you sure it's her?"

"Who else could it be? The name on the house is Gerard. Maybe Smith really is her maiden name. Maybe it's all fake. I'll have to find out who she really is and how she's tied to these killings." He paused. "It might not be easy. Her tracks might already be covered. I don't know why Picot's helping her, but if there's anything in the police files, it's most likely gone."

Justine considered. "So she still might get away clean."

"Yes, she might."

She looked at his face and allowed herself a thin smile. "She won't," she said. "You won't let her. No one ever beats you, Valentin."

He didn't know what to say to that. He got a sense that she wasn't just talking about the ne'er-do-wells whom he had run to ground over the years and decided it was best to let it pass.

Justine stirred her coffee absently. "And what about after?"

"After?"

"After it's finished. Whatever happens. What will you do then?"

He got quiet, staring moodily into his cup. "I don't think I'll be able to stay in New Orleans. Not after all this. I went against Tom Anderson, the police, the mayor's office. They won't let that pass. I'll be finished here."

She nodded slowly, as if she had expected it. For a brief second, she felt her heart dropping and fought an urge to weep. "And what about Ville Platte?" she said in a muted voice.

"Nobody will touch you," he said. "I'll make sure of it."

"You think you can do that?"

He shrugged. "Nobody beats me."

She gave him a sharp look, saw that he wasn't mocking her.

He put his cup aside and stood up. "I'm sorry," he said. "I don't have much time. I have to finish this today."

"Shall I stay here?" she said, keeping her gaze averted.

"No. Go back to Girod Street." He saw her shoulders heave. "I'll come see you later."

When she got up to go, she wanted to say something, or touch him for a moment. Then she saw his eyes had turned inward, intent on the task at hand, and she left without another word.

The offices of the *Picayune* were in a block building on the corner of Camp and Poydras streets. As always, the Sunday edition was posted in the front windows of the building, and at the moment three men stood reading, two with their hats tilted back and their hands in their pockets, the third, an older gentleman who perused the front page with a magnifying glass that would have done Sherlock Holmes proud.

It was Valentin's habit to read the newspaper every morning without fail. He realized now that he hadn't seen one in days, so he stole a quick glance as he passed by. There were no screaming headlines. He hadn't missed any catastrophes. He glimpsed at a story about the Bryan-Taft race for the White House, another about problems with sugar imports from Cuba.

He hadn't come there to read the news, and he walked around the side of the building and then into the alley that ran in back. A set of stone stairs led down to the basement. He peered in through the dirty glass, then pressed the button that was mounted on the jamb. He had to ring three more times before a face appeared and then the door opened.

Valentin had known Joe Kimball for years. They traded information: Kimball picked up useful whispers from the newsroom, and Valentin passed along talk from the street, which Kimball then used for his own purposes. The man would have been a star reporter, except for his appetite for Raleigh Rye, so prolific that it put the rest of the guzzling staff of newspapermen to shame. He simply could not be trusted to put two coherent sentences together when he was into his cups, which was most of his waking hours. So he tended to the paper's morgue, dealt in information, wrote the occasional brilliant story, and drank his poor liver into oblivion.

There were those who whispered that Kimball was Bas Bleu, the mysterious and infamous scribe who wrote a column that eviscerated everyone of importance in uptown New Orleans, including, at times, Tom Anderson himself. Valentin didn't believe it. No one who drank like Kimball could keep anything secret for that long.

He was a useful source, though. Especially at times like this, when Valentin needed background in a hurry. Drunk or sober, Joe Kimball was a walking library of information about the citizens of New Orleans. What he didn't know, he could find in his basement cavern. He was a red-faced, red-haired, short, and burly sort who liked to fight almost as much as he liked to drink. Almost.

When he saw who was at his door, he grinned, crooked a finger, and led his visitor through a file room that was crowded with rows of steel cabinets and into his office. Valentin moved some newspapers off the second chair and sat down. He reached into the pocket of his suit jacket. "Something to brighten your day," he said, and handed over a pint of Raleigh Rye.

Kimball cocked an eyebrow. "Well, aren't you a kind fuck?" he said. He opened a desk drawer. "Join me?"

"Not right now," Valentin said.

"Ah, yes, you probably had your fill last night, eh?"

Valentin was startled. Kimball laughed as he put a dirty glass on the desk, unscrewed the cap from the bottle, and poured. "I heard about it, and I said, that ain't Mr. Valentin St. Cyr. No, sir." He pronounced the name the American way: *Saint Sear.* "No, no, I said, he's up to something." He took a drink, smacked his lips. "Is it about those murders?" Valentin nodded. "Something you can let an old friend in on?"

"Not yet," Valentin said, still amazed that the news had traveled so far so fast. He wondered if he had overdone it.

"So, what will it be?" Kimball said, spreading his arms to take in his little domain.

"There's a party on Prytania Street. Twenty-six hundred block. Name of Gerard."

Kimball's brow furrowed and Valentin could almost hear the pages flipping inside that round head. "That would be... *Louis* Gerard," he said. "Old French family. Their money was in...shipping, I believe."

"Was?"

"There's not much left of it. There are three sons. Louis is the only one who amounted to anything at all. He's a state court judge, but not a very good one. It was some sort of political appointment. He takes care of the money that's left. He's a stick."

"What about his wife?"

"His what?"

"He's got a pretty young wife."

Kimball tilted his head to one side and frowned. "He does? I thought...he was a widower. And I never heard about any second marriage. Are you sure?" His face got all serious. It wasn't often he didn't have the dope at his fingertips. He drained the last inch of liquor and stood up. "I'll be back in a few minutes."

It was closer to a half hour. Valentin spent the time reading the Sunday paper that he found on the desk.

When Kimball did come back, he didn't bring much. "Well, I still have a brain after all," he quipped. "It's like I thought. There's nothing about Louis Gerard getting married a second time. No announcement at all. No recording of a license. You sure the woman is his wife?"

"She was wearing a gold band."

"They might have been married somewhere else." He thought for a moment. "Or..."

"Or?"

"There's one other reason that licenses don't get announced," Joe Kimball said with a sneaky grin, and went about refilling his dirty glass.

Valentin knew that any stranger on the avenues of the Garden District would be noticed and reported. So he couldn't linger on the Prytania Street banquette for too long. Someone would surely call the coppers, or they might have Pinkertons on the payroll. New Orleans was full of private police forces.

He didn't have time to wait anyway. By his reckoning, the last of the murders had been committed, and he still had nothing but pieces. With every passing minute, it became more likely that the guilty party would get away clean. Valentin had come to it too late, and all he could think to do was to push on until something gave way. If that didn't work, the killer would go free, Valentin would have failed, and Justine's history would have been exposed for nothing.

His instinct told him that the woman in the house across the street was his only chance. He guessed that she was the one he knew as "Emma Lee Smith." She might have committed the murders, though he didn't think so; at least not all of them. She wouldn't possess the strength to hold down a hulking man like Noiret or to wrestle someone the size of Treau Martín over the railing of a ferry. Nor did her husband, Mr. Louis Gerard, seem up to such tasks. Of all the players, only Picot would have that ability.

In the lingering mist from the rain, 2623 Prytania Street looked like something out of a storybook. It was one of those charming bungalows that had been well kept over the years. There was still color from the flowers in the garden and in pots on the gallery.

At that moment a Negro was raking wet leaves into piles along the fence and a woman, most likely his wife, was sweeping the gallery. It was a common domestic tableau for a Garden District home, though not usual for a Sunday. It could be that they were expecting company later. Valentin wondered if the man had noticed any footprints in the soggy earth.

He was fidgeting about, expecting the coppers to show up at any moment to chase him away, when the front door opened and Mrs. Gerard leaned out to speak to the Negro woman. He watched for a few seconds, then stepped off the banquette and into the cobbled street. It was time to play his hand.

The man working in the front garden caught movement, raised his head, and regarded the stranger approaching the gate. The two women on the porch stopped talking and turned their heads. They all stared, though not one of them looked surprised, almost as if they had been expecting him.

The lady of the house, a mental patient who had supposedly died two years ago, looked down at him with a challenge in her eyes.

"Sir?" the Negro said, taking a step closer.

"I'm looking for a woman named Emma Lee Smith," Valentin announced.

Mrs. Gerard didn't flinch. She said, "Thomas, let the gentleman in."

Thomas laid his rake against the fence, unlatched the gate, and held it open. Valentin stepped through and walked halfway up the stone walkway. He stopped and said, "Emma Lee Smith."

"I don't know anyone by that name, sir," the white woman said.

Valentin was about to draw it out and anger the woman by asking the Negro couple if they knew such a person when there was a rustle of movement at the side of the house.

Two men came around the corner, one a high-yellow mulatto, the other dirty white. They were large men, thick in the trunk, with flat, sullen faces adorned with mustaches. Both were dressed in poor-fitting suits and each wore a derby. They fixed cold eyes on Valentin. Either a signal had been passed or some feral sense told them there was an intruder on the grounds and they had come sniffing.

As soon as Valentin laid eyes on them, he experienced a wrenching moment of clarity, as if the blanket of gray mist had been pulled back from that small plot of land.

He knew the men; or at least he knew their type. They came out of one of the city's foulest corners, places like Gallatin Street, where they grew up mean and stupid, with whatever dim conscience they might have possessed beaten out of them at an early age. They would leave school, if they ever went in the first place, roam the streets in packs like animals, and do prison farm time sooner rather than later. They would go to sea to befoul and bloody ports from Helsinki to Havana. When they were not on the water or in stir, they spent their nights in the cheapest sporting houses and saloons, and their days doing dirty work for their betters, including acts of murder.

Now two of these creatures had appeared on the Gerard property, stalking like alley dogs to stand at the bottom of the gallery steps and lock their stony stares on the Creole detective who had trespassed onto their territory.

Valentin's mind fell still with the stark realization that these two, singly or in tandem, had murdered the four musicians, the landlady on Philip Street, and Dominique. He felt his pulse quicken as he stared from one to the other, probing their faces for the one who had brutalized her. It was the white one; he had a raw and guilty look about him. Valentin knew that he was the one who had come to Magazine Street looking for a Creole detective, met a black-skinned girl who put up a fight, and proceeded to strangle her to death.

The detective ran down his chances for taking them both if it came to that. This day, he had thought to pack his full arsenal—sap, stiletto, and pistol. He could only imagine what kind of weapons they were toting and wondered how much damage he could do before they got to him. These thoughts passed in a matter of seconds, and then the tension in the air broke suddenly as the lady of the house stepped to the edge of the gallery, just back from the still-dripping eaves.

"Did you say Emilie? Why, that's my name." She spelled it out for him, enjoying the game.

Valentin pulled his gaze off the two toughs and looked up at her. "That's a coincidence," he said easily. "But this is 'Emma Lee.' The last name is Smith. Or at least that's the name she used. I'm sure it's a fake. The woman was a mental patient at the Louisiana Retreat on Henry Clay. I want to locate her."

He thought he saw the woman's face flush a shade. Her gaze never flinched, though.

"Thomas," she called out. "Do you know anyone by that name? Or with such a history?" Thomas didn't answer. "Maybelle?" she said over her shoulder.

The woman whispered, "No, ma'am."

Mrs. Gerard's voice grew an edge as she addressed the roughnecks stationed at the bottom of the steps: "What about you, Mr. Dawes?" The white man turned his head slightly. "No? Mr. Williams? Is that name familiar to you?" No response was expected and none offered as the pair continued to glower. Throughout the little performance, the woman's brownish eyes never left Valentin's face as they shifted from demure to carnivorous. Now she shrugged and said, "I'm so sorry, sir."

"Well, I must be mistaken, then," he said, and turned around. Thomas was still holding the gate open. As he passed through, Valentin glanced at the Negro and saw the tiniest sign of warning in the dark visage. He nodded slightly as he stepped onto the banquette and walked away without looking back.

He got on a St. Charles Line car and found a place in the back where he could sit alone and think.

There wasn't a lot of time before they would be coming after him. He had smelled it in their sweat, read it in their faces, and he had heard the vicious little shriek that was hidden beneath the white woman's quiet patter, as taut and shrill as a plucked wire. He was the last thing standing between her and the rest of her life as the judge's wife in the lovely house on Prytania.

The raw truth of it was a relief. This was no chess game anymore. He would have to fight it out with the two animals and match wits with a very clever female. If he was going to finish it.

By the time he stepped off the car at Poydras Street, he had settled down enough to have the inklings of a plan. First came an absolute necessity to stay ahead of them. If he got cornered, he'd be dead.

He came up on the intersection at Magazine Street and crossed over where a half-dozen carriages waited for passengers who were having Sunday dinner at the Banks' Arcade. He picked out one of the drivers, a Creole who looked like he knew what he was about. He slipped him a Liberty dollar with instructions to watch the street door at No. 330 and give a whistle if anyone went in.

The driver agreed with a quick grin of gold teeth and then proceeded to demonstrate his whistle, a screech so loud and sharp it gave the horses a start.

Valentin hurried across the street and up to his rooms. He changed clothes, packing his weapons again: the whalebone sap in his back pocket, the stiletto in a sheath strapped to his ankle, his revolver in his coat pocket. The pistol was loaded, but he took no extra cartridges. If six didn't do the trick, he'd be through anyway.

He had been going over the details of his plan in his head and now set it in motion. He went out, locked the doors, and with a wave to the Creole driver, walked down to Bechamin's to use the phone.

He still had one critical weakness: Justine. They might go after her; though that would surely bring Picot's little house of cards down. If they had any sense, they'd leave her alone. The thought gave him no comfort.

He finished his calls and left out of Bechamin's to walk to Girod Street, checking over his shoulder for a tail. He sensed someone lurking, but he couldn't be sure. Most likely, it was one of Picot's people, which suited him fine. He would have left a trail of bread crumbs if he'd had any.

When he got to the Girod Street address, he found Paul Baudel's Oldsmobile parked at the curb. At Valentin's approach, the driver straightened from his slouch against the fender and made a move toward him.

The Creole detective held up a hand and said, "No one's going to be harmed," and waited. The driver studied his face for a few seconds, then shrugged and let him pass.

Valentin went inside, climbed the stairs, and knocked on the door. When Justine opened it, she gave a start, her eyes going wide. He stepped past her.

Baudel was standing in the doorway to the bedroom in a silk dressing jacket. He said, "What is this? Who are you?"

"I'll just require a moment," Valentin said.

Baudel said, "Justine?" in a demanding voice.

She said, "Paul, please," with a tone of familiarity that stung Valentin.

"You need to leave, sir," the Frenchman said.

"I'm going to talk to her first," Valentin said.

Baudel threw up his hands. "Then I'm calling the police," he said, and marched to the corner table that held the telephone set.

Valentin dropped his voice. "Don't stay here tonight. It's dangerous."

"What are you talking about?"

"You're in a fix right now. Just don't stay here tonight."

"Where am I going to go?"

"Miss Antonia's. She's got men watching the doors. I've already called her. It's just for tonight."

She watched his face. In the corner, Baudel was griping into his telephone set about an intruder on the premises at 966 Girod Street.

Valentin said, "You'll do it, then?"

Justine sighed and nodded. "All right, yes."

Baudel put down the phone. "The police are on their way."

"I'm leaving," Valentin said.

"No, you are not, sir!" the Frenchman snapped, and reached out with a clumsy hand to snatch his cuff.

Valentin whipped his hand away and let out a blunt laugh that this dandy was playing tough. He wondered what kind of fool Justine had fallen in with. "You'll want to stay out of it. You understand?" His eyes were so hard that Baudel took an involuntary step back, looking like he was about to swallow his Adam's apple whole.

"When the police show up, you can tell them my name is Valentin St. Cyr," the detective said. He looked at Justine, who appeared not to know whether to cry or laugh over this little drama. Then he walked out and closed the door behind him.

When he got to the banquette, he nodded to Baudel's driver and sauntered away. It would be at least another ten minutes before a patrolman would show up, and by that time he would be long gone.

———

One of his telephone calls from Bechamin's was to ask Whaley to find Beansoup and then meet him back-of-town, with or without the automobile. He also told him what was going to transpire and gave him the opportunity to refuse. The man had a family, after all.

Whaley wouldn't hear of it. Not only did he feel an obligation to Valentin for helping him find a situation; he was still enough of a copper to want to see a couple of murdering miscreants taken down. Valentin didn't miss the edge of excitement in his voice. Doing the bidding of a ward boss had to be boring work.

TWENTY

It was seven o'clock when he turned the corner onto Rampart Street and saw the Ford parked there and Whaley and Beansoup pacing up and down. They shook hands solemnly all around, though Whaley and the kid could barely hide their excitement. When Valentin tapped the bulge under his jacket, Whaley pulled back the lapel to reveal a Colt .38 double-action in a shoulder holster.

Valentin laid out their plan and sent Beansoup on his way. Then the detective jerked his head and he and Whaley left the car and stepped into a saloon two doors from the corner called Johnny's Spot. As they went through the door, Whaley said casually, "You see who's across the way?" He laughed. "Little sot name of Tyler. You know that one?"

Valentin said, "Oh, yes, I've been expecting him."

With Beansoup stoking the fires, the whispered word went ahead of them along Rampart Street.

Valentin St. Cyr, the Creole detective, the one who had not a week ago had a woman murdered in his rooms, was back on Rampart Street with a onetime copper in tow. Those who might not know him from Storyville remembered him from the days when Bolden was roaming the same haunts, blowing jass so hot and loud it could wake the dead.

They started at one end and worked their way west. They hit all the saloons, and at every one there was music playing. Downtown New Orleans and even Storyville might be quiet on a Sunday night, but out on Rampart Street, it just kept going. If there was any day of rest, it was Monday.

Musicians from every corner of back-of-town New Orleans would show up because they could still play whatever they wanted there. There were few whites, some Creoles and Italians, many colored. The music they made was fast, loose, and raw, the way it was supposed to be.

Valentin and Whaley hadn't been on the street more than an hour when Beansoup caught up with them and passed the word that a couple of brutes had showed up and looked to have mayhem in mind. They were tossing saloons, slapping customers, demanding information about a Creole named St. Cyr, who was somewhere on the street, accompanied by an Irish copper.

For the next hour, Valentin and Whaley stayed one step ahead of Dawes and Williams. Beansoup sprinted back and forth, all red faced and sweating as he dropped hints in one direction and delivered reports of the miscreants' progress in the other.

The two had been throwing down whiskey at every stop, getting drunker and meaner as they passed over Jackson Avenue, Freret Street, then First and Second streets.

Now it seemed that the detective and his partner had turned into ghosts. Everywhere Dawes and Williams went, the word was "just missed them" or "just left out." Some street Arab kept chattering that St. Cyr and his partner were only one door ahead.

They could never quite catch up, and so by the time they reached the saloon on the corner of Rampart and Fourth, they were so drunk and angry that they were ready to either kill the next person who crossed them or turn around, go home, and forget about this rich people's mess.

Then they stepped back out onto the corner, looked across the street and saw the prey they'd been stalking, standing on the opposite banquette with his hands in his pockets. The other one, the red-faced Irishman, was nowhere in sight.

The two criminals exchanged a greedy leer. The mulatto Williams moved a few paces to his right to cut off an escape. Though they all knew if St. Cyr ran now, he'd never live it down.

A few doors back, a jass band started up with the merry tootle of a clarinet over a rattling drum and a thudding bass and then, like a call to battle, a braying trumpet. When Valentin heard the raucous music and realized that they were going to perform their bloody ballet to horns and drums, he couldn't help but smile.

"What's funny, you?" Dawes called over. A half second later a hammer cracked and he jerked his head around to see Whaley standing to one side of Williams with his Colt pistol pointing directly at the mulatto's temple.

"I think that right there is amusing," Valentin said.

The saloon door opened and two fellows stepped onto the banquette, saw what was happening, and dove back through the door. Five seconds later it banged again, and a dozen men came tumbling out to watch the action.

Williams croaked, "Dawes? What the hell?" Sweat was running down his face.

"Go ahead and shoot him then," Dawes muttered with a bloodshot glare. "You think I give a good fuck?"

Williams cried, "Shut up, goddamnit!"

"Go ahead," Dawes repeated. "He ain't nothin' but a no-good nig—"

The word was cut in half as Valentin stepped up in a blur that Dawes barely caught out of the side of his drunken eye to

crack him on the jaw with his whalebone sap, a sweeping up-
percut that fractured the bone as it tore it out of the socket and
knocked him off his feet and onto his back. Then, in a motion
that had both Whaley and the man he held at gunpoint in open-
mouthed gapes, Valentin switched the sap to his left hand and
drew his pistol with his right, leveling it at the middle of the
broad forehead.

Dawes grunted through his shattered jaw, a harsh animal
sound. Valentin stared down into his eyes, saw the same hollow
darkness that Dominique must have met in her last moments of
life, without a spark of pity, nothing human at all. Even now,
Dawes was too stupid to be afraid, lying there and looking up
with the blank gaze of an idiot.

Now heads were poking out of saloon doors all around the
intersection, and pedestrians stopped to point and stare. They
were gathering a crowd. The next five seconds hung suspended,
as the raging, crazy, faraway sound of jass played on. Valentin
had a gripping urge to pull the trigger, feel the percussion, hear
the roar and see the hole explode in Dawes's brain, then watch
the cold light in those eyes die.

Instead he said something, one word that no one quite
caught, and abruptly backed away. From far off came the winding wail of a police siren. He was out of time. He looked over
at Whaley. "Can you hold them?"

"I've got them," Whaley said. "And it would be my pleasure
to shoot either one or both."

A few seconds later Valentin had disappeared, evaporating
into the darkness in such a sudden moment that no one on the
scene could testify as to which way he had gone.

The rain had started falling again, the sort of cool and silky
drizzle that visited New Orleans in those days just beyond the
end of summer's tail, but before the cold of winter set in. It fell
from the night sky in thin, lazy drops, drenching the Crescent

City from the Irish Channel to Metairie. Everything that was moving slowed. At any given window, a silhouette might appear as someone looked up at the misty moon. It was that kind of rain.

Anyone who happened to be at a window near the corner of St. Charles Avenue and Fifth Street would have seen one citizen who appeared to be in a hurry, a Creole-looking fellow in a gray suit, his shoulders hunched, as he strode along the banquette in the direction of Prytania Street.

Valentin ducked under the boughs of the live oaks, thankful that they still held some foliage and wishing for once that he wore a hat. He turned the corner at Prytania Street and walked to No. 2623.

The gate creaked and he followed the stone walk to the gallery. He had barely set foot on the first step when the front door opened. Maybelle filled the doorway, her face severe as she looked him up and down. Thomas stood a few feet behind her, wearing an expression that was beyond wearied.

Valentin stepped onto the gallery and waited. Thomas whispered something to his wife, and her eyes welled up and her dark face softened with a grave pity. She stood back to let the detective pass, bowing her head now, as if in prayer.

He had stepped into a sitting room that was appointed with heavy, elegant furniture. A crystal chandelier hung overhead. There were sconces on the walls and a portrait of a respectable gentleman in midcentury dress mounted over the mantel, glowering down at the living in their foolish and hopeless travails. The dining room Valentin had seen the night before was to his left. It was as much as the detective could discern, as the room was in dim shadow, the lamps turned down low.

Thomas spoke up. "Did you kill them two?"

"They'll be dead soon enough," Valentin told him. "You can go to their hanging."

"Lord, have mercy," the woman murmured.

Valentin looked at Thomas and the Negro said, "They in the room in back, the study. Both of them." He gestured to the doorway on the other side of the room. "It's that way."

Valentin walked to the doorway that led into a corridor. Thomas said, "She carry a gun. One of them Derringers. A two-shot."

Valentin touched his pocket and felt the hard outline of his own revolver, the Iver Johnson that had been his firearm of choice since he was on the force. He had fired it at another person only once, and that one time had finished the life of Eddie McTier. He had come within a breath of putting a bullet in Dawes's head back on Rampart Street. Now, as he moved along the hallway and pushed the door to the study wide, he wondered if he would have to draw it—or use it—again.

He found them seated on café chairs on either side of a small table that was set before the window. Louis Gerard was on the left side, Emilie sat opposite. The husband was turned in profile, like he was sitting for a portrait, and did not turn to look at the man in the doorway. Emilie was facing the detective, her hands folded modestly in her lap. She seemed neither surprised nor concerned to find him standing there dripping rainwater on her polished floors. Indeed, her face was clear of any emotion at all. Together, the two of them could have been waiting for the maid to serve tea.

The room was as well appointed as the parlor, with not a speck out of place. Bookshelves with volumes in fine bindings occupied the walls on each end, with a library table before one of the stacks. Rain ran down the window like veins that glistened against the darkness outside. It made quite a picture.

Valentin felt a rush of anger at these people and their privilege. There were six men and women dead because of them, and yet they sat primly, unaffected, as if secure in the knowledge they weren't going to pay. They did not plead innocence. They did not hang their heads with guilt. They did not rage or cry for mercy. They simply sat, waiting to see what would transpire next, patient, but all too ready to be done with this unpleasantness.

Or maybe not. Looking closer, Valentin detected something lurking beneath the gray flesh of Louis Gerard's face and stirring in the eyes of his young wife. They were both working to hide tempests that were raging behind their stolid expressions.

One way or another, Valentin didn't care anymore. It was time to finish it.

"I've come about four musicians who were murdered. And the landlady of a house on Philip Street. And a woman...a woman named Dominique Godet."

Emilie now cocked her head slightly, as if he had finally said something that had caught her interest. Her husband did not move or give any sign of having heard.

"Please put the pistol on the table," Valentin said. Neither of the Gerards moved. Valentin went into his coat pocket, pulled out his own revolver, and thumbed back the hammer. It sounded loud in the quiet room. "Put the goddamn pistol on the table," he ordered.

Emilie frowned, all peevish, and then opened her folded hands to reveal the Remington Double Derringer she'd been concealing. She put it on the table and crossed her arms like a pouting child deprived of a favorite toy.

Gerard gazed down at the pistol, then turned his head to look at Valentin with an expression of elegant distaste. After a baleful moment, he said, "You should have left us alone."

Valentin said, "Those people are dead and you and your wife are responsible."

Gerard snapped a demonstrative finger into the air. "If I'd had anything to do with those crimes, I would have been within my rights," he said. "Those niggers had at her. At a time when she was not well."

Valentin thought it bizarre the way he spoke about her as if she wasn't sitting right across the table.

"They took advantage of a deranged woman for their own pleasure," Gerard went on. "They held her captive and they molested her repeatedly."

"That's not how I heard it," Valentin said.

Emilie shot him a sudden hateful glance, her copper-colored eyes narrowing. Valentin looked at her more closely. There *was* something familiar—

"And how did you hear it?" Gerard said, his thin lips tightening.

"It doesn't matter," Valentin said. "Because even if what you say is true, you could have called in the police. There are laws against colored men consorting with white women. They would have been hanged."

"No...vengeance was mine," Emilie muttered darkly.

"That doesn't account for the landlady," Valentin said, his voice thickening. "It doesn't account for Dom—"

"They passed her around, you know," Gerard broke in, as if he hadn't heard a word Valentin had said. His wife turned to him slowly, her face darkening.

Valentin said, "I'm sorry, what?"

The man gazed at him, his brow stitching. "Those men passed her around," he said. "She told me about it. They took turns at her. All five of them. Sometimes they went at her two at one time. It went on for a night and a day and another night. Then they threw her out on the street. Do you understand what I'm saying?"

In a monotone, he went on to describe the details of his wife's consort with the musicians. He spoke as if he had been there, describing how she had been undressed and then placed this way and that so that the men could do what they wanted to her. It was a bizarre recitation, delivered in a calm voice that rankled with a slight disgust. All the while, the blue eyes glittered eerily.

"I am a state court judge," Gerard stated with firm conviction. "My family has a sound reputation in this city. Which *she*"—he waved an accusing hand in the direction of his wife— "would have ruined with her behavior. Those men had to be punished and they had to be silenced. If anyone had ever told..."

He went on, now describing the damage to the family name and then switching back to the intimate recitation of the acts she had performed with the jass men in Prince John's rooms. It was Valentin's mistake to be so transfixed by it that he failed to move in time.

The judge had turned yet another corner in his monologue when Emilie said, "That's *enough,* damn it!" snatched up the pistol and shot him the chest, abruptly ending the sordid tirade.

The explosion rattled the windowpanes. There was a scream and rough shout from the front part of the house. Valentin ducked back through the doorway as Louis Gerard let out a grunt of shock, threw his thin arms into the air, and toppled sideways from the chair.

The echo faded and smoke drifted upward from one of the Derringer's barrels. The detective peered around the jamb to see Emilie holding the tiny pistol loosely and staring pointedly away from her husband.

Gerard gasped loudly and struggled like an insect someone had stepped on, trying to raise himself as blood blossomed on his fine white shirt. Then his head fell back on the rug again. He gurgled a final wrenching breath and was still, his eyes open and fixed on the cherubs and angels that had been carved into the cornices of the ceiling.

Thomas came stumping down the hall, with his wife right behind him. Valentin held up a hand and they froze. He stepped back into the room, keeping his Iver Johnson leveled on the woman at the table.

Emilie glanced at him, then looked down at her husband. "Well, that's over," she sighed ruminatively, as if she was talking about a bothersome chore. She laid the pistol carefully back on the table.

Valentin took two steps inside the room, moving to her right side and turning her away from the weapon. He tipped the barrel of his own pistol up so as not to startle her. He heard footsteps retreat down the hall and guessed that Thomas or his wife had run to call the coppers. He wouldn't have much time before they arrived. Still, he stayed quiet until she lifted her head to meet his gaze.

"Why are you looking at me like that?" she said in the sharp voice that superiors used to reprimand their servants.

Valentin kept his own tone neutral. "You're responsible for those killings."

"Those monkeys committed those crimes." She shrugged her elegant shoulders. "Dawes and Williams."

"You got them to do it. And your husband knew about it. He participated."

She glanced at the body on the floor. "Well, now he's paid for his sins, hasn't he?"

"Yes, he has," Valentin said. "But you haven't."

"I think a judge will see it otherwise." She came up with a weird smile. "I mean another judge."

He had to allow that she might be correct. They would have friends in high places. She was, by every indication, insane. She had been molested in unspeakable ways by five low-down niggers.

That addressed the jass men. Cora Jarrell and Dominique would be another story. She would probably claim insanity on them, too. As for her husband, she could say that he was nursing rage over the incident, and she shot him dead in order to get relief from his constant abuse. Valentin could tell by the look on her face, by the expression, almost childishly haughty, that she knew she would get away with it. It was that look that made him decide at that moment to pull her mask apart, bit by bit, and destroy her.

"The problem for you is that the justice you're talking about applies to white people," he said.

She jerked a little, as if she had just received a slap, and her copperish eyes narrowed. "What did you say?"

"You know what I'm talking about." He stepped closer. "To begin with, there wasn't any rape. You went looking for those jass men. And once you got going, you didn't want to stop. You couldn't get enough of them. And they couldn't get you to leave. Prince John had to put you back on the street."

Some of the color drained from her face and she swallowed tensely. "You don't know wh—"

"Even if a white woman behaved like that, the men would still be guilty of a crime." Valentin went on, "They'd hang for sure. But not if the woman is colored."

"What are you *talking* about?" Her voice was rising.

"There's no record of your marriage in the newspaper. No license in the city of New Orleans. Why would that be? Either you're not married at all or you're hiding something. Like you didn't want anyone to know that you're colored."

In one harsh moment, her shoulders shuddered once like a cold wind had just blown through and her eyes got a little wilder. She let out a soft moan and he wondered if she was going to faint on him. Then she gathered herself. She pointed down to her husband, a rude gesture.

"He told me that it had to be done," she said. "You heard him. It was a matter of honor. I had ruined his *family*. He said he wanted children. But after that happened, he told me there weren't going to be any children, not ever, because he would not curse them with my blood. And he'd never know if they belonged to him or some no-good jass player." Her eyes slid sideways. "He took care of that guitar player himself. He wanted to do it. That was after Williams and Dawes got rid of that one in the house on Philip Street. He got me to bring him outside, but it didn't work because that fat man come along and called him away. He sent me home after and then he waited for him. After that, he said he wasn't about to do no more. It made him sick. He said I had to take care of the rest. He said he would put me out on the street unless I fixed it. He said he was going to send me back where I came from."

"Which was where?"

She stared at him with the dazed expression of an animal that has been poleaxed prior to slaughter.

"Well, your name's not Smith," Valentin said with a short laugh. "You might as well tell me. Because it's all over. You're not getting away with anything. You're going to pay for those murders. You think that Dawes and Williams won't talk? They'll throw you over before you can spit. You'll hang right beside them."

There was the briefest moment's hesitation and in that second he knew exactly what she was going to do and so when it happened it was like he was seeing it again. She dropped her eyes to the floor in fevered concentration. Then she set her chin resolutely and began to move.

He said, "Don't," as she snatched up the Derringer and brought it around with the barrel pointing dead at his heart. Without a thought, his finger twitched and his pistol went off. The bullet caught her just below the chin and went all the way through, breaking the window behind her. Her head snapped back to reveal a bloody black hole. She gagged and then pitched forward, her face slamming onto the ornate carpet. Her out-flung right hand landed on her dead husband's forearm, as if he could now escort her down the path to hell. She gasped a few more times as blood ran over the rug and onto the oak floor. Then she was still.

Valentin caught the wail of a siren and then the clatter of a wagon rattling over the cobblestones and coming to a stop in front of the house. A few seconds passed and he heard a familiar voice shout. Footsteps came pounding down the corridor. Picot rolled into the doorway, took one look, and came to a sudden stop.

As Valentin watched in astonishment, the copper's taut mask of anger melted into something awful in its shock and what appeared to be grief.

Picot took staggering steps forward and dropped onto his knees. Two uniformed coppers stepped into the doorway, and Valentin gestured for them to back away. Their eyes switched from him to the lieutenant, who was crouched on the floor, his shoulders now shaking, then back to him. They retreated into the hall.

Valentin moved up behind Picot. He did not want to behold that face at the moment, and he guessed that the lieutenant would not want him to witness his anguish.

"You done shot her," Picot said, and for the first time since he had known the man, his clipped tone gave way to something rougher; country, in fact.

"She drew down on me," Valentin said. "She was about to snap that pistol in my face."

Picot didn't argue. His thick shoulders heaved.

"She wanted me to do it," the detective said. "She knew she was finished. She wanted it over."

"No." Picot let out an eerie-sounding moan.

"Who is she, Lieutenant?" Valentin said.

Picot came up with an agonizing groan. The detective began to see the strings connect to other strings, and he wanted to hear the man crouched on the floor finish the construction.

"Who is she?" he repeated.

Picot let out a strangled sound, between a gasp and a sob, and hung his head farther. His shoulders began to heave. "She's my...She's my sister."

The detective said, "Jesus Christ!" It was one of the few times that he had been stunned beyond his craziest notion.

The copper kept his head down. A long minute of dead silence passed. Then he said, "She's been passing since we left home."

"You and her both."

"Yeah. Her and me both."

Picot reclaimed himself somewhat, but it was agonizing business. He finally managed to get to his feet, though unsteadily. Valentin went to the cabinet in the corner and pulled down a bottle of brandy. He poured a glassful and handed it over. The copper swallowed it down.

His round ball of a head dipped in a slow nod, and Valentin felt a wave of pity for this man who had made his life difficult since the day he had first stepped on Basin Street as a private detective.

In a disembodied whisper, Picot said, "We were out of Baton Rouge. My mama was colored. Whoever my father was, he was white. We never knew him." He glanced over at Emilie for a moment. Then he sighed and continued.

"There was always something wrong with her. She was wild from the moment she came of age. Wasn't no one who could handle her. She was in and out of hospitals. She was so much trouble that I had to get her out of Baton Rouge. I put her in Jackson for a little while. They said she was cured. By that time, I had come to New Orleans and she came after."

"How'd she get with Gerard?"

"I thought I could keep her away from the rounders and the jass players and all them. That's what I thought." He took a shuddering breath. "I knew Gerard from court. He was by himself. I went to see him and told him there was a young lady, new to New Orleans, who might like to make his acquaintance."

"And what did you tell her?"

His voice tightened. "That this was her chance. If she behaved. It looked like it might go all right. I was hoping he would just keep her somewhere, like your...you know. I didn't have no idea he was going to want to marry her. I thought that would fix her for sure."

"But it didn't."

Picot shook his round head. "She wouldn't settle down. Or she couldn't. It didn't take her no time at all, and she was back on the street."

"And that's where she saw Prince John."

"That no-good goddamn voodoo nigger! He used her and then turned her out for the others in that damn band. They all of 'em had her. After that happened, we put her in the Retreat."

"You didn't speak up as kin?"

"I couldn't." He swallowed. "She wanted out. So I said we needed her to testify in court. I signed her out of there. We made up a story that that night she hung herself. That fellow at the morgue did the papers."

"So who's in her bier?"

"I ain't got no idea. We got lots of bodies around here. Too damn many."

Valentin poured more brandy and the copper drank it off.

"It should have been left alone," he went on. "But Gerard wouldn't have it. He told her she had to get rid of those fellows before someone recognized her. Them jass men was showing up in Storyville. Next thing you know, they'd be in the Vieux Carré. He couldn't have that."

"So he found Dawes and Williams in court?"

"That's right. They done the...work. Tracked them down and murdered them, one at a time. They goddamn deserved it, after what they did to her."

"Dominique didn't deserve it," Valentin said.

"They shouldn't have done that...That was the end." He stood up. He did not look at the detective but kept his eyes on his sister's body. When he spoke again, his voice had come down from its jagged heights and had flattened and cooled. "She would have been better off if we would have just let it be. But colored wasn't good enough." He looked at Valentin. "It ain't good enough, is it, St. Cyr?"

"It's good enough, Picot," Valentin murmured. "What about these damn white people? You see what they do every day."

The copper shook his head resolutely. Now he did look at Valentin, and the familiar mask of cold disdain began creeping back across his face.

"No, sir, it's not. It ain't ever gonna be. I gave her the chance to live a good life. All she had to do was behave herself. She would have been rich, happy...She would have done better than any of us." He glanced at the body again. "She couldn't do it, though. And so she's dead." He drew himself up. "Now you and I have something to discuss." Valentin waited. "You're gonna keep all of this under your hat. And in exchange, I'll never say nothin' about your quadroon and Ville Platte. You understand that?"

Valentin gave him a dim smile and said, "She walked out on me, Picot. Do what you want. I don't care."

He said it just to see the look in the copper's eyes, the spike of fear at the thought that Valentin would sacrifice Justine just to see him taken down. Some seconds passed and Picot got the trick. He produced a glower that Valentin knew too well.

The detective said, "I understand, Lieutenant. I agree to the terms."

He went into the hallway where the two officers were huddled with the servants. He told one of the coppers that it would be best if he called the precinct and asked for another wagon. Then he went out into the night and the rain.

He didn't want to go home. He didn't know if he would ever go home again. He rode a streetcar away from the Garden District. It was all but empty on this rainy Sunday night. A good thing. He had just shot a woman to death. He knew that he might have blood on his clothes. He didn't want to look, though. He didn't want to think, either. He just wanted to hide somewhere.

A Canal Line car carried him to Villere Street. He ducked along the storefronts until he reached the Frenchman's.

Most of the crowd that had been there that night two weeks ago were about. They were winding through a gentle ragtime number when he walked in, and in a few jagged notes, the music stopped.

There was a long silence as Valentin went to lean on the bar. Someone produced a clean glass and filled it. It was passed along from one man to the next. Valentin's hand shook when he lifted it to his lips.

He took a sip. "It's all over," he announced in a quiet voice.

Nobody said anything for a long time. Then someone started up the first notes of the tune and the others joined in once more.

He listened to the music for an hour or so, until he had his fill. They stopped playing again when he got up to leave. There were murmured good-nights, small waves of respect.

By the time he had crossed the street, the music began again, a racy number, full of crazy notes that broke open the quiet Sunday night.

TWENTY-ONE

Monday dawned bright, with the first bit of chill in the air as summer finally began to surrender.

Valentin had woken up so many times during the night that he'd lost count. The last time, he sat up, yelled, "Enough!" and heard his voice cascade through his empty rooms. It was something about that echo that told him it was finally over. After that, he slept and didn't wake up until after noon.

It was quiet on Magazine Street, with the usual midday traffic. He made coffee and found something to eat from what Justine and Dominique had left behind. He thought about going out for a newspaper, just to see what the *Picayune* had reported about the killings, then decided that he didn't care.

He sat for a while, trying to think about what was ahead rather than what lay behind him. Then he went in search of one of his books and spent the afternoon hours reading. He hadn't done that in a long time. Later, he got cleaned up and dressed and went out, walking around the corner at Poydras and north to Girod Street. He stopped along the way for a drink.

When he climbed the stairs to knock on Justine's door, it was Paul Baudel, the wealthy Frenchman, who opened it. Valentin looked past him, saw another gentleman on the love seat.

"What do you want?" Baudel said snappishly.

Valentin said, "Is Justine in?"

"No, she's not. You might try Antonia Gonzales's. Isn't that where you told her to go? Well, she went. But she never came back. And she's not coming back, is she?"

He closed the door in Valentin's face.

Tom Anderson called for his automobile and rode down Canal to Magazine Street, the Winton bumping over the cobbles and streetcar tracks. The broad boulevard was buzzing with internal combustion engines. Only a few years ago, there had been no more than a handful of automobiles on the street at any given time. Now it was becoming crowded with them. He wondered what it would be like if these noisy contraptions eventually took over from the hacks and carriages. What a raucous, smoky mess that would be.

His driver pulled to the curb across from the Banks' Arcade. Anderson stepped down and tipped his hat to the gentlemen who were standing in front of the building, waiting for their own automobiles or carriages to roll up. Even at that distance, he caught the sudden buzz of chatter. Tom Anderson, the King of Storyville himself, had appeared right there on the corner of Magazine and Gravier.

Anderson strolled up the block and opened the door next to the tobacconist's shop. His footsteps made a slow shuffling clop on the stairs. When he got to the landing, he found the door standing open.

Inside, placed precisely in the middle of the floor, was a brown leather satchel that looked worn from years of use. There were sheets covering the furniture. He heard the sounds of movement in the back of the apartment but waited, his derby hat in his hand, until the Creole detective appeared.

Valentin came into the room holding a small leather kit in his hand. He didn't appear surprised to see the King of Storyville in his front room and crossed to the satchel, dropped the kit inside, closed and clasped it. He straightened to regard Anderson with an expression so blank he looked like a blind man.

"So, Mr. Valentin," Anderson murmured. "Where are you going?"

"I don't know," he said. "Away from here."

"I'd like you to tell me what happened." When Valentin didn't speak up, he said, "I need that information."

"I know you do."

Anderson said, "Well, then?"

Valentin sat down on the couch. He didn't bother to remove the sheet. He gestured to the morris chair, and Anderson sat down and placed his hat in his lap.

He told the King of Storyville about Emma Lee Picot, as the lieutenant had related it to him. Then there was the incident in Prince John's back-of-town rooms. And the collusion between husband and wife that demanded that they be punished and silenced.

"And so she got those two fellows to hunt down the musicians?"

"That's right. I don't know what she offered. Maybe just money. Maybe a regular fuck. Anyway, they did it. It would have been easy enough if they spent a little time in the saloons." He paused for a moment. "They thought they were being smart about it by changing the method for each of the victims. I guess it didn't occur to them that I'd find out about the band and connect the killings that way."

"So she didn't actually commit any of the murders."

"I don't believe so. She set up Noiret and Mumford. She lured them to their deaths."

"Just those two?"

Valentin shrugged. "Lacombe was a dope fiend and Martín caught religion, so she couldn't get at them. I'm just guessing, though. Maybe if Dawes or Williams talks..."

"And what about the landlady on Philip Street?"

"We'll never know for sure, but she probably saw Emma Lee with Noiret. She might have tried blackmail. Or maybe she just tried to tell someone about it before she got out of town. It didn't matter; she had to go. After that, they went after the others. Mumford, Lacombe, Martín. They had to work fast, because if word got out, whoever was left would run for cover. When they found out that I was poking around, they came after me." He stopped again, drew a breath. "If I had gone home that night, instead of going to Fewclothes, Dominique would be alive."

"Or you'd both be dead," Anderson commented.

Valentin turned his head to stare out the window at the darkening sky. "So, the only one who escaped was Prince John, and he's the one who started it all."

"I understand he's lost his mind, though."

Valentin nodded. "That's a fair claim."

"Seems like a fitting end. Just like Bolden. I'll be glad when this damn jass business is over with. And the sooner the better."

Valentin knew he was wrong. He could see and hear what the King of Storyville, for all his wits, could not. That jass wasn't going to retreat back to Rampart Street and then fade away. No, it would soon sweep out of the District and flood New Orleans and drag all its joys and all its troubles with it. The way it had taken bits and pieces from everywhere and made something that was never there before had already made it too potent, too bold, too hardy, too *American*. It was too late to stop it now, no matter what Tom Anderson believed. There was no point in telling him so. He'd find out soon enough.

They were quiet for a few moments. Then the King of Storyville said, "They won't be prosecuting Picot, Valentin."

"I know."

"Because he's still got—"

"I said I know, Mr. Anderson."

The white man sat back. "All right, then." He came up with a smile of his own as he rolled his derby through his hands. "What are you going to do? New Orleans is your home."

"Not so much now," the detective said. "I've been here a long time. I just think it's time to go."

He sat for another few moments, then stood and went to pick up his satchel. At the door he said, "Will you watch out for Justine? She's at Miss Antonia's."

"I know where she is," Anderson said.

Valentin laughed quietly. Of course he did; the King of Storyville didn't miss anything that went on in his little empire. The Creole detective murmured a thank-you, then walked out the door and down the stairs.

He carried his satchel to the station and paid to have it put in storage. Then he went to stand before the big board that held the slats of wood, each emblazoned with the name of a city or town. He stood there for a long time, then stepped to the ticket window and purchased a one-way fare to St. Louis. He had no reason to go there; it was just a place to stop. From there he could head north, west, or east. He knew only that he wouldn't be going south for a while.

The train didn't leave for a few hours, so he walked across Basin Street and stood on the corner of Iberville, looking down the line, watching as the carnival began once again. There was light and motion, and swirling around it all was sound, laughter and applause and music everywhere.

He walked into Hilma Burt's parlor to find Jelly Roll at the white grand. There were no customers downstairs, so he played for himself and for the doves who wandered through while they waited for callers.

When he saw the Creole detective walk in, he stopped. Valentin pulled up a chair.

He explained it as briefly as he could. When he finished, the piano man said, "Jesus...who would have thought?"

Valentin said, "Now that I've told you, you can't ever speak about it, Ferd."

Morton's brow furrowed. "Can't what?"

"You can't ever repeat what I just told you. No one can know about Picot's sister. If it gets out, he'll turn on Justine and she'll be arrested."

"Arrested for what?"

"It's old business. But Picot has the goods on her. Do you understand? I need your promise."

Morton looked unhappy, but he nodded. "All right, then. I guess it don't matter. I'm leaving out in a few weeks. Going to Chicago." He glanced at Valentin. "What about you?"

"I'm getting on a train in an hour." He settled back. "So, if you don't mind..."

"I don't mind at all," Morton said, and went to playing, a march of notes to a hot rhythm, so bright that it drew the doves from upstairs and from the other rooms to listen.

When Valentin stepped out onto Basin Street, he found Bean-soup waiting for him. Without a word, they crossed over and went into the station. They walked through the terminal to the platform where his train was waiting. Valentin went into his pocket and handed over a ten-dollar gold piece. The kid studied it for a long moment, cupping it in his dirty palm.

"I'll keep an eye on Miss Justine for you," he said.

"I'd appreciate it."

"What if she asks where you went?"

"Tell her I'm traveling. She'll understand."

"And what if she asks when you're comin' back?" There was an odd catch in his voice.

"I don't know. I can send a letter now and then. In care of Miss Antonia." He smiled. "For you, too."

Beansoup grinned. He stuck out his hand, all manly. Then he turned and sauntered away.

A few minutes later, they called for boarding. The cars weren't very full at that hour. He found a seat that was away from other passengers and watched out the window as they chugged away from the lights of Storyville and then turned north into the Louisiana darkness.

Prince John sat up half the night, smoking hop and tippling a bottle of moonshine whiskey from those he kept under the floor. He lay down on his pallet for his usual raw and fitful sleep, invaded by bad dreams. He kept on thinking that someone was coming to his door. He imagined a body rustling through the bamboo, footsteps creeping closer, a shape looming. When he forced his eyes open, though, there was nothing there.

At least, nothing he could see. He knew that the dark of the night could host all kinds of creatures. Before, voodoo was just something he used, like the music, to play his game and get what he wanted. Then he came to believe in the power and believe that he had it.

He needed it now. Something was creeping closer. That Creole detective had found him. Who knew who else might be appearing? It was time to move. His voodoo skills could not make him invisible. He should have quit New Orleans back when he was having all that trouble.

Now the sound came to him again, the padding of footsteps on the sand outside his door.

"Who's out there?" he called, hearing the dry creak of his own voice. A breeze came up, rattling the strings of gourds that hung from the eaves. For some reason, the sound frightened him. He wished he had another piece of the good Chinatown hop to calm his nerves.

Now he heard a voice, someone murmuring. There was no mistake about it. His fear turned to anger and he stood up, stretching his creaking bones, and slipped to the corner, where his makeshift washstand stood. He found his straight razor, opened it, and stepped along the thin wall of the shack toward the doorway.

He stopped there, listening. He heard nothing now, no voices or steps, just the wind through the bamboo. He stood still for a minute, two, three. Nothing. He licked his dry lips and reached for the block of wood that served as a latch. He turned it with the care of a safecracker, then grabbed the leather handle with his free hand. He raised the razor and jerked the door open.

He heard a rustle in the bamboo, the occasional lap of water down on the bank of the lake. He stared into the darkness. Nothing moved. He dropped the razor to his side and let out a long breath. He was just about to close the door again when he got a sudden sensation. Someone was in the shack. He wondered how that could be and then he thought of the back window, covered with nothing but burlap. He heard a sharp breath and the thump of a footstep and turned just in time to see the dark shape close in on him.

Early that morning, in the pearly mist of dawn, a fisherman who had just pushed off from the shore of the lake spotted something in the water that he first took to be a rolling log with branches attached. Then he thought it might be a dead nutria. When he passed closer, he saw that it was the body of a man, in a gentle slump, like he was sleeping on the quiet current. The green eyes were open and piercing, even in death.

The fisherman, a superstitious sort, thought to paddle on as if he hadn't seen it. But he was also a Catholic who believed in proper attendance to a body. He still didn't want it in his boat, so he hooked the shirt with one of his tenders, tied it off, and rowed back to shore. There he dragged the body up onto the bank and went to call for help.

About the time they were collecting the body from the water, Valentin was waking up to a gray north Mississippi morning. The conductor passed by to say that they'd be in St. Louis in just a few hours.

ACKNOWLEDGMENTS

Many thanks to those who have made and make me better than I am: my editor Jen Charat, Kati Hesford, Liz Parker, Marissa Riccio, Sara Branch, Jodie Hockensmith, Erin DeWitt, and others at Harcourt unnamed but dedicated all the same; and to my agent Laura Langlie.

To Alecia Long, Bill Ferris, Don Marquis, Bill Meneray at the Tulane Library, and the staffs of the New Orleans Public Library and the Historic New Orleans Collection, for helping me steep it in history. The errors are mine only.

Finally, deep thanks are due the members of *my* jass band, sterling performers all: Joanne Arbogast, Barbara Bent, Nancy Bent, Wendy Bosley, Katie Bourne, Larry Cohn, Allison Davis, Ilene Dyer, Jack Dyer, Jennifer French Echols, Barbara Eister, Joe Hynes, Lynn Johnson, Karin Koser, Steve Loehrer, Joanne Mei, Suzanne Mercier, Mary Anne Mitchell, Heidi Nietert, Shelly Paul, Michael Riley, Barbara Saunders, Ebbie Sekulski, Leo Sekulski, James Taylor, Lynn Taylor, Virginia Velleca, Rebecca Wallace, John Weatherford...and Trudel Leonhardt, lost and found.